# BIND ME

## IMMORTAL VICES AND VIRTUES: SHADOW SHIFTER BONDS

## MILA YOUNG

# CONTENTS

**People Are Strange**

*The Dead South*

**Don't Fuck With Joe**

*The Blackwater Fever*

**Revolution**

*Unsecret, Ruelle*

**This Is Only The Beginning**

*Steelfeather*

**Monalisa**

*OsMan*

**Babel**

*Gustavoa Bravetti*

**Come Hell or High Water**

*Steelfeather*

**Wicked Game**

*Witchz*

**Black Sea**

*Natasha Blume*

**Cold Blood**

*Valen*

**Hide and Seek**

*Klergy, Mindy Jones*
**Deep in the Water**
*Spelles*
**Ghost Down**
*Layto, Neoni*
**Dogs of War**
*Blues Saraceno*
**Tides**
*G Voz*
**Hoise the Colors**
*The Wellermen, Ebucx, Eric Hollarway*

**Listen to the Soundtrack on Spotify -
Bind Me playlist by Mila Young**

# BEFORE YOU ENTER

**Bind Me** is a paranormal romance and is not a dark book, but there may be triggers for some as it has violence, torture, grief, death of a family member, miscarriage, trauma, and details of the death.

# BIND ME

**Fate shattered my world in a heartbeat.**

As a bounty hunter, I've hunted the supernatural, yet nothing prepared me for the truth about my bloodline.

Exiled by a harsh twist of fate, I'm thrust into the cold heart of Norway. Here, amid ancient forests and icy waters, I'm supposed to start over. But shadows from my past cling tighter than ever.

A mission that was supposed to be my redemption throws me into the path with *him*—a man as dangerous and mysterious as he is infuriating. He's hiding secrets that will get me killed, revealing he's my fated mate.

Unbelievable!

His touch sparks a flame inside me, leaving me questioning everything.

Together, we stumble upon a dark conspiracy, centuries in the making, binding our fates together. As truths surface, we're forced to work together.

As lines blur between us, I'm faced with a choice. Can I trust the man who awakens my soul but might be my ultimate undoing?

# PROLOGUE

SASHA

Daddy's shouting, and I jolt awake on the plush red couch that's still built like a fortress of pillows and toys.

My heart's thumping loudly as his angry voice pierces the warm silence. It's late afternoon, the sky outside the window bright in pinks and oranges, but inside our tiny living room, it feels like midnight.

Clutching Mr. Fluffy, my teddy bear, I get to my bare feet and stumble across the cold wooden floor to the back fly-screen door.

"Mommy? Daddy?" My voice is thin.

No one answers me, but my heart's racing faster now that they're arguing. Mommy's always angry at us, which makes Daddy shout.

*Things have been hard,* I've heard them say in the past, but I hate that they yell all the time. I may be only six years old, but I understand plenty and know it has some-thing to do with not having *enough.* I'm just not too sure what *enough* is, but I pray most nights for the universe to give us more *enough* so that they'd get along.

Looking outside through the fly-screen door, I see them all the way down by the water's edge, where the river rushes past our backyard. Our house is all by itself in the woods. Our neighbors, who have a cat I play with, are a long walk down the river, so they won't hear them. Mostly out here, any noise is just from cicadas and frogs.

Daddy's arms slice through the air, animated and angry. I've never seen him so mad, not even when I spilled paint on the carpet in my room. Mommy stands there, her back as straight as the tall trees that line our property, but her face is wrong... like she's wearing a mask, one that smiles with no warmth, no love. No Mommy in it.

A gust of wind tugs at the curtains on the open window, drawing my attention. When I look back outside, Mommy is stepping toward him, her hands reaching out, trying to hold him like she always does. But he's shaking his head, stepping away from her.

"I don't even know you anymore," he shouts loud enough for me to hear the words. "How many have you taken so far?"

What is he talking about?

I just want to yell, to tell them to stop, to tell them I'm hungry, and to ask when dinner is. My voice feels like I've got peanut butter stuck in my throat. They've told me before not to butt into their talks. *They are for adults only.*

Daddy is shouting again. Then he grabs her by the arm and starts to drag her toward the house, his face red, as if he's about to turn into one of those monsters he says don't really exist.

My breaths are going too fast now, and my hand is on the door handle, pushing down on it.

"You need help." Daddy's voice is a thunderstorm, loud and scary. "How could you let yourself be used like that?"

Is Mommy sick? Did someone hurt her? The idea has my stomach cramping up. She's smiling strangely again, and the breeze has the hairs on my arms lifting. Last time I felt that way, I was in the woods, face-to-face with a large snake. Luckily, Daddy came in time to save me.

Mommy suddenly pushes him away, her hands driving against his chest. It's not a little shove like when you want more room on the couch, but strong enough to send Daddy stumbling backward. His arms fly out to catch something that isn't there.

A scream rises inside me when Daddy suddenly steps on a slippery, dead branch and falls over.

"Daddy!" I shove myself out into the yard to help him. My bare feet hit the cold, rough earth as I rush away from our home. The wind picks up, howling, tugging my clothes. I can't leave Mommy and Daddy out here fighting.

I have to stop them.

They will listen to me.

Trees are swaying crazily, the leaves shivering, as though even the woods are angry today.

Mommy doesn't pay attention to me hurrying toward them. I drop Mr. Fluffy and run faster.

She turns to my daddy and leaps at him, then drags

him into the water by his arm. He barely has time to get his balance and get up. Except, she doesn't look right... or normal. Not with how she takes fast, jerky movements, how she pulls my daddy so easily, seeing as she's smaller than him.

"What are you doing?" I scream louder this time, my voice barely breaking over the wind and the splashing river.

"Get back in the house," she yells at me, but I don't stop.

I can't believe what I'm seeing. She has been mean to me in the past, even hit me a few times, but she never attacked my daddy.

"Mommy, let him go."

She's suddenly got her hands on Daddy's neck, pushing him under the current. He's fighting, his arms swinging, striking her, but it's as though she doesn't feel him hitting her.

I reach the riverbank, the mud squishing under my feet, making me slip a little as I stop at the edge. The water looks darker than before, almost black, as if all the woods' shadows have decided to go for a swim.

And in the water, Mommy is still on top of Daddy in the middle of the river, pushing him down as if she's trying to bury him in the river.

"Mommy," I scream, my eyes stinging with tears. "Stop!"

She doesn't listen to me. She keeps drowning him while he's kicking and thrashing. He's bigger and stronger than her, so I just don't understand why he doesn't get up.

I move quickly into the water, its coldness crawling up my legs as I tremble, but I don't care.

"Daddy, I'm coming," I yell, tears blurring my eyes as I see his hand reaching out of the water, splashing, struggling. I'm moving too slowly, the mud sucking down on my feet.

"Mommy, stop hurting him," I cry out, trembling. "Don't hurt my daddy."

The river is cold, its rushing waters swirling around my waist as I move deeper. Each splash against my face feels like icy fingers trying to drive me back to the shore, but I can't stop now... not when he needs me. My hands keep wiping my eyes, smearing the tears and river water together until I can barely see.

Inside me, a strange sensation stirs, and a tingle travels through me, whispering of my mermaid side. That part of me wants to come out, to take over and save Daddy, but I'm not strong enough, not a strong swimmer. Daddy always said it takes time to grow into my resistance and abilities and not to rush it. But I need them now!

"Mommy, stop," I scream again, my voice desperate. "Please stop drowning him!" If only Daddy was a full merman. If only he could breathe under the water. But his family are wolf shifters, strong and fierce on the land but not made for the water.

Mommy, still shoving him underwater, suddenly turns her head, her gaze locking on to mine. There's no warmth in her eyes, no flicker of the mother I know. She's more monstrous... a stranger wearing my mommy's face.

My heart pounds against my throat.

With a cry, I reach my parents, my small hands clumsy in the water. I shove at her, my fingers grasping for her arm, trying to scratch her.

"Stop!" I strike at her, my fists seeming to do nothing. "You're going to kill him." My voice breaks, each word like a shard of glass in my throat. Tears stream down my face. I'm crying and screaming as I shove, hit, and plead.

Mommy's like a statue, her body hard and unmoving against me.

Daddy's face surfaces briefly, coughing and spluttering, panic twisting his expression. He's halfway through shifting into his wolf, his jawline starting to stretch out, fur spreading across his shoulders and arms. Yes, good, but when his gaze meets mine, wide with fear and confusion, panic bubbles in my stomach. There's a silent plea in his eyes, a scream for help that I'm trying to answer but failing. I'm shaking, crying, desperately reaching my hands out for him.

"Daddy!"

Instead of driving him back under, Mommy leans in and kisses him, inhaling sharply.

I watch, horrified.

He flails about and his face pales, his cheeks hollow. It happens so quickly I don't have time to react, to stop her. But I know what she's doing—killing him with her mermaid's death kiss.

The water sloshes around us as she pushes them both underwater, still kissing him. The river grows colder, deeper, where I can barely touch the ground. I scream, pushing against the water to reach them.

"L-let him g-go!" I scream over and over. I'm shivering, teeth chattering, and I can't stop the tears.

Suddenly, she emerges from the water, drenched, smiling in my direction.

Under the gray sky, I'm crying hysterically, my chin trembling, my insides feeling like someone has cut them up.

Daddy's limp body bobs to the surface of the churning water, face down in the river, not moving. A scream escapes me, raw and haunting, as I reach for him. Before I can touch him, Mommy grabs my arm, her grip tightening, nails digging deep into my skin.

I wrench my stare up at her, furious with her.

"I hate you," I splutter.

Her face is shifting, cheekbones more pronounced, eyes darkening... this isn't just her mermaid form emerging. She's beautiful in her mermaid form, the most beautiful person I've ever seen. Now, there's something dangerous in the way she stares at me, as if she's no longer my mommy. She's changing, becoming a siren. Daddy told me all about them. How scary and dangerous they are.

"Don't," I cry, trying to pull free from her hold.

For a split second, her gaze softens and lulls me into believing she's coming back to me and will help Daddy.

"Get away from me, little fin," she groans, using her nickname for me, her voice sounding desperate. "I'm sorry."

A whimper slips past my lips at seeing the mommy I remember.

In that same second, she pushes me away with a

painful shove to my chest. I stumble and lose my footing in the mud and swirling eddies of the riverbank. I catch myself just in time to see her transformation into a siren complete.

She looks like my mom but different, like she's lost weight in her face, her eyes darker, her teeth sharper, her fingernails pointed.

In a heartbeat, she dives toward Daddy, and a dark, iridescent pink tail splashes out. It's so much darker than her usual bright pink one. The water accepts her quickly, and they're both gone, Daddy dragged under by her.

I cry out, the sound tearing from deep inside me. My mermaid form bursts forth, tearing my clothes off me, a response to everything I've seen. I dive into the murky, restless river, searching through the silt and shadows for any sign of them. Left and right, I swim frantically, beating my small tail and screaming in the water.

But there's nothing... only the cold depths.

I surface, crying while the current tugs me away from the house that no longer feels like home. With every ounce of strength, I swim, my tail beating against the push of the water and my arms slicing through the chill until I reach the bank, breathless. Collapsing on the muddy shore, I curl into myself as water sloshes across my tail.

The truth of what my mommy did rains down on me, settling into my heart like a stone.

Mommy's become a siren—a creature many fear—no longer able to change back into her human form. Her transformation is complete.

Daddy must have been her final victim because he

said once a mermaid drowns a number of victims with a kiss of death, they will eventually become a siren. Then they'll never be able to return to being a mermaid.

Is that what Daddy was arguing with her about earlier?

The sea calls her now, the wild. She's not my mommy anymore. I hiccup a cry. She's now the monster who killed my daddy.

I curl up tighter, unsure I'll ever be able to stop crying again.

**Fifteen Years Later**

"Are you sure this is the place?" Scout's voice cuts through the creeping fog rolling over one of the oldest docks in South Africa.

"Yep." I keep my gaze fixed on the dimly lit warehouses along the dock that give off an unsettling vibe, as if the weather is holding its breath, waiting for something menacing to happen. These old docks we're walking along seem stuck in time, the place weather-beaten under the weight of the damp air, the moored ships nearby groaning like ghosts. And this strange green tint to the fog spreading over us makes the gas lamps along the dock stretch out like long, twisted shadows.

If I weren't at work, I might have enjoyed the creepy vibes more, reminded of the noir murder mystery books I like to devour. Instead, I'm focused on the target we're hunting down—an animal-trafficking asshole who's skipped bail.

"If I were on the run, I sure as fuck wouldn't be hiding out here, of all places." Scout scrunches his long nose at the dilapidated building we're nearing, which looks ready to fall into a heap any moment. To me, it's the perfect hiding spot.

"Does it matter?" I say, speeding up, scanning for building numbers, searching for A32. "We're taking the bastard in today." I have no doubt in my ability... as long as we find him first before another bounty hunter does.

I've been working for Prime Bonds Recovery for the past five years and have an excellent track record for catching more targets than anyone else in the company. I suspect that's why the boss sent me on this high-profile mission.

But why he threw in Scout as my partner for this task is a joke. The guy started at the company four months ago, yet his father is filthy rich and is buddies with my boss. Of course, that's the reason. I can't help but cut Scout a side glare.

I worked my ass off for years before I was trusted to retrieve big targets... unlike some people. Evidently, knowing the right people can escalate your seniority at work.

Except this mission isn't about me. I want this target taken down. The guy's been caught red-handed illegally importing and selling animals from different Houses around the globe. There are whispers of him trafficking children as well, but without proof, he was released on bail.

I want him brought in.

The other Houses want him taken down, too, and seeing as he resides in South Africa, in the House of Gold and Garnet and under the reign of King Kaspian, who is personally interested in this case, we have the added pressure of ensuring we don't fuck this up.

Our king controls several countries, though he's located at the headquarters in Reykjavík, Iceland. Our House represents wealth and prestige and is also a place where the largest concentration of mercenaries and bounty hunters can be found. So, if anyone can find a criminal, it's one of us. It's also why so many other Houses around the world hire experts from the House of Gold and Garnet to carry out their *dangerous* missions.

So, to succeed in this House, you have to be better than the best.

Oblivious to me glaring at him, Scout groans under his breath. "There's something bad about this place. I feel it," he mutters.

I roll my eyes. "Are you letting a bit of fog spook you?"

He shoots me a narrowing stare over his shoulder, almost challenging me, and suddenly, he's moving forward quickly to prove his point that he's not afraid. I chuckle under my breath, and as the last droplets of rain patter against the cobblestones, I speed up my walk along the docks. I feel the weight of a taser on my belt and the blade in my boot.

Approaching A32, my insides tighten like they do on every mission. I scan the building for security cameras... none that I can see.

Even at five foot three with bright aquamarine hair, I'm a storm to be dealt with.

The groaning sounds of the docks fade behind us, replaced by the soft squelch of our shoes against the damp planks.

Pressing my shoulder against the cold, wet wall of the warehouse, I glance over at Scout with a pointed look. I signal for him to move, and he goes left. I go right, each of us slipping through the shadows to check the perimeter.

My pulse is racing frantically on the off chance that I cross paths with Zane, our target. The guy's a hybrid, half horse shifter, half bird. And every inch an asshole for the atrocities he's committed.

On fast feet, I reach the rear of the warehouse, where a looming silhouette of a rusted crane hangs overhead. The air is cold against my skin, the wind picking up and blowing through my ponytail. My breathing is speeding as Scout steps out of the fog, his short hair combed off his face, broad forehead creased, and the edges of his mouth pinched tight with his worry. The guy's in his midthirties, married, and fierce to prove himself, but I don't trust him. Something about him irks me.

"All clear," he whispers, leading to the rear entry into the joint.

Clenching my teeth, I steady my nerves. "Stay close and don't wander off. Got it?"

He nods, his jawline tight. He stands at five-eight, and I can see it in his posture. He hates taking orders from me, but I'm the senior bounty hunter on this mission, so he can go fuck every damn last drop of his ego.

Taking a deep inhale, I reach for the door handle, my fingers wrapping around the cold metal. I ease it open gently, the hinges giving a faint groan that has me freezing for a moment. When no one comes running for us, we slip inside, our movements as silent as the fog outside.

The thing with our job is that most of our time is spent tracking down criminals, sneaking up on them before they know we're onto them. Once they see you, there's only a few seconds to secure the target, or they'll be long gone.

The inside of the warehouse is vast and shadowy, divided by walls into three sections. The one directly in front of us is open-plan and filled with stacked wooden crates. The other two areas lead into opposite rooms. One has the door open, and it's pitch black inside, so I have my gaze swinging on the one to my left. There's a dim light coming out from the ajar door, almost inviting us.

Shivers crawl up my arms, and I pull out my taser, noticing Scout does the same. One zap and we take our target down long enough to pounce on him and tie him up. It's the quickest way to bring him down with minimal damage.

We move steadily, our steps measured and silent, while I scan every dark corner and potential ambush point. Peering through the ajar door, I find a large open space. Five offices are to our left, and the nearby ones seem to store a bunch of cages. It's dark inside, except for the light pouring in through the open doors. Across from the offices stands a small forklift and more crates.

My ears strain for anything that might reveal Zane's presence. Nothing, only the soft creak of the building settling and the escalating wind outside.

I signal for Scout to join me in checking the offices with a flick of my hand, seeing as the rest of the place is open space and not hiding anyone. Step by step, we approach the first office, and inside, there are at least a dozen animal cages tossed inside. There's a feral, powdery, barnyard smell in here, and I scrunch up my nose.

"This is the place. I knew he'd hide in here. I can smell the animals," Scout whispers the obvious, completely contradicting himself from earlier.

I nod and don't bother answering as we move to the first few offices, finding more cages, as if someone has been fast to transport animals through here. My chest tightens at the thought of these monsters hurting inno-cent animals, propelling me to take Zane down faster.

By the time I reach the fourth office, tension builds. I open the door slowly to a dark room smelling heavily of animals, but there's also a charged electric stink. I can't see anything but a couple of empty cages on the floor, lit by the dim light behind me. The rest of the room is pitch black. Just as I move to step inside, a sharp, unmistak-able sound slices through the silence behind us.

I freeze, then spin around in the doorway, expecting to find Zane. Instead, I catch sight of Scout making a quick dash across the warehouse area. He's near crates and a forklift, heading for another office door I'd missed.

"Scout, what are you doing?" I whisper, but he doesn't respond.

I barely have a moment to process this when another sound grabs my attention, coming from the front door of the building. My gaze shoots in that direction to my far left as the door lets out a drawn-out groan that pierces through the space.

I dart into the office, swallowed by shadows. Crouching in the darkness near the doorway, I leave it slightly ajar to watch who's entering. I peer out quickly to Scout, who's fiddling with the locked door.

*I'm going to murder him. Idiot. If he fucks up this important mission for me, I'm going to be pissed.*

My heart pounds against my ribs. Scout suddenly lunges to hide behind the forklift just as the front door swings fully open. Jerking back into the confines of the shadows, crouching low, I watch a tall man stride into the warehouse. His black coat flutters around him like he has the wings of a dark angel, his steps determined and fast. The keys in his hand jingle, and his black hair is drawn back.

Except that's not Zane.

Crap! Did we miss him, or is he already somewhere in the building?

Instead of heading toward my hiding place, the stranger veers into the next office over—the one I haven't checked yet. Part of me breathes easier, grateful he's not on a collision course with Scout. My plan is to wait and see if Zane appears.

As I steady my rapid breathing, the smallest sound, a faint shuffle, catches my attention. It's close, too close.

Heart in my throat, my gaze darts around the dark room I'm in, when the sound comes again.

*Fuck.*

I'm not alone in the room.

Adrenaline surges through me. I can't believe I didn't search the area properly before throwing myself in here. I blame Scout for distracting me with his stupidity. With my back to the wall, I reach for the small flashlight I keep with my house keys.

With a cautious flick, light sputters to life, casting a weak beam across the room. Except it's not just any room—I've stumbled into a lab.

The beam dances over shelves packed with jars containing murky liquids and powders. Along the length of the room runs a long table cluttered with all kinds of scientific equipment, while on the floor, cages are haphazardly stacked. Their bars imprison animals that we're here to stop Zane from trafficking. Tiny eyes stare back at me. A pair of green squirrels, twitching nervously, three-legged frogs with small horns. The poor things were terrified, stuck in a metal cage, too scared to even move. But they don't look harmed, which is good.

When I rise from my crouched position, another cage with an animal on the table catches my attention. It's small, curled up, its fur patchy, skin marked with splotches of raw, irritated flesh. The creature's eyes meet mine, filled with pain and fear. It whimpers softly.

It's an otter.

The acrid smell of chemicals becomes more distinct now, more disturbing.

As I stand there, the ache in my heart deepens as I

stare at the otter, leaving me completely devastated for the little thing being tested on. I've always had a soft spot for animals, caring for strays and volunteering at shelters. So, the sight in front of me stirs a deep anger that drowns out the earlier tension of the hunt. I now want to really hurt Zane and his accomplices.

Still huddled in the corner of his cage, the otter's terrified eyes stay locked on mine as it trembles uncontrollably. Tears prick my eyes while fire burns my chest. As I step toward the trembling otter, intent on easing its fear, the room suddenly erupts with a sound like thunder. A spark explodes, and I sense the sharp bite of magic coursing up my arms.

I flinch back, heart pounding against my ribs, fearing I've accidentally triggered a trap. Before I can even begin to make sense of what's happening, a loud click resonates through the room, eerily similar to the sound of a gas oven igniting.

In seconds, flames shoot up from the base of all the walls in the room, racing upward as if the walls are lined with kindling. Heat engulfs me instantly, the heavy stench suffocating.

Panic throttles me, and I'm shaking furiously. I stumble backward, my head spinning with dread and confusion. The heat intensifies, slamming into me like a physical blow while the cries of the animals in their cages pierce through the chaos.

From the doorway, I desperately scan the warehouse. Fire is climbing the walls out there, too, a monstrous, ravenous entity consuming the building. It's clear that something triggered the inferno. Was it me?

Through the growing blaze, I spot Scout in the open doorway of the other office across from me, and I know instantly the disaster is his fault. The door handle is half hanging near him, a clear sign of forced entry into a room locked and secured by a purge trigger. He's stumbling forward as the wall behind him catches in flames.

"Idiot!"

Break into the office, hit the trigger, and the whole place lights up, destroying every bit of evidence and potentially killing anyone inside to cover Zane's tracks.

Anger and fear drum through me. We need to get out... now!

Before I take a step forward, Zane races into the warehouse from the rear of the building, a massive figure with a handlebar mustache that does nothing to soften his bulldozer-like appearance. He rushes toward the front door, screaming out something about collecting some files. I assume he's screaming at his friend in the other office.

Shit!

That's when his gaze swings in Scout's direction, then mine, finally spotting us... the intruders.

"Son of a bitch, fucking bounty hunters," he growls, and he's suddenly bolting to the front door as his buddy emerges from the other office, looking terrified with panic twisting his features.

I'm running after them in a second flat, even while the fire grows fast, too fast. The place is going to collapse in seconds. With my taser extended, I shoot, needing to slow him, but despite his size, he dodges with surprising agility. Scout's there, and the heat is becoming unbearable, my throat raw, my nostrils stinging from the smoke.

"Stop them," I yell out at Scout as the wall to one of the offices shatters, collapsing with a tremendous thud near the forklift. It's also when the heartbreaking sound of cries behind me stops me in my tracks. The animals, still trapped in their cages, grab my attention, their actions growing more frantic the worse the fire inflames.

Zane and his friend dart outside the front door, Scout on their heels.

"Sasha, hurry the fuck up," he yells, then he's gone.

I know this is my chance to catch Zane, that he can't get away from us, but I glance back, my insides aching at the sounds of the animals crying, knowing they *will* die.

I promised myself that when someone's in need, I'd always help them, and it goes double for animals. For a split second, everything else fades—the heat, the smoke, the collapsing building—and I'm consumed by the urgency to save innocent animals.

Ignoring the searing pain on my skin and the smoke scorching my lungs, I dash back into the lab room. I can't leave them here, not like this. I reach the cages just as the walls around us begin to crackle and spit larger flames. The metal bars are hot to the touch, and I wince as I grab them, but the urgency pushes me forward.

"I've got you. Just please don't try to escape from me," I coo to the critters in the cages on the floor. "I need to get you all out of here, please," I whisper. All cradled in my arms, I set them on the lab table. Despite the walls on fire and feeling like we've entered hell itself, they stay close.

Turning my attention to the otter, still curled up in the cage, whining, I flick open the lock and wrench the door open. The poor thing whimpers and shrieks back.

"Come on, little one, I just want to help. Don't bite me, okay, and I promise to get you out."

Just then, a deafening sound erupts behind me. I twist my head as a crumbling wall outside the room collapses under the assault of the fire. With no time to hesitate, I stick my hand into the cage deeper, reaching for the critter. With a gentle, quick swoop, I scoop him into my hand and cradle him against my chest. I collect the other small animals as my heart shatters at their vulnerability.

I lunge outside the room, only to find the front doorway to the warehouse blocked. Half the wall falls away from the structure. Despite shaking and feeling like I'm burning alive, I dart toward the rear entry, cowering forward to shield the animals in my arms. A plank of wood crashes down not far from me, and I scream, flinching back instinctively.

The crackle of fire intensifies, deafening me. The heat is unbearable, and my throat burns with every breath I take. Dodging the flaming debris, I run like a maniac toward the rear door... just as a great explosive creak sounds behind me.

I burst out the back door, stumbling into the cool air as I suck it into my starved lungs. I'm choking frantically. Behind me, part of the roof caves in, and I dart farther away from the building that's coming down fast. Sirens wail in the distance from what I assume are firemen coming to put out the flames.

My mind races, terrified at how close to disaster I came. I check on the little guys in my arms, who are all cradled close and silent with huge eyes. So, I turn my attention to finding Zane and Scout.

The foggy, cool air is sharp against my heated skin while my arms tighten around the small, trembling bodies of the six critters.

The docks are obscured by fog and shadows, the aftermath of the fire casting everything in ash and harsh, surreal light. As I hurry away from the collapsing building, my heart thunders with desperation and anger. The animals cradled in my arms are quiet, their small bodies shaking against me.

I pass a hulking ship, its massive hull throwing long, dark shadows across the wooden planks of the dock. It's there, in a dark spot, that I find Scout sprawled on his back.

"Scout, are you okay?" I call out, dropping to my knees beside him as he groans, a hand reaching up to his face as he tries to sit up. Blood trickles from his mouth, and one eye is already swelling shut, coloring with the dark purple of a severe bruise. "What the hell happened?" I ask, scanning him for more injuries. We're trained to handle ourselves in any situation—to fight and defend.

"The question is, where the fuck were you?" he snarls. "You're supposed to have my back." His voice is rough with pain and fury. "We could have had Zane, but what?" His gaze lowers to the animals in my arms. "You saved those fucking things but let the criminal escape? You made us lose him."

"Me? You went against my orders and opened that damn office, tripping the purge trigger."

He sighs, his good eye closing, not even hearing me, yet his accusation leaves me furious.

"These animals are innocent. Last time I looked, we're not monsters... well, at least not me."

Scout pushes himself to his feet, wincing with every movement. "You compromised the mission."

"Shut the hell up. Now, which way did Zane go?"

He shrugs. "How the fuck should I know? After he turned into a horse and kicked me, I almost passed out. I could have died because of your dumb decision." He's practically shouting at his stage, his face shaking with fury.

Sure, I feel horrible for him, but him blaming me is not gaining him any brownie points.

"Sometimes, being a hero means deciding who needs saving the most. So, I made the choice," I retort.

Silence stretches between us as he glares in my direction. Shuffling the animals to be cradled in one arm, I offer him my free hand to help him, but he knocks it aside and limps down the docks.

Great! Sighing heavily, I just know this is going to come back and bite me hard in the ass.

"Wait, are you serious?" My voice shoots up an octave as I lean forward in my seat, staring across the desk at my boss. Mr. Daniels is the epitome of a fitness fanatic, his slick hair and sharply tailored suit giving him an air of unapproachable perfection. His fae ears peek out just enough to hint at his magical heritage, though he plays it down, never really owning up to coming from a powerful family of fae.

"It's for the best, Sasha. Consider it a new start," he replies with that smoothness that I'm starting to loathe. He takes a sip from his cup of special mushroom tea, which he swears is the elixir of life or something. In the corner of the room stands his fancy bicycle, leaning against the wall, reminding everyone of his healthy lifestyle. Most days, I can ignore his arrogance. Today, I'm pissed.

I blink, my mind racing. "I haven't had a chance to put my report in about Zane, but—"

"It's not needed," he interrupts, setting down the cup with a grimace as if the tea tastes like hell. "Scout filled me in, and considering you didn't bring Zane back with you, it now puts me in a very compromising situation because we promised to have him caught. But now, he's on the run, probably gone into deep hiding."

I pinch my lips together, fighting the urge to roll my eyes. Trust Scout to run straight to the boss before I even had a chance to get into the office and explain. The moment I arrived, I headed downstairs, submitting the animals I'd saved to animal handlers for safe transport to ensure they are returned to their original country.

"So, because Scout, who decided to turn a simple capture mission into an episode of *Let's Trigger Every Alarm Possible*, gave you his version of the story, I'm getting relocated? And here I was, thinking we were supposed to work as a team!"

My boss scowls, yet his expression is surprisingly heavy with resignation.

"The issue is that your priority was the target, not the animals, and you let him escape. Scout is still new, and he needed your backup to take him down. So, you made a huge mistake in your choice today, which unfortunately is going to cost you."

The room feels smaller suddenly, the walls closing in as the reality of his words sinks in. Even his framed motivational posters on the walls, screaming about teamwork and vision, now silently mock me.

Swallowing hard, I shift uncomfortably in my seat across the desk from Mr. Daniels. I don't regret saving those animals from the fire. My conscience wouldn't have allowed me to walk away, but that burning side of me flares up, a mix of anger and injustice.

Staring at him, a desperate urgency curls up inside me that I'm being sent away from the team I've worked with for the past five years, from my friends in the place, not to mention the embarrassment of being kicked out.

"I've never failed a mission before," I begin, hating that I'm sounding more desperate than I want to reveal to my boss. Weakness isn't a trait suitable for bounty hunters, but I'm fuming at Scout, dreading to find out where I'm going to be sent. I'm picturing some small office in the middle of an isolated town, tucked away like a broken artifact.

He sighs, leaning back in his leather chair. "My manager is now asking for an explanation on how such a straightforward mission went awry, and I can't let your failure taint this department."

"But... I should never have been paired with Scout. He's a newb," I argue, the words tumbling out in a rush.

"You're not seeing the real issue here, and that's the problem. You put your personal feelings before the greater good of Prime Bonds Recovery, and that makes you a liability and untrustworthy."

My mouth falls open, his words striking like a punch to my solar plexus.

"I-I've put years into this, brought in so many targets, and this one time, I didn't catch my target..." My mouth dries, my chest tightening.

His shoulders soften slightly as he leans back in, his folded arms on the desk in front of him.

"Look, I'm sorry, Sasha, but management is fuming, and they want to see heads roll over this as King Kaspian himself wants results. The best I could do was get you transferred instead of losing your job. Prove yourself with a clean record, then we can relook at you coming back after twelve months in Norway."

Twelve months! Norway! Reality hits me like a blow, and I almost fall out of my seat, shock jarring through me. I manage to steady myself, gripping the arms of my chair and forcing myself to breathe.

"Norway," I echo, the word tasting sour on my tongue. "A whole year?"

"Yes." He nods, his gaze unwavering. "It was a tough situation negotiating with the team there, but it's a chance to really prove that you can prioritize and handle big cases again. Think of it as... a test of your dedication."

I narrow my gaze at how mocking and condescending he sounds. Years of loyalty meant nothing to this company!

I'm mindlessly fiddling with the gold bracelet on my wrist, a charm in the shape of rolling waves joining the chains around my wrist. Unlike most who wear family crests in the form of pendants, charms, or rings, I chose this design myself for the peace it brings me. Now, it feels like a cruel reminder of how quickly life can change, how everything I value can be ripped away without warning. It brings back memories of losing my parents and the realization that, once again, I have no control over my life.

As much as I'd love to quit on the spot and storm out, I'm not exactly swimming in riches, and I don't have any inheritance from my parents.

But maybe I'm looking at this wrong. It's been over a year since Billie, my BFF, moved away to Finland, drawn by the pull of her fated mates, and Norway is a damn lot closer to Finland than South Africa is. I grasp onto that beacon of hope while I feel like I'm drowning. Up on my feet from the seat, I stumble toward the door, feeling dizzy.

"Sasha," Mr. Daniels calls out. "Make me proud. I know you will do great in Norway. Just don't get distracted. Oh, and the team there will be sending me regular updates on your progress."

I exhale loudly at being treated like a newb. My anger simmers, and I hate the tears stinging my eyes from the fuckery of the day.

"Thanks," I mutter bitterly as I push the door open. The large open office in front of me is bustling with staff, and most are avoiding looking at me. Which means they all know. Of course they do.

Fucking Scout. I spot him across the room, two desks down from where mine used to be. He's laughing with someone but glances my way with the widest grin. I curl my hands into fists, furious that he got me relocated. I want to rip that damn smirk off his face. Rage and betrayal boil over as I glare at the man who cost me so much, yet he walks away unscathed.

All because of one mission, because I chose compassion over cold duty.

Fuck you, Scout!

# TWO

## KADEN

"Asher, watch your back!" I shout as movement in the forest to our left catches my attention. Two men, armed with blades, charge as fast as the wind, coming right for my friend. "Looks like our welcoming party's arrived!"

We had just set foot in Norway, traveling by boat, and no sooner had we left the harbor and started down the long road for my grandfather's place than we'd gained unwanted attention.

Sure, we recently got out of Tartarus, the prison where we were born, and it had royally messed us up. So, when the opportunity to leave arose a year after the portal in the prison opened up, we did what we had to do. We lied through our damn teeth to get through a tedious, drawn-out interview with the guards, and finally, they opened the portal to let us out of that world.

But I'm not complaining. No fucking way in hell. The shadow creature inside me, born from the prison's darkness, had twisted my shifter side into something more feral, more primal. Sometimes, I don't know where the beast stops and I begin. But there's one thing I'm sure of —the only way to keep it from taking over completely is to find my fated mate.

So, here we are, fresh out of Tartarus, and we're already being ambushed.

It's like another day in Tartarus, really, except I had hoped things would be different out here.

I swing toward the newcomers, my feral beast rising through me at the promise of bloodshed, pressing against my insides, wanting control.

*Back the fuck down.*

The air crackles with energy when three more men spring out from the woods, their attention on me.

I grin, a chuckle rolling past my lips.

"Does it say a lot that I'm excited for a fight?" Asher growls, lunging for his attackers. He moves with terrifying ease. He only partially transforms, as if he's not even trying, and this is too easy for him. With hellhound claws and fangs, he rips through the men like paper, his snarls booming through the trees.

"You're as fucked up as me." I throw back a laugh. I could shift into my beast form, but that would be too easy. I want my hands dirty and, most importantly, not tell the whole fucking country of Norway we've arrived. So, for now, I'll keep it low-key.

The smaller man coming for me shifts into a black wolf and charges while the other two lunge at me from either side.

I rush to meet them, my body moving with the force of an avalanche. I slam a shoulder into one man, sending him sprawling into a tree with a sickening crunch. He doesn't get back up. The wolf shifter reaches me next, and I snatch him by the throat. I twist and snap him like a twig with two hands. His earlier growl flatlines, and I toss him aside as I swivel to the third attacker.

He's got a blade out, plunging it at my chest. Lightning fast, I jolt out of the way, but not before the blade slides across my arm. It stings, but fuck it. It's a surface wound, and I'll survive.

Fury burns through me, my beast punching forward with ferocity. I snatch the man's wrist and haul him toward my fist, which collides with his face. He falls backward like a plank of wood, and I lunge at him, fists raining down on him, each fueled by the anger, the frustration, of centuries spent locked away. His cries become muffled, but my beast keeps pushing me, craving destruction.

Suddenly, a hand touches my shoulder, and I spin around, a snarl ripping through my throat, fist raised.

It's Asher standing there, unflinching, his dark gaze unwavering.

"Pull the fuck back," he says firmly, his voice cutting through the chaos in my head. "Guy's gone. You can stop now."

His words anchor me back to reality. I glance down at the lifeless body beneath me, the massacre I've left behind. I push to my feet, breaths coming in ragged gasps.

I don't feel remorse for those who wish me harm.

That part of me was lost long ago, back when I was a kid and my dad threw me into the woods he nicknamed *Death's Door*.

"You're no son of mine if you can't fight, if you can't be stronger than the rest," he barked at me, hammered into me, beat into me.

I fucking hated him, loathed him, but I learned that living in Tartarus changes you. Like me, my father was also born in a supernatural prison, brought up ruthlessly by his father.

My grandfather... the reason our family line was cursed into Tartarus.

The reason I'm in Norway, of all places. To uncover who the fuck betrayed him and threw him into the prison. My father and grandfather might have been assholes, but they never lied. It didn't mean they always revealed all the details, but what they did, I trusted.

Turns out, my grandfather was falsely accused of a crime he didn't commit. And I'm going to find out who cursed us.

Asher's staring at me, and I snap out of my thoughts.

"We're good?" he asks, extending a hand toward me.

"Yeah, I'm fine." I accept his help, not because I need it, but to show him it's me and that I'm calm.

We both come from the same darkness, come in touch with Tartarus's magic, and we're both shadow shifters now. And not tamed easily. Back in Tartarus, the full moons there forced my shift, whether I wanted it or not. Same with all the other shifters in the place. With it came the maddening craving for a mate, a savagery that tries to rule me.

That's why I need to track down my fated mate before I go insane. And Asher's got it bad, too. That's why he joined me. Otherwise, we're both fucked.

"Thanks for that." I throw the words over my shoulder.

"Don't worry about it."

He's strolling over to the guy I'd tossed into a tree. He now slumps against the trunk, his groans echoing through the clearing. I move to wipe the blood from my hands on one of the fallen men's shirts, then straighten up and head over to Asher, who's grilling the guy for answers.

Just as I get there, the man gurgles, "You fucking idiots, you think you can waltz into our House without repercussions? Every damn mercenary will be on your tail. Get the fuck off our land while you can. No one wants you here."

I exchange glances with Asher, who's grinning at the news.

"Well, I didn't expect that. Looks like we're in for more fun, then."

Asher leans in closer, fisting the guy by the hair, wrenching it sideways harshly. "Who's in charge of this House, then?"

The man grins, his teeth stained with blood, clearly in no shape to get up anytime soon. "King Kaspian," he manages to rasp out. "And trespassers are free game."

With a grimace, Asher puts the man out of his misery with a blade to the throat. Quick and merciless.

In no time, we're leaving the bodies behind. They

might serve as a warning to any other mercenaries who think about crossing our path.

Asher releases a low rumble in his voice. "How did these fools find out about us so fast?"

"I bet that dick of a captain on the ship sold us out," I reply, recalling the way the man eyed us suspiciously on the trip over. "He never trusted us."

Asher cracks his neck. "Fuck, he shouldn't trust us."

I chuckle, scanning the woodland around us and the snow-tipped mountains in the distance. We were dropped off at a small port far from the city of Bergen, specifically to avoid drawing attention and to slip into the country unnoticed. We've learned enough to know the new world is divided into Houses, and joining one requires approval by those higher up and isn't as simple as just walking in—though that's exactly what we're planning on doing.

Asher strolls beside me, shoulder to shoulder, his hands stuffed into the pockets of his pants, looking beyond calm, reminding me of when I first met him in Tartarus at a market. I was in the middle of a fight, and he stepped in to give me a hand—especially since there were twenty men against one... me. He wore a grin on his face the whole time, not worried. Just like now.

Turned out we had more in common than I expected, one of them being our shared desire to get the fuck out of that prison and find our fated mates.

"So," Asher murmurs, his dark eyes glinting my way. "Where do we start?"

"Tracking down my grandfather's place, see what's there, what family still exists, and start digging into exactly what the fuck happened five thousand years ago, before he got shoved into Tartarus." Thing is, many supernaturals, including my family, live for thousands of years, so there's bound to be someone in Norway who remembers my grandfather.

Asher chuckles and slaps my back, his laugh deep. "I don't envy you that mammoth task."

I laugh along, knowing it's going to be near impossible, but I'm a determined bastard when I set my mind to something.

The road ahead twists and winds around a mountain. We press forward. The sunlight filters through the dense woods on either side of our worn path, and descending before us, the city comes into view.

It sprawls at the base of mountains with towering peaks and houses of varied colors gathered together by the water. Even from our location, the harbor shines with the sun. The whole place feels like a mix of old and new, buildings fitting into the curves of the mountains and the edges of the water.

Sunlight reflects off the homes and the sea, and it's hard not to compare this world to the one I knew in Tartarus. Darkness had been a constant companion there, consuming the land. No sunlight, no natural warmth, no seasons—just a dull atmosphere and weather. Unless my father spoke of the outside world from his learnings or stories we'd heard from elders, I wouldn't have known any differently.

Now, the touch of sunlight on my skin, soft and warm, is a sensation I'm slowly growing to appreciate. The bright colors of the land and vibrant greens of the forest all feel new, almost surreal. Even the smells are sharper and crisper, like the pines, the fresh grass, and the soil.

After growing up in that darkness, I adapted, learning to accept that world—after all, it's the only one I'd known. I even found ways to care for people there, especially those who bent the knee to my family out of loyalty. After my parents died, that dedication only grew stronger around me.

I lived comfortably in Tartarus after I moved out of my parents' home. Yet, everything became mundane, repetitive, and I craved more. So much more.

I focus on the city ahead of us, eager to discover it.

"Notice how even the air smells different out here?" I say, then take in a long breath.

Asher grins at me, inhaling deeply. "It's sweeter than back at Tartarus."

My response dies in my throat as we approach several wooden cabins, and ten men spill out, each carrying blades, their attention fixed on us. I'm furious at the captain for revealing our approach. He must've gotten paid well for it for word to spread so fast.

"Go, dart around the back of that building," Asher mutters in hushed whispers, lifting his chin to point to the closest cabin to my right. "Cut across the field to the city. I'll find you."

"Hell no," I respond, already pushing up my sleeves, ready for a fight. "And let you have all the fun?"

"Listen," he insists, his tone serious for a change. "They're going to follow you to your family home and won't leave you alone. I'll distract them so they lose track of you."

I blink at him, momentarily stunned. Sure, we'd helped each other out before, but this is the second time he's saved me when he didn't have to.

"Why?" The question spills out. A part of me always doubts anyone who wants to do something for me.

He shrugs. "Because I have nowhere to go aside from searching for my fated mate, but until then, I'm going to have some fun." His grin grows wicked, and I see the glint in his eyes, the hunger for fights, for hunting. He craves it, just like he did back in Tartarus.

"You sure?" I ask.

He laughs, already sizing up his enemies as the cool breeze ruffles his short, dark hair, the muscles in his arms bulging, his shoulders rising.

"I'll lead them away while you work on the reason your grandfather was framed. Sound like a deal? We'll bump into each other again." He smirks, one of his eyebrows arching, as if he can't wait to get into the battle with the mercenaries.

I'm stunned but appreciative. Not many people surprise me, but Asher is different. That's why we hit it off from the start. Neither of us ever tried to betray the other; we were in such similar situations that there was an unspoken trust between us.

"You've got a deal. You always have a place at my home if you need it. Always a helping hand for anything. Come and find me." Then I quickly rattle off the directions to my grandfather's place as my father gave them to me.

With a nod, Asher takes off for the mercenaries, calling out, "Perfect day for you all to die."

I dart into the woods toward a cabin nearby, knowing some mercenaries won't take his bait and will follow me. And they'll be dead men soon after.

But it's good to know that in a foreign country, in a new world, I already have a loyal friend. I'm not alone out here.

"How the hell did I even end up here?" I grumble to myself in my magic-fueled sedan, staring up at my new workplace in Bergen, Norway.

Last week, my biggest issue was deciding what to wear to work. Now, I'm in a foreign country, feeling more alone than ever. I grip the steering wheel, glaring at the two-story white building where I'll be working for the next twelve months. The place looks pristine and too perfect, but in truth, I'm still pissed at Scout and Mr. Daniels. To hell with them both. They think they've put me out, but I'll show them. When I return to South Africa, Scout better watch out because I can hold a grudge like nobody's business.

I take another glance at the manila folder on the passenger seat with details on my target—yep, I'm out on a mission already. They don't mess around in Norway.

Streets are bustling with traffic and people, but it's strangely calm compared to the chaos I'm used to back home. The whole drive through the city toward my target in the woods, I replay the last few days in my head. How I could have done things differently, yet I keep coming to the same conclusion. If I had gone after Zane, the animals would have perished, and that's not how I dance.

Exhaling loudly, I decide to make the most of what I have because, hey, I still have a job, right?

As I turn the corner from the main road in the city, the buildings fall behind me. I'm greeted by an explosion of open land, winding roads, monstrous mountains in the distance, and glimpses of the famous fjord looming farther ahead. I roll down the windows, taking in the fresh air, and for a moment, it's beautiful in a wild, untamed way. As if, somehow, it calls to me as though it's familiar.

"Welcome to Norway," I whisper to myself, sounding pitiful even to myself.

Around me, the landscape unfolds like I've stepped into a fairy tale. The water in the fjord—a deep inlet carved by the glaciers long ago—is like a dark mirror, reflecting the overcast, stormy sky. It shimmers and farther in the distance slices between steep cliffs that seem to pierce the low-hanging clouds.

The location is breathtaking.

There's something comforting about leaving the city behind, in only having an occasional vehicle pass me while the wilderness spreads outward. A few homes peek through the dense woodlands that stretch away from the water's edge around me, painted in browns and reds, some stark white or yellow.

I read up on Norway on my flight over. Part of the town of Bergen has been preserved, deliberately rebuilt to reflect the lives of humans who once lived here so long ago.

Back when humans were in charge of Earth, a bunch of portals popped up all over the place, letting magic flood in. It caused a real ruckus—wrecked a lot, killed off a bunch of humans—until things sort of settled down. That was when they came up with the Houses, assigning all of us supernaturals a spot to belong. Now, you have to be in a House, basically.

And while other Houses around the globe might've kissed goodbye to things like planes and all those travel methods, in the House of Gold and Garnet, we've still got those amazing items. Thanks to some expensive magic and living under King Kaspian, we get to enjoy all those high-end luxuries.

Following a narrow path along the thick pine woods, I pass a broken and rusted metal gate, yet it's exactly where the coordinates are bringing me. Shadows darken the area, the place ominously silent.

Eventually, I pull up near a rocky edge by the water, barren of any homes nearby or across the fjord on the other side. It's isolated and gorgeous. I park by the trees so the car isn't easily spotted, then climb out of the driver's seat. I stare out at the open tranquility, at the mountain looming behind me, where farther up and tucked in its embrace is a house—a once majestic red mansion now worn and weathered. Unlike the rest of the location, this place hasn't been restored.

I grab the notes from the passenger seat, flipping

through the pages to the section about my target. According to the brief, Belu has been seen along the fjord on a boat in this vicinity, stopping at the shore, behaving erratically but then always vanishing when authorities arrive.

Now, this location offers an easy view, and evidently, my task is to watch out to gather information if he returns. Of course, I'm pissed that it's not a hunt-and-capture mission, but I'm not going to ruffle feathers on my first field day.

Studying the notes, I flip through them, stopping on his profile page. The guy's a large, lofty man with dark hair and blue eyes, and he is a merman. That last bit piques my interest since I tend to keep my distance from my kind. Mostly since they're not common in the town I'm from in South Africa. And I'm not especially fond of other merpeople's initial questions, asking who my parents are and what our bloodline is.

It's none of their damn business.

Yet my stomach twists into knots at the mention of my past, at the nightmare I've lived with for years.

"Deep breath," I murmur under my breath.

Daddy's face flashes in my mind. He's choking and spluttering, his panicked expression tearing at my insides. I still see the terror in his eyes as he looked at me. That crushing helplessness still destroys me. I'm stretching my hands out toward him, desperate to save him, but it's not enough.

Tears well up in my eyes, and my hands tremble. Each breath feels heavy, as if I'm right back there, pleading with my mom to stop.

The vividness tears into me, and I know I'm spiraling. I've learned to stop myself from going into a full-blown panic attack. Forcing my breathing to slow, I anchor myself to the present, the car I came in, the woods surrounding me.

*I'm here now, not back in that horrible moment. I'm strong enough to push past the pain.*

Calming slowly, I stare at the document shaking in my hands, needing my attention on something other than my thoughts.

I've been practicing meditation and Tai Chi to learn to calm myself, and it's been working. But sometimes, the darkness sneaks up on me.

Taking a deep breath, I shake the thoughts back and refocus on the papers in my grasp. There's an image of Belu in the top left-hand corner of the file, which could have been hand drawn. It's barely more than a shadow, but it's enough to give me an idea of his strong face and jawline.

The dossier doesn't say much more, just that he's been elusive, and he was out on bail despite being under investigation for murder. Ah, another asshole who knows someone in power.

Tossing the papers back into the car, I exhale deeply and scan the area, then make my way down to the water. I tread carefully on the rocky shore, my gaze sweeping my surroundings for any sign of movement. The pier is just ahead, the wood worn and extending into the dark water. A few birds fly overhead; otherwise, it's eerily silent. The cold in the air wraps around me, yet on the inside, I'm scorching hot. I loosen my leather jacket, at least to try looking more like a tourist who might have wandered here for a great sight instead of a mission.

As I near the pier, a splash of brown catches my attention. There's no boat tied up, but there's something there. Moving closer, I stumble over a pair of male boots carelessly abandoned near the shore.

Tilting my head to the side, I smirk. Who else but a merman might ditch his shoes to take a dip in freezing waters? Except, what about his clothes? Regardless, what if he's hiding something underwater?

I grin to myself and make my way to the right-hand side of the rocky shore. Without a second thought, I start shedding my clothes. If I'm going after a merman, I'm diving in on equal footing. I'm a lot more powerful and dangerous in my mermaid form.

Boots, jacket, pants, bra, underwear—everything drops in a pile on a rock by the pier. One last scan to confirm I'm alone, and there I am, butt naked in the open. With a deep breath, bracing myself, I rush to the water's edge and dive in. The cold fjord water embraces me and is startlingly frigid. My skin tingles from the freezing water rushing over me.

With a single willing thought, my change pushes forward, my legs fusing and stretching into a powerful aquamarine tail. A familiar tingling sensation cascades down my hips and lower as scales shimmer into existence. The water feels different suddenly—as if it recognizes me, welcoming me back. It clings to me, not as a chill but as a warm coat, embracing me, making me whole. It's not just a return to the water but a homecoming. A sensation I will never tire of when I enter the water and transform into my mermaid form.

Instantly, everything around me changes. My vision shifts and sharpens, and the murky depths become less blurry. Subtle movements in the shadows grab my attention to the quicksilver dart of fish nearby. Each swish of water, each distant call of marine life, echoes in my ears.

There's something calming about uniting with the water realm, and it never gets old.

Calmness washes over me.

This is where I belong, where I feel more powerful, more alive—underwater. With the small lines of gills at the edges of my neck fluttering subtly, I breathe in the water effortlessly.

For many years after losing my parents, I avoided the water, refusing to transform, reminded of my mother, but once I started my work as a bounty hunter, my best friend, Billie, pushed me to face my fears. I miss her so much. I make a mental note to get in contact with her soon.

I dive deeper, slicing through the water and barely making ripples around me. The fjord deepens, and the water darkens. If Belu is out here, I'll find him. Fjords are known to plunge thousands of feet, where not even sunlight can reach, but my mermaid eyes are sharp, built to pierce the dark as long as there's a sliver of light to work with. If I can't see clearly this far down here, then neither will the merman... or so I hope.

As I push deeper, the water grows colder, icy on my skin. With a flick of my tail, I pivot sharply, but as I do, a dim light flickers through the deep water. I dart toward the beam, my tail beating fluidly just as a school of mackerel darts past, their silver bodies a flashing glint against the darkness around me. I can't help but grin, missing the whole swimming in the wild with the marine life, but I push those thoughts aside.

Sharpening my focus on the glow, it quickly becomes clear there's something else deep down here, something man-made—or mer-made, I guess. Nestled against the underwater cliff is a huge cave, its mouth agape. A light blazes from deep inside, cutting through the water the nearer I get.

Creeping closer, I realize something even weirder—some kind of invisible barrier that arches in front of the cave is keeping the fjord's icy waters at bay. It's like a magical force field, a clear, shimmering wall that seals the cave off from the rest of the underwater world. Just outside the cave is a ledge that stretches left and right, along with a path directly in front of the opening. It leads right into the wall of water.

Remaining farther at the side of the barrier, I peer in and can just make out two figures inside the cave, talking, the murmur of their voices barely reaching me. They're still too far away to really hear exact words or discern their features, but they're definitely not swimming. They're just... standing there as if on dry land.

As I float closer, my tail working overtime to keep me still against the currents, I can't help but wonder if I've just stumbled upon the merman's lair. Is this where he's bringing his victims? Despite the seriousness of the situation, I'm slightly impressed. This spot is genius—hidden in plain sight, accessible only to those who know exactly where to dive, and invisible without light.

I hover, shrouded in the murky darkness, concealed by the shadows, as a man emerges from the cave, giving me a perfect vantage point. He's strolling onto the ledge, hands deep in the pockets of his pants, before he pauses to stare into the rippling wall of water before him. I'm hidden, but my eyes are locked on him, taking in every captivating detail.

My gaze follows him from head to toe, and a delicious jolt shoots through my entire body.

Tall—very tall—with broad shoulders and lines of muscles tensing under his black button-up shirt. Oddly, his clothes look bone dry, his pants clinging to his solid thighs and outlining a large package right where I can't stop staring, where my mouth might have dropped open.

Who the hell is this guy?

Dark chestnut hair, shoulder-length and loose, frames a face that leaves me breathless. He's the most beautiful man I've ever seen. My heart's thudding a wild beat as I take in his brilliant blue eyes that resemble crashing waves and savage storms, the strong jaw shadowed by light stubble. Curls of tattoos spill out from under his shirt collar, trailing along his tanned collarbone and neck.

Is that my merman, Belu? The killer?

As much as my head screams danger, my libido and eyes can't stop drinking him in. He looks less like a man and more like a god—every inch of him dominating the surroundings, even seeming to command the waters at the edges of the magical barrier, as if they're trying to reach out to him. To be fair, I can't see him clearly from my angle, but it's enough to know he is devastatingly handsome. I could easily surrender to a man like that.

Then a snap of semi-sanity shoves me back to reality, reminding me my last ex was the king of jerks, and this sex god is most likely the killer I'm here to track, the one I need to bring in to prove to my bosses that I'm not easily distracted, that I won't fail my mission.

As he turns slightly, catching a reflection in the water, the light grazes his features, highlighting the angular perfection of his profile. My breath hitches all the way down to the pit of my stomach.

My ex left me sour on dating bad guys. He had been one of my targets, but I started dating him. Though I'm not even sure if I can call him my ex, considering we went on two dates before I discovered he lied about who he was, and our breakup ended up in a chaotic mess I prefer not to remember.

Yet, here I am, drooling over the next criminal, my entire body reacting to him, sizing him up as a prospective lover. Something's very wrong with me.

*Sure, he's insanely gorgeous, but I'm not interested.*

I repeat the mantra a few times in my head, especially as I watch his chest puff out with each breath, signaling his irritation. What's got him all worked up?

Just as I'm trying to convince myself of my total disinterest, she appears.

A woman steps onto the ledge from within the cave, joining the mer-manliness, and suddenly, I feel as if I'm watching a show live from the best seat in the house.

Of course, she's stunning. Turquoise hair cascades

over her shoulders like a waterfall, shimmering, while her silvery skin seems to emit a soft glow. Iridescent scales glitter along her arms and down the outside of her impossibly long legs, visible thanks to the audacious slits in her body-hugging dress, which reveals a lot of skin with every step she takes. I think about the scales I have, hidden away where no one can see them. They feel like pebbles compared to hers.

She's staring at him, and from my angle, I can only catch the side of her face, but enough to see her beauty is absolutely stunning.

"You will return with me," she states with authority and a power that seems to command the very air around her. It's not a question but a decree, her tone implying that no isn't an acceptable option. "That's fair payment for your unauthorized intrusion. With me, you will have access to every ocean to your heart's desire."

My pulse kicks up a notch, and while I'm clueless about what's going on, I'm all ears. And what's this about intrusion? Is this her cave?

The man says nothing at first, just stands there, holding her gaze. He doesn't seem fazed in the slightest, which is either a sign of confidence or complete foolishness, as I feel like this woman could eat any man alive.

He rubs his jawline, saying, "That's not going to work for me."

My body weakens at the sound of that deep, guttural, rough sound that screams his manly dominance. Fuck me, but I have a weakness for guys with deep, dark voices. And this merman's voice has me shivering with need.

Her shoulders tense, just slightly, but it's enough to tell me she's not used to resistance. I can tell she's a woman who controls, not one who is controlled. Yet there's calmness in her pose, confirming she's more than capable of handling whatever this guy throws at her.

"Oh," she murmurs almost softly, the gentleness in her tone surprising me—and I've only just met her. "You will have the space you need, not confined here. It's the least you can do as part of your payment for your intrusion."

He doesn't answer right away. Instead, he turns and walks toward the other end of the wide ledge outside the cave, his movements deliberate. The woman follows, her stride confident and poised as they move to the opposite side from where I'm hidden in the shadows. Her voice carries again, forceful, yet I can't grasp the words, and he's shaking his head in response. Not angrily, but firmly.

"Until you pay your debt," she says, her voice louder, more commanding now. "You will remain in my service. I'm being hospitable by personally visiting you. I don't want bad waters between us, but there must be respect shown."

He moves back toward the open mouth of the cave. "And if I agree to join your House, then you will let me out of your service?" His tone is cautious, probing the terms of his negotiation. "I will need to remain here in Norway for as long as I need to deal with family affairs."

Intrusion? Family affairs? Who exactly are these two?

When she doesn't respond, a half smirk plays on his lips.

"If not, then I will seek residence with King Kaspian. I hear he's a reasonable king and will no doubt understand the power of welcoming someone like me into the House of Gold and Garnet."

Wait! What? So, the merman isn't from this House?

She emerges from the darkness, stepping into the flickering light of the cave, and her face becomes visible to me. My stomach drops, and my insides turn to mush.

My heart's in my throat—not just because she's the most stunning woman I've ever seen, but because I've seen her before... well, paintings of her.

For a split second, my heart locks up, and a cold realization spreads through me at having someone like her standing so close to me.

Asbesta.

The Queen of Sirens, of Mermaids, of the Oceans. She's a goddess, a powerful and intimidating one with a dangerous reputation. Stories speak of her voice being so deadly it could lull someone into doing anything she asked. Just staring at her could have that impact, and here I find myself frozen in place, caught in her presence. Unease spreads through me. Fuck, I definitely don't want her to see me. I've heard stories of her ruthlessness.

As the Siren Goddess, she rules the waters in our world from her House of Sea and Serpentine. Those of us from different Houses—like me—are forbidden from entering her domain without permission, a.k.a. the oceans and rivers and fjords.

I did it many times back in South Africa, staying close to the shore, figuring no one would see me.

Yet, here I am, tucked away in the shadows of her

fjords, uninvited and unnoticed. And from what I can tell, this merman has done the same, been caught, and now she wants him to pay a debt by joining her House. I have no idea why Asbesta would want the likes of a merman who's being investigated for murder.

Disdain flickers across Asbesta's face, yet I admire the merman's guts. He's got some serious brass balls to stand up to her like that.

A sudden flutter of the school of mackerel rushes past me in such a flurry that it has me flinching and missing out on part of the conversion. Exhaling and trying not to draw attention to myself, I refocus on the pair.

She takes a deep breath, and even furious, she's drop-dead gorgeous.

"Accepted. When you complete your affairs, you are to relocate to the House of Sea and Serpentine immediately," she states firmly. "With your committed loyalty, you have uninhibited access to the fjords. You will uphold your agreement."

He nods once, a sharp, quick gesture, and without another word, he strides back into the cave, leaving the Siren Goddess alone on the ledge. Time seems to freeze for a moment, my heart still thundering in my chest, and I honestly have no idea what she's going to do next.

She turns abruptly to face the wall of water surrounding her domain. For a heart-stopping second, her gaze sweeps my way, and I lock up, my veins turning to ice.

Has she spotted me?

Fuck! Fuck!

I don't need to be punished for being in her territory when I'm already trying to fix my work reputation.

Just as quickly, she shifts her focus back to the water and steps gracefully off the ledge, disappearing through the magical barrier and into the water.

I withdraw farther into the shadows, watching and waiting until the last glint of her iridescent scales vanishes in the dark fjord. Once I'm sure she's really gone, I slowly move closer to the cave to look for any sign of the merman.

Of course, he's no longer there.

And just like that, the light flicks off in the cave, and a great rush of water surges around me, wrenching me forward as if I've just plummeted down a waterfall. I grunt as I crash into the hard wall of the fjord, panic rising through me as the force of the water pins me against it.

I fight against the flow, convinced I've been caught by the Siren Goddess, my mind spinning on an excuse. When nothing more happens, it hits me that with the light going out, the cave has not only closed, but the pocket of air has been replaced by water.

Frantically, I swim to the surface, more confused than ever. My head breaks the surface, already transforming back, and I've never scrambled out of the water so fast.

As I wring out the last drops of fjord water from my hair and frantically dress, which is hell when I'm completely drenched, my thoughts circle back to Belu. The more I replay the encounter by the cave, the more something doesn't sit right with me.

The handsome man's demeanor, his brazen defiance in the face of divine authority, the fact that she permitted him to use her waters, which is rare for an outsider— well, this isn't exactly the behavior of someone skulking away from having missed bail and hiding from a bounty.

No darting glances, no jittery nerves that usually mark the guilty. He was too composed, too... regal.

Could I have been wrong about him being my target?

If so, then who in the hell is that guy in the cave?

# FOUR



The moment I step out of my car, the first drops of rain kiss my face. I stroll toward my rented cabin, nestled on the edge of the woods, loving it when it rains. With the sun already descending, coating the sky in a dark golden hue, I'm contemplating a quick swim in the pool at the back of my place. The fjords brought something out of me today, something I missed—that connection with nature. Something I hadn't done for a few months back in South Africa from a lack of time.

"I'm home, Chowder!" I call out as I shut the door behind me.

Instantly, there's a scramble of claws against the hardwood floor, and then, like a tiny furry hurricane, Chowder bursts into the living room. The little otter, with his gleaming eyes, mouth stretched in an almost smile, never fails to brighten every single day since I made him mine.

My heart beams at his cuteness, at his eagerness to see me.

Brown fur, richer along the top and the cream color underneath, glints in the hallway light. Seeing that Chowder wasn't fully recovered from his injuries caused by that jerk, Zane, I picked up a cozy little vest for him. The fur along his back took the worst hit and hasn't quite grown back yet. I wanted to make sure he stayed warm and comfy while his fur gradually returned.

I bend down and scoop him up into a hug, his body still long and lean but getting stronger every day. "How was your day, little one?" I ask, holding him close. I couldn't bear the thought of handing him over after rescuing him from that cage, not with the risk of him being put down because of his injuries. So, here he is, having snuck into my life and now a part of it.

"Did you miss me?" I murmur as he nuzzles his face and cold nose into my neck, making little chirping sounds.

"Food?" he squeaks out. "Who's hungry?"

It's astonishing, really. Whatever Zane was doing with these animals wasn't just trafficking—but experimentation involving magic, and now, Chowder can speak. It's basic, sure, and usually phrased like a question, but it's clear evidence of a mind working beyond animal instincts.

"Always food with you," I joke, walking us both to the small kitchen. The cabin isn't huge, but it comes with two bedrooms and a bathtub—perfect for Chowder to have a place to dip into water any time of the day or night.

I place him down on the counter and reach for a can of chowder from the cupboard. The first time I brought him home, I'd made a fresh batch, and he was all over it, starved, so I let him polish it off. That's when I decided it made for a perfect name.

Watching him eat, I stroke his head, loving that I no longer come home to a lonely cabin. Moving into the bedroom, I start undressing from my semi-wet clothes when a heavy knock comes at my door.

Who's that?

I grab a robe, pulling it around me, calling out, "Give me a sec."

I hurry to close the sliding door to the kitchen, Chowder still devouring his meal and unbothered.

Who could it be? A neighbor? The landlord? The cabins nearby are spaced well enough for privacy yet close enough that a visit isn't uncommon. A knot tightens in my stomach as I open the front door.

Instantly, a shiver runs down my spine.

There stands a wide-chested man in a dark guard's uniform, a blade at his hip, and the unmistakable emblem of the House of Sea and Serpentine emblazoned on his chest.

My heart's thundering in my chest.

Oh, fuck!

Half of me expects Asbesta herself to float up behind him, but when she doesn't, I count my blessings. Hopefully, she's gone back home to Brazil, as far from Norway as possible.

With his eyes fixed on me, I muster my composure and lean casually against the door frame as if his appearance is the least startling thing of my day. He's a towering figure, his face set in a stoic mask that looks like he hasn't cracked a smile in years. He's stern, rigid, his brow furrowed.

"Can I help you?" I manage, biting back the sarcasm itching on the tip of my tongue.

He clears his throat. "You have been caught illegally trespassing in sacred waters belonging to Asbesta, and I am here for reparations."

I swallow hard, the dryness in my throat making it difficult to speak smoothly. The idea of pleading ignorance flashes through my mind, but making an enemy of the goddess could be a death sentence. For all I know, she's still lurking nearby, ready to exact whatever punishment she deems fit for intruders.

"In truth," I begin, "I was in the fjord out of necessity for work, chasing a murderer, not for pleasure. I can offer confirmation from my place of work. Surely that must be taken into consideration? I believe this man I was chasing has entered her waters illegally, and my intention was to bring him to justice."

He glares at me, unimpressed, with a slight rise of one of his eyebrows. "We don't accept excuses. Even if you run into the water to save your life, you are still breaking the rules and must pay."

My thought flies to the gorgeous guy in the water and how he was asked to join the House of Sea and Serpentine for his errors. Is that what's going to happen to me?

"Look, I've just moved here, and I'm not ready to swap alliances to another House."

He raises both eyebrows that time. "What makes you think we want someone like you in our House?" he sneers.

I instantly hate him. His arrogance has me glaring in response. My shoulders shoot back in a bristle as he steps forward, muscling his way into my cabin. His sheer size forces me back a few steps.

"First, you'd be lucky to have someone as skilled as me in your House," I snap back. "And secondly, I never said you could come inside."

But he's already shutting the door behind him with a decisive thud, sealing us in together, and I flinch at the sound.

"I'm not leaving until you pay your fine, even if I have to take it by force." His voice deepens, a rumble that fills the small space, meant to intimidate.

I meet his glare head-on, standing my ground. "I'm not scared of you." I've faced bigger assholes than him. In the back of my mind, I'm already calculating the distance to my bag, where my taser is tucked away.

"Go on, then," I spit out when it's clear he's not going to respond. "What's the payment? Then I'll decide if I pay it. Then you can get the hell out of my house." I take a casual sidestep toward the table by the window where my bag lies, then another.

"It's a binding agreement the moment you enter our waters," he affirms, locking eyes with me.

I just meet his stare, waiting to hear it.

"Let's get this done," he says. "You will pay Asbesta two of your mermaid scales." He heaves a heavy sigh, his broad chest rising and falling.

I balk, a scoffing sound spilling past my lips. "Are you kidding? You want to ruin my tail?" I haven't lost a scale in years and spend a lot of time taking care of it. Plus, it takes ages for my scales to grow back.

He chuckles, seeming amused by my reaction. "It's our currency in the House of Sea and Serpentine, and like I said, you hand them over, or I take them by force."

I blink at him, irritation flaring. I'm starting to really hate the smirk playing across his lips. He's clearly enjoying this too much.

"Fine," I say grudgingly, despising the thought of damaging my tail. But facing off against the goddess herself seems like a worse option. "I'll get it done. Are you happy now? Where do I send them?"

"Nope," he cuts in. "You're going to pay right now."

I inhale sharply, grinding my teeth. Mermaid scales are precious, valuable beyond many other currencies, so of course they'll demand them as payment.

"Stay here," I mutter, turning toward the bathroom. "I'll go do it."

But he steps in my path, blocking me. "I need to see you doing it so I know they're your scales."

I glare at him, frustration boiling over. "Sure. You can watch me in the tub."

He shakes his head, his annoying smirk deepening. "You're doing it here, now. You're wearing my patience."

"Forget it," I snap, well aware that transforming into a mermaid outside of water is possible but is excruciatingly painful. "You're being a real jerk," I add.

He reaches for my arm.

At that same moment, a movement from the direction of the now open kitchen door catches my eye. It comes so fast, a blur of motion, that I barely have time to register it.

"Chowder, stop!" I shout, lunging for him as he launches at the guard, a growl in his throat.

All I see then are his teeth—two rows, sharp like a shark's, his jaw expanding and growing at a monstrous rate. I'd seen him do this once before when I first brought him home. Another magical trait forced onto Chowder by Zane in the labs. He's a little attack dog.

The guard reacts too slowly.

Chowder is fast and latches onto the man's two last fingers and chomps them right off.

"Oh, fuck," I murmur.

My insides freeze.

The guard howls and shouts, his voice erupting like a volcano. Blood spurts wildly all over the floor and him from his flailing hand.

Chowder spits out the digits, hissing venomously at the man, his fur bristled up in aggression. His transformed, oversized mouth is a terrifying sight.

My head spins for a split second, shocked and unsure what to do next.

Then, I rush to grab Chowder as the guard tries to kick him away. Swooping him up, Chowder snaps his teeth at the guard, furious and frightened. I'm holding him close.

"Chowder, no, don't attack him." I'm gasping for air.

"Bad, bad man hurts you."

The man is wailing, "What the hell is that thing? You

dare harm one of the goddess's guards? You will pay for this severely."

Panic surges through me. I rush and shove Chowder into the bedroom, closing him inside, despite his growls echoing. I'm back in the living room within seconds, facing the guard who's clutching his bleeding hand, his howls filling the space.

"Shit, we need to bandage that properly, and the fingers can be reattached," I mutter, more to myself than to him.

I grab his arm and drag him into the bathroom. He's too shocked to resist, trailing behind me in a daze. I rummage through the cabinet, which is mostly empty, but manage to find a roll of bandage and some tape.

"Hurry," I urge, directing him to place his hand in the sink. Blood is spurting out so fast that I'm genuinely worried he might pass out.

"I will personally cut off your fingers. An eye for an eye, and for that feral thing that attacked me..." he cries out with pain in his voice.

Nope, it's fine if he passes out.

"It's not my fault you got attacked. You were being aggressive, and you entered my home uninvited," I explain with a wobbly voice, my hands shaking as I wrap his hand. It's a mess—blood all over the sink and mirror. I'm trying not to gag. I somehow manage to use the entire roll, securing the bandage so the bleeding stops. While he leans against the wall hurling insults, I'm already climbing into the tub filled with water, sitting on the edge. My whole body trembles. I want him out of my place, so I'll give him what he wants.

Why do things always end badly for me?

Calling forth my mermaid form feels urgent, desperate. The transformation sweeps over me with a rush, every inch of my skin responding to the need.

"Look, I'm giving you my payment," I say softly, hating every moment of it. "Then we can just forget this incident."

"For this, I'll take your whole fucking tail, bitch," he retorts.

With trembling hands, I reach down to the base of my aquamarine tail, which glints in the light, where the scales are smaller, less noticeable if missing.

"Don't think about it," he growls menacingly. "I want the two big ones, the golden ones right in front..."

"You ass," I spit back, the words hissing through my clenched teeth. This whole situation is spiraling out of control, and I'm left bargaining with my own body parts to appease this brute. I touch the shimmering golden scales and slip my finger under one, then I grip it tightly and tug hard. I wince at the sharp pain, like being cut with a blade. I make quick work of the second scale next to it, and already I see the hole they leave behind in my tail, sticking out like sore thumbs.

I almost laugh at my own sarcasm when the guard, snarling, stumbles out of the bathroom. Just as quickly, I call back my human form with a single thought, my body tingling with the fast transformation. With the bottom half of my robe also soaked, I rush after him.

He's stumbling, his shoulder banging against the walls in the hallway. I pass him and dart into the kitchen, grabbing two small containers with lids from the kitchen.

In one, I gently place my two scales, my heart already mourning their loss. Then, I'm in the living room and gingerly picking up his severed fingers from the floor. I drop them into the other container. Gross.

Locking eyes with him, I grumble, "Well, it was terrible to have you visit. Now I think you should leave." I shove the containers into his pockets as his face pales, then I open the front door. "Want me to take you to the local medic?"

He growls a no and pushes outside. "You'll hear from us again, and when I return, you'll be sorry for the fury that Asbesta will bring down on you."

My half smile feels forced, my insides quaking. "Okay, have a nice day," I say sarcastically, shutting the door behind him and freaking out. Of course, he's going to heal, and magic medicine is amazing these days. That's not what I'm worried about.

I pace back and forth.

Chowder's scratching at the bedroom door. I dart down the corridor to let him out, noting his sharp teeth are gone, and he darts into the living room, searching for the guard.

"Oh, Chowder, I adore you, and thank you for protecting me," I murmur, lifting him into my arms.

"He can't hurt you," he says, licking his mouth, which still has a bit of blood on it. I might have cringed if I didn't find him super cute.

"This may just plunge us into major trouble." I hold on to him in my arms, contemplating my options. Go into hiding? Or maybe come up with a plan to explain to Asbesta that it was all a mistake after the guard forced himself into my home, threatening me? Already, I'm running through the details in my head.

Blood is on the carpet and the walls, so I jump into doing the one thing I can control. I start cleaning it up before I completely break down. As I scrub the floor, Chowder tries to help me by mimicking my actions.

The truth of what might come next looms over me like the growing murky clouds outside. Whatever happens, I know one thing for sure. A huge, dangerous storm from the House of Sea and Serpentine is just beginning, and it's headed straight for us.

CHAPTER

# FIVE

KADEN

Ironic how I've spent a lifetime hunting for a way out of Tartarus to find answers on who betrayed my family, yet here I am, hunting for the mermaid. She'd been spying on me in the fjord earlier in the day, and whether she wanted it or not, she got my attention. Waters talk to me, sending ripples of awareness through to me even when I'm on land. Her presence in the fjord had raised every hair on my body from the pull to her.

Right now, she's in the swimming pool at the rear of her cabin, and I'm in the woods surrounding her property.

Watching.

I'm darkness, desperate to capture her.

A growl vibrates in my chest.

She's fucking stunning, a surprise I wasn't expecting, and a great one at that, considering the uncomfortable conversation I had with Asbesta earlier in the day. I said what she wanted to hear, to appease her, but I bow to

67

nobody's commands. I'm no idiot and know having someone like me in her House gives her a great advantage over her enemies, so of course, she lets me use her fjords while I remain here.

Whether I return to her House once I'm finished with my business in Norway is a completely different matter. If she wants to bring war down on me for it, I'll show her exactly why I'm not someone to be fucked with. Sure, I may not survive against her powers and army, but I sure as fuck will have fun trying.

I shake off the unease clinging to me and refocus on something delicious.

I followed my little mermaid from the fjord to uncover who she is. I wasn't letting her out of my sight. Now, primal curiosity pushes me to get closer, to claim her, and I'm grinning, knowing it won't be long until I do.

Her aquamarine hair catches the moonlight, shimmering like the surface of the water as she splashes playfully in the small pool. Her tail, vibrant blues and greens with hints of gold, splashes in and out of the water, drawing my attention to every flick. Besides her, some small creature frolics, its significance lost to me.

There's a pull, a nearly physical ache that courses through me toward her, toward the water, a thirst only joining her can fill. Yet I'm standing on land, feeling the distance like a dry crackling in my throat.

Back in the Tartarus prison, many stalked and kidnapped their mate. That same temptation simmers under my skin, but I'm biding my time, needing to first understand if she's my true mate. My cock's already hard, close to losing control, so I'm not under any illusion that this could just be me being horny as fuck and needing to sink into that gorgeous mermaid.

Compelled by a need to see her closer, I begin to move. Each step down the sloped hill is calculated to avoid making any sound.

I've been in Norway for a couple of weeks now, finding a very different world from Tartarus, but I'm adapting quickly, finding my footing, setting up Grandfather's home as my own, and slowly putting out feelers as to his past dealings on how the fuck he ended up in Tartarus.

The night air is cool on my skin, and each breath feels warmer as I approach the pool. I pause within the line of trees in her yard. I stay hidden in the shadows, yet my view is crisp.

Tracing her every movement, I watch her gracefully pull herself up to sit on the ledge, a side view to me. Her hair drops down her back, cascading like liquid, and under the moonlight, her skin almost glows with a silvery luster, her tail shimmering with each movement. She's mesmerizing.

My gaze falls to her exposed breasts, large enough to fill my hands, firm and curvy. Aquamarine nipples are hard, and each time she moves, they jiggle in the most hypnotic motion. I lick my lips, and the desperation to pull them into my mouth, to suck on them, to make her moan is pure torture.

Just as I adjust my cock and shift my stance, a small twig underfoot snaps. The sound is slight, but in the stillness of the night, it carries. Her head snaps up, those piercing eyes scanning the woods in my direction.

I lock in place, waiting to see if she'll notice me, ready to step out of the darkness.

Her brow creases as she scans the woods, but when she doesn't spot me, she lowers her gaze to her lap. Part of me is disappointed she didn't see me.

She's absolutely breathtaking, the kind of mermaid I'd crash a hundred ships just to be ensnared by her.

Then I see her still leaning forward, focusing on a dark hole in the shimmering scales of her tail. Her beautiful skin is exposed where there are missing scales.

I've seen a mermaid being completely scaled back in Tartarus, tortured, and it was horrendous.

Seeing this beauty suffering, a primal fury kindles inside me, especially when I hear a whine softly escape her lips as she runs a finger over the wound.

A fierce instinct to protect her flares in me.

With my gaze still on her, I notice as the little critter from the water, her apparent companion, sidles up to her, nudging against her gently. A knot twists inside me at seeing her pain.

As my mind races, I recall the sight of one of Asbesta's guards leaving her cabin not long ago, his hand wrapped and bloodied. Could he be the cause of her pain? Was that why she retaliated and hurt him?

Fuck, he's lucky he's still walking because if I'd been there, his head would be rolling.

Breathing heavily, I can't quite explain my sudden obsession with this mermaid, but something feels right about her. It's satisfying, has me buzzing, and I want more.

Watching her for a few moments longer, my anger flares at what might have happened to her.

Taking one last look, imprinting her on my mind, I turn and dart from my hidden spot, disappearing into the night. Each step is driven by a storm of fury, my chest thumping louder, and suddenly, I feel more alive than I have in decades.

**Sasha**

I flinch awake with my heart hammering, my eyes snapping wide, and stare at the wooden ceiling. The remnants of yesterday's events cling to me, cold and terrifying, as I keep picturing Asbesta coming for me.

Chowder makes a small whining sound as he curls up alongside my legs in bed.

I glance over to my bedside table to see the time, but instead, my gaze lands on something entirely unexpected—a container. My breath catches in my throat.

Wait, is that the same container I used yesterday, the one I put the guard's fingers into? Except he took it, and I didn't leave it on my bedside table.

My chest tightens, and a chill sweeps through me as I struggle to breathe. How did that get here?

Frantically, I jump out of bed, stirring Chowder out of his sleep with my sudden movement. My mind races with thoughts of Asbesta or perhaps the guard breaking into my place while I slept. My heart thunders louder as I check the front door—it's still locked. I rush through the house, finding nothing else amiss, no windows open, nothing tossed about.

Back by the bed, I stare at the transparent container, starting to realize something even more unnerving— there are no fingers inside, though a bit of blood on the inside confirms it's the same box. There's something else in there.

Tentatively, I pull back the lid, and inside, to my utter disbelief, I find the two scales from my tail. The ones I plucked out yesterday as payment.

I blink at them, a mixture of confusion spinning in my mind.

"What the hell is going on?" My hands shake, the box trembling as I hold it. All of a sudden, everything feels unsafe—the room, my home, the world outside. Yet as I curl my fingers around my scales, I'm deeply appreciative of having them back. I can't reattach them, but just holding a part of me, a part I thought I'd sacrificed, softens the ache.

I don't know what happened or why, but I'm on my feet, pacing the room. Someone broke into my house as I slept, most likely watched me sleep, and then headed out. And not even Chowder noticed, or he would have made enough noise to wake me up.

That's fucking creepy. So why the hell did the guard or Asbesta return them?

With Chowder now stirring and watching me with his big, curious eyes, I rub the top of his head.

"Feel like something to eat?"

"Who isn't ready for chowder?"

I smirk at his cuteness and get up, my mind on fire.

If someone really wanted me hurt, they would have done it while I slept. And while that doesn't ease the chill on my skin, it helps stop the panic crawling through me. Tonight, I'll be setting up the house with some trip wires and sleeping with my weapons.

After a rushed morning, I head into the office, trying to shake off the events of last night.

Now, I'm leaning against the kitchen counter in the office at work, chatting with my boss, Ada, who looks every bit the seasoned bounty hunter. Dressed in jeans and a leather jacket, she's tall and looks like she can handle herself in the field. But it's her smile that catches me off guard—soft and welcoming. Her lion shifter heritage is apparent in the slitted, golden eyes and the taut pull of her blonde hair in a tight bun, which really brings out their brightness.

"Your report on yesterday's findings was intriguing, especially with discovering that underwater cave," she says with a grin. "Smart idea to explore the fjords."

I nod, grateful for the recognition but also slightly regretting going down there, considering the reper-cussions.

"I think I need another day or two out there to see if Belu shows up," I suggest, leaving out any mention of the handsome merman or Asbesta. Maybe if I find the guard again, I can ask him why he returned the scales. Not that I'm looking a gift horse in the mouth, but something feels really strange about it. And I hate being in the dark on anything that involves me.

"Mr. Daniels informed me of your hard work and tenacity, and I see it." Ada's hands cradle a cup of a steaming hot brew, her expression earnest. "And agree on a few more days. If you see him, bring Belu in or call in for backup. There's no shame in asking for help."

"Will do," I say, proud that she trusts me with the target. Edging toward the door to get started, she calls out, stopping me in my tracks.

"That property you're checking near the fjord," she states. "It has a lot of history. Dark history. Be careful. I've heard rumors that a family member might be in town. Use your ID to show you have authority to be there if you are confronted."

My mind instantly flashes to the merman from the cave. Belu. Could that be him? I turn to face her. "What do you know about the house up on the hill and who lived there?" I ask, curiosity piqued.

Ada shrugs, sipping from her drink before saying, "Honestly, not much. It's been abandoned for thousands of years, yet a team has continued to keep it maintained. From my understanding, the grandfather of the family committed a crime so heinous that he ended up thrown in Tartarus."

Intrigued, I stand there, absorbing her words. Tartarus is a prison where only the worst of the worst are sent, and they never come out. It's said to have become a sort of settlement, with new generations born and raised within its confines. Imagine growing up in a prison.

"Good to know. I'll keep an eye out. Going to head out, then," I call over my shoulder to Ada, but she's already engaged in another conversation with someone else. The office isn't too different from the one back in South Africa—open plan, desks lined up for bounty hunters who come and go from missions.

As I make my way out, two of the girls I met on my first day smile my way.

Stepping outside, I make a beeline for my sedan, beyond curious about those who lived in that house near the fjord. As I drive back to the spot I visited yesterday, I'm going over my boss's words, curious as hell about what someone would have had to do to end up in Tartarus. I've heard enough tales to know something terrible would have had to happen to be sentenced and end up there.

Parked, I scan the rocky edge where I last saw those abandoned shoes. Now, they're gone, with no trace of anyone.

It's silent.

Calm.

I take a moment to scan the surroundings—the calm fjord waters, the chilly breeze curling through my hair, the eerie sensation of being watched.

I'm definitely not alone here.

My gaze eventually drifts toward the huge house perched on the hill behind me. Maybe there's no harm in checking it out. For all I know, Belu could be hiding there, or maybe he's in cahoots with the family member rumored to be in town.

I stroll past my car near the woods and follow a stone path, now overgrown with wild foliage. Encroaching trees and underbrush make the walk clumsy as it curls uphill toward the house.

As I reach what must have once been a gate, I find nothing left but the open yard. It's a wild tangle of plants and trees desperately in need of trimming. The enormous mansion itself looms farther ahead and is grand, bigger than it appears from down by the water. It's been diminished by the years of neglect. Those needing to fix it clearly haven't been working on the exterior of the house.

With a cautious step, I cross the threshold of where the gate once marked the entrance and approach the home. Long grass folds under my steps.

The quiet of the old mansion is suddenly shattered by a sharp snapping sound.

I flinch around as something tight cinches around my ankle, yanking me right off my feet. Instantly, I'm wrenched upward, my feet going up first, and a cry bleeds from my throat.

"Fuck, are you kidding me?" Here I am, suspended upside down in the air, dangling helplessly from a thick rope secured around my ankle. I walked right into that trap. "Great job, Sasha."

I thrash, reaching for my pocketknife, but as I fumble, my blade and keys slip from my pockets and clatter to the ground. "Damn it!" I stretch my arms down, but I'm too far up to reach them.

I always come prepared, and as I strain up to reach my ankle for my other knife, a flicker of movement in the shadows of the surrounding woods catches my eye.

Someone is definitely there, shifting silently between the trees. My heart thumps even louder, not just from the effort of hanging there but also from the realization that I might have just fallen for their trap.

And whoever they are, they're coming toward me.

Fuck!

# SIX

### KADEN

H ere I was, grumbling about heading into the yard to deal with another damn mercenary after the trap went off, so imagine my surprise to find myself staring at the gorgeous beauty from the other night instead.

She's wriggling, hanging upside down from a branch by the rope around her ankle. My traps are all over the yard, a habit I picked up in Tartarus to avoid intruders, but I've never been this pleased about a catch before.

I can't wipe the foolish grin off my lips or the speeding thud of my heart pounding against my rib cage. Something about her sets me off, and I'm fucking engrossed.

Where did she come from, and more importantly, did she follow me to my grandfather's home because she couldn't get me out of her mind? Ever since watching her in her pool, she's been a constant in my thoughts.

Her gaze finds me in the shadows of the surrounding trees, and she stiffens, her eyes wide, brow furrowed with what I can only imagine is frustration. Long aquamarine hair swings down, brushing the ground. She's wearing a deep scowl, and somehow, she's so damn adorable when she's angry. Her round face, ice-blue eyes, and delicious lips call to me. Leather jacket zipped up and black pants tight around her curves remind me of her in the pool, her breasts bare. That hunger in me stirs awake again, my cock throbbing in my jeans.

I step out of the shadows, pausing by the tree she's dangling from, grinning at this mermaid who is so much more captivating close up. They're known for their magical beauty, the kind that can render most weak in their presence, but there's something about *her* almond-shaped eyes, those full red lips, her tiny nose, the curve of her neck... something that's going to ruin me. I feel it already, yet I can't walk away.

"If I knew trapping mermaids was this easy, I would've started long ago," I say, resting a shoulder against the tree she's hanging from, studying her intently.

Her eyes narrow as she swings gently, still hanging upside down. "How do you know me?"

I grin, taking my time with an answer. "You insult me, thinking I don't know you were spying on me in the fjord the other day."

She stares at me sharply, her mouth opening and closing while she spins slightly on the rope. She doesn't respond immediately, telling me she thought she got away with sneaking around underwater.

Adorable.

"I wasn't spying on you," she finally answers firmly. "I stumbled across you."

Her voice is a song in my ear, each word playing across my skin, a cadence that's like velvet against me. I can almost feel the spark of her magic in her voice, an irresistible allure that can easily convince someone to speak the truth. Yet she's barely using it to her full potential, as though she has no idea she has such a power. An ability that won't impact me, but others would be fair game if she came into her full strength.

Does she even have any idea of the impact she has on others?

I've heard it said that people either fall under a mermaid's charm and adore them, or if they resist, they despise them. Then there's the whole connection to how they become sirens... it's fucking dark. Of course, there are a bunch of rumors about mermaids, and not everything is based on truth.

I nod, still grinning, well aware that she stayed underwater long enough to watch my conversation with Asbesta, but I don't call her out on it. Instead, I keep my smirk fixed on her.

"And I'm guessing you live here, in your family mansion?" she murmurs. "So, why do you have this stupid trap in your yard?" she grumbles, attempting to reach up to her ankle but failing as the breeze pushes her into another spin.

"I have more than one trap, but I guess you were unlucky enough to step on one."

"Story of my life," she mumbles, and I catch the

words. "Anyway, are you going to keep me hanging here all day or what?"

I chuckle, enjoying the sass in her voice. "All right, all right, I'll let you down."

"Do you have a name?" she blurts out as I slowly push off the tree.

"Kaden Vinter. You?"

She blinks my way as her spin settles, and she's facing me, as if seeing me for the first time. Was she expecting someone else?

"I have legal permission to be on your property, but if you just help me down, I'll be on my way."

I can't take my attention off that cute face, the sinful body, rather enjoying seeing her tied up for me.

"You never told me your name," I say, curious what she's doing here and in the fjord the other day.

"Not important, especially when you're not a man of your word and haven't gotten me down yet."

"I'm sure you've heard the stories of mermaids and sirens hunted, tied up by their tails once captured." I lift my gaze to her bound ankle. "My grandfather once told me that if you capture a mermaid and release her, she will be indebted to you."

She bursts out laughing, the sound like honey, sweet and delicious, yet she rolls those hypnotic blue eyes.

"Sorry to disappoint you, but I'm not a genie in a bottle granting wishes. Nice try, though. Think your grandfather spun you a lie."

"He usually did." I nod and grin, suspecting the story had been fabricated.

She wrenches herself upward once more, bending at the waist and reaching for her ankle.

I step toward her to help, but she jerks around to face me, sending herself into another spin. Something slips from her grasp and tumbles into the grass—a black object with metal prods at one end.

"Oh, look, you dropped your weapon. Was that meant for me?" I tease.

She narrows her eyes, gaze unwavering. "You can never be too careful. There's a lot of psychos around."

My curiosity is piqued. What makes her so afraid that she carries weapons around? And the fact that she does tells me she's single—otherwise, her match would be around to protect her, and she'd have nothing to worry about.

"Hold on," I say, grabbing a blade from the back of my belt. I reach up to the rope, keeping her tied up, and cut it quickly. Moving lightning fast, I drop the blade behind me into the earth and catch her before she falls headfirst. My arms wrap around her back and knees, bringing her head up, so she's cradled securely against me.

She's light as anything, but she wriggles in protest. Her face twists. Suddenly, she shoves against me, her hands against my chest, instinctively trying to get down. I release her legs from my grasp, and they fall.

When I don't let her go completely, she knees me in the thigh, way too close to my precious jewels, and my knee wobbles. Before I know it, we're both tumbling to the ground, her beneath me.

We land with a soft thud on the grass, her gasping

while I have my elbows on either side of her shoulders, pinning her down. Face-to-face, she's beneath me. Her eyes enlarge as she attempts to escape.

Me? I'm in heaven, lost in the way she looks up at me, her breaths coming in quick gasps. I smile, and it's completely uncontrollable. Her cheeks flush as her gaze locks with mine, and for a moment, neither of us moves. The closeness, the undeniable connection—it's electrifying. The instant my skin had touched hers, sparks flew. And she knows it, too. I see it in her eyes.

Adrenaline rushes through me, and every nerve in my body comes alive. Cock twitching, heart pounding, something inside me shifts... my shadow beast recognizes her instantly as ours. I must have saved up all my good luck by suffering the last thousand years in that hellhole prison to finally find her.

"Get off me!" Her voice is lined with venom.

I can't help but smile, my heart racing in my chest. "You're not making it easy," I tease, refusing to release her just yet, rather enjoying the feeling of her soft body, those delectable breasts against mine.

"I swear if you don't move..." Her hands press against my shoulders, trembling as she struggles to push me away.

From her quivering touch, the way her eyes dilate, and her intoxicating rising scent of roses, the ocean of nectar tells me all I need to know. The warmth that's coiling around my heart, squeezing, embracing, and compelling me can't be ignored.

"Mate," I mutter, the word slipping out on its own.

"Excuse me?" she retorts, eyes blazing with defiance, despite her position beneath me.

I lean in closer, my voice soft but firm. "You heard me."

"Don't get any ideas," she fires back, her tone sharp. "You're not my mate. Hell no, I don't have a fated mate. Not now or ever!"

"Maybe you're not ready to accept it yet," I say, smirking as I release her and roll off to the side. "But you know it's real. You feel it deep in your soul, don't you? And I'm willing to wait."

She scrambles to her feet, brushing herself off, flicking the grass and dead leaves off her pants. Then she snatches her weapon out of the grass. I half expect her to use it on me, except she tucks it into her back pocket.

"You're delusional," she mutters, but the way she avoids my gaze tells me she's not as sure as she's pretending to be.

"Time will tell." I get to my feet, my gaze never leaving her as I dust off my shirt.

"Time will tell that you're an idiot," she scoffs, clearly unimpressed.

I laugh, thoroughly amused by her feistiness. "Maybe, but I'm your idiot now."

She shakes her head, incredulous. "Don't say that."

"And yet here you are," I say, my amusement never fading. Stepping closer, I'm drawn to her. My head's whirling with the high, with the notion that I found the one thing I left Tartarus for.

She backs away as her scowl deepens, and the fire in

her eyes only makes my yearning for her stronger. She's fierce, determined, and utterly intoxicating.

She's my fated mate.

Whether she likes it or not, she's mine.

**Sasha**

Fated mate?

No, this can't be happening. I've always figured I'd just keep dating until maybe I found someone special, if ever. Finding your fated mate? That's supposed to be a one-in-a-billion chance. Something inside me isn't ready for something so serious—so permanent—that it might destroy me if I lose them... or if I hurt them.

My thoughts flash to my parents, to the river, to my mom's kiss of death to my dad, stealing his life. I shake those images away because I'm not her, I'm not...

Kaden stares at me with that ridiculously sinful smile, and my knees are close to buckling. I hate that he smells so good—like the fresh cut of lawn, the ocean in a storm, and masculine sexiness that leaves me close to swooning.

Sure, I've been attracted to lots of men, but this is something else, something terrifying in how my body is responding as if my insides are pushing me to get closer to him.

I force a step backward instead.

On the bright side, this guy isn't my target, Belu, so one point for me in not falling for a criminal again.

"My little mermaid, what brings you to my family mansion? To find me?" His voice is deep, the kind that slides over my body, slipping between my thighs, teasing me, grasping onto me as though he has me pinned beneath him once more. Whatever he's doing to it, it's almost like being strangled into submission... and part of me wants to give in desperately.

For a moment, I forget how to breathe.

My thoughts fly to the conversation I had with my boss about this very property. She mentioned it held a lot of dark history, and I assume this man is the family member who returned. I also remember my boss, Ada, saying his grandfather had been sent to Tartarus.

Does Kaden know what his grandfather did to end up there?

When I notice he's staring unblinking, waiting for my response, I manage to murmur, "W-work. I'm here for an investigation. I'm searching for someone." My voice comes across steadier than I feel, but the casual flicker of his eyebrows shows he senses the nerves in my voice. He steps close, a challenge written all over that gorgeous face.

"In my yard?"

I meet his steely gaze. "Could be. He was last seen down by the water recently."

Kaden runs a hand through his deep chestnut hair,

which glints in the light. It cascades around his face and falls to his shoulders, and it's almost impossible not to stare. How can someone be so handsome? The way the sunlight catches his features almost seems unfair.

He's tall, too, close to six foot two or three, and broad, massive. I feel so tiny next to him. He could easily overpower me, yet he seems more interested in watching me, as if I should just fall to my knees before him.

The idea of accepting my fated mate is incredibly tempting. The attraction, the invisible pull to him, my body responding to his scent, his touch... it's my body telling me I'm meant to be with him. Imagine having by your side the kind of man who nobody would dare challenge.

I shake myself back to reality, to the fact that this is happening too fast, and I'm not ready.

"Who are you looking for?" he asks, his head tilting slightly to the side, the breeze fluttering through his hair. I can easily frame in a photo now where the slight frown at the bridge of his nose just adds a darker edge to his beautiful face.

"You wouldn't know him," I say, keeping my gaze fixed on him as I try to decipher the nature of his supernatural essence. Given that he had a cave underwater, he's some sort of water being. A merman, maybe? But then, on second thought, curiosity gets the better of me.

"Actually, do you happen to know someone by the name of Belu Jonsyn?" I'm torn about whether I should have mentioned my target, but if there's a chance Kaden knows him, I need to find out.

He shakes his head. "Can't say I do. I'm new in town.

But I prefer to talk about us, not another man." There's almost a growl in his voice.

We stand there, the moment stretching awkwardly—or maybe it's just awkward for me because he's studying me with a smile in his eyes that's breathtaking. My heart hammers in my chest, every beat echoing that tingling sensation I've been told you sense when you meet your fated mate. They say you'll know instantly.

Well, I hate that it feels so overwhelming, confirming what he suggested earlier.

He's my fated mate.

Fuck!

Now what?

Do I just assume it's all going to be happy-go-lucky, then wait for whatever curse overtook my mom to claim me next? How long before I give my fated mate the kiss of death? The fear is relentless, gnawing at my insides. My mom once told me about the allure of a mermaid's death kiss, about the intoxicating feeling of taking a life. She said it's addictive, empowering, and so easy that you wouldn't realize you were hooked until it was too late.

I've mulled over her words for years, every sentence she said, every horrific memory from the night by the river, pondering if there's something sinister in our blood.

Truth be told, I've already used my powers three times for work, taking lives in dire situations where it was life or death... It's frighteningly instinctual, and I'm beginning to worry about how much I enjoy it.

The thought's been constantly on my mind, the concern consuming me, yet when it happens, I'm filled with a strange elation, as if it's a natural thing to do. As though another part of me is coming alive... and I keep thinking that's my siren side calling to me already.

Kaden's gaze is on me, and it's as though he's staring right through me.

"Well," I begin, trying to tamp down the intensity billowing inside me and focus on the current situation. "If you do happen to hear anything about him, I'd like to know."

"Of course," he states, standing tall. "And if I find him, should I dispose of him, or do you need him alive?"

A gasp slips past my lips. "Don't kill him. I need him breathing. In fact, don't find him at all. Forget I even mentioned it."

He nods as if he's taking a mental note, standing there like a warrior on the battlefield, broad, huge, and for some reason, the universe saw fit to make him my fated mate.

My thoughts are out of control, and I don't know what to think except to get the hell out of here.

"I need your name, by the way, sweetheart."

I blink at him. "Sasha," I mutter, already edging toward the broken gate, taking backward steps. "Okay, well, this was interesting, but I need to go."

He watches me intently, a half smile playing on his lips, but he doesn't follow. I'm barely holding back from bolting out of here. My breaths come fast, and I'm freaking out on the inside, but I need distance so I can breathe again and make sense of what I'm feeling.

As I turn to leave, he calls out, "Sasha."

The sound of my name in his voice is commanding

and tempting, a tingle of arousal spiraling through me. Why does he have to sound so incredible?

"I'll find this Belu and drag him to your doorstep. And if I discover he's hurt you..." His voice trails off, and there's a sudden intensity in his voice that sends shivers down my spine.

The threat left hanging in the air has me second-guessing his intentions. He might very well be one of those psychos I'm trying to avoid.

My head is spinning, and I can barely make sense of it all.

Without another word, I rush off his property and head down the path in the woods, my pulse on fire. Traveling downhill, I start to feel the tight pinch around my ankle from that stupid rope trap, but I'm not stopping until I'm far from this property.

I'm in the car in no time, driving away. My cheeks and insides are burning up, oddly calling for him, which is insane. All the while, my stomach dances with butterflies at the thought of such a man implying I'm his...

This is insane.

I grip the steering wheel tighter, trying to focus on the road ahead, but my thoughts are back at that mansion, back with him. The idea of him hunting down Belu, possibly putting himself in danger for me, is both terrifying and appealing. I've never had anyone fight for me. Though, I also know I'll need to return there to track down Belu, to show my boss I can complete this job.

The road stretches out before me, winding the lush Norwegian landscape, and I try to steel my resolve. My time in the country is a brief stop until I return home to

South Africa, yet since arriving, I've felt like things have been getting more complicated for me.

From getting the Siren Goddess's attention to Chowder chomping off two fingers of one of her guards, and now a beautiful, dangerous stranger, who looks like he could take down a small army, is my fated mate.

*Hey, Universe, give me a freaking break!*

As the landscape blurs past, a sudden thought strikes me... wait! Kaden said he'd come tell me if he finds Belu, but does he know where I work?

I swallow the thickness in my throat.

Or where I live?

# SEVEN



It's been two days since Sasha, my fated mate, appeared on my property, and it's been hell trying to stay away from her. I'm doing my best to be less of a psycho, as she called it, and give her the space she needs. She looked pretty shaken by the notion of being paired with me—though I prefer to think her shock was more about the surprise of finding a fated mate, not that it's me specifically. That's why I'm keeping my distance... but it's been fucking killing me. I can still feel her touch on my skin, hear that singsong voice, and smell her honeyed scent that lingers in my memory.

That's how I know this is the real thing—I even woke up with a smile on my face this morning. That rarely happens.

Right now, I'm heading into the city after having just hired a business for major restorations on the mansion's exterior. Those hired to maintain the place had kept the interior fit for a king, but they let the outside decay. Evidently, the appearance did its job in keeping others away, but now that I'm back, I want a home. All while working on digging up as much information as I can about my grandfather.

Speaking of which, I've found a fae from my grandfather's era who is still alive. All the family members are long gone, but this... this is a step forward. He said he'd meet me at a local bar, so let's hope this isn't a complete waste of my damn time.

I tug down the hood over my head to hide my face as I march up a street with grand homes on one side and a brilliant view of the ocean in the distance beyond the cliff.

The vast blue waters hold my attention. Back in Tartarus, the oceans where I lived were dark, an endless abyss. But here, the sea is a vibrant, inviting blue, sparkling with sunlight. I sense it calling to me as my skin ripples to slip into its embrace, to unleash the beast within, and explore this new world that promises freedom.

The sight of the ocean fills me with a heavy longing, but I push past the sensation and keep walking up the sloping road. The cool sea breeze mixes with the salty air, invigorating me.

I think about the last few interactions I had with my grandfather when I was a child, when he told me stories of his adventures. Most of the places he mentioned no longer exist, but I do recall that he spoke fondly of others. So, maybe this visit will give me the lead I need.

Up ahead at the corner of the road stands an old wooden building with a pointy roof and a dangling sign out front, swinging in the breeze.

*The Drunken Kraken.*

It has a painting of a tipsy kraken, eyes slightly crossed and smirking like a fool. Its tentacles are sprawled out lazily, with one casually clutching a pint of beer.

I chuckle to myself, remembering all the times my grandfather would be piss-drunk, reminding me very much of that image. At the building, I reach for the door handle, and a sudden surge of images floods my senses. In a heartbeat, I'm no longer standing on the threshold of a bar, but instead, I find myself on a deck at the rear of a house overlooking the ocean.

*A younger version of my grandfather is there, no longer the weary old man I remember. His hair is dark and neatly cropped, muscles defined under the fabric of his sky-blue short-sleeved shirt. He's seated at a rustic wooden table, a large glass jar of beer before him. Opposite him sits a woman radiating beauty and warmth. Blonde hair tumbles in soft curls down her back, a small beauty spot just above her lip adding to her pretty smile. Her eyes, bright and affectionate, are locked on my grandfather.*

*Despite her saying something, his attention often drifts back to his drink.*

*The woman leans forward. "Everything ready?" she asks.*

*He nods slowly, taking a gulp of his drink. "The new shipment's coming in tomorrow. I've got it all lined up, and we're going to finally grow our team." His face beams as he talks about his work.*

*For a moment, he studies her, then he takes her hand. The*

*gesture might look tender to anyone else, but his touch lacks sincerity—I know him well enough to see the tightness around his mouth, the tension in his muscles, the way he doesn't lean forward.*

*"You think anyone will notice the shipment coming in?"*

*"It'll be fine. Things are going to change for us. You'll see,"* he asserts, though his voice lacks conviction. *"We'll grow the business faster this way, to the point where no one can touch us."*

*Her grip squeezes slightly as she smiles, leaning toward him more. "Then maybe we can finally make our fortune and let someone else run the business for us,"* she murmurs, *staring at him as if waiting for his affirmation. "I've had no sleep for days as we wait for the shipment, worried to hell we'll get caught."*

*"Lilia, you worry too much. It's going to work out well. You'll see." He grins, but it's a hollow gesture.*

*Lilia accepts it, though, her smile widening.*

As fast as it came, the scene blurs around the edges, the focus intensely sharp, then instantly it fades into insignificance, leaving me standing in the cool breeze outside The Drunken Kraken bar, hand still on the door.

I shake off the dizziness, taking a deep breath.

*Who's Lilia? I haven't seen her before in my visions.*

I steady myself as the residue of the past clings to my thoughts.

Genetic memory my father had once called the ability—a gift that runs in his family line—where random snippets of my ancestors' experiences are passed down to each new generation. Strangely enough, these memories only ever come from my grandfather, never my parents. I spent a lot of time with him as a child, often seeking refuge from my parents, and that closeness must have chosen me to imprint on. It's said memories can only come from someone you've known in your life.

Not that anyone in my family had ever wanted to talk about the ability.

Why the fuck would they do that when they can pretend it doesn't exist? A source of family secrets that were better off left undiscovered, unspoken about. I recall how my parents cut off all communications with my grandfather, though they never explained why. And even after he passed away, he was never to be spoken about in the family.

Yet I always found myself drawn back to him. He was never cruel to me. Instead, he became the person I escaped to.

With the vision settled and making no sense to me, I push open the door, stepping into the bar. The inside strikes me as though I've walked into the belly of an ancient ship.

Wooden beams run overhead, like ribs of a hull, the walls covered in nets and old fishing gear that haven't seen the sea in decades. Salt, beer, and the musky odor of damp wood linger in the air in a place that only has half a dozen men at tables, drinking.

Navigating deeper into the long bar, I spot Joe at a secluded table in the rear corner. He's exactly as he'd described himself—wild white hair that fuzzes out around his head like sea foam. He's built like a bear, which is unusual for a fae, hinting at some mixed heritage.

Joe has two empty glasses on the table, so I make a quick detour to the bar and order two of what's on tap, the frothy heads spilling slightly as I carry them over to his table.

"You have to be Kaden?" he asks with a crackly voice as I set down the glasses.

"That's me. Thanks for agreeing to see me," I answer, sitting in the chair across from him.

He studies me with a sharp gaze, a smirk breaking his stoic expression. "You look similar to your grandpa, son. It's bringing back memories from so long ago." His eyes, bright green, seemingly carry the weight of his memories.

Lines etch his face, wrinkles deeply set around his eyes and along his neck. Despite the clear signs of his age, the man is undeniably tough, reminding me of my grandfather. Joe has to be over five thousand years old to have been around before my grandfather got tossed into Tartarus. They truly don't build them like they used to— just like my grandfather.

"I've heard people say that we looked alike." I take a long drink of my chilled beer, the perspiration running down my fingers from where I'm holding the glass.

"So, tell me, son, what brings you to Bergen? I heard rumors you were in town."

The bar around us hums with a low buzz of conversations, but I lean forward, lowering my voice. "I'm not going to waste your time, so I'll be upfront. I'm trying to find out how my grandfather ended up in Tartarus, as I've heard it might not have been for reasons everyone thinks. I'm told he was framed."

Joe sets his glass down. "That's a heavy piece of history you're digging into," he says, his tone darkening.

"Yeah, I know," I acknowledge. "But it's something I need to understand." Not to mention, I spent one thousand goddamn years in that prison for simply being his family line and being born in there, just like my parents had been. They met in prison, married, and had me.

Thing about Tartarus was that once you're in, you couldn't leave, and neither could any children you gave birth to in the place.

It's lineage sentencing, and it's fucking unfair.

So, someone not only fucked up my grandfather's life, but mine, too.

I refocus on Joe. His weathered face is marked by the lines that seem to deepen with his frown.

"Look, it's not a good path you're thinking of going down," he utters.

I take a long sip from my glass, the cold beer doing little to ease the tension knotting my muscles. Across from me, Joe studies me carefully. He groans, his mouth twisting in disapproval that I'm not backing down.

"I see the same damn stubborn streak in you as I'd witnessed in your grandfather. And I heard and saw enough about him to stay away from the likes of him."

"What did you hear?" I ask, curious. Neither my grandfather nor my parents told me the full details of how he ended up in Tartarus, just that he was set up. When I prodded them about who it was, I was told I was too fucking young. Then they damn died on me, and I was left with too many questions and not enough answers.

Joe shifts uncomfortably as I study him carefully, waiting for him to tell me what he knows.

"Your grandfather wasn't seen by many as a decent man." His fingers trace the rim of his now-empty glass. "He was involved in all sorts of illegal activities—theft, fighting, hurting anyone who stood in his way, whatever it took. He was as shady as they come, and he was involved with someone just as damn shady."

"Who?" I ask eagerly, my thoughts flashing back to him sitting at the table with that blonde woman.

Joe shrugs. "I don't know who. Like I said, I kept my distance. But most knew he ran some kind of racket in town, and every time something terrible happened, he was somehow involved. But it was a long time ago." He pauses, his gaze meeting mine squarely. "Son, he got tossed into Tartarus... maybe he got what he deserved."

"A life in hell for him and his family seems like a grave price to pay for stealing or roughing up some people." From my understanding, he'd been involved in importing illegal materials. Perhaps it was drugs or fuck knows what, but whatever happened, he was betrayed by someone. His partner in the business is my first thought, except I have no fucking clue who it was. He never spoke of a partner.

"Son, it's better not to dig into some pasts." Joe chuckles darkly, then groans as he rises to his feet. "You might not like what you find."

I swallow hard, my jaw clenching.

He steadies himself by leaning a hand on the table, then he walks away and out of the bar. I'm left grappling with the whirlwind of confusion. I sit back, the chair creaking under the shift of my weight, and the room suddenly feels claustrophobic.

I have no doubt there's more to the story of my grandfather, and I know the answer is within reach. I just have to know where to look.

Exiting the bar, my mind churns with the new information—my grandfather had a partner in crime, potentially the very person who betrayed him. It's always those closest who wield the sharpest knives, isn't it? I need to find more people like Joe and dig deeper. He can't be the only relic of those days still kicking around this city.

I wander up the road, where quaint shops begin to line the streets. The place is surprisingly modern, far from the backward world I'd pictured in my youth, listening to tales inside prison walls. Here, in the House of Gold and Garnet, one of the wealthiest districts, magic is as common as dirt, used to provide all the comforts of life, regardless of the cost.

As I navigate through the quiet streets, movement catches my eye in a shadowy alley between two buildings. I pause, peering into the dim light. There's Asher with his foot planted on a man's chest.

"Told you I'd find you again," he jokes, spotting me.

I grin, stepping closer. "Still having fun, I see."

"I've been enjoying myself tremendously, just as I promised myself." His laughter cuts through the chilled air, dark hair fluttering with the movement. "It's been fucking insane. The freedom to hunt is everything." He glances down at the man under his boot, who's groaning in obvious pain, face bloodied, eyes fluttering closed from pain or fear, possibly both. He's in bad shape. "These fuckers have been keeping me busy and entertained."

Asher smirks, practically buzzing with energy. He loves his hunts, just like he did back in Tartarus.

"You're going to make these mercenaries extinct." I chuckle.

His laughter booms again, resonating between the narrow walls. "I'll take that. Better to be a guardian from hell than some fluttering cherub. Anyway, this jerk was on your tail, so I dealt with him."

The man pinned down with Asher's foot tries to mumble something as he spits up blood, but a sharp look from us silences him. He's one of so many mercenaries who think we're free game for entering their territory, and they've been swarming us like ants.

"Come on, let's get out of here," Asher states. "Any progress on your grandfather?"

"Small steps, but I'll get there, even if I have to scour the whole damn country and speak with every single person."

Asher peers down and notices the guy is passed out but still breathing. We leave the mercenary behind. Perhaps he'll think twice before coming for us again.

We weave through the back alleys of the city with voices farther in the distance. Asher mentions a temporary place he's found for himself, secluded, sounding like the kind of spot a man looking to disappear when necessary would have.

My thoughts keep drifting back to Sasha... her fiery spirit, that spark in her eyes, the way she felt up against me. Finally, I cut in, unable to keep it to myself.

"I found my fated mate."

Asher pauses mid-sentence, his expression shifting from casual interest to shock in an instant. "You fucking lucky asshole."

"Yeah," I say, the word hanging between us.

"Well, fuck, man! That's huge!" He claps me on the shoulder, a solid, affirming smack. "And here I thought we'd just lie low and go to town on the mercenaries."

"I thought so, too," I admit, shrugging slightly. "But she just walked into a trap... literally."

Asher laughs, the sound booming around us. "Only you could find your mate because she stumbled into one of your traps."

"I've never reacted this way to anyone."

"Well, you're not going to let her go, right?" Asher's tone turns serious. "She's moved in with you already?"

I sigh. "Not yet, but that's the plan. She just doesn't know it yet. Something about her makes me want to rush things, like I need her in my life now!"

His grin is fierce, an approving look.

As his laughter fades, a thought pops into my mind —an idea that might help me handle things with my fated mate without scaring her off. Doing her a favor of sorts.

I turn to Asher, querying, "Feel like a scavenger hunt?"

His gaze sparks alight with interest. "What do you have in mind?"

"There's someone in the city we need to find. We only have a name and the fact that he's been skulking around my place recently."

His grin widens, the thrill of the chase already igniting his blood. "I'll track his scent!"

"Perfect." A familiar surge of adrenaline I used to feel in Tartarus floods me. This thrill, this anticipation for the hunt, it's part of who I am. "Let's flush him out."

**B**arely awake, I rub my eyes as I head out the door early in the morning when the sight in front of me has me yelping.

Right there, at the base of the three steps leading up to my cabin, is a man—tied up, gagged, and grumbling through the cloth in his mouth. His face is a mess of bruises, his clothes are spotted in blood, and he's sprawled on his stomach, wrists and ankles bound behind his back.

"Oh gods!"

At first, I freeze in place, unsure what to say or do, trying to process what in the world is happening. Then I rush down the steps to help him, but before I can reach him, Chowder darts out of the house, tilting his head curiously.

"Who left us him?" he asks, wearing his tiny vest, standing up on his hind legs. All he's missing is a detective's hat to really look the part. He sniffs around the man, adding, "Who would trap him?"

Good question, yet my suspicions are off the chart, flying right in the direction of Kaden... evidently my fated mate, who seems to have a crazy streak to him. Something I'm still coming to terms with.

My chest tightens, and my stomach swirls with butterflies as I recall the encounter from the other day. Sleep escaped me that night while I tossed and turned, consumed by the idea that I might actually have found my fated mate. The thought both thrills and terrifies me.

I wondered if staying away from him might make these intense feelings calm down. Perhaps the deep ache in my chest for him might eventually fade. The pull toward him is unlike anything I've ever felt—powerful, insistent. It demands my attention, refusing to be brushed aside.

And now this. I stare down at the bound man... Did Kaden have something to do with this? I shake my head. No, he wouldn't. Would he?

I crouch down next to the guy, pulling the gag from his mouth. He gasps, a string of groans tumbling out.

"Fuck!" he spits out, wriggling. "Untie me, now!" His blue eyes, familiar somehow, dart frantically under the dark fringe of his hair.

Wait, I've definitely seen his face before. Right then, it comes to me like a tsunami—from the mission files at work.

"What's your name?" I ask immediately.

He makes a grunting sound like he's attempting to clear his throat. "What the fuck has that got to do anything. Get me out of these ropes!"

"Not happening. I need a name."

"B-belu, are you fucking happy? Now help me," he almost spits the words.

"Belu Jonsyn?" I query.

The man's gaze pierces into me, a lightbulb clearly going off in his head that I know exactly who he is. Then he's trying to roll over but failing, bellowing in pain.

Chowder scrambles up on Belu's back now, sniffing at the ropes binding the man. He immediately leaps up on the back of the man's head, his little paws petting around.

"What the hell's on my head? Get it off, get it the fuck off me!" Belu shouts, thrashing about and trying to shake Chowder off. But my little otter hangs on, gripping his hair as if he's a bull rider.

"Why is man tied?" he asks a bit louder to be heard over the man's wailing.

"I'm guessing he's here for me to find," I murmur. I'm pretty sure I know who's responsible, and I pinch my lips together because it's my fault for opening my fat mouth around Kaden.

Belu's freaking out still, and I glance at him.

"Hey, hey," I say, clicking my fingers at him. "Focus now. Seriously, talk to me. Who did this to you? Who brought you here?"

He grumbles something unintelligible, still trying to dislodge Chowder, who's casually hopping off him.

"I don't fucking know," Belu snaps, trembling. "Two psychopaths jumped me, then forced me to run so they could chase me through the woods. They were mental, and I saw my life flash before my eyes. They made me run from them the whole fucking night!"

Two guys? My mind races. Maybe it wasn't Kaden? But no one else knows I'm hunting Belu except for my boss. Could it have been Kaden with a friend? The thought twists in my gut, partially grateful he might have helped catch my target but also irritated that he dared to interfere. Belu was mine to claim.

Exhaling, I pick up Chowder, snuggling and kissing his head. "You're amazing at detective work," I murmur, walking him back into the house.

"Hey, don't just leave me out here," Belu's yelling behind me. "I told ya what you wanted to know."

"Hold your horses," I call over my shoulder.

Chowder snuggles against me, then asks, "Why do ropes smell of a different sea?"

I blink at his question. He sniffed them on Belu; that's for sure. And as much as I know Belu is a merman, Chowder's smelled something else on Belu. More like someone else, like Kaden perhaps, who also carries the scent of the ocean.

Setting Chowder down on the couch, I grab my taser from the dining table, figuring I might need to employ a bit of intimidation to get Belu into my car and to my workplace. There, I can officially check him in and close this case.

There's something satisfying about proving to my boss that I can complete a mission, though part of me feels disgruntled, as if it's cheating. Then again, I'm not one to look a gift horse in the mouth. I march outside, taser in hand, and approach Belu with a newfound determination.

"Time to get moving," I say firmly, lifting my taser and wriggling it in my hand for him to see.

He squirms in response.

"Now, are you going to play nice when I remove the ropes?"

"On one promise," he blurts out. "I don't want those two fuckers anywhere near me ever again!"

"Deal. Now, don't make a run for it, don't mention them to anyone, and you won't ever see them." Last thing I need is for my new boss to ask me about the two hunters who tortured Belu all night.

"Fine, fucking fine, just untie me. The ropes hurt like a bitch."

I get him in the passenger seat, ankles and wrists tied and secured to the door by rope, then jump into the driver's seat. And we're off, despite his constant murmuring to himself. What the heck did Kaden do to this man last night?

My thoughts remain on Kaden because I have no doubt he's involved. He has that intensity about him where he'd keep his word when he commits to something, no matter the consequence.

I focus on the road ahead, ready to deliver Belu to the authorities.

Looks like this morning is already turning out to be anything but ordinary, and somehow, I have a feeling it's only going to get crazier from here.

Evidently, bringing in Belu earned me brownie points because my boss just handed me an urgent case. The last bounty hunter got roughed up, and now it's my turn to bring in the offender —a selkie shifter named Moore. My boss suggested backup, but after how badly things turned out with Scout, I insisted on going solo.

So, here I am, skulking around the back of a seedy motel, the kind that makes me check my belongings in my back pocket every so often. The hallway reeks of garbage and something sharply chemical with a spark of magic—probably drugs—but I'm not cleaning up anyone's crap. I just need to find Moore.

The number of water supernaturals popping up around this city by the sea is intriguing.

Like moths to a flame or selkies to a shore.

I grin at my own joke.

Finally reaching his apartment door on the ground floor, heart thumping, I take a deep breath. Taser in one hand, bounty hunter badge in the other, I rap sharply on the door with my knuckles. Hands hanging by my sides, hiding the taser for now, I plaster my best friendly neighborhood smile.

Two knocks later, the door swings open to reveal a woman, maybe nineteen or twenty years old, in nothing but pink underwear and a thin white tank top that hides nothing. Her eyes are glazed, her body swaying like she's about to fall over. She's definitely high on something.

Behind her, the room is a disaster. Clothes strewn all over, a mattress on the floor that's seen better days, and rubbish.

"Is Moore inside?" I ask quickly.

The girl squints at me, suspicion etched on her face as she yawns. "Who the fuck wants to know? You better not be another of those girls he's fucking because—"

I cut her off by lifting my badge, and instantly, her eyes widen. As if finding a sudden reserve of energy, she yells out over her shoulder while shoving the door in my face, "Moore, they found you."

Fuck!

I shove my shoulder into the door, driving it open, to see the woman backing away, her face as pale as milk. Just then, a thin man in nothing more than pants bolts deeper into the apartment from the kitchen. My pulse kicks up a notch as I dart after him, adrenaline fueling my chase.

He nearly slips on a magazine as he lunges for a window, smacking it open with such force that one hinge snaps free. He scrambles out, moving fast—but I'm quicker.

Tucking away my taser and badge, I surge forward like a missile, scrambling through the window and leaping onto the front lawn. I spot him taking a corner around the next apartment building and charge after him, just catching a glimpse of him slipping out the back. I find him fighting to open a locked door.

"Hey, we don't have to do this the hard way! Just turn yourself in." Breathless, I charge on, dodging fallen trash cans and skidding closer to him.

He turns to face me, desperation scribbled on his face as he does a fast scan of the enclosed yard to realize there's no way out but past me unless he scales the tall fence.

Suddenly, he charges at me like a madman.

I throw myself forward, ducking his swinging arm at the last second, and whip around, aiming a swift kick to the back of his knees.

He stumbles slightly, and fortunately, the wall of the building is there to catch him. Before he can fully regain his footing, I capitalize on the moment. In a fluid motion, I twist around to his front, my taser already in hand, and with a decisive shove, I push myself into him, driving him against the building. His back hits the brick with a thud, and he winces, caught off guard by my force.

With one hand, I clamp down on his throat, my mermaid grip iron-tight, his skin already reddening as he gasps for air. The taser is pressed firmly against his balls over his pants.

He thrashes, his hand half-raised, ready to punch me in the face.

"Don't fucking think about it," I hiss, jamming the weapon harder against his jewels. "Ever wondered what happens if your balls are tasered? You're about to find out if you don't do exactly as I say."

He grimaces, a wincing sound coming from his throat, as he lowers his hand.

Even in my human form, I can draw on the strength from my mermaid side, pinning him to the wall with greater ease. At times like this, I wonder how much stronger I'd be if I carried some of my father's wolf-shifter abilities. Wish I had them some days for my job, but I don't.

I ease my grip on Moore's throat only ever so slightly so he breathes.

Just as I have Moore securely pinned to the wall and am preparing to cuff him, a shadow falls over me. My heart leaps into my throat, fearing someone's about to jump me. I flinch, twisting my head in that direction, tensing from whatever's going to happen next. Instead of a confrontation, I find him...

I roll my eyes hard. "Are you following me?"

Kaden leans casually against the building beside us, his elbow propped like he's merely watching an interesting street performance. A sinful smirk plays on his lips while the butterflies in my stomach are doing somersaults, and my knees wobble.

"Hello, mate!" he states in that dark voice.

That word, *mate*, rolls over my thoughts. The man I'm destined to be with is this huge guy who melts my insides from his mere presence. I can't keep staring at the curling edges of his mouth.

"Go away," I manage, releasing Moore's throat and reaching for the cuffs on my belt while still holding him prisoner in place with my taser.

"I'm loving this darker side of you. It suits you well."

The tension, the arousal that awakens instantly in his company, doesn't completely leave my body, but irritation flares up.

"Not the time, Kaden," I snap, though a part of me can't ignore the amusement in his azure eyes. I keep my taser pressed firmly on Moore's balls, but he's eyeing Kaden warily.

"Who the fuck's that?" he groans.

I level a brief stare at Kaden while lifting my cuffs.

"Just pretend I'm not here," Kaden replies. "I'm simply watching my gorgeous fated mate at work," he quips, then turns to me with a more serious tone. "So, this is your job? Catching bad guys, then? Just like you were searching for Belu?"

His words trigger a sharp response from me, the memory of finding Belu tied up on my doorstep that morning flashing through my mind.

"It was you, wasn't it? You caught him and dumped him on my doorstep," I gripe, my voice tight.

His grin widens, confirming my suspicion without a word. Despite the anger threading through me, his lips slightly part, as though he's about to speak, then chooses not to. The breeze that carries his scent over me—the ocean in a storm, undeniably masculine—makes me involuntarily inhale deeply, my body tightening with an unbearable need despite the situation.

At that moment, Moore shoves me hard and bolts across the yard toward the towering metal fence. I stumble back, but Kaden's arm is viper fast and loops around my back, catching my balance.

"Fuck, look what you did," I growl at Kaden, frustration boiling over, pushing away from him.

"Me?" Kade feigns innocence despite his evil smile. "I'm irresistible, and I don't know why you're fighting fate."

I don't have time to argue. I sprint after Moore, reaching him just as he throws himself up against the fence. I don't hesitate this time—raising my taser, I zap him right in the ass. He yelps and falls onto his side, curling up, shuddering, and making strange noises. Once the electrical cycle ends five seconds later, he collapses to the ground, still quivering and groaning.

"Told you, fuck with me, and I'll tase you," I say, leaning down and pulling out the taser barbs. He cries out, and yeah, it hurts bad, but he'll heal quickly enough. I nudge him in the side with my foot. "Will you behave now?"

He groans, clasping his rear, and Kaden steps closer, grimacing.

"Oh, you really are dark, aren't you?" he says, almost admiringly. "I'm adoring this in you."

Exhaling loudly, I collect the strings with the prongs and wrap them around the taser. I'll replace the cartridge in the car. Holstering my taser, I fix Kaden with a look that's all serious. Then I bend down and cuff Moore's hands behind his back.

"Sometimes, you have to be dark to get the job done," I answer, my breath still catching from the chase.

"And you enjoy this kind of job?" he asks, one of his thick eyebrows rising.

"It's what I'm good at, and it pays the bills," I reply honestly, looping an arm under Moore's to heave him up. As Moore struggles to rise, Kaden is suddenly at his side, grabbing him by the hair and yanking him to his feet with ease.

Moore whines, cringing from the sharp pull.

Kaden leans in close to his face. "Today's your lucky day, buddy. You ever lift a hand to my mate again or disrespect her by not doing as she asks, I'll rip your fucking spine out." He then gives Moore's shoulder a patronizing pat. "We good?"

Moore's eyes widen, face draining of color as he nods vigorously.

"You don't need to do that," I say, but Kaden's all smiles.

"I will never stand back when I see anyone mistreating you."

It's hard to hate that, in all honesty, especially when a torrent of excitement bubbles in my chest at hearing his protective promise.

"O-okay, let's get going," I manage, tightening my hold on Moore's arm and dragging him toward the main street. My car's parked across the road.

Kaden strides alongside me, and I feel his gaze on me, analyzing and studying.

"You have a fierce warrior side I admire," he comments as if his approval means something to me. "It will serve exceptionally well when I breed you."

I gasp, choking on my breath, while Moore snorts a chuckle. Scowling up at Kaden, I glare, and I expect him to smirk, but he's utterly serious.

"Don't say shit like that, ever!" Shaking my head in disbelief as I reach my car, I fling open the back door and shove Moore inside before slamming it shut. The locks click, ensuring he can't open the doors from the inside.

What the hell is Kaden thinking? I keep telling myself I can't have a fated mate and risk becoming a siren and killing him, yet he's talking about breeding. Has he lost his mind? Heaving for breath, I turn to Kaden, and he's right there, in my face.

"Why not? It's the truth."

Instinctively, I push my hands against his chest to shove him back, but the moment we touch, a shock of electricity jolts through me. It races up my arm and pierces my chest, leaving me breathless. I find myself studying him as though he holds all the answers to the universe.

It's the fated mate effect; it has to be. Nothing else could make my heart race this fast or my body react so viscerally to his proximity. The intensity of the sensation leaves me momentarily helpless, as if only he can save me.

He moves in closer, trapping me against the side of the car, his body inches from being pressed to mine, and I'm really not that averse to the idea. Except, are these my feelings or the blooming attraction our destined fate is awakening between us?

Kaden notices the change in my expression, his own face softening.

"I know it's a lot," he murmurs, his voice a low rumble that seems to vibrate through me. "But we don't need to figure it all out today. All you need to do is accept that we're together now and move in with me at my mansion."

His words, meant to be reassuring, only tighten the knot in my stomach.

"Why would I move in with you?" I ask, my question steadier than I feel on the inside. Around him, half the time, I'm trying to just concentrate and not get distracted by the feelings he brings out in me, the ones that have me gawking at him, that leave me buzzing with unbearable need.

The bridge of his nose creases. "Because you're my fated mate, Sasha. I'm not living apart from you," he states as if it's the most obvious thing in the world.

He's closer now, his warm breath caressing my face. I inhale deeply, and his crisp ocean and masculine scent encases me—so intoxicating it leaves me wavering on the spot. I feel the hardness of his muscles each time he moves. I crane my neck back to hold his stare. He steps down from the curb, his legs straddling mine, so he comes down in height slightly to meet me.

Hands against his chest, the muscles shift beneath my touch, and I'm beyond mesmerized. I've had my share of boyfriends, but none have been as big and built as Kaden. I should be pulling away. Instead, I'm failing spectacularly and peering into his eyes, which swirl like the deepest parts of the ocean, drawing me in.

I can almost believe I'm out in the sea, being this close to him, as though he is the epitome of the great sea itself. I've never met anyone with such a powerful connection to the ocean.

"What are you?" I ask, heart racing, my insides tingling. I realize I still have no clue what supernatural creature he is.

His finger gently lifts my chin, tilting my head back, and his lips find mine without hesitation. The world suddenly falls away at his kiss. It crashes over me like waves, taking over my senses, inhaling every inch of me. My toes curl in my boots. The power he expels is intense and impossible to resist. As our lips move in sync, I can't help but kiss him back with fever. Part of me is surrendering to him, giving in to the pull that I've fought so hard to resist.

I run my hands through his hair while his huge arms coil around me, lifting me off my feet, or perhaps it just feels like I'm floating. It's really hard to tell at this stage, as every fiber of my being is lit up. Fire ignites through me, burning with a blaze between my thighs as our lips are mashed together, kissing as if we're starved.

He licks my lips before pressing into my mouth, and there's something so fucking sexy about sucking on his tongue. I moan, softening, and am rewarded with a growl vibrating in his throat, the kind that leaves me utterly hopeless and at his mercy.

He pulls back just enough to gaze into my eyes again, his forehead resting against mine.

"See?" he whispers with that husky voice. "We're inevitable."

"I've never been kissed like that before." I shouldn't have said that part out loud, but I'm still floating, still lost out in his sea. Despite all my fears and doubts, at that moment, I couldn't hide from the truth in his words. I barely know the guy, yet right now, it feels as if this is what I've been missing in my life. My resistance melts a little more, leaving me wondering if maybe this isn't such a horrible thing and I should perhaps embrace it.

The loud knock from the car snaps me back to reality. I glance down to see Moore scowling at us from in the car, having clearly used his head to smack into the window. I untangle myself from Kaden, his warmth leaving me just as quickly—and I hate that I miss it already. My heart is racing, that unbelievable kiss leaving me swooning.

"Okay," I manage, feeling a flush spread across my cheeks. "I gotta take him in. I-I'll think about what you said."

That spectacular grin splits his lips, his white teeth flashing, the corners of his eyes crinkling. It's hard not to fall head over heels when the most gorgeous man I've ever seen stares at me like that, especially when I can still taste his sweetness on my lips.

"I'll be seeing you soon, Sasha." He starts to walk away.

Impulsively, I call after him, "You never answered my question!"

He glances back at me, a sly smile playing on his lips. "I'm surprised you haven't worked it out yet."

I give him a deadpan stare, waiting for more.

"I'm your kraken, gorgeous little mermaid," he says with a wink, then takes off.

I'm left standing there, gaping after him. "Are you kidding me? No... no way in hell," I mutter under my breath.

My last boyfriend claimed to be a kraken, the beasts of the sea everyone fears, and I stupidly believed him— only to find out he was a mere seahorse shifter. I know the size and type of shifter shouldn't matter, but I hated that he lied to me. And now this again?

"Kraken?" Is that what all men are using these days as their pickup lines? I shake my head, a sarcastic laugh escaping my throat. "Yeah, right, kraken. Might as well tell me you're Poseidon next," I murmur to myself.

Shoving the last of my disbelief aside, I open the car door and slide into the driver's seat.

From behind me, Moore says, "Nice make-out session with the devil there."

"Shut it," I snap, starting the car. The engine roars to life, drowning out any further comments from him. As I pull away, the last traces of Kaden's scent linger, a reminder of the most beautiful kiss I've ever experienced.

Kraken or not, there was no denying something deep and wild had been awakened, but I wasn't sure if I was ready to dive into those waters just yet.

Especially if I find out he's lying to me.

CHAPTER

# NINE

SASHA

I woke up with a craving to go for a swim.

Not just any urge—all-consuming, unlike anything I've experienced before. Sure, I've longed for ice cream and chocolate, especially brownies. Thinking of my favorite thing in the world—fudge brownies—makes me drool. But this desire to swim is intense, and I know it's the need to be in salt water... just as I'd been in the fjord waters.

However, to avoid being charged by Asbesta again, I'm settling for fresh water this morning, splashing in the pool behind my cabin. I dip under, my tail propelling me the length of the pool, then come up less than a foot from Chowder. He's on his back, smacking a rock into a large clam he has balanced on his chest. I had to buy him a bunch on the way home yesterday because I know he loves them.

He makes that adorable chirping sound, like he's chuckling. "Who wants clam?"

"It's all yours," I answer, rubbing his head. I don't eat

seafood, but growing up with a wolf shifter for a father, I enjoy all kinds of land-based meat.

The sun is rising, flooding the skies with a blood-orange streak, the light breeze rustling the trees behind my cabin. Floating in the water, the earlier anxiety fades from my body. I didn't sleep well again, contemplating yesterday's events, and most prominent was Kaden and his comment about me moving into his mansion.

He was kidding, right?

I barely know him, and as we get to know each other better, we should live apart. Plus, look at my place. I glance around the cozy wooden cabin in the woods, neighbors not close, and the main road out of sight. It's perfect for me. And Chowder loves it.

Just then, I spot two uniformed guards—those who work for the city, who are responsible for maintaining some level of peace. Except why are they at my place?

Having seen me, they make their way toward us in the backyard. I swim quickly to the edge of the pool, mostly to avoid flashing them since I'm in my mermaid form. I'm sure they've seen my kind before, but that doesn't mean I'm comfortable with having them leering at me.

With scowls and darkness under their eyes, they don't look pleased. Something in my stomach unsettles.

"How can I help you, Officers?" I ask, keeping my voice light, feeling slightly awkward seeing as my breasts are bare, but I use the side of the pool to cover myself.

"Sasha Snow?" the tall one asks.

"Yes, that's me," I answer.

"We need to bring you into the station for questioning."

My heart drops into my stomach. "Excuse me?" I splutter, glancing at Chowder, who seems as confused as me. He's no longer on his back but swimming closer to the guards, eyeing them suspiciously.

"There's a case that requires your cooperation."

"What case?" My thoughts are on fast-forward, thinking if this has anything to do with the fjord trespassing and Asbesta's guard, who lost two of his fingers to Chowder.

"For what?" I continue incredulously.

"We'll explain everything once we get to the station," the officer replies. "Now, you can come of your own accord or by force." He touches the cuffs on his hip.

I swallow hard, stunned, my pulse thumping under my skin, that things keep going from bad to worse for me.

"I've done nothing wrong," I mutter, shaken up. "Look, I need to get out of the pool and get dressed. I'll come with you, no trouble. Just... can you look away?"

They both shake their heads in unison. I heave a sigh, wanting to argue but not in the mood to be manhandled while naked. Already pulling back my mermaid form, I frown and swim to the steps. At least, I manage to give them a side profile of me naked as I climb out, feeling their leering gazes all over me. My skin crawls as I hastily grab my towel and wrap it around myself.

"I guess you're coming inside with me while I put on some clothes."

They nod; of course they do. Assholes.

Grinding my teeth, I call, "Chowder, let's head indoors."

He swims over rapidly, his gaze narrowing at the men. I pick him up, holding him close under my arm. The last thing I need is a repeat of what happened with the last guard who came to my house.

Ten minutes later, after the most awkward dressing session of my life, trying to keep the towel around me while pulling on clothes, I head into the kitchen. I give Chowder extra food and close him indoors before being guided to their car by the officers.

The whole trip, they don't say a word, and I don't bombard them with questions, knowing they're just the messengers. But I have no idea what the hell is going on.

Finally arriving at the station, the silence continues as they lead me inside. They guide me along a narrow hallway to a small, dimly lit room with a table and a couple of chairs. One of the guards motions for me to sit.

"Wait here," he says curtly before they both leave me alone.

I flop down on a seat, the metal chair cold, even through my clothes. My thoughts are still spinning out of control with confusion. What could they possibly want from me?

The door opens, and a curvy woman walks in. She's wearing a crisp burgundy dress with buttons running down the front, her hair is pulled off her face in a ponytail, and her expression is serious. She takes a seat across the table from me, folding her hands on the table.

"Do you know why you're here?" she asks, her thin eyebrows arching on her round face.

"Not a clue," I answer, leaning back in my chair. "What's going on?"

"Where were you last Wednesday morning, before midday?" she asks, jumping right into it.

I think back to almost a week ago, barely remembering what I had for dinner last night. Then it hits me—it was the day I went on my first mission in Norway, when I went into the fjord. The beginning of all my troubles.

"I was on a work mission, investigating a location by the fjords. Did something happen?" Part of me wonders if this is all related to my time in the fjord and Asbesta.

"Do you have anyone who can corroborate your whereabouts?" the officer asks. "We spoke with your boss, and she said you were in the office after midday, but before that, she hadn't heard from you."

"You spoke with my boss?" I stammer, feeling a bit of panic rising that I'll get fired for drawing the authorities to my workplace, for appearing like I'm causing trouble.

The woman in front of me just stares with huge brown eyes, her expression stern.

"Okay, look, you're asking questions that don't make sense," I mutter.

She leans forward, lips tight. "I'm going to be straight with you, Sasha. We know you're a bounty hunter, a mermaid, but you could be in a lot of trouble. Last Wednesday, a ship close to shore washed into the docks with seven crew members butchered."

"And?" I blink at her, confused. "What's that got to do with me?"

The woman releases a heavy breath. "Two sailors on

the boat place you at the scene as the mermaid who attacked the men and pulled their throats out."

I laugh almost hysterically. "You've got to be joking."

"The thing is, no one can place you for several hours from the morning until lunch, and that's enough time to reach a boat that was attacked not far from shore."

"Wait, why would I even do that?" My gut is churning with a sick feeling.

"That's what I'm here to discover." She tilts her head, studying me.

"Well, I didn't do it," I state, feeling like I'm in a crazy town.

"Two crew members who survived both swear they saw you in town the other day and reported you as their attacker."

"I don't understand." I shift in my seat, stunned and confused. "This has to be a mistake. I was doing my job, investigating a case by the fjord, and I sure as hell wasn't out at sea. I mean, I went for a swim in the fjord, and if that's a crime, I'll accept my punishment. But I didn't attack any ship or its crew."

My knees are bouncing under the table as perspiration rolls down my back. I shouldn't be nervous when I'm innocent, yet she's staring at me like I'm under a microscope.

The woman's gaze doesn't soften. "I need you to come with me, because right now, you're a prime suspect."

"There has to be some mistake. I would never—"

"We'll get to the bottom of it," she says, cutting me off. "For now, please come with me."

"Fine." I swallow hard, my pulse speeding. "But I'm telling you, this is all a huge misunderstanding."

The officer takes me into a stark, cold room where three other guards stand watch. Two men are seated across the room, and they look rough, dressed casually. One has tattoos snaking up his arms, and the other has a scar running down his cheek. Their eyes lock on to me with a mix of fear and hatred, glaring my way as though I'm some kind of monster.

"That's her!" one of them yells, his face turning pale as he points a trembling finger at me. He reels back, hitting the wall behind him, his eyes wide with terror.

I feel a rush of confusion and fear. "I didn't attack any damn ship!" My words shake, but I try to keep my composure.

The second guy's hands are shaking, too. "It's definitely her. I'll never forget that face."

Before I can react, one of the guards steps forward and wrenches my hands behind my back before slapping cuffs on my wrists. "You're under arrest, Sasha Snow." It happens so fast I barely have time to register it. The metal bites into my skin, the cold sting sending a shock wave of panic through my body.

"You can't do this!" I shout, trying to twist free. "I'm innocent!"

They don't listen. They drag me out of the room, and I fight against their grip, my heart pounding in my chest.

"You're making a mistake, please!" My voice is desperate, pleading.

The officer in front of me pauses outside a closed

door to what appears to be a cell, holding up a photo for me.

"The men's identification of you confirms our other evidence," she states, her response cold. She thrusts the photo farther into my face. "One of the sailors on the ship took this while you attacked his colleagues as proof. Otherwise, no one would believe him."

I stare at the photo, my breath catching in my throat. The image is slightly shaky and slanted, but it clearly shows a horrific scene. One of the crew members is about to fall over, his throat ripped out by a woman with aquamarine hair standing almost facing the direction of the camera, holding the bloody throat in her grasp. She's completely naked, blood sprayed across her chest.

But it's her face that grabs my attention.

She looks so much like me—same almond-shaped eyes, same facial structure. It's uncanny, but as I look closer, I realize it isn't me.

The icy, hard truth strikes me hard.

"Fuck, wait!" Is that my mom? She's a siren, not a mermaid! And she appears like she hasn't aged at all. Tears prick at the corners of my eyes at the past rearing its ugly head, but I blink them away.

Flashes of images of her stealing my dad's life, the look on her face, her transformation into a siren... it's right there, fresh on my mind, still coiled like barbed wire around my heart. She's in this photo, appearing as though she's miles away in her thoughts, yet she just killed a sailor... seven, apparently.

My whole body trembles with anger and confusion. My mind aches with dread, swallowing me, as I try to piece together some explanation, some way to prove my innocence. I can't let this happen. I can't let them think I did this.

"You asked me if someone can corroborate my whereabouts for last Wednesday," I blurt out. My words are breaking, heat churning in my gut. "I wasn't alone when I went to investigate the fjord. I have proof that it's not me in the photo." Even as I speak, I can't get my mom's image from that photo out of my head. "You can contact them for my alibi."

"I will need their details," she states.

My thoughts are consumed with why my mom is attacking a boat, killing sailors. That's not normal siren behavior. Sure, she might kill one or two, drowning a sailor, but it's rare. Seven is beyond unusual, especially doing it openly on a ship.

"The person in the photo isn't me. It's my mom," I state.

The female officer pauses, glancing at the other guards before looking back at me. The stern woman narrows her gaze. "I'm listening."

My thoughts spin with disbelief, and it takes me a moment to track my voice.

My mom... A wave of nausea washes over me, my insides twisting in knots.

"She's a siren," I whisper. "I considered her dead for years, but that's definitely her, not me."

The officer's expression softens a fraction. "That's something we will investigate, too, but until I speak with someone about your alibi, you're not going anywhere," she explains firmly.

It feels like the ground has been ripped out from under me, being blamed for something *Mom* did.

The cuffs dig into my wrists, and tears are stinging my eyes from everything she took from me and what she's about to destroy now. I try to stay calm, but the panic is overwhelming. I glance around, trying to find something, anything, that makes sense, but there's nothing. Only cold walls and stern faces.

And the stabbing ache of seeing my mom after so many years...

CHAPTER

# TEN

KADEN

"It's a step forward," I say, guiding Sasha out of the building, my arm securely around her lower back. She's not pushing me away, but she's trembling, her face as pale as a ghost, clearly frightened by being wrongly accused of a crime.

"What is?" she finally answers, glancing up at me with those huge doe eyes, then she stares back at the busy road as though she's unsure where to go.

"For you accepting me as your fated mate."

She cuts me a piercing stare, then blinks, looking elsewhere as if she's lost.

"Thanks for testifying that I was with you last Wednesday."

"For you, I'd reach up into the sky and drag the moon down if it made you smile again."

She glances over, the corner of her lips attempting to curl into a grin, but it never makes it.

"What did they do to you?" I ask, leading her down the street, my hand slipping into hers, covering it completely. She doesn't pull away, which is a good sign, but she's shaking. Something scared her. I grind my jaw, determined to find and destroy it.

Her lips are pursed, and she's not answering me. The furrowed brow and gaze are lost in the distance, telling me she didn't hear my question. Or she refuses to answer it.

I jumped at the chance to come for her the moment the authorities arrived at my house, saying Sasha needed my help. Fuck, I would have run into the city, bowling over anyone who stood in my way. And now, I'm not letting her go.

What I found fascinating was that once I notified the authorities of who I was, they were hesitant to let me testify, asking more questions about my approval to be in the House of Gold and Garnet. I have none, yet the moment I clarified that I'm Sasha's fated mate, they welcomed me without another issue. Does that mean she's my gateway to staying in the country without gaining formal approval?

I sure as fuck wish someone would tell the mercenaries on my tail that. Found two more in my yard this morning.

Anyway, I arranged for someone to drive Sasha and me back to my place, but she insists we go to hers. Something about a chowder, which I am led to believe is a meal. She must be hungry.

Sitting next to her in the back seat, our legs close, she blinks a lot, hands curled in her lap. I stroke her thigh tenderly, my body hyperaware of where we're touching, the need consuming me to take her into my arms, but I resist… for now.

"Want to talk about it? I can hurt them for wrongly blaming you. I'll burn down the whole damn building."

After a pause, she shakes her head, not shooting my idea down right away, which says a lot about her state of mind. It's hard watching her this way when I'm used to seeing her being strong, fighting me. I adore the fuck out of that, but this side of her, the vulnerability, squeezes at my chest. It brings out a primal desperation to wrap her up, protect her, and keep her safe.

"I'm here to protect you," I remind her.

Her shoulders slump a bit. "Except you can't protect me from my past."

I wait for her to elaborate, but she doesn't. I exhale heavily, fighting back the urge to insist that she tell me what's going on. Except I'm trying not to terrify the girl.

When we finally arrive at her place, she climbs out of the car without a word, and I take that as my cue to follow. I get out, telling the driver to leave us. Then I follow her into the tiny cabin in the woods.

The place is as I remember—small, cozy, and with minimal furniture. My hunting lodge back in Tartarus was better furnished than this. We might have lived in a prison world, but after thousands of years, those stuck inside made the world their home with all the comforts.

This cabin Sasha lives in is only temporary. I've already dug into her background. Sure, I may be new in the city, but I have a way of convincing people to give me the information I seek.

What I discovered is enough to know she's from a

place called South Africa, but she's now in Norway for her job, and this cabin is under a rent-by-the-week plan. So, she doesn't have any real attachments to it, and it'll be easier for her to move out.

Shutting the door behind me, I turn to the scattering sound of nails on the wooden floor. From somewhere in the house comes running a little... rodent or something, wearing a blue vest. It skids to a stop in front of me, lifting on its hind legs in my direction. I don't need to know what sort of creature it is to instantly sense it's water-based, something I respect.

Sasha rushes to the critter, swooping it off its feet. Swinging it away from me, she whispers to the creature and kisses it on the cheek.

"Now remember, no more biting, okay?"

"That thing isn't going to hurt me," I state.

She faces me, laughing sarcastically, sounding high-pitched. "You'd be surprised. Chowder is rather fond of biting off fingers, so watch out. And he's an otter."

I chuckle. "That little thing?" So that's the critter's name, not food. I don't recall seeing an otter back in Tartarus. I suppose for something tiny and wearing a vest, it's kind of cute.

Chowder keeps eyeing me, as though he's sizing me up.

"Nice to meet you, little guy."

She sets him on the floor, and he makes a small hissing sound in my direction. I raise an eyebrow, impressed by his bravery.

"Feisty little thing, isn't he?" I say, stepping closer.

"He's just protective of me after I saved him from a

lab doing experiments on him," she retorts. "He doesn't trust easily."

"Neither do I," I admit, my gaze locking on to hers.

There's a moment of silence, my attention remaining on Sasha, at the way she stands, hands stuffed in her pockets, smiling down at the otter, to how she nibbles on the edge of her lower lip. There's something captivating about her mannerisms, the way she tucks her blue-green hair behind her ear. The girl is spectacular, a beauty I can't get enough of.

Already, my feral side, my beast, is pushing me to claim her as ours, wanting to claw to the surface to destroy anyone who upsets her. It's admirable how quickly he's taken to her when, most of the time, he wants to destroy anyone new we meet.

"So, what's the plan?" she asks, breaking the silence. "Are you going to just stare at me?"

"Sounds good to me, though I'd like some food. My gut's grumbling." I reach down to pat Chowder, but he shrinks away from my touch.

"Don't touch his head. He doesn't like it, especially from strangers," Sasha says, watching me closely. "Let him approach you first. And I'm not a restaurant."

Fair enough.

Chowder tilts his head, his whiskers twitching, saying, "Hello again."

I blink, genuinely surprised. "All right, now I'm impressed by this otter. He talks."

"Chowder, what do you mean by *again*?" She stares at the otter, then glares up at me. "He must have seen you drop off Belu in front of our door."

I shrug, chuckling. "I guess."

Crouching next to Chowder, she strokes the fur around his neck. "They did something to him during the experiments. That's why he speaks, among other things."

"Who the fuck would do that?" I ask, frowning, my hackles raised. I will kill anyone for looking at me wrong, but hurting animals, that's a line I won't ever cross.

"A jerk I was meant to catch for my last job," she explains. "Bastard got away, but I saved Chowder and kept him because he deserved the best life."

I admire her for her caring nature, something I'm not necessarily used to.

"So, are we going to talk about what happened back at the station? What did they accuse you of?"

"Does it matter?" she says, her tone weary. She goes to sit on the curved couch in the corner, tucking her legs under as she makes herself comfortable.

"It matters," I state, strolling after her, eyeing the seated cushion right next to her. "If you're in danger, then I'm going to fix it."

She half laughs, even though she furrows her brow. "This isn't something you can fix. Trust me."

I go to sit, but Chowder leaps up just before I do, pressing himself against her hip and stretching out his body across the cushion, taking my spot, glaring at me with narrowing eyes.

*You little shit.*

So, I sit a bit farther away but still close enough to squish him in his location.

"Tell me more," I insist, curious. Lounging back, I

drape an arm across the back of the couch just as Chowder's back leg kicks my thigh, as if he needs more space. I chuckle, gazing down at this tiny otter with the personality of a damn kraken.

Sasha's face hardens, and her attention shifts to the floor.

"They think I killed seven men on a ship that crashed in the docks recently," she says quietly. "But it wasn't me. It was my mother, who, long ago, turned into a siren. So, you see, there's nothing to really address. Mistaken identity, that's all." Her voice cracks, her posture curling slightly forward.

Her words hit me hard, remembering when I lost my mom, murdered along with my father by a gang he'd crossed. Exhaling deeply, I push the past aside, leaving it as that.

"She's a siren, then?" Everyone knows once a mermaid has enough drownings under her belt, the darkness inside them manifests and changes them permanently into a siren.

"Happened when I was a child." Her eyes glisten, but she quickly wipes them and puts on a forced grin.

I reach over to catch the tear rushing down her cheek, suddenly feeling the hard slam of Chowder, jamming those little feet into my side, hissing. I almost adore the otter for his tenacity.

She doesn't pull away when I wipe the tear.

"Family is so fucking complicated," I add. "They give us life, but then go and fuck us up."

Twisting my way, she glances at me with those

expressive pale blue eyes. Up close, I notice the golden-green flecks in her irises.

"You can say that again. I lost my parents when I was young and feel like I've been looking out for myself ever since. I just never expected my mom to transform, or in the way she did. It still affects me so long after."

Her voice shakes, and she falls silent, the weight of her words hanging between us. A physical ache spreads through my chest, matching the pain in her eyes.

My hand is on her thigh, even if Chowder is nudging it with his body.

"I lost mine when I was younger, too," I confess, a roughness tracing my voice. I hate talking about the past, about them, but for Sasha, I will. "My father was always doing deals, always involving himself with the wrong people. So, to know that his decisions lost both his and my mom's lives..."

She looks me in the eyes, a softness behind hers. "It's like they leave us with their messes to clean up."

I nod, remembering the shit fight I faced when the gang came after me for my father's payment, for blood. I shake those memories away. I did what I had to in order to survive. It gained me a reputation for making many afraid of me, but in a place like Tartarus, that's a godsend.

She places her hand on top of mine, and for a moment, we're two broken souls, realizing we're not that alone.

"Thanks for being here for me," she murmurs. And aside from Chowder, who hasn't ceased his nudging, the cabin falls silent.

"How about I head out and bring us food from one of the nearby shops?" I offer, lightening the heavy mood.

Shaking her head, she gets up and straightens her posture.

"Look, it's best if you go. I need... just some time alone to process everything."

I study her, every inch of me dying to lean in and hug her, to chase away her worries. My gaze lowers to her luscious lips, and I can't forget our kiss, how she tasted like the sweetest honey, how I'm craving to discover if the rest of her tastes as delicious. I'm not sure how much longer I can be a patient man, especially if my beast has any say in it.

But her quiet worries me that there's more she's not telling me.

"Are you in any kind of danger? Call me paranoid, but I always expect the worst."

A half grin pulls her lips up. "The only danger is me dealing with memories I buried long ago, along with my mother I thought I had known. I told myself she was dead so I could move on..." She literally shakes herself.

I stroke her arm, stepping closer to take her into my arms, but she moves away. It leaves me with a stabbing ache in my gut.

"Really appreciate your help," she states.

It's frustrating as hell to have her push me away. My fated mate. Nope, this isn't going to do.

The creak of the door suddenly sounds, and I turn to find Chowder pulling it open, eyeing me with daggers.

"How fast can he leave?" he says in his chirpy voice.

"All right." I admit defeat, but worry seeps through

me that my fated mate shouldn't be grieving on her own. That ache burrows through me. It strangles me. But I'm going to rectify this once and for all.

"I'll be seeing you real soon, Sasha." I stroll out of the cabin, Chowder seeming to almost smile at seeing me go.

I chuckle to myself because they have no idea how much more of me they're going to be seeing real soon.

CHAPTER

# ELEVEN

SASHA

Chirps and squeaks are the first things I hear as I wake up. A smile tugs at my lips at Chowder's cheerful noises. I push myself up from the bed, feeling as if I've had the best night's sleep for the first time in who knows when. It's as though the bed has somehow become softer, embracing me.

Once I blink my eyes open, I stare up at a black ceiling, and I startle at the fear that collides with me.

I'm not in my bedroom or my bed—or anywhere I recognize.

Heart thundering, I frantically scan the room, grasping the bedsheet tightly as if, somehow, it'll give me the answer. Three of the walls are arched windows, looking out into an aquarium with faint lights illuminating the water, casting a serene glow. Fish of every color—magenta, sun yellow, sky blue—swim gracefully, weaving between rocks, stones, and plants.

Am I in an aquarium and the fish are watching me? Is this a dream?

Panic crawls up my spine as I try to remember how I got here. I'd crashed in my bed from exhaustion, trying to forget the police encounter and me being mistaken for my mom in a murder investigation. I took a sleeping pill to ensure I slept, but clearly, that worked too well.

So, where am I?

A subtle smell of roses fills my nostrils, mixed with a powerful masculine scent that brings my insides to life. I know it instantly.

*Kaden.*

"Is this his room?" This can't be the dilapidated mansion by the fjord. Can it?

Chowder is by the window, tapping the glass, making those chirping sounds, probably wishing he could reach the fish. Did he sleep through the transport, or is he a traitor now, taking Kaden's side?

Pushing the blankets back, I'm still wearing my PJ shorts and tank top.

My feet touch the glass floor that has more fish swimming underneath, making it feel like I'm floating in the water. For a few moments, I forget about the whole being kidnapped from my home and brought here. Instead, I'm taking in the most glorious room I've ever seen.

The bed is covered in plush, silken sheets in deep ocean blues. Crystals glint from the chandelier, casting tiny rainbows across the room. The wall without the windows is adorned with intricate themed artwork of waves crashing, the pattern carrying over the closed door.

The situation washes over me. "Great," I mutter

under my breath. "He's finally gone all serial stalker, hasn't he? Just what I need."

Chowder chirps again, and I walk over to him, the glass cool under my bare feet. "Gorgeous view," I say, running a hand over his soft fur.

He turns his head up to me. "Who doesn't like this place?"

"Right. It's gorgeous, but we don't belong here." I make my way out of the room into a hallway that leaves me gasping. This place is built for a god.

Intricate carvings continue on the walls out here, the rolling waves that seem to move under the frosted, aqua-colored arched ceiling. More chandeliers hang from above, casting a soft, enchanting glow. As much as I need to speak with Kaden, I can't help but be awestruck by the beauty of this place. It must have cost a fortune to craft something so elaborate.

Passing by closed doors, I peer into one and find an extravagant bathroom made of amethyst crystal for the bathtub, with black marble on the floor and walls and more windows to the aquarium. I stand here, my mouth dropped open, imagining how amazing it would be to have a bathroom like this. It's easily bigger than my entire cabin.

At the end of the hall, I follow the curve to the right and enter a large living area. It's circular, with bookcases made of dark wood lining the walls behind leather lounges facing each other. The shelves are filled with books, and there's a fireplace nearby. Overhead, the arched ceiling is made of glass, with fish swimming above and small star lights resembling a night sky underwater.

I'm stunned, unable to believe this place exists. The carpet cushions my feet as I step out farther while Chowder bolts past me and darts onto one of the couches.

"What place is so magical?" He's lounging against a cushion like he's some baron.

I giggle, turning toward a half-circle bar, complete with stools and more glass windows, looking into the aquarium. It's darker inside here, with most of the light trickling in from the water outside the bar.

The whole place is surreal, a scene from a fantasy novel.

Sensing movement from my right, I turn toward a figure standing in a shadowy doorway, filling the space.

"Morning, my little mermaid." Kaden steps out of the dark, sporting a devious grin. "Welcome to our home."

"I don't know where to start," I admit truthfully. "This place is absolutely breathtaking, yet you kidnapped Chowder and me, bringing us here against our will."

He strolls into the room, not seeming bothered one bit by my words.

"Is it kidnapping if you are my fated mate and in danger? This is now as much your home as it is mine. Here, I know you're safe. Out there, I can't protect you all the time."

I blink, taken aback by his honesty.

"You can't keep me prisoner here."

He turns to face me, sitting on the end of a couch, legs crossed at the ankles, hands gripping the armrest he's leaning on.

"You're not a prisoner, but there's no way my fated mate is living in a separate home from me. And your cabin isn't big enough for me and all the space I need."

The weight of his words leaves me frustrated that all of a sudden, we're living together.

"I'm… I'm not ready."

"I know you're not," he admits. "Which is why I've given you the master bedroom. I'll sleep in one of the spare rooms until you're ready."

Anger slithers through me. "I have my belongings in the cabin, I have a rental contract, and—"

"I've already paid it for the term of you giving notice, and your items will be packed and delivered here," he interrupts, speaking smoothly, as though he's had this planned for weeks and I'm supposed to just go along with it.

Hell no!

"I didn't give you permission." I blink at him, feeling a burning inside me. "And what if I don't want to move into this fancy mansion but want you to move in with me?"

"You do?" he asks.

I notice Chowder hasn't moved from his cushion, just watching us.

"No." I pause. "Maybe… I don't know, but what I'm saying is you can't kidnap me because I bet you wouldn't like it."

He studies me, lips tight, his dark hair sitting messily around his face, a few strands hanging over an eye. Dressed in black pants and a matching button-up shirt, it's hard to ignore the muscles that push against the fabric and how the curled tattoos peer out, spreading across his collarbone and thick neck. The guy is pure muscle, and he's the most gorgeous man I've ever seen. Yet I'm fighting him because I'm scared of how fast things are going.

The whole true mate is not a joke. We're talking about a forever decision, and it kind of freaks me out every time I come face-to-face with it.

"I know how being ripped out of your house feels more than anyone. I left the only home I knew back in Tartarus, a world away, and moved here."

"Wait, what did you just say?" Coldness slides through me. "You're telling me you're from Tartarus? And you escaped? Because no one walks out of Tartarus." I'm suddenly pacing and shaking all over. Of course my fated mate is also a criminal. It's my track record of love interests.

"They opened the portal, and after interviewing me, they released me."

He's talking like this isn't a big deal. My thoughts are rushing ahead. My boss told me that his grandfather was put in there for a crime he committed, and anyone born in that place stays there, serving a life sentence as well. So, Kaden had no choice. I jumped to conclusions, but can you blame a girl?

My response is jammed in my chest, mostly because I want to keep being furious at him, but instead, a sliver of pity fills me. He would have been forced to grow up in a prison for no wrongdoing of his own... I swallow hard, trying to process this revelation.

"So, you were born in Tartarus, raised in that hellhole?"

He nods, his gaze steady.

"But still," I protest, anger and confusion swirling inside me. "You can't make decisions for me. I have a life, a job... responsibilities. How can you do this?"

"I'm not taking anything away from you," he replies calmly. "I'm giving you a better life, a safer one."

A hitched breath spills past my lips. "I don't need saving. I've looked after myself this far and did pretty well."

His head tilts to the side, studying me, most likely pitying me, and I grizzle internally at the notion.

"I know you can," he says softly. "This is about giving us a chance to get to know each other and without danger."

I shake my head, but he's on his feet.

"My little mermaid, we'll make this work, no matter what I have to do. You tell me anything in the world you want, and I will move oceans to make it happen."

"Not everything," I murmur, mostly to myself.

His words hang in the air, and there's almost sorrow in his voice, disappointment. I won't deny that the idea of not making it work with my fated mate squeezes my chest, shortening my breaths. Deep down, I want this so badly, but what happens if I turn? Will he face the same fate as my father?

"So, you're saying if I want to leave, I can go?" My

inhales are coming faster now, my thoughts flinging about in my head between giving him a chance and hating that I'm losing control.

He doesn't respond immediately. His jaw is tight, his chest is sticking out, and there's no denying he's a predator who gets his way.

"You want to leave me?" he asks in a cold voice, striding across the room, stealing the space between us.

I stand my ground, even as his fingers reach out and stroke the length of my throat, running along my jawline. Goosebumps race over my skin, covering me, as an excited shiver zips down my spine.

I half expect Chowder to go all feral on him, but he surprises me, staying on the couch quietly, studying us. Has he completely betrayed me and already taken to Kaden?

Glancing back up at Kaden's dark expression, my insides squeeze, knowing I've pushed him too far.

When I don't speak, he drags his thumb across my lips.

"It will devastate me if you ever leave."

His touch has my body melting, ready to give in to him. It's the fated-mate connection between us that weakens me. That has me wanting to fall to my knees before him.

"You're confusing me." My words tumble out in a whisper. "I can't leave, then?"

"Of course you can. You head to work, go anywhere as you wish," he explains. "But you return to your home here."

Fear and allure twist inside me. "I'm not your possession."

Silence meets me as his intense, deep blue eyes burn into me.

"You are mine, Sasha, my fated mate, my everything. You think I won't fight for that?" he states with a growl in his throat.

His hands slide down my arms, gentle yet firm in their hold. I can barely breathe, hating how vulnerable I feel, how desperately I stare at his mouth, needing him.

As if reading my thoughts, he leans in, our lips meeting, our kiss a clash of worlds—intense, tearing through me, anger and lust fight for power. I grasp his shirt, pulling him closer, needing to taste him, lifting myself up on my tippy-toes, though I'm also secretly hating myself for falling under his charm so quickly.

I suddenly rip myself from his kiss, somehow having found a sliver of strength to fight the infatuation consuming me. Kaden is stubborn, and whether I want to ignore the situation or not, he's my fated mate. And he's not going to leave me alone either, is he? It also doesn't help that part of me craves him insatiably.

"Fine," I exhale the word, my pulse thundering. "I'll give living here a try."

Kaden smiles, a dazzling, relieved grin that has my heart doing an involuntary flip, yet I see the tightness around his eyes that says it's not exactly the response he wants, but that's all I can give him right now.

"A man like me isn't capable of letting go of something as precious as you, something that belongs to me."

His hand slides into mine, our fingers intertwined. "Come, I've arranged for breakfast."

An overwhelmed sensation washes over me as if I've now completely lost control of my life. Except, who am I kidding? I lost that the moment I moved to Norway.

# TWELVE



"Chowder, where'd you go?" I whisper in the main living area, my voice barely cutting through the silence. It's past midnight, and the bedroom door cracked open when I woke up. Chowder wasn't in the bedroom, so now I'm worried about him getting lost or in trouble.

Stepping into the hallway, the darkness presses around me as I move slowly through the unfamiliar house, wondering where he's vanished to. I head through the next doorway and into the kitchen, flicking on the lights.

I blink against the bright light in the expansive room. Chairs and tables are on one side with white marble walls glistening under the light. Chandeliers and paint-ings are on the walls, displaying ships at sea during wild storms. The other end has a small island in the middle of the kitchen, complete with pots and pans hanging from the ceiling. There's a U-shaped counter, and everything is made of white marble, the doors and the counter adorned with thin lines of gold.

It leaves me thinking back to Kaden telling me he was a kraken, and as much as a large part of me doesn't believe him, a small part does... mostly due to the huge chip on his shoulder and the way he carries himself as though nothing can touch him. Even my seahorse-shifter ex, who claimed to be a kraken, never pulled off the level of Alpha prowess Kaden carries effortlessly.

I'm curious, though, to discover the truth.

If I'm moving in with him, then I want to know exactly who my fated mate is. Anyway, back on my search, tracing my steps, I remember how much Chowder loves the bathroom in my cabin.

I'm there in seconds, pushing open the door. Light from the aquarium beyond the glass window gives the room a glowing haze, and there, inside the amethyst bathtub, I find Chowder. The tub's half-filled with water, and he's floating on his back, fast asleep. I hadn't put the water in there, so was it Kaden? I creep out to let Chowder sleep, a soft smile tugging at my lips at how easily he's adapted to this mansion.

Just as I start to head back to bed, a great splashing sound comes from somewhere in the house. I freeze, feeling like something huge just entered the aquarium. Curiosity and a bit of dread gnaw at me, so I follow the sound back to the living area and down another corridor that shoots off from the kitchen. The hallway is elaborately decorated with carvings and paintings of the ocean, with more closed doors, yet it's eerily quiet.

The hairs on my arms lift at the stillness.

I reach a set of grand stairs that lead both upstairs and downstairs. I've yet to see a front door, so I assume it must be upstairs. When another great splash sounds again, I know with certainty it's coming from downstairs. I glance down at the spiral stairs, its wooden banisters intricately carved with flowing wave patterns, while glowing sconces pierce the darkness.

I can't see anything down there, not from my angle, and when something splashes again, sounding louder, a shiver races through me. Is Kaden in his true form?

With a deep breath and a bucketful of curiosity, I slink down the stairs, each step silent. The darkness thickens around me, but I press on.

At the bottom of the stairs, I find myself in another hallway, this one dimly lit with soft, glowing sconces on the walls. The splashing sound is louder now, coming from behind a large, ornate door at the end of the hall. My heart pounds as I approach, pushing it open slowly.

No sign of Kaden.

Inside, I'm greeted by the sight of an underground room that has me stunned. It's as though I've stepped back in time to when kings and forbidden lairs existed.

The room is enormous, the walls a deep blue marble that seems to absorb the light from the sconces dotted overhead. Lofty pillars, engraved from floor to ceiling, line the walls, creating an air of majesty. To my right, the floor dips into the water, shimmering under the low lights, glowing bluish. There's a narrow walkway in the middle of the water that leads directly to an arched open way that I instantly recognize as the cave from the fjord waters. Except I'm inside the cave now, and past the opening, it's pitch black. The fjord waits out there.

Farther on my left stands a decorative stone, almost resembling an oversized gravestone, yet so much more beautiful. It's smooth and carved, and the center is hollowed out several inches, revealing an exquisite painting of a mermaid. Red hair flows like fire, her gold-and-green tail sparkling and curving beneath her. The stone is etched away in spots, the painting missing small bits here and there, yet it's still breathtaking.

In front of it are several steps with a flat stone table —more of a solid, oversized sacrificial table. At least, that's what comes to my mind. I really hope I'm not right about that, yet that's all I can think about now.

I move into the room, stepping closer to it, noting that on either side are more paintings on lofty stone murals. One of a kraken taking down a ship, its tentacles wrapping around the vessel with terrifying might. The other shows a siren with dark, piercing eyes that feel like they're following me. My skin crawls, the image of my mother flashing in my mind.

"What in the world is this room?" I murmur to myself, a shiver running down my spine. I drift closer to the mantel with the paintings, thinking there might be something more I should know about Kaden. I run my hand across its smooth surface—cold to the touch. Walking around the stone table, I notice a dug-out section behind it. A shelf catches my eye, something glinting back at me. A blade.

My stomach hardens.

*Well, this isn't creepy at all. Just a casual sacrificial table in my new fated mate's mansion. Totally normal.*

This place, beautifully disturbing, feels ancient and dangerous.

I draw in a long inhale, sensing the faint pull of belonging as it ripples over my skin. I rub the chill out of my arms when another splash behind me makes me twist around.

My heart leaps into my throat because, in the dim light of the room, it takes me a few moments to see a figure emerging from the water.

I freeze at first, trying to work out who it is.

Then the light hits his strong face, that powerful jawline, the piercing eyes.

Kaden.

Muscles, dark hair washed off his face, abs that go for miles, well-built thighs, and... I might just fall over at his size.

He's completely naked, water running down his chiseled body. And I've suddenly forgotten how to breathe.

He's carved of muscles, so many of them. Powerful and built, all those angled lines, and I realize how much larger he is when he's not hiding behind clothes. The V at the front of his hips, the one that makes most girls go wild, is sharp and pulling my attention lower and lower.

His eyes glint as they find me, like a predator catching sight of its prey. I'm trying my damn hardest to ignore how casual he is in his delicious nudity. If I thought I had problems ignoring him before, I'm completely distracted by all the flesh, by the huge thing dangling there.

I gasp for air, and he suddenly picks up a towel I hadn't noticed discarded near a pillar and wraps it around his waist, coming my way.

Partly relieved, I pinch my lips, still grinning like a teenage girl about to fangirl at seeing the most gorgeous man in the nude.

He strolls toward me, arms dangling by his sides, and I fight to find my breath, my words, my sanity. Heat pours through me, a force so powerful I'm left burning up. My reaction to him... it's the fault of this cursed fated-mate bond, isn't it? Here I am, trembling, trying really hard not to lower my gaze to the bulge pushing against his towel but holding his intense stare.

There's something different about him tonight. He's normally got that "I'll destroy you" look on his face, but tonight, it's cranked up to maximum. It's overwhelming, potent... and it's affecting me on a deeper level that leaves me quivering for him. Yet he hasn't even touched me.

"You shouldn't be here," he mutters, his voice a low rumble. "Sometimes, I can't be trusted around you... and especially on such nights." His gaze devours me, strands of dark, wet hair falling over his face. He's still dripping wet, beads of water rolling down his muscles. It's almost hypnotizing to watch.

Words slip past my lips. "What sort of night is that?"

A curl pulls at the corners of his lips, the kind I've seen on someone who knows they're out of control but having way too much fun to rein themselves in.

"Where I can't sate my beast, where he craves something I won't give him." He steps closer, towering over me, the fire from his body leaping onto me.

I back against the stone table, and he leans in closer, propping a hand against it, partially caging me in on one side.

My heart's beating frantically, my nipples hard points against the fabric of my tank top as I squeeze my thighs together. My exhales grow ragged at his proximity while my brain panics. Without thinking, I slip from him in the opposite direction from where he has me locked in. He's intimidating, but that's not the part that scares me.

It's the energy pouring off him, the sheer force of his presence, that I grapple to push away or ignore.

What the hell is up with him tonight?

"And why's that?" I take quick steps back around the table, then quickly descend the three steps across from him, putting distance between us. "Because you're going to go all kraken on me?" I say sarcastically.

Feet away from him, I glance back at him with a grin. He hasn't moved, yet darkness seems to have gathered around him. The water near the cave's entrance turns turbulent, lapping at the shores as though something massive has disturbed it. Except it's more than that... I watch it splashing up, seeming to reach out for Kaden.

Shivers snake down my spine at his power.

"Sasha," he growls in that dangerously deep voice, almost sounding like a warning.

"Look, I'll let you do your thing... whatever you were doing down here," I murmur, rushing toward the door, unsure what mood I've just stumbled on.

When he doesn't respond, I turn and hightail it out of there. But in a heartbeat, something snaps around my middle, something soft, cold, and extremely strong. It wraps around me so fast, wrenching me backward with a speed I barely keep up, but it's almost as though it carries me as my feet try to keep up.

A cry flies out of my mouth, dread surging through me as I shove my hands at the restraint to get it off me. When I do a double take, I notice it's a large octopus limb, complete with those thick suckers sticking to my skin.

Dread comes alive inside me as I realize how wrong I've been to not believe Kaden.

I'm twisted on the spot and now standing at the base of the steps. He's partially transformed, still mostly in his human form, but spearing out from his back are long, dark, sinuous tentacles. They're a deep, inky gray, glistening in the low light, with suckers lining their undersides.

It's impossible not to panic, especially at the glint in his eyes, as if he's teetering on the edge of fully transforming.

My breath catches in my throat. "Gods, you're a kraken."

No one's really seen one as they are rare as fuck, but everyone's heard stories about how gigantic they get, how unstoppable they can be, how they can command even the ocean itself.

So much makes sense now about Kaden. Why Asbesta, the Siren Goddess, wants him in her House.

Having a kraken as an ally gives her a tremendous advantage.

Kaden laughs, the sound dark and low, as if my shock and fear bring him pleasure. He doesn't answer immediately, his eyes unreadable. The octopus arm tightens slightly, but it's not painful, just firm.

"You chose not to believe me," he states, his voice rumbling with a primal edge. Standing up on the steps, he fits in with his surroundings. All he's missing is a throne to rule the waters and fishes.

There's definitely something else—something raw and restrained—about him.

"So, this is your way of dealing with your out-of-control night? By grabbing me with your... kraken arm? What's next? Sacrificing me on this table? Is that what you do?" I shove hard against the tentacle, but it doesn't budge.

"Sacrifice you?" His eyes flash with amusement, a dangerous glow behind them. "No, not that." His smile widens with all kinds of implications of what he'd like to do with me.

Is it bad that it turns me on to think about what he'd do to me?

He suddenly draws me up the steps, where the tentacle releases me, and I catch my breath, yet he's now holding me firmly with his hands on my hips. I'm suddenly off my feet and sitting on the side of the table, bringing me face-to-face with him.

I swallow hard, trying to calm myself while placing a hand against his chest to keep our distance.

He pushes against me like I'm no obstacle, his breath on my cheeks, his lips sliding over to my ear, leaving me quivering with need.

"You always fight me, little mermaid."

"I don't know any other way to be. And didn't you just tell me I shouldn't trust you on such nights?"

His hot breath is on my neck as he chuckles. "Trust and fighting me are two very different things."

"I beg to differ." I gasp the words, my body heating up, the fire between my legs soaking me. Fire burns off his body, and he's so close now, inches from kissing me, from claiming me, that it's becoming impossible to think straight.

One of his tentacles starts slithering up my leg, the touch cooling against my skin, while another winds around my waist, dipping under my top, finding skin.

A moan slides over my throat at the sensation of his touch, at him holding me in place.

"Trust is knowing I won't harm you, Sasha. Fighting me... well, that's just foreplay."

I snort, half out of nerves, half out of frustration. "Is that what you call this?"

His lips graze my ear, and my chest pushes out toward him as if even my body betrays me in my need for him. When another tentacle slides up my other leg and pulls them apart, I can already feel my resolve weakening.

"You're mine, Sasha." His grip tightens on me. "You're never leaving me. You belong to me." Then he licks my earlobe, tugging it into his mouth, sucking on it, leaving me completely helpless.

As much as I desire him, as much as I desperately want to give myself to him, I also want him to know he doesn't control me.

"Kiss me," Kaden urges, and Universe help me, I lean in closer to him at his command.

The glint in his eyes and the mischievous grin from the power he knows he carries over me make me weak. He runs a hand from my waist over my ribs, his thumb grazing across my stiff nipple over the fabric of my tank top, leaving me breathless. Lust curls up to my gut, holding me prisoner for him.

I push a flat hand to his bare chest, the skin still wet yet on fire, but he reaches for me, grabbing me by the wrist.

"Kaden," I say with as much warning behind my voice as I can manage.

"You don't resist me, little mermaid." His tentacle is gliding up my inner thighs as he steps between my spread legs, me sitting on the sacrificial table, my ass on the edge. My pajama shorts are drenched with the arousal that consumes me.

Shaking my head, even as I spread my legs a bit

wider, the hunger I feel for him is becoming unbearable. Of course, my body betrays me, and I tilt my chin up to meet him, my eyes closing. The pulse deep inside me throbs.

His mouth is on mine, his breath racing, his tongue meeting mine. He kisses like a demon, forceful and taking what he craves, never relenting. He isn't letting me go; he said so himself.

And he isn't allowing me to leave him tonight, not until I give him what he desires.

Something I've yearned for since first meeting him, since our first kiss, since he claimed me as his fated mate.

Fireworks burst behind my eyelids as he suckles my tongue, a pleasing groan grazing my throat at the way he cherishes me. I can't escape the anticipation of what he'd be like when we take things further... because I'm not a fool. I feel his erection against my inner thigh, how mouthwateringly hard he is for me. I've never been this wet for any man.

I can't help myself. I know I need to show him he doesn't rule over me, but I've never felt this horny, this intensity, over anyone.

My hands trace up to his neck, pressing closer while his tentacles wind in and out of my shorts and my tank top, tugging at the fabric, pulling them off me. In a heartbeat, his hands fall to my waist, and he lifts me off the table long enough to have my shorts ripped off me and down my legs. My eyes flip open, a starved sound in my throat.

He leans in closer, setting me back down as he licks

my lips. Then he breaks away from me so his tentacles can wrench my tank top up and over my head.

And there I am, naked, shivering with uncontrollable need, my legs spread, granting him full access.

His stare undoes me. His tongue pushes out, dragging across his lips as his gaze dips down my body.

"This is how I love to see you, how I've dreamed of this moment. It's what my beast has been torturing me for... to make you ours."

"Please, Kaden, give me what I need, then." I swallow the thickness in my throat, barely able to stand the arousal deepening in my gut at how the smallest breeze across my pussy has me shuddering.

He's wearing that smile again as he leans in, his mouth on my neck, whispering, "I never rush a meal."

He covers me in kisses across my collarbone, then lowers himself to my breasts and gently bites down on my nipple, making me cry out. His hand finds my other breast, squeezing it, pinching my tip. He takes the nipple into his mouth, sucking down hard, his breath over my skin. I can tell he's enjoying himself, the grunting sounds of someone struggling to contain himself.

But he has more control than me, taking his time.

An inferno washes over me, my head back, and I'm trembling with need. The urgency to have him touch me is excruciating.

"Lie on your back, my beautiful little mermaid. Let me worship you."

I quiver, every inch of me hyperaware of his fingers tracing the insides of my thighs, of the tips of his tentacles brushing around my ankles, making me an offering to him. I lie back, knowing I've gone too far to stop myself now, but that doesn't mean I won't remind him he's not the only one in charge.

He lifts my legs gently, knees bent, his tentacles holding them up and apart, essentially tying them up.

"Fuck, Sasha." His hand falls between us, fingers tenderly running over heated lips, over the silky arousal, and the sensation is tantalizing.

Moaning, I arch my back off the table while his tentacles hold me open for him. Quickening breaths have me cranking up my neck to find him getting to his knees before me, his gaze fixed on me. He pushes a finger into me, smiling at his action, while the tension thunders through me like a volcanic eruption. I'm so far gone already, so needy.

"Your tight pussy is mine. All of you is mine."

My body trembles as I clench around his pumping finger sliding in and out of me as if he's made for me.

I'm rocking my hips, my clit pulsing at the sensitive skin. His face is so close that I feel his breath as he takes a deep inhale.

"So fucking beautiful. Your slick is dripping. I love seeing you like this, your delicious cunt bared for me."

"Stop teasing me... you know what I need," I say breathlessly, squirming with unrest, with agitation at him taking his time.

He laughs at me, which has me narrowing my gaze. Grabbing my ass, his fingers dig into my flesh, lifting my hips slightly as if he's about to dive into his meal—me.

I gasp for air as his exhale dances across my sensitive folds.

That mouth, the savagery in his eyes

A whimper strokes my throat.

His gaze lifts to mine as he moves in closer, his tongue finding my pussy. He traces me all the way from my entrance up to my clit.

He unleashes the growl of a protective animal, guarding his food, while I moan out loud, the world drifting away from me. I'm falling headfirst, driven mad by his mouth.

Sinking in closer, he holds me, his fingers pulling my cheeks apart as the flat of his tongue teases me, over and over, licking harshly as if he's sampling me. When he pushes it into me, I cry out, my back flat against the stone table. Its coldness barely keeps the blaze inside me at bay.

Then he dives in, devouring me like a beast possessed, fingers burrowing into my flesh, his tongue fucking me. Two tentacles snake up my body and circle my breasts, their tips curling around my hard nipples and squeezing just firmly enough to leave me screaming from the arousal about to ruin me.

Grasping the sides of the table, I shamelessly grind myself against his face as whimpers tumble from my throat.

He plunges his tongue back into me just as one of his fingers pushes into my ass, sinking in deeper.

Nipples tugged and my pussy devoured, I stand no chance as tiny electrical pulses fire through my body. And that heaviness building up deep in my gut busts, crashing through me.

I scream, tilting my head back, body arching, my legs

shaking as an orgasm claims me. Any attempt to pull my legs together, to clench them, fails miserably as he holds them apart, refusing to release me. But I'm too busy quivering and coming all over his mouth to fight him.

Crying out, the room around me blinks in stars like I might pass out... that's how incredibly hard I erupted, and it doesn't end but continues as Kaden remains between my legs, lapping me up.

My pussy trembles under the ferocity of his tongue. Then he's sucking my swollen clit, tugging on it, his teeth lightly grazing it. Just when I think I might be floating back down, unstoppable desire rises through me once more.

"Kaden," I call out as part of another scream as my body thrashes.

He releases me, and I collapse, my breaths racing, his tentacles falling away from my breasts.

"No one's ever made me feel that insanely wonderful before," I whisper.

"Then you've been with the wrong men who don't know how to cherish a body like yours." He gets to his feet, his lips, nose, and chin glistening with my slick.

He glances back down at me, grinning that spectacular smile that's put a spell on me.

"You taste of honey and sex, and I'm already starving for more. But I'm hungry for something stronger." He rips his towel off, dropping it on the floor.

Of course, I push myself up on my elbows for a real look, doing what I've craved since seeing him emerge from the water.

My eyes widen at the sight, my pussy quivering at

what he's packing. His cock is erect, thick, and damn long, but it's not just the size that intimidates me. It's that he has built-in speed bumps running up both sides of the shaft. He's ribbed, and I'm not sure what to make of them.

He chuckles when I glance up to meet his gaze.

"They're for your pleasure, my little mermaid, for when I stretch your tight little pussy. You're going to be screaming my name, begging for more."

My mouth parts as I stare at that huge cock once more. I must be delusionally drunk on arousal because I grin.

"Then show me, my kraken lover, what your magical cock can do to me."

He chuckles loudly, the sound booming against the stone walls.

"That's my beautiful mermaid." He palms himself, moving in closer to where I'm dripping.

I feel the lust controlling me, craving him.

"You make me so wet I can barely stand it," I admit.

He brushes the tip of his dick against my pussy.

"I plan to never let you go. With your scent in my head, your taste in my mouth, there's no turning back."

That darkness he wears so well returns in his voice, in his obsessive stare.

"Maybe stop talking and show me."

He doesn't waste a second, pressing the head of his cock into me.

I flinch at the strong push into my cunt, at his impatience, at the devious grin spreading his lips.

"So tight... so fucking tight," he growls as his hands grip my thighs, dragging me closer to him.

I quiver as he slides deeper into me, unsure how in the world it's even fitting. Each exhale rasps from my lungs from the overstimulation of those ridges he sports and being stretched to the point of shock. I grip the table with my life.

"You take me so well," he crows. "I'm going to fuck you in front of a mirror one day so you can see how wide I've got you spread."

"Oh, I know," I breathe out. "I'm feeling it."

He gives a final thrust, shoving himself all the way into me, not really taking his time to ease that massive trunk where it belongs. Yet my pussy's shivering with desire, dripping, starved to be fucked ragged.

Powerful hands grasping my hips, Kaden takes no pause, fucking me in and out like a maniac. I thrash on the table, my body shuddering at the friction he ignites with each plunge. He holds me firmly, his gaze glancing down at himself going into me, spreading me.

His growls are music to my ears, the elation on his face doing something to me. To see a man as dominant as Kaden falling under my control does something to my ego. It's empowering, telling me he loves everything he's seeing and feeling.

"Fuck," he snarls, his eyes rolling back as he hammers into me.

I'm rocking back and forth, cries raw in my throat to be fucked to where I'm so full that I feel every inch of him pushing me wider.

He's going at a speed I've never experienced, and I might be floating, darkness dotting the edges of my vision. The energy, the sexual power he radiates, is making it impossible to think straight. My heart's charging in my chest, pounding in my ears, as are his growls and my moans.

Those dark blue eyes of his lock on to mine, and I swear I feel the power he wields running over my body. It's electrifying, overwhelming.

"This is how it's meant to be," he assures me. "You and me as one, fucking, together, forever."

The heaviness of his words and the way he stares at me make me feel both cherished and possessed. His admiration is intoxicating. It's a losing battle inside of me with the desperation to give in, to let him take control.

Then something in his words reminds me of his comment from the other day about intending to breed me. And here he is, going insane, me wriggling, my own lust pushing me to the edge of a second orgasm. I'm tingling all over, and each time he slaps into me, the sound resonating around us, I shiver harder.

Beneath it all, panic starts to swell, and my voice spills past my lips.

"Kaden," I breathe heavily, barely able to get the words out. "Are... tell me you're not thinking of breeding me."

He grins, a predatory smile that makes my stomach flip. He's pounding into me almost quicker, his grip tightening, holding me tighter. The thing is, I feel trapped, yet part of me yearns for more.

"You bastard," I call out, followed by a delicious cry

as his fingers rub my clit in small circles. He's unrelenting. The hard part is that I want everything he offers, but the battle inside me is serious.

*Breeding...* gods, no. This is too fast. I need to have a say in it.

At that moment of being torn between euphoria and freaking out, I remember the weapon I spotted earlier under the sacrificial table. I slowly shimmy closer to the left side of the table. He doesn't seem to notice, and I move just enough for my arm to dip down over the side. My hand pats the air, searching blindly.

His eyes widen, spotting my action. Just as he leans over me, reaching for my arm, snarling, "Gorgeous little mermaid, don't make me chase you," my fingers graze the metal hilt.

I snatch it, wrapping my fingers around it firmly. I whip the blade up and out as he's practically lying on top of me, and I press the length of the knife to his throat.

His eyes enlarge in surprise, a flicker of something dangerous crossing his face.

"Good girl," he growls. "I needed something to tame my beast."

His words leave me partially confused, but I keep the blade pressed to his throat.

"Don't think about breeding me. I'm not ready, and you don't get to decide everything for me."

For a moment, he pauses fucking me and stares down at me. I honestly have no idea how he'll react, but I'm not lowering my blade. Then he releases a slow, measured exhale, his gaze never leaving me.

"You keep the blade to my throat while I fuck you, and I won't fill you with my seed."

I blink, trying to figure him out and if this is some kind of fetish or if he seriously meant what he said about his beast, his kraken side, driving him to breed me.

I nod. "Now, don't you dare stop what you're doing because I'm so close. Gods, Kaden, that cock of yours is the world's gift to women."

He laughs, dark and playful. "My cock is only for one woman... you. And I had no intention of letting you go until I fucked you into loving me."

"Wait, what?"

But he's already thrusting back into me, distracting me, his hands on the table on either side of me, a growl in his chest.

I hold the blade to his throat, but he's not bothered that we're both moving about as he slams into me, as I cry out from having him completely dominating my pussy.

He moves faster now, and it's as if a switch flicks on inside me as the tsunami of explosive orgasms rattles me from the core. It tears through me with lightning speed.

I notice a few red droplets rolling down his chest, dripping onto me from the knife. I barely have time to register that as the euphoria wreaks havoc on me, and I'm screaming my pleasure.

Lowering the blade to the table beside me, not trusting myself to not slice his throat in my excitement, he suddenly pulls off me.

In a swift movement, he draws out of me and flops that massive cock, soaked in my juices on my stomach.

Instantly, the warmth pours over my stomach, spraying over my breasts and my neck. Some of it reaches my face.

He roars like a damn lion, seeming rather proud of himself, pumping his cock with his hand to get it all out. White ribbons of cum spew out, coming fast and hard.

It's warm against my skin, his manly scent intoxicating. I can't stop myself from licking the two drops that hit the corner of my mouth, tasting his salty, masculine elixir. Delicious.

Still buzzing from my own climax, I'm taken by the elation on his face, where there's no anger, no domination, just the most beautiful man I've ever seen floating on a high, still consuming both of us.

I take a deep breath, trying to steady my racing heart. Tonight has taken me to places I never expected. As I lie sprawled on the sacrificial table, covered in kraken cum, I can't help but let out a dry, sarcastic laugh.

"Well, I guess this table's finally getting some use."

# FOURTEEN

## KADEN

"I'm capable of walking," my little mermaid insists as I lift her into my arms. That feistiness of hers that I adore roars to life.

"I know," I answer, carrying her across the expansive cave underneath my mansion to where the water laps at the edge of the stone floor. She's so light and yet glaring at me. "You're not going anywhere until I clean you up. You're covered in my cum, and it's going to get everywhere if you try to walk."

She bursts out laughing. "Oh, that's what you're worried about? Surely a kraken like you has the ability to command the water to wash the mess you make."

I grin at her quip. "What fun would that be?"

Stepping into the cold water brings me to life. Something about the iciness awakens me and my beast. Though for the first time in too long, he's calm... sated from getting exactly what he's craved—me fucking Sasha.

She's cradled against me, wriggling to get out, but I tighten my grip. In my eyes, she's the most beautiful woman in the world. She's all I see, all I need.

Moving deeper into the waters has her flinching as the cold laps up against her naked body. She presses against me, leaving me as the happiest man in the world.

"Are you sure you're a mermaid?" I tease and dunk us both beneath the water. She squirms, and I bring us back up, with her splashing me in the face.

"That's freezing," she yelps. "I don't have thick squid skin like you. Give a girl a warning before you ice her to death."

I laugh again, finding her beyond amusing. "Squid— is that what you think a kraken is?"

"If the tentacle fits," she murmurs, then pinches her lips as if holding back a smile. "Sure, I know you're not, but you're annoying me. In fact, I've actually read up on how many sailors back in the day would mistake giant squid for kraken, and clearly, things got mixed up with your origin. Though I'm not sure why the kraken destroyed all those ships."

I watch her mouth, still tasting her on my lips, wanting more. Instead, I lower her to her feet in the water that reaches just under her full breasts. I start splashing her across the chest and collarbone, my large palm wiping her clean of my cum.

She pushes my hand away as I grope her breast, unable to resist. When she pulls completely away from me, I snatch her arm and haul her to my side.

"Thing is... kraken have a wild temperament."

"Oh, I can tell." She pushes against me again as my arm wraps around her, wiping clean my stickiness from her chest and stomach, especially around those delicious breasts with her dusty pink nipples. I remember them being aquamarine in her mermaid form, and I look forward to tasting them that way, too.

"When those boats fished in their waters," I explain, "they threw waste into it, so the kraken burst into fury, and, well, they destroyed the boats. Can't really blame them. What would you do if someone came and threw their garbage into your home?"

"Or came into your home and took you away from it," she attests sarcastically.

"Sasha," I coo, drawing her against me. I drop myself to my knees, so I don't tower over her, wrapping her in my arms. She's soft, so warm against me, and I can't get enough of her body pressed against mine, skin to skin. "This is your home; you just didn't know it at the time."

She rolls her eyes while I smirk and run my palm down the valley of her breasts and over her stomach and right to between those beautiful thighs. In a heartbeat, my fingers are on her sweet pussy, running the length of her seam, the silkiness covering her from her own arousal.

"Hey," she reacts in a split second, shoving against my shoulders.

"I'm making sure you're thoroughly clean." I have a tight grip around her waist.

"I don't need you to do that!" she gasps. She's still fighting me, pushing against my arm, but I'm not pausing.

"But I do, my sweet. When I make a mess, I'll fix it up. It's either in the water here with my hand, or I place you back up on the table and use my tongue. Your choice."

She blinks while I slip a finger between her pussy folds, leaving her trembling, those nipples tightening for me once more.

"You wouldn't."

"Try me." It'd be so easy to claim her right here, over and over. My cock's already throbbing at piercing her tight cunt again.

I chuckle, holding her firm, keeping my word, and finish stroking her gorgeous pussy free of her slick, my cock hard as a rock, ready to fuck her. I contemplate bending her over for being a bad girl and fucking her hard, that adorable ass in the air, my finger pushing into it.

Grinding my jaw, I'm torturing myself.

Her expression belongs to a serial killer, yet her body sways, leaning into me. So sweet, loving me playing with her little pussy.

When I finish, I release her and she stumbles from me, then tosses water at me in anger.

"Don't ever do that again. I can take care of myself."

"Not promising that because now you've got me looking out for you as well," I reply, smirking as she storms out of the water. My gaze lowers instantly to that curvy ass that's calling for my touch, for my cock, each cheek wiggling with the fast steps she takes.

"For all I know, I'll wake up in the morning tied up on that sacrificial table. That's what it's for, right?"

Her tenacity is admirable. "The table belonged to my

grandfather, as did the whole mansion. He built it, I was told."

"So, I'm not wrong, then, hey?" Daggers fly at me from her gaze. "Sacrificing is in the family line."

I chuckle at her anger; she's so damn adorable. "I can't speak for my grandfather because, for all I know, he did use it for that. Me, I haven't found the need... yet."

She heads for the doorway.

"Going already?" I call out sarcastically.

She twists toward me, and I admire her full-frontal nudity. She's absolutely spectacular, dripping in water. I especially love that small patch of hair between her thighs, a darker shade of her aquamarine hair.

"Yeah, I've had my fill of possessive crazy for one night," she declares.

I hold her stare, admiring her strength to stand up to me. And I can't exactly deny her accusations when they're plain as day true.

"Good night, Sasha," I say, then turn from her, already feeling my beast pushing out of me. The transformation comes effortlessly, as easily as changing clothes, my body growing, extending. Knowing that my intention isn't to remain in my cave in my kraken form, I dive into the water, the cave open, as is the enormous underwater passage carved out from the stone, large enough for a kraken to swim through.

It's liberating, fucking freeing to unleash him, to swim unrestricted. I enter the fjord with black water, the moonlight somewhere overhead, but as I propel myself ahead, my thoughts remain on Sasha.

It seems there's something in the coming times to

look forward to. My kraken is obsessed with her, and maybe, just maybe, I can see a future where she's by my side, taming the beast within me.

My thoughts remain locked on my mermaid, her taste on my tongue, her scent fogging my head, and yet, I swore I felt something different about her, something I can't quite pinpoint. It's an energy deep inside her that I haven't sensed before, something primal, definitely not what I've picked up with any mermaid I've fucked.

Maybe it's our fated-mate connection bringing forward this undercurrent of power she carries just below the surface. My curiosity heightens. Whatever's going on with her, it's something I'll keep an eye on, determined to understand why she feels so different.

The cold fjord waters ripple around me, my massive tentacles sliding through its darkness. Gliding through the depths, I let the current carry me when a surge of images suddenly crashes into my mind, dragging me away from the present. The fjord fades fast, replaced by a vision that feels too real.

*I'm standing on the edge of a natural hot spring located in a valley surrounded by rocky, snow-tippled mountains that rise imposingly into the sky. Steam curls up from the blue lagoon, creating a mist that hangs in the air.*

*My focus is drawn to my grandfather and a red-haired woman in the water. She's splashing playfully, her gold-and-green tail calling out to my grandfather, her voice singsong and filled with laughter.*

"Water's so hot it's beautiful," she says, her piercing green eyes gleaming with joy.

Recognition strikes me instantly.

Is it her?

The mermaid painted down in the cave beneath the mansion, near the stone table? The sacrificial table, as Sasha called it. A table that is used by some sea creatures in the waters I lived with in Tartarus as a birthing altar. Some also call it a celebration altar for when fated mates mark their first mating... something I was fully aware of when I fucked my little mermaid on there. It's all ritual, nothing with magic, but I'm not above inserting some customs into my life.

With my attention back on my grandfather, he appears slightly older but unmistakably himself. He strips in seconds and joins her in the water. The hot springs ripple around him, seemingly aware of his power as a kraken. He reaches the mermaid in moments, drawing her into his arms. Her beauty is striking but doesn't come close to comparing to Sasha's.

"I'm so happy you brought us here," she chirps.

He spins her away from him so her back is flush against his chest, his arms wrapped around her. His chin rests on her shoulder as he steals a small kiss that leaves her giggling.

"I needed to get away," he admits, his voice softer than I've ever heard it. "Business has been demanding as we keep growing it."

"You work too hard," she answers. "Though I really want to know what you do. It's been eight months since we met, and you still won't tell me." She pouts.

He kisses her on the cheek, breaking into loud laughter that echoes off the surrounding rocks. "It's boring, trust me.

*The last thing I want is for you to see the dull things I do, then you'll think that's me."*

*She faces him, eyes locked on him, clear she absolutely adores him. "Nothing you do could ever be dull. Not you, my love."*

*He cups her face. "I've never loved anyone before, but now you have my heart, Nixi."*

*I groan inwardly at the sight of my grandfather being so romantic. It's slightly sickening, but it makes me wonder if this is how I appear when I'm sweet to my Sasha. The thought is both amusing and unsettling.*

*The real question gnawing at me is who is this red-haired mermaid Nixi? My grandfather never spoke of anyone he loved, not even the female kraken he impregnated in Tartarus. They never stayed together, so when she passed from an illness, he took my father under his tentacle.*

*But the man was a closed book, offering nothing of himself or his past. Yet here he is, with this woman, sharing a moment so intimate it feels like an invasion to witness it. I don't doubt his love for her, especially not when he'd had her mural painted in the basement of his mansion.*

*So, what happened to her? Why didn't he ever mention her?*

The vision fades, and I'm back in the fjord, the cold water wrapping around me, though the image of my grandfather lingers in my mind, more vivid than any memory. I glide forward, the dark waters swirling around me, silver fish darting away from me, while a Greenland shark coming directly in front of me jolts to the side, vanishing into the dark with speed.

Still, I can't shake the image of my grandfather and the red-haired mermaid. The secrets he kept, the women in these visions—how do they all connect to his imprisonment in Tartarus?

# FIFTEEN



**B**ack in Kaden's bedroom, I'm breathless, trying to make sense of what just happened downstairs. My attraction to Kaden is mind-blowing; that's clear. Even now, I'm tingling all over, unable to believe how quickly things have escalated between us. Not that I regret a single scorching hot moment. Well, putting aside the whole "controlling me" aspect, trying to breed me, and then cleaning my pussy in the water with his hand without being asked to do it.

What the hell!

The thing is, I'm not even that upset about it… more shocked. The guy has zero concept of personal space. Maybe moving in with him was too fast, giving him the impression he can do whatever he wants.

On top of all that, my mind is stuck on seeing Kaden shift into his kraken form. The sheer size of him, even though I knew it still wasn't his full form, left me trembling. The guy's terrifying. I ended up standing in the doorway long after he dove into the icy waters of the fjord, trembling at the reality of who my fated mate is. The image of those massive tentacles unfurling, his body expanding, the raw power in every movement... it's something I can't easily shake off. My skin prickles from fear, from being awestruck.

In my room, I find Chowder sleeping in the bed, stretched out like he owns the place. With the towel I grabbed from the bathroom on the way, I dry myself quickly and get changed into leggings and a hooded crop top. Deciding to return to my cabin in the middle of the night feels like the right thing to do. Sure, Kaden is my fated mate, but this is too fast for me.

Luckily, my belongings from my place only just got here, and they're still packed. Makes for an easy getaway.

A light chirp sounds behind me, and I twist to see Chowder on the edge of the bed, standing on his hind legs. "Who is upset?"

I go to him and throw my arms around him. "We don't belong here. We need to go back to our home."

He pulls out of my embrace. "No."

I sigh, seeing him shaking his head. "You like it here? But he's overbearing."

Chowder stares at me, that tiny nose of his twitching, and I realize he may not understand what *overbearing* means.

"He's just—"

"Good to you. Good to us," he completes my sentence.

"Is he?" I sit on the bed, my heart racing.

Chowder scrambles onto my lap, lying there, and glances up with those soulful eyes that make me smile.

"You're confusing, you know that?" I say, scratching behind his ears. "One minute, you're all grumpy at him, and the next, you're defending him."

Chowder groans in response, making me laugh despite myself.

"So, you think he's good for me, huh?"

He nudges his head against my hand, his way of saying yes.

I take in the room that's both luxurious and suffocating.

"It's just... I don't know if I'm ready for all this."

Chowder, tilting his head, says, "What will we do?"

"I don't know," I admit, leaning back on the bed. "Part of me wants to stay, to see where this goes, but the other part... I feel like I'm losing myself. It worries me."

He snuggles closer to my side, offering his support.

"Why does everything have to be so hard?" I mutter, running a hand through his fur. "I don't know. Maybe it's better we leave? So, little buddy, I should get our stuff ready to go."

Chowder's head pops up, staring at me with almost disappointment on his face.

"How can we leave? When he brings back your scales."

I blink at him, pushing up to a sitting position.

"Wait, what are you saying?" My mind charges back to the two scales from my tail I found on my bedside table. And Chowder is telling me Kaden was responsible?

"Did you see him bring them back?" I ask softly.

"He sneaks past me. But he scratches me, and I'm a

good boy," Chowder says, almost smiling. "So, Kae'en is good man."

I grin at his mispronunciation of Kaden's name, but I'm sitting here torn into dozens of pieces. Getting up, I go to my bag and pull out the scales, still in their container. I can't part with them, and I stare at them. Kaden did that for me? Something so deeply personal when he barely knew me.

Chowder nuzzles against my hand while he remains on the bed. "Stay here?" he says. "Kae'en is good."

I exhale loudly, stroking his soft fur. "I don't know. Maybe?" Flopping back onto the bed, I feel the weight of everything. "Here, I thought you hated him."

Chowder scrambles onto my chest, staring down at me, a world of emotions behind those tiny eyes, and I can see exactly what he wants.

For us to stay here.

I laugh softly. "All I can promise is that we won't leave tonight, okay?" I'm torn in two directions, figuring I'll sleep on it.

Chowder gives a chirping sound, hops off me, and goes to curl up on one of the pillows.

I glance at the scales one more time before tucking them into the bag.

Kaden keeps surprising me, and I can't tell if that's a good thing or a disaster waiting to happen. Either way, I feel as though things are going to get very interesting.

I curl up next to Chowder, stroking him, and close my eyes, thinking that Kaden did something for me and never bragged about it or even told me. There's something almost humbling about that.

I must have crashed because it's already morning. I stroll out of the bedroom after realizing Chowder is not next to me. Hearing laughter through the house is what initially woke me up, and I'm curious about what's going on.

I stagger into the kitchen, where I find the two men in my life. Chowder eating a full, raw trout off a plate at the table, standing on a chair. Kaden sits across from him, devouring his meal. The table's flowing with food—meats, bread, eggs, pancakes, fruit, fish. Everything I can think of is available. My stomach growls in response. In all honesty, I can't recall the last time I ate. I'm starving and take a seat at the round table.

"How'd you sleep?" Kaden asks with a devious lift at the corners of his lips.

"Stirred all night," I answer with a lie, refusing to let him know he affected me so much.

"Not true," Chowder pipes in. "You snore heavy. Sleep like log."

Kaden laughs while my cheeks are burning. I never thought I'd have them both against me.

"And you?" I break the attention from myself.

"Best night's sleep in years. I needed *it* last night." His eyes never leave me as he takes a bite of his bread smothered in jam.

Is he referring to the sleep or our fucking session? Most definitely the latter, leaving me breathing quicker, unable to forget the most incredible orgasm I've ever experienced.

"So, I hear good news that there's no plan for you and my buddy here to be leaving the mansion," Kaden murmurs, leaning back in his chair, the streak of sunlight pouring in from the window lighting up those dark blue eyes. A light stubble covers his jawline, his dark hair messy around that ridiculously gorgeous face, and that white tee he's wearing pulls taut across his pecs, his muscles unmatched.

I shift my gaze to Chowder, who doesn't even notice but is devouring his fish, making a mess of his whiskers.

"Is he a spy for you now?" I murmur in Kaden's direction. I serve myself a couple of fried eggs on thick pieces of toast. Most mornings, I grab fruit on the way out the door.

"Believe it or not, guys do talk about their feelings," Kaden responds, a smirk playing on his lips. "Chowder was very vocal about wanting to stay here."

"I gives otter of approval," Chowder blurts out, staring at us.

"Do you mean seal of approval?" I ask.

He's shaking his head. "I say correct. Who likes seals?"

I burst out laughing, unable to help myself.

"Okay, you got me there," I say. He's been hanging out with me too long and picked up on my sass.

Kaden watches us intently. "See? It's like a family breakfast already."

I roll my eyes but can't help the warmth spreading through me. Despite everything, despite my reservations, there's something undeniably comforting about this moment.

"You're pushing it," I say.

"Even Chowder sees it." His grin almost reaches up to his eyes, enjoying himself way too much.

I swallow hard, trying to ignore the fluttering in my chest. "We'll see," I say, focusing on my food. Deep down, I know he's right. This place, him, it all feels inexplicably right. And that scares me more than I'd like to admit.

I take a bite, savoring my meal as Kaden pours me some juice. He seems to be enjoying the domestic routine far too much.

"So, I've heard some things, too. Like you returning my scales without telling me."

He tilts his head slightly, but that strong expression remains fixed on his face.

"I would never stand back and watch someone hurt you or take anything from you. I've told you this."

"Yes, but why didn't you tell me you retrieved them for me?"

"Sasha, I don't seek approval or praise."

"Who said I'd praise you?" I affirm instantly, my voice snappier than intended. He brings out many things in me, including that challenge to always best him.

"I see it in your eyes. And you're welcome." His feet reach mine under the table, and I draw them away.

I chew on that for a moment, realizing what he did was before he knew we were fated mates, yet he still looked out for me.

"Well, thanks. I appreciate it. Hopefully, that doesn't

bring down the wrath of Asbesta on your doorstep because of me." The thought alone tightens my middle.

Kaden smacks his lips, swallows, and reclines in his chair.

"She would never harm you. Trust me. As my fated mate, she will do well to keep as far from you as possible, and she will know this."

"Why? Because you agreed to join her House?"

"Nothing's set in stone," he explains. "But sometimes, it's easier to appease someone until you work out your next move."

"So, you're not planning on moving?"

"Unless you intend to relocate with me, I'm staying by your side." He's wearing that stalker grin again.

Chowder, finishing his fish, looks between us. "Are we moving house, all three?"

"No," I say firmly.

Chowder gives me a pout.

"If that's what we need to do," Kaden answers, his tone equally resolute.

"You can't just make decisions for all of us." I glare at him, irritation bubbling below the surface along with something warmer.

"I'm not," he replies calmly. "I'm offering a solution. Your safety is my priority."

"Me, too," Chowder chirps in, his eyes wide and innocent.

Feeling outnumbered and slightly overwhelmed, I murmur, "I don't even know how to process all of this."

Kaden leans forward, his gaze intense but softer than before. "Embrace it, little mermaid."

"We family now?" Chowder suddenly blurts out.

"No," I say at the exact same moment that Kaden says, "Yes."

Chowder shakes his head. "Confusing."

I can't help but laugh.

"We're... figuring it out," Kaden adds.

I park the car at the side of the busy port, the hustle and bustle of the docks in clear view at the bottom of the street. Reaching over for my backpack on the passenger seat, I prepare to grab just the essentials, but my hand lands on something unexpectedly fluffy. I flinch, my heart skipping a beat, only to glance over and find Chowder popping his head out of my bag, his eyes bright and inquisitive.

"Hello," he chirps.

"You little sneak," I murmur. "When did you get into my bag?"

He makes a low grunting sound, which I've learned is his attempt at laughing, replicating the sound I make.

I giggle, ruffling his fur. I'd been in such a rush this morning that I didn't even think anything about my bag feeling slightly heavier than normal. I blame Kaden and his words from breakfast distracting me.

"I can't exactly leave you alone in the car. Looks like you're coming with me." A part of me really hopes this won't require any chasing down the bad guy. After all, it's just a checkup on my new target.

Chowder's chirping now, chin high, his little paws grasping the top of my bag. "I ready to work," he tells me.

"Well, let's see how we go today, all right?" He nods, and I grab my bag with him sinking inside. "You just need to remain low, okay?" Once I'm out of the car, I slide the bag onto my shoulder and make my way down to the docks.

The sun shines brightly this morning, the salty sea breeze whipping through my hair.

Today's job is easy—collect the whereabouts of a twenty-year-old guy due to check in in a day's time because he's a high flight risk. The idiot got busted smuggling stolen jewels from the House of Air and Amethyst, thinking he could hide out in the House of Gold and Garnet, living off his treasure. So, we're tracking him to ensure he doesn't skip town.

He was last seen working down by the docks.

The place is bustling, merchants dragging in fish, other workers milling about. From my understanding, those who go out on the boats are from House of Sea and Serpentine and usually drop off catches on the wharf for locals, and those running the docks are meant to ensure no one enters the House of Gold and Garnet if they don't belong here. How well that's policed is something else unless, of course, mercenaries get wind of those illegal entries and go hunting for them.

My target works on the docks, so I'm hoping to catch a glimpse of him. Pulling down my cap over my eyes, I dressed casually in jeans and a hoodie, blending in easily.

I spot a bunch of men chatting near the edge of a

jetty, the sound of their voices growing clearer the closer I get. I'm hoping my target is nearby as there are workers coming and going from that ship, unloading cargo. Fishing boats bob in the water nearby. Seagulls squawk overhead, and the air is thick with the smell of the fish—lovely, just what I wanted to start my day.

Walking past buckets of cod and hake flopping about, I can't help but feel a bit of a pang. I mean, people eat fish—fine, I get it—but seeing them like this, gasping for air, tugs at something in me.

I sense Chowder flipping around in my bag, which I assume is in response to the strong fish smell. Hopefully, he has some self-control, considering the huge meal he had for breakfast.

Passing two fishermen, their conversation catches my attention. My heart skips a beat, pausing by a stack of fish, pretending to be interested in them.

"All crew dead as doornails. Third one in town in as many weeks," one of them says, his voice gruff, pausing me in my steps.

"Aye, I heard. Rumors sayin' it's them sirens turnin' deadly. Anyone on the water ain't safe no more," another adds, shaking his head, his beard bobbing with the movement.

Sirens? Three attacks? My mind flashes back to the mistaken identity involving my mom, who eliminated seven men recently. Could it be her? Or is this something else entirely?

"Somethin's changed in the waters," the other agrees. "Heard a while ago of this happening farther north in the country."

I feel a chill run over my skin. This isn't normal siren behavior at all. As the men wander off, I travel down another busy dock, eyes scanning for my target while my mind's hooked on the news I'd just heard.

Sirens don't massacre groups of sailors like this. Maybe one here and there... So why are they acting this way?

How is my mom involved? I tell myself she's no longer my mom, that she most likely won't remember me, yet my chest tightens at the memory of the photo the authorities showed me of her killing those men.

The need to discover the truth billows inside me.

As I walk faster, hands in the pockets of my jeans, my gaze lands on a new ship recently docked. A group of men emerge, making their way down the wooden ramp, and behind them, an older woman follows. Blonde hair pulled back in a no-nonsense bun, a beauty spot above her lip, and she's dressed in gum boots and jeans. She's managing to look both stern and completely at home on the dock.

I stride over, putting on my most approachable smile.

"Hi there," I start, hoping my cheerful tone will melt her ice-cold demeanor. "I'm doing a piece for a local journalist company about the fishing industry. Do you mind if I ask you a few questions?"

She gives me a once-over, her eyes narrowing suspiciously, but her stare lingers on my face a bit too long, leaving me uncomfortable.

"Why do you want to know?" Her voice is as gruff as her expression.

"I'm trying to understand more about the local industry and some of the challenges you all face out here," I lie, keeping my tone light and professional. "You know, for the readers."

She crosses her arms, still scrutinizing me. "You don't look like any journalist I've ever seen. What paper did you say you're with?"

"Uh, the *Fjord Times*," I reply, hoping it sounds credible enough. "We're doing a special series on the impact of recent events on the local fisheries. Along with a rumor spreading that..." I glance around me to see if anyone is nearby, mostly for effect. "There's a siren attacking sailors, killing them."

In the meantime, Chowder's rummaging about in my backpack, and suddenly, his head pops up, making a tiny chirp as though he's coming up for air. Being super dramatic.

The woman's attention flips to the bag over my shoulder, her eyes landing on Chowder.

"Cute otter," she mutters, feigning more interest in him than answering my questions.

"Yeah, he's my partner in crime for the day," I joke, trying to keep the conversation light, not wanting Chowder to start talking and draw more attention to himself, considering his background. "Okay, Chowder, back to your nap." I reach over, nudging him back inside, which he does, thankfully.

When she glances at me again, her eyes narrow, and she stares at me longer than feels comfortable. There's a flicker of recognition—or maybe suspicion—crossing her face, making me uneasy.

"Look, I'd caution you against following rumors from sailors. Best you don't get involved where you don't belong," she states, her tone heavy with implication. "Some things are better left uncovered."

Not waiting for me to respond, she turns on her heel and marches away, leaving me blinking after her, my radar going off the charts. That woman knows something.

As I watch her stride away, I turn my attention to the ship where the men she was with are carrying closed boxes off the ship, taking them straight to the back of a van. They're not selling their catch at the small market by the shore like others.

I stroll over to another dock, my mind racing about her standoffish behavior. Of course, it could be that she hates journalists sticking their noses in her business. Most people despise them.

As I approach, I catch sight of my target in the distance, a wiry guy with a perpetual scowl etched on his face unloading boxes off a boat. I slide behind a group of men, trying to blend in. The last thing I need is for him to suspect I'm here checking on him and bail.

The older woman's warning echoes in my mind. Something feels off about the whole thing, and I decide I need to dive into some research. In particular on the north shore of Norway.

For the second half of the day, I take Chowder back home and return to the office. I bury myself in admin work, catching up on training modules and trying to distract my wandering thoughts. The morning keeps replaying in my mind—the deaths, the sirens, my mother.

Tomorrow's the weekend, and seeing as I'm not working, I have plans to start investigating what's really going on. As much as I tell myself it's not my business, not to get involved, I can't walk away when it might explain why my mother turned on my father, why she killed him out of the blue.

On the drive home, my mind miles away, I find myself parked in front of my cabin. My brain went on autopilot as I drove here without even realizing it.

I sit there, staring out at the small wooden home, nostalgia lingering inside me. It appears empty, as though no one has moved in yet. Knowing I still have the key in my bag, I get out of the car to check for any of my belongings missing. Plus, something about it makes me miss living out here, where it's nothing but peaceful.

I stroll up to the front door quickly, key in hand, and let myself in. The cabin's exactly as I left it—well, except for all my belongings, which are gone. The furnishings were already here when I moved in, but it feels strange staring at a hollow place I once called home. My gut churns at the thought of being moved out without a say.

Deciding to do a final check, in case anything of mine was left behind, I do my rounds. Fifteen minutes later and a small bag of items—a couple of books, a forgotten hairbrush, and a stray sock—are all I find. With a sigh, I lock the door and head back to my car. The drive back to Kaden's mansion takes me through the city and into the woods near the fjord. The sun is beginning to set, casting long shadows that add to the eerie ambiance.

Once at the mansion, in the run-down, foreboding yard that screams dilapidated house, a single light illuminates its creepy appearance. With my key, I enter a mansion that feels like a fantasy. The hallway upstairs is lined with paintings of ships battling stormy seas, each one more dramatic than the last. As I reach the stairs to go down into the main living area, a loud knock echoes through the hallway.

I freeze, a spike of fear running down my spine. Did someone follow me?

Slowly, I turn and walk back to the door, my heart pounding in my chest. The knock comes again, more insistent this time. I take a deep breath and grip the doorknob, my hand trembling slightly. I pull the door open a crack.

"Who's there?" I ask, my voice soft.

A man stands on the doorstep, his face partially hidden in the shadows. "Delivery," he states, holding a large, flat, square cardboard box. There's nothing printed on it, but instantly, I'm hit with the most delightfully delicious aroma of food I've never tasted before. "For Kaden."

"A delivery?"

The man shrugs. "I just deliver the packages, ma'am. Are you Kaden or not? Otherwise, I need to cart it with me all the way back to the car. Why do you live so far away?" His voice dips with his clear frustration.

I nod slowly, opening the door wider to take the package. "Yeah, that's me. Sasha Kaden. Thanks." I'm too curious about what smells so good to let him leave with the package.

"About time." He shoves it over and storms away without another word. I watch him go. There has to be food in this box, and why does anyone deliver food? Wait, what if it's poisonous? I turn back into the house, only to come face-to-face with Kaden standing behind me, glaring outside.

"Please tell me you ordered this, because it smells divine."

He's still staring outside in the direction the delivery guy went. "Sasha, my job is to make you a goddess, treat you as one while I stand behind you like a beast ready to destroy anyone for ever disrespecting you." He steps out through the open door, frowning, shoulders rising.

"What are you talking about?"

"The delivery boy." Kaden faces me, his brows pinched together. "He dared speak to you so disrespect-fully. I should rip his tongue out for that."

"The delivery guy? He wasn't really that mean."

"He was," he says firmly, still glowering.

"He's probably having a hard night," I murmur, hoping to calm him down. "If I had to deliver packages to people's homes, I'd be pretty pissed, too."

Kaden shrugs, exhaling loudly, then his gaze falls to the box in my hand. "I wanted to surprise you with a unique human meal called pizza."

"Oh, so they bring food to your home here? I've never seen that," I say, never experiencing it in South Africa. "And pizza smells so good."

He finally smiles my way, locks the door, and then takes the pizza from me. He reaches down and plants a kiss on my lips, surprising me more than what just happened.

"Are you ready to eat, Sasha Kaden?" He smirks at me, winking, and he's probably dying to tell me I'm his again.

"Haha. Anyway, I'm starving." And by the time we're at the kitchen table, the pizza box open between us, I'm starving. Many human-style foods aren't as popular as they once were, not to mention they aren't easily available to purchase.

I follow Kaden's lead and pick up a slice, the cheese stretching.

I'm salivating, even if I've never eaten anything like this before. Kaden watches me as I take my first bite, the savory flavors swirling in my mouth, and with the crust crispy, it leaves me moaning for more.

"Hmm, this is really good," I say, taking another bite. Kaden examines his piece, then takes a big bite. He's nodding in no time.

"Not bad. A bit greasy, but I can get used to this."

Chowder, perched on the table, sniffs at a piece of the crusty edge I offered him. He nibbles on it, then makes a face and pushes it away.

I chuckle. "Someone's not a fan. You're more of a clam guy." He sits there, watching us eat this meal, and in all seriousness, I've never devoured anything so fast.

"So, I did well?" Kaden asks, eyeing me as he grabs another piece.

"Yes, I love *these* kinds of surprises." The longer we eat, chatting about what toppings the pizza has, I come to realize that this place isn't so bad. It's a far cry from my cold cabin. And as Kaden serves me another piece, showing me sides of him that aren't all rigid or demanding, a sense of belonging I hadn't expected rises through me.

I try not to think too much of it, but what if this is where I'm meant to be?

When I was young, my parents always told me fate would guide me in life. After losing them, I stopped believing in such things, thinking it was a comforting lie. Now, sitting here with Kaden and Chowder, I can't help but wonder if everything has happened for a reason.

# SIXTEEN



Heading out of the work building during my lunch break, I decide to make a visit to the city *bibliotheca*, a place filled with all kinds of books of history from around the world, including news articles. We had one back in South Africa, but I never used it. Now, I want to read some articles on fishing boat attacks, and it's the perfect place.

I reach my car in the work parking lot when someone calls my name.

I glance back, thinking it's a work colleague, but end up staring at my landlord from the cabin, across the parking lot, swerving around parked vehicles to reach me.

"Good, I caught you," he says, out of breath. The man is short, plump, and a porcupine shifter. His face is round and almost looks like one in his human form.

"Is everything all right?" He's always been kind to me, and I feel slightly bad that Kaden had me leave so abruptly, though he confirmed he paid any outstanding charges.

"I was in the city and wanted to come see you." He rubs his cheek, a nervous tic I noticed he has, especially when he's anxious.

"Yesterday you came to the cabin," he states, and it's not a question.

"That's right. I was checking if I left anything behind. I hope that's okay?" I dig through my bag for the cabin key, as I still haven't returned it to him.

"Of course, it's fine, but as I have cameras on the street in front of all cabins for security, I had seen you arrive. As soon as you went inside, I noticed another vehicle pull up several blocks down. I thought nothing of it at the time," he says, his breaths racing.

I glance up at him, cabin key in hand, unsure where he's going with this. "Did something happen?"

"Well, after you left, I had dinner with my family, then did my usual late-night checks on all my cabins, as you can never be too sure. But when I drove past yours, that's when I noticed it had a smashed front door."

I gasp. "It was perfectly fine when I left it. I swear."

"I know," he says, almost flustered. "But when I looked back at my footage, two men in black hoods emerged from the car after you left and entered the property. Twenty minutes later, they rushed out and drove away."

"Oh, shit." My mind's sparring in dozens of directions. Had someone followed me home, maybe tried to steal from me? Except they would have been sorely disappointed, seeing as Kaden had all my belongings packed and delivered to his home already.

"The place was mostly empty," I state.

"Well, what's strange is that they tore up the place, smashed windows, tore the upholstery on my furniture, slashed the mattress. And they sprayed your name on the wall in red paint. With a message."

My heart's thundering, fear worming in my gut. "What did it say?"

He's rubbing his cheek again. "Sasha, I see you."

"What the fuck does that mean?" A shiver jolts down my back, but with it comes a roaring anger as I don't bow down to threats or bullies.

My ex-landlord shrugs, looking more spooked out than me, his face paling.

"I thought you should know that you may be in danger. Maybe something you've done recently? I don't know, Sasha, but you've been a good tenant, never causing trouble, and thankfully insurance will cover the damages. But just be careful. Norway has a lot of deadly people in the shadows you may not be aware of. So much of this country long ago survived on the backs of thieves and murderers, and those old ways haven't all vanished."

"Thanks for letting me know." I hand him the key, and he takes it with a tight grin before scuttling away. Climbing into my car, my mind races with the warning left at my cabin.

Why would anyone threaten me? *I see you.* What the hell?

So, I'm being watched, but why? The strangest thing I've done recently is move in with Kaden, but he's new in town, and I'm not sure if it's a jealous partner. He seems the obsessed, stalker kind who doesn't jump partners too much. So, it doesn't feel like it's related to him. My mind skips to my last few days and right back to the dock, where things felt odd.

The warning from that sailor woman, the words from those sailors I eavesdropped on... did someone see me doing it? But it's not like I learned anything new... Unless it has to do with Asbesta. Except Kaden was adamant she wouldn't dare touch me, seeing as I'm his fated mate.

Whoever it is, I'll be ready. Until then, I'll be extra diligent. I can only assume they don't know where I've moved to if they attacked the cabin... at least for now.

I arrive at the bibliotheca soon enough, devouring an apple in the car before rushing into the three-story building. Made of stone, it appears as though it's come out of Ancient Greece—spectacular with its huge wooden double front door and large glass windows.

Once out of the car, I can't help but scan around me, a sense of paranoia skidding down my back.

Inside, I find out where the news article archives are and head up to the second floor, where it's dead quiet. I dive into my research on northern Norway, curious about what those men were talking about by the dock with regard to more attacks. I scan physical articles bound together, each page covered in a clear, hard substance that gives off small sparks of magic. Of course, they're protected from damage. I go through the folders I initially pulled off the shelves, looking for anything about attacks on ships and sailors out at sea.

Twenty minutes later and not a single article. I sigh. Perhaps I need to go back beyond ten years.

Up on my feet, I move from the tables against the wall to the wooden bookshelves packed with archive books from years upon years filled with articles. Evidently, I might be spending more time in the library at this rate.

I shove the books back on the shelf where they belong and run my fingers across the thick, leather-bound spines embossed with the dates of news articles. The smell up here is less like books and more musty. Shadows fill the aisles, and I doubt anyone comes up here, not even the librarians, based on the dust on some of the shelves. I move to several aisles farther back, where it's darker, away from the steps that lead to the lower floors. I find older folders, from roughly fourteen years ago. With no real clue to follow, I randomly select a folder to begin with when the wooden floorboards creak.

I glance up to the end of the aisle, where a large figure stands, blocking out the light. Panic saws through me, thinking whoever went to the cabin found me. I shake so hard that the folder slips out of my grasp, hitting the floor near my feet.

I reach for my belt, not feeling my taser. Right, it's in for repairs.

The brawly figure steps forward, and the light hits a gorgeous face.

"Fuck, Kaden, give a girl a heart attack!" Catching my breath, I release a deep exhale, still clutching the shelf.

He struts forward with a grin. "Why are you in a place like this? Don't tell me my mermaid loves books."

I glare at him. "Are you following me?"

He gives me one of his shining smiles that melts my knees. "Maybe I am. Or maybe I just happen to find the same interests intriguing."

I roll my eyes. "Right. Because the ancient mansion with the hidden kraken cave wasn't enough for you?"

Kaden steps closer, his presence filling the narrow aisle. "I'm a man of many interests. And right now, my main interest is you. After I saw you coming into the library in a mad rush, I was curious about what was going on."

I cross my arms, trying to tamp down the heat rising in me. "Wait, you were already in here?"

He nods, those dark, stormy eyes admiring me, smiling. Then he stretches his body, his chest expanding with his intake of air, arms over his head, muscles bulging. Is he doing that on purpose to show off how buff he is?

"I followed to ensure you were safe."

"So, you've been watching me this whole time?"

That devious nod again.

"Has anyone told you how creepy you can be?"

"Why, thank you." He has one hand resting on a bookshelf, the other in the pocket of his black pants, one leg crossed over the other at the ankle, appearing right at home.

"Why are *you* really here?" I ask, trying my best not to show him how much my body yearns to lean in toward him, eager to press in against him. It's ridiculous how out of control this fated-mate thing makes me feel.

"Research."

"For what?"

"My family line. There's a whole section downstairs on Norwegian family heritages."

I narrow my gaze at him.

He grins again, yet there's seriousness behind his eyes. "It's the reason I'm in town, to discover who wrongfully got my grandfather committed to Tartarus all those years ago."

I find myself gravitating toward him, my hand on his arm, feeling his muscles shift under my touch. Something in me wants to show him support. Kaden spent his life in prison for someone else's doing... not to mention if his grandfather was wrongly accused, that would sting like hell.

"Really sorry your family suffered for so long. Did you find anything in the archives?"

The side of his mouth twitches like he's unsure how to react to sympathy.

"Can't undo the past, something I learned a long time ago. What happened is fucked, but now's my chance to make up for it, especially making whatever son of a bitch is responsible pay for it. If they're still alive, I need to know the truth to get closure."

"I get that." His hand is on mine, warmth stretching up my arm.

"And you?" he asks. "Are you going to tell me what you're doing here?"

He's fast to change topics off him, so I give him a quick rendition of my trip to the docks and what I'm searching for. I leave out the whole cabin thing as I'm not sure what that's related to yet, and I don't need him going more psycho-possessive over me than he already is.

"So, yep, I'll be spending a bit more time here," I prattle on. "Who knew libraries were such hotspots for discovering drama?"

His gaze never leaves mine. "I'll help," he vows, his hand skipping up my arms, over my shoulder, to the back of my head, bringing me closer to him.

I resist him, of course, digging my heels in, but he swivels us fast, my back instantly kissing the shelves of the books, and he's in front of me, both hands now on the shelves on either side of my shoulders.

My breaths are on fire in my chest, our proximity always leaving me breathless.

"Look, you can't help me if you're going to trap me against the books. Back off, will you?"

"You'd be surprised how much this can help." His eyes crinkle at the edges of his smile.

"Oh really?"

As he shifts closer, my hands shoot up to his chest to keep him away because I know what happens next. He gets too close, and my brain becomes lust-foggy, and before I know it, I'll be with my pants down, my legs wrapped around him in the middle of the library. That's the kind of control I lack.

He suddenly pulls back with a thick book of articles in his hand, plucked from the shelf behind me. He arches an eyebrow at me.

I glare at his games.

"This looks like a promising start," he exclaims, flipping through the folder. "So, we're looking for anything about sailors at sea attacked by sirens?"

I shrug. "Not too sure. Maybe, but it could be just missing boats, sailors found dead with no explanation. I'm just trying to find a pattern to what's happening here with the sirens." With my mom...

When he reaches over and moves a strand of hair caught in my eyelashes, the edge of his hand grazes my cheek. The touch is innocent, yet it sparks a fire inside me, igniting it, and an involuntary growl rolls in my chest.

Whoa, that's new. My mermaid doesn't growl, ever, so that's an interesting development with our fated-mate connection.

He leans in closer. "Whenever I'm near you, I'm completely caught off guard, every damn inch of me needing us connected. I won't lie. Skin to skin is preferred, to hear you purring in my ear, begging me to fuck you."

"Gods, don't say that stuff in public," I murmur, my pussy quivering.

"It's a very long way down in the ocean, and that's how I feel with how fast I'm falling for you, Sasha. But I'm embracing it, letting the dark side of my obsession with you own me. You shouldn't be afraid of yours."

That sexy voice of his is gruff, yet leaves me swooning, and he knows the effect it has on me. All I smell is his earthy, manly scent, the furnace burning off his body embracing me—I want to smother myself in everything that's him.

His gaze darkens, and I shouldn't feel awful for

craving such a handsome man. Those stormy eyes flick over my face, searching for a response, for something.

"It sounds like a really deep fall." I realize that I'm gripping the shelves behind me as I steady myself from the explosion of images of us on his sacrificial table last night. I still feel that beautiful ache in the apex of my thighs from being fucked too hard, too damn hard, that I'm wet just thinking about him buried inside me.

"You smell so sinful," he purrs, pressing his face against my neck and taking a deep breath.

While I struggle to take air into my lungs, squeezing my thighs, heightening the sensation that tingles through me.

"Did you enjoy my cock last night?" he whispers in my ear in that gravelly voice. He gropes my breast, fingers pinching my nipple.

Moaning, my head tilts back. I want to be fucked and used by Kaden.

"Yes," I gasp in response, tingling all over, my bravery escalating with the explosion of arousal licking every inch of me. "I want you in my pussy, in my mouth, in my ass."

"Such a good girl you are." His words are like the kind of praise I can't get enough of, his acceptance of me.

Yet, as much as I tremble, it's hard not to blush at admitting those things out loud. Even after what we did last night, I'm practically begging for it again. It's confusing as hell because, despite the fear, I know what I crave, what my body needs.

His breathing picks up, hands falling to my skirt, tugging the fabric up to my waist, and I don't stop him.

Those hands, his tongue, his cock, I'm craving release. The world fades away, and it's only us two, staring at one another as his fingers slip under the elastic of my thong.

"Maybe not here," I murmur just as he drags it down my legs, crouching in front of me.

"Lift your leg, my little mermaid."

I oblige; of course I do.

Electricity sparks between us as he lifts himself, one hand stuffing my thong into his back pocket, the other tracing my inner thigh, brushing the tips of his fingers over my soaking seam.

"You are everything to me," he coos, pulling me by one shoulder, then pushing the other back, turning me to face away from him.

Butterflies are bursting through me, aware of this dance. The way he's touching me, running those large palms under my skirt and over my ass cheeks, leaves me shaking. I never want him to stop.

"Now be a good girl and don't scream," he whispers, stepping back from taking me with him, all while a large hand slides across my back, pushing me forward, bending at my waist. "Hold on to the shelves."

"Ah," I murmur, unsure how much I trust my voice when I'm already buzzing on an arousal so high I'm on the verge of coming. If I'm going to let myself have fun, then I'm going to enjoy every damn second of it.

His hand falls between my thighs, and I feel sexy as fuck right now. Kaden's fingers spread my lips, tracing my slick to my clit, teasing it, rubbing it, leaving me rocking my hips.

"Such a tease," I quip, really hoping no one stumbles up here and finds us.

I glance at him, pulling open his pants and unleashing his huge kraken cock—thick, erect, and covered in pre-cum. My pulse speeds up in anticipation.

But he's not wasting time, and the fat head of his cock is already pressing into me, sending shivers through my body as though I've been waiting for this moment for a lifetime.

"Just promise me, no breeding," I say over my shoulder.

He chuckles to himself.

"I promise." Then he slams into me. It's rough and harsh, that massive cock of his close to splitting me in half. My head bumps into the books on the shelf. A guttural moan spills past my throat, louder than I should have made.

"You know what finding you so drenched does to a man? Feeling your slick seeping down your inner thighs, your scent so strong, intoxicating me with desire?" His fingers squeeze into my hips, gripping me firmly, buried so deep I struggle to breathe from how absolutely full to the brim I feel. "All night, I dreamed of sucking on that sweet pussy of yours, rolling my tongue over your clit, listening to you cry out from pleasure. Knowing that you're soaking because of me, and you're barely holding it together, desperate to beg for my cock."

He draws out of me, those perfect bumps on his cock rubbing me, stroking my entrance, making me a puddle of shuddery gasps.

I want to tell him I'm not the kind of girl who begs

for anything, but as he picks up his momentum, pounding into me and spreading my inner walls with each plunge, only a whimper comes out.

He thrusts into me, a powerful motion that has my whole body rocking forward. Fingers gripping the shelves, I hold on, with a clear view of the stairs leading up to this floor from my position. Just seeing that no one's arriving has me moaning for more.

I've never felt this full with any man before, my body tight, trembling with arousal. He fucks me hard, shoving himself into me over and over, his hands on my hips like iron.

Breaths short, those whining sounds graze my throat as he growls like a beast behind me, going so deep into me that he's taking me to a completely different level of euphoria.

I'm reeling, close to screaming with how near my orgasm is. I claw at the shelves as he fucks me against the books, his grunts filling the silence. I'm dripping from the excitement owning me, and he plunges faster, as if sensing my own crescendo rising.

That savage speed makes me hold my breath as a tornadic orgasm rips through me, unleashing itself while he keeps going, unrelenting.

"Fuck," I breathe just as I notice movement across the room near the steps. Someone's coming up here. My heart freezes, all while I'm convulsing with the best orgasm, while Kaden hasn't stopped pounding me, my pussy squeezing him with each pulse of my climax.

I wriggle to get away from his grasp, and he must

have sensed something because he releases me and pulls out his massive cock, breaking away from me.

My gaze remains on the older woman who isn't coming this way, thank the universe, but is at another set of shelves on the other side of the room.

I've barely recovered from the orgasm, trying to breathe again, when Kaden's strong hands are around my waist, lifting me up. He turns me around with ease, his eyes locked on mine, and gently pushes me down onto my knees. His smile is both predatory and amused, making my heart race.

And there, in my face, is this massive cock, glistening with my arousal, the thick vein running the length of his shaft, bulging like he's on the brink of exploding himself. I lift my gaze to him breathing heavily, deeply, one hand on the base of his cock, the other moving to the back of my neck.

"Taste yourself just like I lapped you up last night."

I move in closer, opening my mouth, my pussy soaked and still trembling with desire, knowing we're no longer alone up here, but I'm at that stage where I don't care. I need his huge cock in my mouth so desperately that being found is the least of my worries.

He pushes himself closer, and I wrap my lips around his girth, sliding him into my mouth. I inhale my aroused scent on him, tasting myself—honey and sex. With his hand putting pressure on the back of my head, I take more of him, my hands flush against his thighs for leverage. Glancing up, I notice his gaze flickering to where I'd seen the woman on our floor moments earlier.

He knows she's there, and fuck, but he's smirking, loving the idea of getting caught, isn't he?

Working him deeper and deeper, I lick the underside of his cock, watching the way his eyes are rolling up, his breaths speeding up. His hips work with me, slowly grinding into my mouth, his hand fisting my head, keeping me prisoner to his cock.

A keening sound rolls from my chest, something I've never heard before, and I blame my body's reaction to him dominating me, but when his cock kisses the back of my throat, I pause, tears springing to my eyes.

He's looking down at me as I swallow, attempting to deep-throat him. With his free hand, he reaches over and rubs my neck and under my chin.

"That's my good mermaid. You can take me farther, can't you?"

With my mouth jam-packed with his erection, his eyes haze over with the sheer arousal pulsing from him.

I breathe in and out, taking more of him, and work him back and forth, holding back from gagging each time he dips past my throat. He's completely in my mouth, my lips at the base of his dick, and I'm absolutely loving the groans he's making. I love holding the power over him and him being at my mercy.

I pause for a moment when his hips thrust deeply into my mouth, and the spray of his explosion floods down my throat, warm and sticky, a salty and sweet taste. Digging my fingers into his thighs, I frantically work to swallow him, and damn, but there's so much. The guy's a cum-making machine.

We both groan.

"You feel incredible," he grunts.

My mind's dizzy from desire, and if I were to suddenly stand up now on my own, I'm certain I'd fall over from the dizziness, from the way my pussy still throbs, from my body beyond being satisfied at being pleased.

Taking every last drop from him, he slips his cock out of my mouth, and I lick my lips clean. He pauses, glancing to his right, and I follow his gaze to where the older woman stands at the end of the aisle, watching us with her mouth gaping open.

"Did you need a book from this aisle, dear?" Kaden asks innocently, except he's got his cock out and me kneeling in front of him.

Her cheeks blush pink, and I frantically wipe my mouth, getting up as the woman scurries out of there and downstairs, moving rather fast for someone her age.

Kaden chuckles, his lips grazing mine. "You're fucking amazing."

I'm kind of panicking, glancing over my shoulder every few seconds, expecting a guard to rush up here and kick us out. Then how will I do my research? I told myself I didn't care about being spotted, but now that it's happened, I regret my decision.

"Let's get out of here," I insist, wondering if they'll let me back in next time. I push my skirt down from around my waist, then move to grab the fallen book of articles from the floor, which had opened on an article with an image of a luxury ship.

I lift it into my hand, Kaden towering over my shoulder, peering down as he tucks his cock back into his pants. I quickly scan the article.

*Tragedy Strikes Again: Expensive sailing vessel Liberty returns to shore with only one crew member alive. Survivor recounts horrific attacks by sirens, claiming the lives of five crew members. The lone survivor describes a powerful siren with aquamarine hair as the leader of the attack.*

My insides ice up. My mom. Is that my mom? I frantically check the date of the folder, seeing it took place only one year after she killed my father and left me alone. So, it's possible that it could be her. Our hair color is rare, and I haven't yet met one person with the same hair highlights as my mom's and mine.

My hands are shaking, and Kaden is there, saying, "We need to go now."

Heavy steps approach from downstairs.

"I... I think my mom is killing people on the ships," I murmur.

Kaden takes my arm, tugging me in the opposite direction of the guard coming upstairs. He takes the book from my hand, setting it down, fiddling with it while I keep an eye on the man approaching. Then we slip quietly across the other end of the bookshelves, away from the guard. As the footsteps vanish into the back of the room, Kaden darts us to the steps and hurries down.

My head's spinning, and even the scowl from the woman who spotted us, now standing near the front counter, doesn't affect me... not as much as the reality that my mom might have been on a killing spree for years!

The realization crashes over me, making it hard to breathe.

I've spent years trying to forget her, yet it's not just my life she's destroyed. A part of me had hoped she'd disappeared forever, but this... this is something I can't ignore.

Kaden keeps a firm grip on my arm, guiding me through the library's exit. The moment we're outside, I take a deep inhale, the crisp air doing little to calm my racing heart. We put distance between us and the bibliotheca.

I can't work out why my mom's been doing this for years. And why in Norway?

None of this makes any sense.

# CHAPTER
# SEVENTEEN

### KADEN

I guide Sasha quickly out of the bibliotheca, noticing the blush creeping up her cheeks. Her shyness about being caught is sexy as fuck. For me, I don't give a shit who sees us; my focus is solely on my little mermaid and bringing her pleasure.

We stroll away on fast steps, the sun beating down on my head and shoulders. I can't get enough of it in my skin, its warmth chasing away darkness deep inside me, even if the breeze is cold.

"Okay, well, let's not do that again," she clarifies, staring up at me with a lopsided grin.

"It's going to happen again," I confirm. "We're in the honeymoon stage of our fated-mate connection, where we're going fuck each other's brains out."

I grin, already growing hard at the idea.

She rolls her eyes. "Well, I can't exactly lose my privileges to the bibliotheca if I need to keep researching. Guess I can go in there with a disguise."

"Don't worry," I confirm. "If we get kicked out, I'll

just build you your own library. A grand one with all the books you could ever want."

She glances over at me, trying to hide her reaction but failing.

"You always surprise me with what strange thing you're going to say next," she murmurs, shaking her head with a small smile. "Anyway, I'm parked over there. I just want to get out of here." She lifts her chin toward a parking area to my left, past a line of short shrubs and benches on the sidewalk.

"Good, you'll give me a lift home."

She nods.

My thoughts are back in the library, with me balls-deep in her pussy, in her mouth. I picked up that primal power inside of her again, raw and untamed. It's a sensation that curls around my kraken, which tells me it's definitely a fated-mate bonding, yet it's so much more. Captivating and wild. Like she's hiding a part of herself, and it's leaving me fucking confused to make sense of why she's coming across that way.

I turn to ask her as we enter the parking area when I catch a flash of movement. Something deliberate emerges from the rear of the car we're passing. Call it paranoia, but unexpected movements set me off, and instinct takes over.

I push Sasha behind me and lunge at the barrel of a man charging our way, the glint of a blade in his grasp. He's taken by surprise, not expecting my aggressive response. I slam into him, shoulder first, jamming him against the car, snatching his wrist, snapping it with a twist until the blade falls to the ground. He groans, the air rushing past his lips.

"Wrong move, asshole," I growl in his face, holding him by the throat as he cries from his injuries.

Out of the corner of my eye, someone else moves toward Sasha from my left.

Fury blindsides me, and I slam a fist into the man's gut in front of me. He tumbles over on the ground, moaning.

Effortlessly, I swivel with rage at the second man, sneaking up behind us, thinking he can take advantage of the distraction. I close the distance to Sasha and her would-be attacker in a heartbeat, but she's ducking and throwing out her leg, slamming it across his shins.

The guy pinwheels forward, and I snatch him by a fistful of hair before he completely loses his balance, pulling hard.

I drive my fist into his chest. A gush of air expels from his mouth, and he gasps for air. Sasha rises behind him, knocking him in the back of his knees so he loses his stance. In that same second, while I hold him, she wrenches his arms back, cuffing them in seconds.

"Who the hell are these idiots?" she snarls, and fuck me, but seeing her in warrior mode has my cock throbbing.

I shift my attention to the whining guy on the ground who hasn't moved.

The second asshole's upper lip curls back. "We're never going to stop coming for you," he snaps, practically spitting the words.

I growl, "Heard it before asshole. Now listen—"

"Fuck you, you have no idea how many mercenaries there are, how—"

"Do you want a blade in your temple, or are you going to fucking listen?" A grunt reverberates in my chest with my frustration.

Sasha studies me, her forehead furrowed, and it's clear she has dozens of questions. But my focus is on the mercenaries in front of me.

"Go and tell all your little fucking buddies that I'm no longer playing nice. Cross my path again, and I'll be leaving a trail of dead bodies." Though I'm convinced Asher is already doing that. So, I can only imagine how many of these rats would be on my heels if he weren't eliminating some of them.

The man's eyes go round, then he glares my way. I like his tenacity, but this isn't a battle he's going to win.

I shove him with my foot to the ground to be with his buddy. "Stay down if you know what's good for you." Snatching Sasha by the hand, we move past them, my ears alert for their approach.

Sasha's eyes are on me as she leads me to her vehicle, her expression hardened.

"Wanna tell me what the hell that was about? Since when do you have mercenaries on your tail? Those assholes won't relent until you're gone."

I shrug. "I'm not afraid of them, but I'm fucking annoyed with their constant interruptions and bothering me."

She raises an eyebrow. "So, what's going on?"

"Apparently, moving into the House of Gold and Garnet is prohibited."

"Wait," she says, studying me as the sun hits her face. "You entered this House without approval first? Hell yeah, they're going to keep coming for you, except..." She lifts her gaze, tapping a finger to her chin. "No, in fact, they shouldn't anymore. It's well known that the moment you find your fated mate, you automatically get residence in the House they live in. That means you are now a citizen of the House of Gold and Garnet." She grips her hips and leans on one leg, looking proud of herself. "You're welcome," she says sarcastically.

I'm well aware she isn't happy about accepting our fated-mate connection yet, but she'll come around to it.

"Well, try telling that to those fuckers who haven't gotten the news."

"Yeah, I guess it's a gray area on how to let them know..."

"Easy," I state, exhaling loudly. "Something I should have already done. I'll pay the king a visit and get it sorted."

She bursts out laughing. "You think you're going to just walk in to see King Kaspian? You've got a rude awakening coming."

Frustration rips through me. Sasha is strolling ahead of me while I glance back to see the two mercenaries across the parking area, going in the opposite direction, one still with hands cuffed behind his back. Smart choice.

"Come to think of it," Sasha purrs, her voice smooth like silk. "I may have a way for you to see the king."

I shoot my shoulders back, rushing to catch up to her as she gives me her most appealing smile.

"Go on," I state as we reach her small white vehicle with four doors. As she unlocks the doors, I eye it, convinced that no way in hell I will fit inside.

"You see, my best friend has three fated mates who have an in with the king. They are half-gods themselves, so perhaps they can arrange an audience for you with King Kaspian. But we'll need to ask them first."

"Good," I state, smacking my hand on the roof of the car more out of finality. It sounds louder than I intended, and her eyes blaze with incredulity.

"Well, then, let's go there now and get that resolved," I clarify.

She almost chokes on her laughter as she gets into the car. I open my door while she pushes my seat back for more legroom. I somehow manage to climb in, pressed in like those sardines in cans, and I hate it already. As I shut the door, feeling compressed, I lean an arm on the door, the other on the middle console as she starts up the engine.

"They live in Finland, another country. We need to fly there," I say.

"All right, then let's arrange this. We'll go together."

Her gaze flashes something my way.

"All depends on if I can get time off work, but I'll ask my boss. And the only reason I'm contemplating this is because I've been dying to catch up with my friend, Billie. Haven't seen her since she left South Africa and moved in with them. Plus, I'm dying to meet her twins."

I nod, shifting uncomfortably. "You need a bigger car."

"This is a work vehicle, so I don't exactly get a choice."

"Fine, but we won't drive in this one anymore. It's too small for me."

She gives me a long stare. "It looks cute seeing you all cramped up in here."

I lower my window for air. "Cute isn't what I'm going for. How am I supposed to get out fast if I need to fight someone?"

She chuckles. "Noted."

As we drive, I can't help but notice how natural it feels to be around her, even in these mundane moments.

"So, Billie," I say, trying to distract myself from the tight confines. "Tell me about her."

"Billie's amazing," she squeals. "She's fierce, independent, and has this way of making you feel like you can conquer the world. I've known her for years, and we lived together in South Africa. She's been like a sister to me, looking out for me."

"Sounds like someone I'd like to meet," I admit, my thoughts returning to Asher and if he's found his fated mate yet. Or is he still having fun destroying mercenaries? I'd consider him a close friend... I don't have many I trust back in Tartarus, so to hear Sasha talk so fondly of a friend has me confirming that with Sasha by my side, she will be my closest friend.

"Oh, she'll love you," she says with a grin. "She has a thing for big, brooding guys."

"If she's your friend, then she's mine, too."

As we drive farther from the library, I reach down

and pull out a scrunched-up paper, which refused to flatten when I unfolded it from my back pocket, smoothing it out on my knee.

"Let's read this properly now..."

Sasha gasps, half swerving across the road in the process. "Did you rip that out of the archive book in the library?"

"Yep. We needed it; they didn't."

"We are gonna get thrown out now for sure and fined." She shakes her head, clearly struggling to stay straight on the road.

"You're cute when you're paranoid," I tease, enjoying the slight flush that colors her cheeks. I lean back in my seat, hearing a sudden crunching sound as my seat slips back a bit.

She cuts me a sharp stare and exhales heavily. I can't help it if I'm too big for this vehicle.

"You know, back in Tartarus, I used to spend my spare time solving murders. A hobby I enjoyed and was damn good at."

She laughs. "Your hobby was doing detective work? Why?"

I shrug nonchalantly. "Keep myself busy."

"Okay, so what else does the article say? Anything useful?"

Lifting the page, I scan it quickly. "Only thing that's of importance is the last line that says this is the third attack in as many weeks."

"So, it *was* happening in North Norway, too. The sailors were right. How good would it be if we were still in the library to check other dates," she states sarcastically.

Lowering the article, I glance over at Sasha. She's concentrating on the road, her hands clutching the steering wheel a bit too hard.

"What happened with your mom? I notice you're more angry than emotional when she's mentioned."

She stiffens, her grip tightening further. There's no response at first, and I don't push her. We've all been broken in this fucked-up world, left with scars we bear until our dying breath. A world of pain we learn how to tolerate, but if I can ease hers somehow, then I'll do what it takes.

Finally exhaling loudly, she murmurs, "Thing is, I never saw her transformation into a siren coming. Maybe I was too young to notice any signs, or maybe she just hid it from my dad and me really well. It happened when I was very young, during an argument between my parents." Her words are shaky. "Things escalated so fucking fast..." she continues, her voice cracking.

I place a hand on her arm, hoping she knows I'm here for her.

"Then, in the snap of a second, she became someone else... She turned on my dad... That day, I lost them both. Lost my childhood, lost it all."

The weight of her words thickens the air in the car. It's as though I feel the raw wound she's carried all these years. I squeeze her arm gently. She must have witnessed her mother murdering her father, and that stings hard.

"Sorry you had to go through that."

She nods, eyes still on the road. No tears, although I suspect she's done her fair share of crying over what her mother did.

Silence beats between us until she whispers, "Thanks," as though that's all she can manage.

I admire her strength and begin to understand her tenacity, her fighting back on everything. She's learned to deal with the loss and the pain by building a wall around herself.

No words needed, I hold her arm and keep her company as she drives me home.

The article in my lap suddenly flutters from the open window. I snatch it before it flies away, my gaze dropping to the image of the ship docked at the harbor. My gaze narrows as I notice a figure standing nearby, as if accidentally caught in the image. I blink, unable to believe what I'm seeing.

No fucking way.

I inspect the grainy image more carefully. That's Lilia from my grandfather's visions, the blonde, her beauty spot above her lip, talking to him about growing his business... his partner in his business.

If this article is around fourteen years old, then there's a chance she's still alive today. Fuck, she lived thousands of years since my grandfather lived in Norway. A sense of anticipation floods me that perhaps this is the clue I've been seeking.

"What's got you hyper-focused on the article?"

I lift my attention to Sasha, and my thoughts fast-forward.

"This woman in the photo, my grandfather knew her, and she might know more about why he got tossed into Tartarus."

She squints her eyes to look at the photo, then back at the road. When she pauses in traffic, she grabs the page and studies it closely. She runs the tip of her finger over the woman, her brow creased.

"Could it be?" she mumbles to herself when someone suddenly honks at us from behind. She flinches, shoves the article at me, and is driving once more. "I-I think I met that woman the other day when I was down at the docks. I swear it looks just like her."

"Are you certain?" I stiffen.

"Pretty sure," she says, her voice filled with conviction.

"She was in Norway the other day. So, if I can find her, then I can find out what the fuck happened to my grandfather." And how I ended up losing my parents, my childhood... and most importantly, who the hell is responsible.

Sasha nods, her grip on the steering wheel tightening. "Then let's find her now."

"Fuck, love your determination." My hand falls to her thigh, my fingers grazing her skin, but my adrenaline is for vengeance. My sweet little mermaid's scent still lingers in my nostrils, her tight, wet pussy still a memory on my cock.

"You helped me, so I owe you one."

I grin to myself, well aware that she owes me nothing, but I'll let it slide.

I lean back, my mind buzzing with the eagerness to

finally find my answer to my grandfather's imprisonment.

When we finally arrive at the docks, the salt tang of the sea fills me, and I take several deep inhales, craving to dive into its depths. But for now, I get out of the car and head down to the docks. Boats bob in their berths, with only a handful of dock workers loading fish into an oversized container.

I track after Sasha, who's hurrying down the farthest dock, but it's empty. No ship in sight. I grind my back teeth, instantly knowing we missed her.

"Shit," Sasha murmurs. "It's gone. Hold on." She strides over to a nearby dock worker, a burly man sorting through nets. Tense all over, I march to another group of workers, drawing the article from my pocket.

The two men turn in my direction, their expressions questioning me for interrupting their conversation.

"Do any of you know this woman?" I ask, shoving the photo forward.

Both of them stare at it, then shake their heads.

"Never seen her."

"Me, neither."

Exasperated, I march back to Sasha, unsure if those fuckers are lying or not, but I don't want to cause a scene right now. Sasha's coming my way, her expression dropped, and I sigh heavily.

"No one's seen her or remembers the boat banked here the other day. I mean, a lot of boats come and go through this port, so it rings true that they might not remember her." She runs a hand through her hair. "But

I'm sure she'll show up again. You've got a lead to follow, at least."

She touches my arm, and that earlier anticipation has morphed into frustration. But she's right. It's my first real clue, and I'll stalk the docks until she returns.

I'll find Lilia and the truth. No one hides from me.

# EIGHTEEN



The small plane hums with the strength of enchantment, the chair beneath me vibrating, the motor roaring. I shift in my tight location, my knees brushing against the seat in front of me. I glance out the round window at the puffy white clouds.

It's been three days since I discovered Lilia might be in Norway, so I spent every moment down by the docks with no sign of her. But once those bastard mercenaries started tracking me there, I knew I had to fix that small problem first.

So, here I am, flying with my little mermaid to a place called Finland.

Tightness squeezes my chest each time I stare outside, and I'm breathing rapidly at the small clouds showing me the land so far down below. Fuck! I'm made for swimming, not damn flying.

A tender, soft hand touches mine, and I flinch slightly, which isn't me. Nothing scares me, yet I'm squeezing the armrests with a death grip. Add to that the sensation of being cramped, and the whole experience is itching on my nerves.

I look over to Sasha next to me, her grip on my hand light, and I breathe slightly easier that she's not frightened.

"How are you holding up?" she asks.

Chowder's head pops out of her backpack in her lap, tilting his head, staring at me as though he's judging me.

"How do you sweat so much?" he says in that chirpy voice.

"I'm fine," I half growl as perspiration rolls down my back.

"No harm in being scared of flying," Sasha tells me. "Lots of people dislike it."

"Then why do it? Nothing about this feels natural." I glance around at the other passengers, noting their tense expressions. At least it's not just me feeling unsettled.

"It's a fast way to travel, and actually, it's quite safe, especially when propelled by magic."

I arch an eyebrow. "Magic can be easily countered and manipulated."

She pats my hand, grinning.

Chowder reaches out his little claws, patting my arm, too. "You be strong."

I eye him. "Like I said, I'm fine," I counter, shifting in my seat again. The sight of clouds so close outside is too much, and I shove down the blind.

Turbulence strikes again, shaking us, and I try to concentrate on anything else. Sasha is leaning against me, her hand resting on my thigh in a comforting gesture. It's hard to keep calm when the plane keeps shaking.

A brunette air hostess in a tight dress pauses at our row of two seats, her eyes locked on me, completely overlooking Sasha. She leans in, a flirtatious smile playing on her lips.

"Excuse me, sir, is there anything else I can bring you? A pillow, whiskey, snacks?"

I can feel Sasha's fiery gaze burning into the side of my face, and I can't resist playing up the conversation a bit. I grin at the hostess.

"Thanks. I might take you up on some snacks."

Her eyelashes flutter. "Of course, sir. I'll be right back."

As she saunters off, I lower my attention to Sasha, whose cheeks are flushed red with fury. I can barely contain my laughter.

"Don't worry," I whisper, leaning closer to her. "I only have eyes for you. You are my beautiful mermaid. No other female even compares."

"Oh, you think I care?" She pulls her shoulders back. "I'm not even that much into you." She shifts in her seat, seemingly accidentally elbowing me in the arm. Then she gives me a death glare that could freeze hell over.

I chuckle, leaning back. "Oh, I see. So, then you won't mind if I go chase down the brunette into the back and rip that skirt off?"

Her face turns white, her eyes blazing with fire. "You do that, and I'll slit your throat."

I laugh, absolutely adoring her to pieces. "There you

are, my fierce little mermaid. Don't pretend you don't care for me when I know you're obsessed."

She tries to maintain her angry facade but ends up laughing.

The hostess returns with an armful of snacks. She beams at me, offering the selection. "Here you go, sir."

I take the snacks, lowering my gaze to Sasha. "Thank you. These are for my wife."

Sasha smirks at me, collecting the snacks, though not as greedily as Chowder, who's half hanging out of the bag.

The hostess blinks in surprise, glancing between Sasha and me. "Oh, of course. Enjoy your snacks."

As she walks away, I lean in closer to Sasha. "See? Only for you."

She rolls her eyes but can't hide her smile. "You're ridiculous."

"And you love it," I tease.

We settle back into our seats, the plane's turbulence shaking me so hard I'm back to gripping those armrests, my knuckles turning white.

Sasha leans in against my arm. "Hey, my dad once told me about a trick on how to deal with fear. Want to try?"

I give her a wary look. "I'm not afraid, but what did he say?"

"Close your eyes," she instructs, and reluctantly, I follow her instructions. "Now, take a deep inhale. Imagine you're in your favorite place, somewhere you feel completely at ease. Focus on the sounds, the smells, the feeling of being there."

"That's easy. My favorite place to be is between your thighs," I state proudly.

She gasps, and I grin, already picturing her blushing.

"Well, thanks, because now everyone on the plane knows that, too," she murmurs.

Unable to stop smiling, I shift to my second favorite place—the ocean. Water rippling and swaying against me, the crashing sound filling the air, salty air in my lungs. The image keeps vanishing each time the plane bumps about, but I bring it back.

After a few moments of failing, I crack open my eyes to come face-to-face with Chowder. He's in Sasha's arms, leaning toward me, staring me in the face. Chowder's so close his whiskers are tickling my nose.

"Fuck! Personal space!"

Sasha laughs at us.

"Why make funny noises?" Chowder asks.

"I'm not," I grumble, though my heart rate is still off the charts.

Chowder scrambles back into Sasha's bag, his head popping back out in seconds. He reclines like he's in heaven, the little shit.

"And you like flying, I suppose?" I ask Sasha, trying to sound nonchalant but failing miserably.

"You bet. There's something incredible about being so far off the ground. Like, I can never fly, but this is the closest to knowing what it must feel like."

I resettle in my seat, trying to look composed. "Well, I'll stick to swimming. The ocean doesn't drop you out of the sky."

The plane jolts again, and I grip the armrests tighter,

feeling the tension coil in my gut. Sasha keeps her hand on mine, her touch grounding me as I count the minutes until we land.

By the time we finally come down with a loud thump, I'm so wound up, so tense, I've accidentally ripped one of the armrests completely out. Sasha's eyes widen in shock at the sight, and Chowder tsk-tsks me.

I tuck the armrest down beside me. "Let's get out of this tin can. I've done my time being confined."

"I have to admit, you handled that better than I expected," Sasha teases. "I expected you to create more damage."

"Next time we're swimming."

She chuckles. "We'll see about that."

In no time, we're heading toward the terminal. I'm ready to meet the king and officially get those fucking mercenaries off my back. Then back to tracking down whoever backstabbed my grandfather.

Outside, a sleek black car waits, the driver opening the back door for us. I climb in while Sasha has a small conversation with him, then joins me. The spacious interior is a welcome change from the cramped flight. I stretch out, lounging comfortably in the back seat with Sasha beside me and Chowder still in the backpack.

"This is more like it," I mutter, gesturing to the luxurious car. "You should request this vehicle from your work."

She rolls her eyes. "I doubt my work will supply me with a limo. Do you know how rare these things are in this world? I guess Billie has connections with her important fated mates to actually source a limo." Her attention turns out the window.

I reach over, placing a hand on hers. Her skin is soft and warm under my touch. Before I know it, Chowder is scrambling out of the bag, his tiny paw resting on top of my hand as if staking his claim. I stare at him, and he stares back, leaning up against Sasha.

"Seems we're back to this old game," I mutter, though I can't help but smile at the little furball's protectiveness.

The scenery outside is mesmerizing—rolling hills, dense forests, and hardly any vehicles on the road. Finland is every bit as beautiful as Norway, maybe even more so.

Noting the tension in her shoulders, I ask, "Are you all right?"

"Yeah, just excited and nervous," she admits, her voice soft. "I haven't met Billie's mates yet. She said they were happy to have us stay with them, but you just never know." Her gaze is filled with uncertainty. "They're half-gods! That's slightly intimidating."

"It's not that impressive," I reply, straightening my posture. "I'm the last of my family line, and from my understanding with my grandfather, we're the largest kraken of any family line left alive. He also hinted that our family was unlike any other. Now, that's impressive."

She studies me, her brow furrowed. "It's not a competition, you know."

"I know it's not." I raise my chin, and she grins, shaking her head.

"Anyway, let's just, you know... act normal in front of them. I'm certain they're all polished and perfect."

She's put these men on a pedestal, but no matter how far up the chain you are, there's no such thing as perfect. If anything, it's the opposite.

"You're overthinking this," I tell her gently. "We'll be fine."

"I'm sure you're right."

Sunlight filters through the window and dances across her face. She's absolutely beautiful, and every day I spend with her, I find myself losing my head to her.

"You're staring," she teases, a blush creeping up her cheeks.

"Can you blame me?" I murmur, brushing a strand of hair behind her ear. She's wearing skintight leather pants and a shirt that follows her curves, the buttons pulling across the chest, constantly distracting me. "You're breathtaking, Sasha."

She laughs again, the sound filling the car with warmth. Then we fall into a comfortable silence on the drive.

We pull up to a lofty iron fence, the car's engine humming softly beneath us. Beyond the fence is an enormous property with a grand yet standard stone building, but farther beyond that, there's a much larger mansion —no, a castle by its appearance.

The gates open of their own accord, and we roll onto the driveway. Sasha and Chowder are practically plastered to the window, staring out in awe. The car stops, and they climb out eagerly, with me trailing behind. The driver starts unloading our bags from the trunk, placing them on a winding stone path alongside the initial building leading to the back gates. Beyond them stands the enormous mansion of dark obsidian stone with lofty windows on all four levels, with a dark, pointy roof. A winding path cuts through a sparse forest of pine trees, leading up to the grand arched doorway. The entrance steps are flanked by imposing gold wolf statues.

"It's all right, nothing special," I say, pretending to sound unimpressed. "Once I complete my mansion by the fjord, it will blow this place out of the water."

"Of course you'd say that. I think it's stunning."

"Let's just see if this place lives up to your hype," I retort, though I can see a hint of a smile tugging at her lips because she's already smitten by the place.

The driver gestures for us to follow him. "This way. You are expected."

As we move closer, someone rushes out of the front door of the mansion, a woman about the same height as Sasha, with flowing white, silvery hair, dressed in tight black pants and a loose V-neck shirt that glints like blue pearls in the sun. She's even more beautiful when she's smiling.

"Sasha! You're here!" she calls out, her voice quivering like she's crying.

"Billie!" Sasha squeals in delight, and without a second thought, she pushes her handbag with Chowder into my hands and rushes toward the woman. The two of them clash in a huge hug, their laughter and grins infectious. There's something so rewarding about their happiness, about having someone so close that meeting them again feels like your whole life changes.

That's Sasha for me. She just hasn't fully embraced that yet.

She deserves this happiness with me, even if she's too stubborn to admit it.

Billie pulls back from the hug, holding Sasha at arm's length. "I missed you so much! You look amazing!"

"It's been too long, and you have no idea how much I've been dying to see you again."

I stand there, holding the bag with Chowder squirming inside, trying not to feel like a third wheel. The driver, with the bags, starts moving them along the path, and I follow, keeping a respectful distance.

Billie looks over at me, her lips widening into a grin. "And who's this handsome fellow?"

Sasha grins bashfully, and I adore seeing her stare at me that way.

"This is Kaden, who I told you about. He's... well, he's..."

"I'm her fated mate," I answer for her. "Nice to meet you, Billie," I say with a friendly nod. I can behave when required.

She's suddenly there, giving me a hug, her friendliness showing me exactly why she and Sasha are so close.

"Welcome to our home."

Chowder's head pops out of the bag, and Billie gives a small laugh at seeing him.

"Oh, and who is this little guy? Is he yours?" She looks at me for a response.

"Chowder," he answers himself. "I don't belong to someone. Especially not him." He cranes his head up toward me.

I chuckle, rubbing his head.

"He's with me," Sasha states, snatching him out of the bag. She tells Billie all about him as they stroll toward the house.

Well, guess that's my cue to get moving.

As we reach the grand entrance, Billie turns to me, her eyes twinkling.

"Come on, let's get you settled in your room. We have so much to catch up on, and I want to hear everything about how you two met."

"Of course, but I have to see your little ones first," Sasha pleads.

Taking Sasha by the hand, Billie glances back at me. "Hope you don't mind that we go see the little ones first then?"

I shrug, smirking. "I'll happily do whatever makes you both happy."

Sasha throws me a grin, and I adore the joy on her face.

As we head inside behind Billie, I find myself liking her more and more. There's something about her openness that's refreshing. Maybe this visit will be good for Sasha. It might even help her accept the inevitable—that she's my fated mate. With Billie's influence, perhaps Sasha will finally see it, too.

So, here we are, rushing through this enormous mansion, with paintings on the wall, spotlights illuminating the art, and green plants adding life to every corner. The place looks lived in and loved. We head upstairs, passing several maids who bow our way, taking a bit too long to stare at me before rushing away.

Once we reach the third floor, we find ourselves in a long hallway. Outside a doorway, Sasha turns to me, handing me Chowder.

"Maybe best if you stay with Kaden for a bit," she suggests and smooches him on the head.

"What's in room?" Chowder asks. I collect him, and he scrambles onto my shoulder. I half throw it over my shoulder, allowing him to lean against me to see what's going on.

"Babies," I answer Chowder, and he just stares at me as if he's uncertain how to register that.

The girls enter the nursery, and I follow them, remaining near the doorway. Two wooden cribs catch my attention first, with whites, blues, and mauves used in the toys and the linen. The walls are painted to resemble the sky, as though we're floating among the clouds, with stars on the ceiling that twinkle from the sunlight. The white carpet gives the impression of fluffy clouds, and I can't help but feel like I'm back on the plane.

There's a blue-and-white-striped couch with blankets and cushions, shelves filled with books and toys, and pristine white cupboards. Above each crib hangs a rotating mobile—one of a gryffin, the other of a wolf. The small baby sounds draw my attention to Billie lifting a baby out of one crib and into her arms.

"So, this is my firstborn, Lucian," Billie explains.

He's tiny with a dark patch of hair, his face all squishy, and appearing quite serious for a baby. As Billie lifts him, he coughs and releases a small explosion of fire.

"Whoa," Sasha states, both of them laughing and cooing over him.

"Well, I didn't expect that," I mumble to myself.

She's smiling down at the baby. "As you can see, he takes after his father, Tallis, with his demon side."

"Can I hold him?" Sasha asks instantly, her voice filled with excitement.

Billie hands Lucian over. The baby sits in Sasha's arms, resting against her shoulder as she coos and kisses him.

My heart thunders in my chest. Seeing her all maternal, clucking over this kid, shouldn't impact me, yet here I am, hungry for our own children. I want a big family.

Billie glances up at me. "Aren't they adorable?" She

gives me a look, and I can tell she's dying to ask me when Sasha and I will be doing the same. If it were up to me, I'd be doing it now.

"Yeah," I murmur, unable to tear my eyes away from her. "Absolutely adorable."

"If you two ever have babies, they will be so beautiful. I mean, look at you both, and the beauty of a mermaid, nothing compares." Billie grins at us both.

Sasha laughs nervously, avoiding staring at me. "We're not... it's complicated." She turns back to the baby in her arms. "You must be so proud of your little bundles."

"It's ridiculously exhausting, but I wouldn't swap it for anything. They're both my little miracles." She moves to the second crib, leans into it, and gently lifts another baby. This one has a very thin layer of hair, lighter in color, and the brightest golden eyes I've ever seen. Even Chowder, who's been silent on my shoulder until now, leans forward with curiosity. The baby, wearing only a diaper, stretches out a pair of beautiful chestnut-colored wings from his back, almost a dark golden hue.

"Why does baby fly?" Chowder mutters, his whiskers twitching.

"Anything is possible," I answer, my voice soft with awe, making me wonder what my child would look like. Powerful kraken limbs, strong jaw like his father, handsome so every girl fawns over him? Our DNA is dominant.

Billie's kissing the baby all over his chubby face. "And this is my bundle of energy, Dante. He takes very much after his father, Eryx, and is a complete handful."

Sasha, holding Lucian, reaches over one hand to stroke Dante's cheek, and both now have their arms full of babies. It's a beautiful sight, and all I can think about is my little mermaid pregnant, her belly round with our child, how beautiful she'll be, how demanding she'll be when she's lusting after me. The thought sends a jolt of excitement through me.

"I can't believe you have two babies. It feels like just yesterday we were back in South Africa, living together," Sasha murmurs.

I glance over at Chowder, who's watching them intently.

Sensing movement from the doorway, I twist in that direction, where a man stands tall and proud, grinning. His long, flowing black hair reaches past his shoulders, and his eyes are as dark as hell itself. A faint smell of burning wood floats around him. He stands like someone in command, someone unafraid, and I instantly know he's the father to the fiery child—a demon.

"Tallis," he says in a strong voice, glancing my way and extending his hand to me. His handshake is firm and powerful. He wears a leather band around his wrist embedded with a golden tree symbol, which I'm guessing is a family emblem. I've seen similar ones in Norway but with different designs. His assertiveness demands attention, and I can respect a man like him.

"Kaden," I answer, shaking his hand just as hard.

"I hear you're a kraken." Tallis takes a step into the room, watching our two women and the babies, then swings his attention to Chowder on my shoulder. "They are rare as fuck… you must feel special."

I chuckle. "Yeah, something like that."

Tallis laughs heartily. "Well, we have a huge lake behind the woods at the rear of our property. You're welcome to use it, and we have heated pools indoors, too."

"Appreciate it. Might take you up on those."

His gaze lifts. "Who's the critter on your shoulder?"

"I am Chowder. And why black eyes?"

I chuckle. "He says what he's thinking and has no filter."

Tallis grins. "I like it. It's refreshing. He and my brother Eryx will get along wonderfully. Anyway, welcome to our home, Kaden and Chowder. Make yourselves comfortable. Later, you can meet my brothers. Eryx is up in the mountains, and Khaos is out with King Kaspian."

My interest is beyond piqued. "Speaking of King Kaspian," I bring up.

He raises an eyebrow. "I heard you want an audience with King Kaspian?"

I nod. "That's my reason for visiting, and Sasha's been eager to catch up with her friend, so two birds, one stone." I raise an eyebrow at Tallis, who chuckles, his dark eyes constantly moving between me and Billie. He's absolutely smitten with her, and seeing a man show that kind of obsession and commitment resonates well with me.

"Since arriving in Norway, I've had a few mercenary issues, and rather than leave a trail of bodies, which I guess the king wouldn't appreciate, I'd rather work things out amicably."

"Well, as long as you respect those who intend you no harm, as my brothers and I are mercenaries, then we'll have no problems. We run a very successful business connecting those around the world to some of the best mercenaries living here in Finland."

"You have my word," I state honestly, head high. "I want them off my back now that I'm a citizen of the House of Gold and Garnet, which doesn't seem to have been communicated."

"Well, my friend." Tallis grins and slaps a hand on my shoulder. "The king isn't easy to get hold of, but I respect your willingness to resolve things peacefully. It shows a lot of restraint."

I chuckle. "Something I often don't have control over. But I appreciate help from you and your brothers. I won't waste the opportunity to set things straight."

We both turn to our fated mates. Billie collects Lucian from Sasha's arms, then hands both babies over to Tallis. Sasha told me that he's a succubus demon, so to see him in daddy mode gives me hope that I'll make a first-rate father myself.

"Come, let me show you both to your room," she offers.

She and Sasha head out of the room, laughing, leaning into one another. Tallis is juggling the babies, one batting his wings, the other coughing flames, which catch on his shirt. They're small burns that go out instantly, and he doesn't seem to feel it.

"Need a hand?" I ask him.

"Or a paw?" Chowder pipes in.

He laughs. "Nothing I haven't done before. Usually

easier when one of my brothers is here, but I'm getting used to it when Billie needs a break. It'll be interesting when the next baby or babies come along. My plan is to hire an army of nannies because these two are already a handful." He grins at me while placing both babies into one crib and turning on the wolf mobile overhead, which starts spinning and singing.

"Billie's pregnant?" I ask, raising an eyebrow, not remembering Sasha telling me this.

"Not yet, but my oldest brother, Khaos, is determined to ensure our next baby is his. And he's taking every opportunity." He's grinning suddenly. "Except Eryx and I have a bet on which one of us will get her pregnant first instead."

I'm chuckling, shaking my head. "Sounds like a hell of a challenge. She must be incredible to keep up with all three of you."

He laughs, deep and hearty. "She's not one to take any crap from us, and I fucking love that about her."

"Something must be in the water in South Africa. Sasha's the same. Well, I better go catch up with them before I get lost in this castle."

"Good luck." He gives me a nod, and I can see myself spending hours with Tallis over drinks. I bet he's got a lot of stories to tell.

I turn and head out of the nursery, my thoughts shifting to Sasha. Following their echoing voices through the grand hallways, I catch up with them in no time. Chowder, half-asleep, is nestled comfortably in his bag, finally catching some rest after staying awake for the entire flight. By the time we reach our room, Sasha and Billie are hugging tightly, and I notice how much Sasha's smiling.

Striding past them into the living area of our guest quarters, I take in the immaculate decor. A sleek leather couch sits in front of a large stone fireplace, and there's a cabinet with decanters filled with various honeyed drinks. The room is fancy, no doubt, but it feels a bit bland for my taste—too perfect, too untouched.

Two doors lead off from the living area into separate bedrooms, and another door reveals a lush, enormous bathroom. This could be a home in itself. I decide that the smaller bedroom will be Chowder's domain. I place him on the bed, still half in his bag, careful not to wake him, and shut the door.

Returning to the living area, I find my beautiful mermaid buzzing around, checking everything out. She's grinning, light on her feet, her energy reaching me.

"This place is stunning. I missed Billie so much. I can't believe she has two little boys... they are just every-thing," she gushes, her joy infectious.

I stroll up to her, taking her into my arms from behind, and lower myself to whisper in her ear, "You looked so fucking beautiful in the nursery. I saw the way you were gushing over those babies." My hand slips under her shirt to her bare skin. "I was going to wait a bit, but I'm going to put a baby in you."

She stiffens, fighting me, but I hold on to her. "Kaden, what the hell?"

"You heard me... all I can think about is you pregnant

and how beautiful you'll be, how much fun I'll have with your swollen breasts, your gorgeous body, how you will make the most incredible mother..."

She twists to face me, her eyes wide. "Whoa, slow down there, cowboy."

I chuckle at her words, having no idea what a cowboy has to do with anything.

"Yeah, I want a family, but not now, so cool your damn jets."

My lips find her neck, and I sense her softening against me.

"We should at least start practicing more."

She pushes against me, trying to resist, but I've been dying to have her writhing beneath me. She throws an elbow into my ribs, and I grunt as she slips from my grasp.

"Damn, Sasha," I groan, clutching my side. "You're going to be the death of me."

"Good," she snaps, though there's a playful glint in her eyes. "Focus on why we're here."

"It's all sorted, but I'm not seeing the king now, so until then, we can enjoy ourselves."

I watch her as she ignores my words but checks out the rooms, her eyes lingering on the luxurious details. "Nice, we have two bedrooms."

"One's taken," I say, smirking. "You're going to have to share with me."

She studies me, the glare she gives me makes my heart race.

So I change the topic. "I find it intriguing that your friend has three fated mates."

She arches an eyebrow. "Do you have a problem with it?"

"Hell no, the more the merrier and I'm happy for her. But I just want to make it clear that you are a one-man mermaid. No one touches you or looks at you with the wrong intention... I don't share. Krakens don't share."

She laughs, shaking her head. "Just calm down, Kaden. I'm a one-guy type of girl, too."

"Good." I take a step closer, stealing the distance between us. "Because I'm not letting you go."

She rolls her eyes but doesn't move away. "You're impossible, you know that?"

"Only because I want you. Seeing you with those babies... it just made me realize how much I want that with you."

Her expression hardens, and she takes a deep breath.

"We're not officially even an item, so how can you be talking about babies?"

"That's where you're wrong. We've been destined to be together from the moment you were born. Don't delude yourself otherwise."

She studies me, not saying a word because she knows I'm right.

"I'm going to go find that heated indoor pool." Stretching her arms above her head, her muscles visibly relax. "I'm desperate to sink into the water."

I raise an eyebrow, feeling a wicked grin spreading across my face at how hungry I am to sink into her. I smirk, grabbing her hand.

"Let's go find the pool."

She hesitates for a second, then nods, her grin matching mine.

"Okay, but just to be clear, this isn't some romantic getaway. We're just finding the pool and relaxing. Nothing more."

"Sure, whatever you say," I reply, unable to hide the amusement in my voice.

*abies!* Is Kaden losing his mind? I glance over at him as he walks alongside me in Billie's mansion, grinning and humming to himself as if he's at home. I noticed him getting along well with Tallis, and it's impossible to ignore that Tallis, one of Billie's fated mates, is drop-dead gorgeous. Although I have to admit, not as stunning as Kaden, even if he's a handful and pushy.

But yes, babies. Nope, I'm not ready to settle down.

"Enjoying yourself?" I ask, arching an eyebrow at him. "This place has a certain charm, don't you think?"

He grins wider. "Absolutely, if you're into white mansions and godlike hosts. But I like Tallis, and Billie's a genuinely sweet person. She's beautiful, but not at your level. I mean, it's hard to compare anyone to mermaids."

I roll my eyes, trying to ignore the flutter in my chest. "Oh, is that so? And that's why you're drawn to me?"

"It's hormones and pheromones, little one. It's destiny. It's the savage hunger that has me so hard for you when you walk into a room that I know we're meant to be."

His words send a shiver down my spine, but I fight to keep my composure.

"Well, how about we make a deal? On this trip, we don't talk about fated mates, babies, or any of that stuff. Just enjoy our short trip in Finland. Depending on how quickly the king can see you, perhaps we can explore a bit, then head back to Norway."

He studies me, a playful glint in his eyes. "Agreed. No talk about relationships, just the lure you have on me and me having my way with you at any chance possible. I got it."

I roll my eyes again, but a smile tugs at my lips. "That's not what I said."

"It's what I heard…" He chuckles.

We seem to be going in circles through the white-walled corridors of the mansion.

"Where are we?" he asks, glancing around a large hallway ahead of us.

"This way," I say, pointing toward a white hallway to our right. "I can smell the water…"

"Right…" He guides me in that direction, then down a set of steps. I must be distracted or something because the steps are suddenly rushing out from under me. I cry out, grasping for him, for the railing. He moves swiftly, catching me so fast it spins my head. I'm in his arms before I hit the steps, gasping as I wait for the painful fall.

"You gotta be more careful." He cradles me in his

arms like a child. "From now on, I shall carry you up and down stairs."

"Now you're being ridiculous. Put me down."

"I will, at the bottom of the steps." And he stays true to his word, even when a red-haired maid goes past, smiling at me, then staring at Kaden a bit too long.

I shouldn't care, yet a lick of fire flames in my chest at seeing the hunger in her eyes for him. I stare into his eyes, their deep, captivating depths, his strong, chiseled face, the way he's studying my mouth like he can't think of anything beyond kissing me. Why is it that a touch, a stare, is all it takes, and I'm burning up with an unbearable need for him?

I wriggle out of his arms before I lose control. "I can walk, thanks."

"Suit yourself." He smirks, letting me go but remaining by my side. "Just trying to keep you safe."

"Yeah, well, I'm perfectly capable of handling a few steps," I mutter, smoothing my wrinkled shirt.

We continue down the long corridor. It's always like this—an electric pull I can't ignore, even when I try to keep my distance.

"So, what's the plan once you meet the king?" I ask, trying to steer the conversation to safer waters.

He shrugs. "Figure out how to deal with the mercenaries without causing a bloodbath. It's all about keeping the peace, right?"

"Sure," I say, unable to hide my sarcasm.

He laughs, the sound vibrating through me. "You have a way with such a few words, Sasha."

I cut him a hard stare. "And you have a way of driving me crazy."

He chuckles.

We reach the room with the huge swimming pool located on the bottom floor, and the sight takes my breath away. It's like stepping into a fantasy world, a cave decorated with lush plants and a blue, oversized pond. The walls are lined with greenery, creating a natural, serene atmosphere. It's the kind of place you'd expect to find in a mermaid's grotto, not hidden away in a mansion. The water shimmers under soft lighting, steam rising gently from the surface. It's everything I imagined and more.

"This is perfect," I say, stepping closer to the edge. "Wow," I breathe, taking in the scene. "You need some of these in your kraken cave so that it's less dark and sacrificial and gives off more mermaid vibes."

I notice there's a wall of shelves with fluffy towels, a few benches scattered around, and even a small bar in the back. I can easily picture the family having fun here.

I turn to Kaden, who hasn't responded, only to find him butt naked and diving into the water. His clothes are discarded behind him. I shouldn't have expected anything less from him.

Head bursting out of the water, he calls out, "Get in here. Water's so warm. I do prefer the icy chill of the fjord, but this is calming. You'll love it on your mermaid tail."

I kick off my shoes and dip my toe in. The warmth curls up my leg, and I'm already feeling at ease. Stripping down to my tank top and underwear, I hesitate at the edge.

Kaden swims over, raising an eyebrow. "What are you doing? You can't come in here with those clothes." A mischievous grin spreads across his face.

"Why not?"

"This is a naked-only pool. Tallis told me so."

"He did not!" I protest, recognizing the lie but still feeling the flush creep up my cheeks.

He's grinning wider now. "You come in here like that, and they're coming off."

I eye him, accepting his challenge even as I'm halfway down the steps.

"Fine," I say, feigning indifference. "I don't need to go in." I turn to leave when one of his tentacles snaps around my waist as fast as whiplash and wrenches me backward.

I lose my footing, a scream caught in my throat, and fall into the pool's embrace. It's so warm, and despite myself, I hate how much I don't want to get out. I wriggle and fight against his damn tentacles, curling around me, pulling at me. The suckers stick to my skin, then pull away, a strange sensation that sends shivers down my spine.

"Kaden!" I sputter, coming up to the surface, seeing that he's still holding his human form while dark, inky tentacles jut out from his back, appearing lighter in color on the undersides. "Let go of me!"

I shove him away, only to see him gliding in the water. His tentacles are spread out gracefully, and two of them are grasping my tank top and underwear. I instantly pat my body under the water and realize he's ripped them off me.

"You asshole!" I shout.

"Told you the repercussions. You chose not to listen," he says, a smug grin plastered on his face.

"Why do you always have to be a horny bastard?"

"Because I am, especially when you keep fighting me," he replies smoothly.

I suddenly feel the gentleness of his tentacles on my legs, swirling around like seaweed, a sensation that sends heat through my body.

"Maybe I'm not ready... maybe it's moving too fast. You're talking about babies and..." I sigh, my words trailing off.

"Then I'll take my time until you're ready." His voice is a soft rumble.

It's like he's trying to unravel me with every look, every word, every touch. And damn it, he's succeeding.

I glance up at him, my heart aching with the weight of my fears.

"And what if I'm never ready? What if I'm the wrong person for you? What if... I hurt you down the track?" I turn away from him, emotions bubbling up inside me.

Memories of my mom and dad flash through my mind, the way their relationship crumbled, the way my mother's choices tore our family apart. I can't repeat that. I can't become like her.

Kaden moves behind me, his body pressed flush against my back, the impossibly hard erection against my ass difficult to ignore. His breath is hot in my ear.

"You could never hurt me."

Silence hangs heavy in the air.

"That's what my father thought, too," I whisper, my voice cracking.

"You're not your mother. You're nothing like her," he says firmly.

He turns me around by my waist, and I see the determination in his eyes. This huge kraken shifter sees something in me that I can't. He's not leaving me alone, and I can't deny the attraction to him. It's magnetic and unbearably hard to resist.

Suddenly, his mouth is on mine. It's a clash, a thunderstorm, an explosion between us. He always has a way of reminding me why I struggle to ever walk away from him. His kiss is fierce, demanding, and I can't help but respond, my hands tangling in his hair, pulling him closer.

We break apart for a moment, both of us panting.

"You drive me insane." My words are breathless.

"Good," he replies, his eyes darkening with desire. "Because you make me just as crazy."

I laugh, a sound that feels foreign and freeing. "What am I going to do with you?"

"Whatever you want," he says, his tone serious. "Just stop pushing me away."

I look at him, really look at him, and see the vulnerability hidden behind his confident exterior.

"I'm scared, Kaden. I'm scared of what this means, of what we could become."

"Fear is normal," he murmurs gently. "But don't let it control you. Don't let it keep you from something that could be incredible."

"I don't know if I can do this." I bite my lip, my mind a whirlwind of conflicting thoughts and emotions.

"You can," he says firmly. "We'll take it one step at a time. No pressure, no rush. Just us."

His words soothe something deep inside me, and I nod slowly. "Maybe one step at a time."

He smiles, a genuine gesture that lights up his face. "That's all I ask."

Kaden pulls me closer, his tentacles wrapping around me gently. "You're safe with me, Sasha. Always."

Doubt creeps into my mind, though my body has other ideas. I'm softening against Kaden, craving the protection he offers, the idea of me no longer being alone, and yet those exact same reasons terrify me.

His lips are on mine again, and I kiss him hungrily, my body flushed with emotions, with desire, with confusion. Yet I don't pull away. I can't because, for those few moments, I let myself believe that this is a perfect world where I have no past, where time stands still, and where all my worries have vanished. Where it's Kaden and me, and nothing else matters.

He gives a low grunt as his tentacles wrap tighter around me, as though he can't get close enough to me.

I absolutely adore that feeling of being wanted. Letting myself relax completely, I push aside those nagging thoughts that I'm making a mistake.

He's encasing me completely, those suckers pulling at my skin as if he's trying to drag me under the surface —something I'm not resisting because I wanted this. I sink into cracks in my mind where I'm broken, and with his kisses sailing to my neck, his breath whispering in my ear like a breeze out at sea, I feel whole.

I close my eyes, clinging to him as his mouth traces the curve of my neck. My body shudders with primal desperation, my thighs clenching tightly. In those few moments where I only inhale him, I swear I'm out in the middle of the ocean.

Free.

His arms and tentacles move over my body like the embrace of the sea. It's as if nothing else exists. The world and all its chaos fade away, leaving just the two of us.

Kaden's touch sends ripples of warmth through me. It's both terrifying and exhilarating, like diving into the deep without knowing what lies beneath.

Those tempting lips travel along my skin, and I'm floating, suspended in this perfect moment.

His gaze searches mine. "I've got you," he whispers.

I moan in response, barely able to take a breath from the emotions he's stirring within me.

"You're every fucking thing I crave," he continues.

I see his smile as he pulls back, our faces still close. It's hard not to fall head over heels when he's the most beautiful man in the world. His features are sharp and defined, like a marble statue, and there's sin in his expression when he studies me. Those vibrant blue eyes remind me of lapping waters on the shore in a tropical ocean... where I want to lose myself.

"You know your eye color changes in various blues," I say, breathless, still caught in his arms, my heart skipping a beat as his tentacles roam over me. "Or am I imagining things?"

Two of his limbs swoop beneath my ass, lifting me off my feet to meet him face to face. My hands are plastered to his rock-hard chest. His eyes glimmer as he leans forward, brushing his lips across mine.

"They follow my mood. The happier I am, the lighter they get. You can see for yourself what you do to me, the sheer amount of joy you've brought me."

"I guess it will show me when you're in a dark mood, too, then?"

He grins ominously. And instead of drawing away, he runs his tongue over the seam of my mouth in a dominating, claiming move.

I'm trembling from his earlier words, from the thrill of his commanding actions—a confident man who takes exactly what he wants... Me.

"Come, my little mermaid," he purrs, a seductive whisper that sends a hungry tremble down my back. "Let me show you how it feels to be loved by a kraken."

Before I can respond, he pulls me tighter against him, his arms and tentacles cradling me. My body tenses up, and then, in one swift motion, we're both under the surface, and he's charging through the water to somewhere behind me, carrying us both.

Panic flares in my chest, and I try to wriggle free. It's not the water—I can breathe just fine. But Kaden has a way of always pushing the boundaries, and as much as I try to stay in control, the unknown terrifies me. His presence is overwhelming, and every instinct tells me to fight, even though I know I'm safe.

We're deep under now, his movements fluid as he propels us to the darker part of the pool. Yet I can still see him clearly, the smile on his lips, the flow of his chestnut hair in the water.

At the bottom of the pool, I find myself beneath him, him leaning over me, his mouth savagely at my neck, licking, nipping, leaving me shuddering for more.

When he reaches my mouth, I kiss him back because I'm helpless around him. His tentacles curl between my legs, spreading them, others glide around my breasts, his large palms holding me prisoner.

I kiss him just as deeply, and the world disappears. It's just us.

His passion is fierce and demanding.

Surrendering to him is a dizzying rush, and I can't deny how right it feels.

He's in control, how he always demands every situation. I clasp the back of his neck with my arms, my legs held wide as his hands slide down to my waist. Something light brushes across my needy clit... something that feels very much like one of his tentacles.

Pulling from our kiss, he makes a growling sound, smiling at me.

"I count myself lucky every day that I've found you." His mouth moves, and I hear his voice—muffled as though it's filtered through layers of the ocean.

It's strange hearing him so clearly down here. My parents always told me not to speak underwater, something mermaids didn't do, apparently. I have no idea if they were lying or why they said that, except that it was frowned upon by them. Curiosity gets the better of me, and I try to answer.

"Do you often speak underwater?" I ask, feeling the words more than hearing them echoing in my ears.

He shrugs, the motion causing small ripples in the water around us. He grins, making me think he's heard me, and it's not just in my head.

"Not often enough for my liking," he replies.

I smile at the novelty of speaking this way when the tip of his tentacle limb strokes the length of my spread pussy.

I shudder, clinging to him, and an unexpected force of a tentacle pushes in past my entrance.

"Kaden," I gasp, stiffening all over, unable to focus on anything but the way he pushes into me.

He's staring at me. "I'm going to give you a mind-blowing underwater orgasm. You can show me your thanks later, gorgeous."

I'm moaning rather than protesting. The sensation of those suckers inside me brings a whole different level of excitement than I ever expected.

"How does it feel?" he asks, watching me like a starved predator. "I feel every sensation of my limbs, you know."

I'm writhing, sensing him moving deeper inside me and his girth stretching me.

"Kaden, this is so unfair," I manage when one of his suckers perfectly attaches itself to my clit. A scream flies from my lips, and he's holding me, his smile practically reaching his eyes.

I'm floundering, nipples tight. I'm burning up,

floating, and completely losing control. Kaden smirks at seeing me falling apart. His gaze trails up and down my body, pausing on my spread legs where his tentacle is fucking me, pushing in and out. Another sucks down on my clit, while others are gently moving over my body... one pushing into my mouth, another sliding to my ass.

He's filling me up, and he's so aroused that I don't miss the way his huge cock twitches for attention.

Kaden floats in front of me, eyes glazed over, enjoying me being tentacle-handled. There's utter elation on his face, intent in his gaze.

"I want to own every inch of you, fuck every hole."

Shaking ferociously in his hold, I can't speak. I'm lost in the beautiful way the sucker on my clit pulls down on me. My hips are rocking, meeting the rhythm plunging into me. I never expected to fall victim to arousal in front of Kaden while he got off on it.

My pussy quivers... every inch of me does. My hands grasp his arms as he still holds me by my waist. I feel incredibly vulnerable while drowning in overwhelming ecstasy.

I keep adjusting, writhing, mostly to accommodate him pushing into me. I'm at his mercy, exactly where he wants me.

He thrusts that tentacle into me, my control completely vanishing, and he's missing his own arousal. I'm glowing, especially between my legs, unable to deny that being taken by his limbs leaves me weak and pleading for more.

"Told you that you'd never forget being with me," he

grins just as my crescendo peaks, and an orgasm crashes through me.

I scream, his tentacle slipping from my mouth as I thrash and fall apart. I come harder than I ever remember doing. Kaden's growling once more, leaving his limb inside of me, those suckers never pausing.

"You're so beautiful when you come. One day soon, I'm going to marry you."

My stomach does a small lurch at his words, while I'm ruined, collapsed in his embrace, panting from the sensation of soaring through the sky. Except his words, they stay with me, pressing down on me... His pushiness to commit, to control, is lighting up my insides for a very different reason.

He's the king of the sea, the man of my dreams, yet I'm freaking out every time he talks about any kind of commitment.

As I wriggle from him, he finally pulls out, his limbs releasing me, and I'm floating on my own, already missing him. Except my head's all over the place.

His forehead furrows, and those bright eyes darken. "Sasha, what's going on?"

I'm swimming backward from him, but I know he's not finished with me. He never is.

"I can't," I manage, my voice trembling. "This is going too fast. The things I feel are happening too quickly." All I can think about is how much love my parents had for one another and how fast my mom became a siren, destroying our lives. What if it's in our bloodline to be more susceptible to becoming one?

His deflated expression is a blade to my heart, and my cold, inevitable rejection starts to crush me.

"I thought we talked about this," he says, gliding through the water toward me.

"Yes, but I'm not feeling myself, and you're... why do you have to make me care so much for you?"

"Be with me," Kaden says softly, his voice filled with sincerity, eyes searching mine as if willing me to say yes.

Instead, panic surges inside me, stronger and more overwhelming than before. My heart feels as if it's being squeezed in a vise. I push him away, shaking my head.

"Please, just leave me..." My voice cracks with desperation, the plea sounding more like a whimper. But as I turn to swim away, he reaches for me again, his hand firm on the back of my neck.

"Sasha, stop hiding from your true self. Embrace who you are, that you're meant to be with me." His voice transforms into a strong command, guttural and deep, resonating through to my bones.

The sound of his voice is a force that vibrates through my very being, rippling through my muscles and my nerves, reaching places I didn't even know existed. It's like being caught in a powerful current, and I'm suddenly drowning in the intensity of it all.

Something strange begins happening. My body turns to putty, no longer responding to me but to him. My legs and arms feel heavy, disconnected, as if I'm floating outside myself. I've lost control, and the struggle is so hard it hurts.

"Breathe," Kaden says, his voice softer now, trying to cut through the storm raging inside me.

But I'm not fully in the room. I'm trapped in my head, and my body is convulsing, racked with pain that's both physical and emotional. It feels like my very essence is being torn apart and reconfigured, and I don't know if I'll survive the process. I'm scared out of my mind, a flare of something different pulsing through me, something foreign and terrifying.

I'm shuddering, the pain shooting through my body as if my bones are breaking, my heart racing as I cry out. It's an agony I've never experienced, and it's relentless, unyielding.

"Kaden!" I scream, a call for help. I'm not even sure I want him to answer.

He's got me in his arms and shoots us upward. We break the surface, and he lifts me out of the water.

He cradles me with a tenderness that feels like a life-line and rushes me to a long seat at the pool's edge. He holds me steady, his grip firm yet gentle. But I can barely see anything through the fog of fear and pain. The world around me is spinning, and I'm lost in my own mind.

What's happening to me?

Kaden is saying something, but I can't hear him when he suddenly jerks away from me.

Almost instantly, a jolt of energy pulses through me, changing my senses into sharp focus. It's like I've snapped my fingers, and I'm no longer in my body. My sight is clearer, crisper, the world around me more vivid than ever. I see the water with an odd clarity, every ripple and wave magnified, glistening with a surreal bright-ness. I can smell Kaden so strongly, his masculine and pine scent mingling with his saltwater smell, and it's as though I can even inhale his blood.

What is wrong with me?

I push off the seat, landing on the floor, my breaths coming in ragged gasps.

*Wait, why do I feel weird?*

A great howl breaks past my throat, primal and fierce, a sound I've never heard before but recognize instinctively as my own. It's a noise that comes from deep within, born of fear and something more—a transformation that I don't understand.

Glancing down, I notice I'm on all four paws!

Paws!

Oh, fuck!

Kaden's eyes widen with shock, and he's rubbing his chin.

"I didn't see this coming."

He moves toward me, but the fear in his eyes mirrors my own. I'm terrified of what I might become. Before I can make sense of it, my instincts take over. I bolt across the room, unsure where I'm going but driven by a force I can't control, propelled by dread and an overwhelming urge to escape.

"Sasha, just take a deep breath. You're going to be okay," Kaden calls out.

My heart's about to burst out of my chest. Everything's a blur—the world rushing past me as I clumsily stumble right into a room I soon realize is a bathroom, not the way out. How in the world does anyone walk on four legs? I bump into the wall, struggling to move straight.

I don't know where I'm going, but the need to get away is all-consuming. The air is alive with tension, and I can feel something inside me shifting, something awakening that I can't comprehend.

The fear is suffocating, pressing down on me from all sides, but I can't stop. My body's betraying me, but I have to keep moving, even if it's stumbling. I rush through the stalls in the bathroom, hoping for a window or something, but there's nothing.

My thoughts are all funneling in on my father... a wolf shifter!

Is that what's going on with me? But why now? What had Kaden done to me?

Pivoting back around, his huge figure fills the doorway.

"Let's not panic," he tells me.

I sneer at him, showing him my teeth. I'm way past the fucking panicking stage.

I'm losing my damn mind right now!

My movements are more in control now, more fluid, more powerful than I ever thought, but my mind is a whirlwind of chaos. My heartbeat is a drumbeat in my ears, urging me to run faster.

I charge for the doorway.

Kaden's eyes widen, surprised by my actions.

"My little mermaid, or wolf, now it seems, I don't want to hurt you, but I'll wrestle you to the ground to get you to calm down."

I'm moving so fast I'm like the wind, and in seconds, he goes to scoop me up. Except I dart right through his parted legs and back into the pool room.

Claws hitting the stone floor, I madly scramble toward the main door we'd left partially open. My sense of urgency doesn't fade. If anything, it grows stronger, driving me forward with a single-minded focus. I don't know what I'm running from or toward, but I know I have to get away.

The echoes of Kaden's footfalls strike behind me, the hot air against me fluttering through my fur, but all of it is secondary to the terror that clings to me like skin. It whispers insidiously in my ear, telling me that I'm losing myself, that I'm becoming something else, something monstrous.

My breaths come in sharp, ragged bursts, my lungs burning with the effort, but I don't dare stop. With a final explosion of speed, I throw myself at the door, rushing through the gap and into the mansion.

I keep running, keep pushing myself forward, away from the terror, away from the uncertainty. Needing to be outdoors... There, in the distance, I spot the side door to the kitchen, which leads to another exit where I can see woods outside.

My heart's soaring, and I'm rushing madly for escape, a strange craving for the wild consuming me.

I glance back at Kaden at the end of the hallway, and he's calling my name, but right now, all I can do is run.

# CHAPTER
# TWENTY-ONE

### KADEN

"Sasha, fuck! Don't run!" I shout as I watch her race down the hallway in her wolf form. Her thick white fur almost gleams aquamarine in the light —matching her hair. I've never seen a more spectacular wolf in my life, and right now, she's sprinting away like her life depends on it.

I run like a madman through the mansion after her, half dragging my jeans up over my hips, doing them up, then pulling a T-shirt over my head, never stopping. I just met her friends, so darting around their home naked isn't going to go down well.

Sasha rushes into a room with a door open to the outside, and in seconds, she's gone.

My stomach drops. Fuck! The thought of losing her claws at my mind. What if she's so panicked that I won't find her again?

I have no idea what the hell just happened. One second, we were in the water, and maybe I'll admit I got frustrated with her pulling away. The next second, I spoke and something I'd never done before happened—my alpha voice rushed out of me, commanding and authoritative. I've heard of this happening before, an alpha controlling his mate, but I never intended to bring out her wolf. It's the only way I can explain it.

She told me that her father was a wolf shifter, but she also insisted she didn't have his ability. Yet the fear in her eyes won't leave my thoughts.

Fuck, this is my fault. What have I done to my gorgeous little mermaid?

Sprinting through the kitchen, I leap outside, where the air is sharp and cool, the skies darkening with clouds. I scan the grounds, trying to get a glimpse of her. To my left is the front of the property, and farther in front is a lofty fence, but to my right, the landscape stretches out behind the mansion, moving into the woods. Of course, she'd be there. No way in hell am I letting my fated mate vanish in such a panicked state. I did this, and I'll damn well fix it.

I run, my bare feet pounding the soft soil that's cold to the touch. When I come around the corner of the house, my sights set on the explosive woodland stretching out, I swear I catch the movement of something white. I almost crash into someone, but at the last minute, I pivot away, missing a collision with a man who's just as tall as me, standing with authority. Wind-blown dark brown hair cut short and tousled, he's wearing dark jeans, a tight shirt, and a leather jacket.

I stumble back. "Whoa," I mutter, steadying myself.

"Sorry there," I say, my gaze fixed on the woods, then back at the man who brims with power. I can feel it emanating from him, and I know he's an alpha, someone important in this mansion.

"My name's Kaden," I state. "I'm your guest, but right now, I don't mean to be rude, but I've got an issue."

The man's lips pinch, but he's concerned, not angry, staring at the woods. "I'm Khaos," he states in a deep voice. "Guessing that white wolf I just saw charge into the woods belongs to you?"

I sigh. "It's a long story, but I need to find her urgently before she's hurt. She's never turned into her wolf form before."

"Well, fuck me. Then we need to find her. I'll help. I can track her down. The woods are in my veins. I'm part wolf shifter."

*The other part a god,* I think to myself, for a second admiring this powerful man who offers his help without knowing me. I know I like him already.

Khaos is already pushing toward the woods when he calls out, "Kaden, this might help you a bit more..."

He points to a black dirt bike at the other end of the yard, looking clean, as if it's never been ridden.

"Keys are in the ignition," he calls out, stripping down to nothing and already throwing himself into the woods, transforming mid-pounce into a pitch-black wolf form. He's huge, massive, as he darts into the woods.

"Well, fuck," I mutter. Rushing over, I climb onto the bike, revving it to life. I'm going to find my girl before she's terrified to death.

The bike roars beneath me as I tear across the open

lawn, heading straight for the woods. The wind whips past my face, ripping at my hair, while the engine vibrates through my body. I lean forward, urging it faster. Every second feels like an eternity, and the fear of not reaching Sasha in time gnaws at me.

The trees close in around me as I enter the forest, the path narrowing, branches whacking against me. The dirt bike handles the terrain better than I expected, but it's still a struggle to maintain speed and control. My heart pounds in my chest at the urgency to find and catch her.

I push the bike harder, adrenaline surging through me, driving me forward. Sasha's image flashes in my mind—her wolf form, so wild and beautiful, her eyes wide with terror. I curse myself for letting things get so out of hand, for not understanding the power of my own voice and the impact it could have on her.

Branches snap under the bike's tires as I maneuver through the forest, the scent of pine and earth thick in the air. Every shadow seems to shift, every rustle of leaves a possible sign that it might be her. I strain to catch any glimpse of white fur, any indication that she's nearby.

The bike skids to a halt as I reach a clearing, but something inside me urges me forward. So, I keep riding, my instincts pulling me in the direction I know she went. The trees are dense, their heady aroma filling my lungs as I speed forward.

A deer darts out of the way, startled by the intrusion, and my heart pounds in my chest. The wind tugs at my hair, the bike growling beneath me like a beast in pursuit.

I hit a slope hard, the bike climbing up a track with ferocity. I catch sight of Khaos in wolf form just as he scales the top of the same hill, and I know I'm on the right path. I gun the engine, the wheels skidding here and there, but I hold on, pushing harder.

As I crest the hill, a small valley opens up below me, a river snaking through it. And there she is.

Sasha, in her wolf form, backs away from the black wolf. Her teeth are bared, a snarl etched across her face. I curse under my breath, knowing she must be terrified, having no idea who the wolf approaching her is. But Khaos was right in that he found her fast, and for that, I owe him.

Halfway down the hill, I stop the bike and discard it, rushing down on bare feet, not wanting to scare her further.

"Sasha!" I call out. "It's okay. He's Billie's mate. He's not going to hurt you. He's helping me."

Her head swings in my direction, the sneer still on her mouth, her eyes wary and wild. She backs away, her hind legs splashing in the narrow river.

As I approach, Khaos lifts his head toward me, nods, and backs away. He rushes back up the hill toward the mansion, leaving us alone.

"Thank you," I say to the retreating wolf, grateful for his help.

Now, my attention is solely on Sasha. She's shaking, but at least she hasn't run from me. The clouds are darkening the sky, casting an ominous shadow over the valley, and all I want is to have her in my arms again, to reassure her.

"I'm sorry, Sasha," I whisper, taking slow steps toward her. "I had no idea you'd turn, but I'm here for you."

She watches me, her eyes tracking my every movement, tense and ready to bolt. I move cautiously, gauging her reaction, hoping my presence will calm her. I take another step, heart in my throat.

"Please," I say, holding my voice steady despite the storm inside me. "Just let me help you."

She hesitates, and I seize the moment. I make a last move to get closer, but she scrambles, trying to escape. I lunge, catching her, grabbing hold of her around the middle.

Sasha turns her head to snap at me, her teeth grazing my forearm, tearing skin. I hiss. Blood bubbles up, the sting sharp, but it's nothing compared to the guilt shredding my insides.

I hold her, one arm looped over her back, the other cradling her chin and head, keeping her against me sideways to my chest. She growls, her eyes locked on mine, teeth bared, but I'm kneeling and won't release her.

"I'm not letting you go," I say firmly. "And I'm not leaving your side until you hear me out. Then, if you want to tear into me and watch me bleed to death, that's your decision."

She pauses, her growling ceasing for a moment, and I know I've gotten through to her. She understands me.

"I feel like the world's worst shithead for forcing your wolf transformation," I confess, my words tumbling out in a rush. "I had no idea, and I didn't intend to use my alpha voice, but it came out, and it all happened in the worst way... Well, not the worst because you are fucking stunning as a wolf. But why didn't you think you could turn? Nature has a way of ensuring all our abilities are of use to us."

I realize I'm rambling, but she's not growling at me. Her eyes are focused, alert, but no longer filled with the same panic.

"Okay, look," I continue, searching for the right words. "I didn't mean to scare you, and I didn't mean to push you into this. But you have to know that I'm here. I'm not going anywhere, and I'll do whatever it takes to help you through this."

I can feel her body soften against mine. Her gaze eases, the wildness receding, replaced by something else —something that gives me hope.

"I'm sorry," I repeat, my voice softer now. "For everything. I never wanted to hurt you. I just want to be there for you, to love you."

Sasha remains still, her breathing steadier, and I hold her close, feeling the rhythm of her heart against mine. I can't change what's happened, can't undo the fear and confusion, but I can be here for her.

The clouds overhead rumble, a low growl of thunder echoing through the valley.

"I promise," I say, meeting her blue gaze. "We'll figure this out together."

She lets out a soft whine, a sound that tugs at my heart, and I suspect she's beginning to trust me again. I stroke her thick fur gently, feeling the softness beneath my fingers, and offer her a small, reassuring smile.

I hold her close, determined to see this through. But

then Sasha pulls back slightly, her eyes meeting mine with a clarity that surprises me. She gives a small, tentative nod, as if acknowledging my words and actions.

I pull her closer, wanting to calm her, waiting for her to settle completely. She gives a small whimper, and I lean down to kiss her head.

"Okay, here's the deal," I say softly. "I'm going to let you go, and if you want to bite me, I won't stop you. But you have to know I would never do anything to harm you."

Slowly, I release my hold, my heart thundering in my chest, muscles tense but trusting her and my instincts. She instantly pulls free from me, stumbling on her feet, and turns to me. Her lips curl in a snarl, but she doesn't run or attack. She just stares at me with those mesmerizing aquatic eyes.

"You're so beautiful in your wolf form, absolutely stunning," I tell her.

After a long pause, she pads back to me, sitting by my side. I don't push it. She lifts her head and releases a howl. It moves me. Something in my chest twists as I'd witnessed her experiencing her first transformation into a wolf.

Other howls echo in the distance, a chorus responding to her call. I grin as she glances at me.

"You've shown your respect to the wilderness, to embracing your true form," I say.

She gives a shake, then settles down, her front legs draped over my lap as I sit on my ass, legs stretched out in front of me. Her chin rests on my legs, and she stays there.

I stroke her head, marveling at the super thick fur and her graceful ears. I'm in awe of her magic form, her power.

"You do realize how magnificent you are," I say. "It's not many who can hold two forms they can shift into—let alone two as powerful as a wolf and a mermaid."

She makes a groaning sound but doesn't move, seeming content, and I don't want to disturb her. We sit there together, the silence around us comforting and serene.

I take a deep breath and continue, wanting her to know how much she means to me.

"I know I can be pushy, and I know it scares you," I admit. "But I've never felt this way for anyone. When I want something, I take it. And I want you to know that we are an item, no matter what. I'll be by your side, always."

She shifts slightly, her eyes meeting mine with a softness that wasn't there before. It's a small gesture, but it speaks volumes, and I feel a warmth spread through my chest, knowing she's starting to trust me again.

We sit there, me stroking her fur, her breathing long and calming. I study the woods, at the beauty of nature surrounding us, thinking back to when I was in prison, where I never thought I'd leave. Fuck, but those days were filled with darkness and despair, a time when hope seemed out of reach. Now look at me!

With my fated mate.

Free.

And while I haven't yet found who betrayed my grandfather, I'm getting closer... I feel it.

"I've been given a second chance," I murmur, more to myself than to her. "And I'm going to make the most of it. I promise you, Sasha, I'll always be by your side."

She lets out a soft sigh, her eyes closing as she rests her head on my lap, and I know she's found comfort in my words.

An hour, maybe more, has passed, and Sasha's fallen asleep, her wolf form nestled against me, warmth radiating off her. I know it's the exhaustion of everything she's been through today that has her passing out. The weight of the transformation, both physically and emotionally, must have taken its toll on her.

As the air grows colder, I shift carefully, lifting her in my arms. She's heavier in this form, her muscles thick and powerful, but there's a softness to her, a warmth that soothes me. With her pressed against my chest, I tighten my arms around her body, under her tail and head. She slumps against me, trusting even in sleep.

"Well, let's get you back to our room," I whisper softly. "Then you might find it easier to come back to me in your human form."

The trek back up the hill is slow and deliberate, and I keep finding myself burying my face in her fur, taking in her sweet wolf scent; beneath it all is the smell of the sea. She's got me fucking hypnotized.

As I reach the mansion, the warm glow from the

windows spills out onto the lawn. I push open the door with my shoulder, careful not to jostle her. Waiters inside pause, their eyes widening slightly at the sight of the wolf in my arms, but they step forward to help, holding doors open as I pass.

"Thanks," I mutter, grateful for their assistance.

Finally, we reach our quarters, and I close the door behind us, shutting out the world. I walk to our room, then lay her gently on the bed. Her body shifts slightly, settling into the softness of the mattress, and I can't help but smile at the sight of her so peaceful and serene. There's no smart-ass commentary either, which has me grinning more.

The pitter-patter of tiny feet catches my attention, and I turn to find Chowder standing in the doorway, staring at the wolf, his head tilted with curiosity. His nostrils twitch as he sniffs the air.

"Why does wolf smell like Sasha?" Chowder asks, his brow furrowing.

"This is her, buddy," I explain, crouching down to his level. "Tonight, she discovered her other ability, but now she needs to sleep."

"She hurt?" he asks, stepping into the room, his attention on her.

I scoop him up quickly, not wanting to risk Sasha's wolf instincts taking over if she wakes disoriented and thinks of him as a snack.

"She's fine, just tired," I reassure him. "We need to give her time."

Chowder's eyes never leave her. Even as I shut the door, he continues to stare in her direction.

"I worry for her," he admits.

"I know. Me, too," I say, setting him down gently. He scrambles up onto the couch, leaning on the armrest, his gaze fixed on her door.

To distract him, I grab a bowl of fruit from the table —grapes, pears, and mandarins—and bring it over. "Enjoy. It'll keep you busy."

He doesn't hesitate, digging in with enthusiasm. I've never seen something so small eat so much, but it's a welcome distraction.

With Chowder occupied, I slip back into the room to find Sasha still sleeping soundly. I don't want her to wake up afraid and alone, so I climb into bed alongside her. I rest my hands behind my head, feeling the purr of her heavy breathing, the warmth from her body beside me.

"I meant what I said before," I whisper into the silence, my voice barely audible. "I love you, Sasha."

The words hang in the air. It's a promise, a declaration I don't give lightly.

I close my eyes, allowing myself to relax, to savor the peace after a long day.

Sleep already tugs at my thoughts...

I wake up to a sudden splash of water hitting my face. It's cold and sharp, shocking me awake. I snap upright in bed, growling, "What the fuck!" My eyes are wide as water runs down my face, soaking my shirt and the bed—where I'm alone.

In front of me stands Sasha, holding an empty glass with a triumphant grin.

"I see you're back in your human form," I say, wiping my face with my hand.

"Thanks for looking after me," she says, a teasing edge to her voice. "It means everything that you brought me back here."

"Strange way of showing it by throwing water in my face," I reply.

She grins, spreading her lips, and I notice Chowder at her leg, scrambling up her body to sit in the crook of her bent arm. He looks at me with bright, curious eyes.

"Oh, the water is for pushing me too far in the pool, for not listening to me, and for forcing my wolf out with your alpha asshole command," she states. "Don't ever do it again!"

I struggle to keep a serious face and smile instead.

"Oh, little mermaid, I know you're mad, but that command was completely accidental. But now we know you can transform into your wolf." I push my legs out of bed, wiping the water dripping into my eyes.

She stares at me deadpan, not giving an inch.

"They're expecting us downstairs for a catch-up in ten, so, you know..." She turns on her heel and walks out, Chowder now perched on her shoulder, gawking back at me.

"Why you wet the bed?" Chowder chirps, his laughter a high-pitched sound that makes Sasha chuckle.

I shake my head, loving that we're back to our playful taunts. As I get up, I know that one way or another, I'm going to get her to break down those walls and realize she can't live without me.

Her strength and resilience inspire me, and as I dry off and change clothes, I'm more determined than ever to show her that we're in this together. Her smile, her spirit, and the fire in her eyes are things I will cherish forever. And I'm ready to prove that I'm the one who will never leave her side. Whether she likes it or not, she's stuck with me for life.

# TWENTY-TWO

Kaden and I are dressed up and heading down to the entertainment room. Billie's instructions were straightforward enough, and we don't seem to be lost yet.

After the whole pool and woods incident and the fact that I turned into a wolf, I'm still reeling in shock. I assumed I'd never transform, yet it appears I have more in common with my father than I ever expected. The realization alone has my heartbeat speeding up because I miss him terribly, even after all this time. I wish he could be here to tell me everything I need to know about being a wolf shifter.

When I woke up earlier in bed alongside Kaden, I was back in my human form, but even now, I feel the wolf lingering beneath the surface, as though she's part of me —and this whole time, she's been hiding from me. It's comforting in a way to have her present.

And sure, I'm annoyed at Kaden for his pushiness,

but then, if he hadn't pushed, would I have ever discovered my wolf side?

"Are you okay?" he asks, genuine concern in his soft gaze.

Chowder's in my arms, just hanging out casually over my shoulder.

"Yeah." I nod, trying to convince myself as much as him. "It's been a long day."

He reaches over and gently pushes a strand of hair caught in my lashes away from my face. Chowder quickly does the same with his little paw, making me giggle.

"You're going to have to learn to share, little man, or we're going to have some problems."

Chowder just stares at him, unmoved by his words. "Why you hurt her?" he asks accusingly.

Kaden's mouth pinches, and he stares at me. "I would never hurt you. You know that, right? I worship the ground you walk on."

"I'm not mad, and I'm still dealing with it all. But let's not talk about this now." I'm eager to avoid another tense moment.

He smiles, and I sense the warmth of it seeping into me. As much as he gets me all riled up, he's also crawled into my heart, and no matter what I want, I can't deny my growing attraction.

"You look spectacular, by the way," he coos, eyeing my outfit. I'm wearing black fitted pants and a dark-pink wrap blouse with a V-neck, tied at the front, paired with pink heels. My hair is pulled back into a messy ponytail. I feel both beautiful and relaxed, exactly what I need after today's fiasco.

"Thanks, you don't look too bad yourself," I reply, smiling as he raises his eyebrows, staring down at himself and giving me that cheeky nod. The one where he knows he's so damn hot that he's lucky I'm not crawling all over him right now. His shirt pulls against the buttons from his muscles, open at his throat, drawing my attention to the ink over his collarbone.

I glance away, schooling my emotions around him.

As we reach the entertainment room, the double doors immediately push open, and a handsome man greets us.

"Perfect timing," he says with a welcoming grin. "I'm Eryx," he introduces himself.

Ah, another of Billie's fated mates. She told me he's a gryffin shifter, and a wild one at that, but staring at him now, he appears friendly, easygoing, and undeniably handsome. His blond hair cascades down to his chest, and he's dressed in blue jeans and a casual deep mauve T-shirt that hugs all his muscles. Those blue eyes are striking. It's as though I'm face-to-face with his animal side, unsure if I'm talking to Eryx or the gryffin.

"Hi," I say, trying to sound casual.

Kaden steps forward, extending his hand with a firm grip. "Kaden," he states, locking eyes with Eryx. "Heard a lot about you. You keep everyone on their toes, much like me."

Eryx chuckles, shaking Kaden's hand. "I do my best. How are you liking our neck of the woods?"

Kaden smirks. "It's beautiful. That's for sure. And I'm

all about trying new things. Never a dull moment here, right?"

"Definitely not," Eryx replies with a grin. "Especially when Billie's involved."

My friend approaches us, smiling brightly. "So good you've arrived," she says, pressing against Eryx's side as he holds her like she's his entire world. He absolutely adores her.

"Where are the little angels?" I ask, glancing around, half expecting to see the twins about.

Billie grins softly. "It's way past their bedtime. They're fast asleep upstairs, which means we can all relax and be adults." There's a mischievous sparkle in her gaze.

"Come in," Eryx says, reaching out to Chowder, who accepts his fist bump. It's the first time I've seen him do that.

"This is Chowder," I explain. "He's part of the family and goes everywhere with me."

"Well, great to meet you, too," Eryx says with a nod in his direction.

As we enter the entertainment room, I take in the gothic style of the room. There's a grand stone fireplace, its flames flickering with a warm glow. A spread is laid out with all sorts of drinks and snacks. In fact, there are two tables just for food. Tallis is already there, dressed in black fitted pants and a button-up shirt, his dark hair cascading over his shoulders. He's helping himself to the food.

Kaden claps Khaos on the back, greeting him with a grin. "Great to see you again."

"Appreciate you helping here earlier. Means a lot."

"Of course."

Tallis calls out his hello, and Kaden drifts over to him by the table of food, along with Khaos.

I take a deep breath, trying to push away the weight of the day's revelations.

"So, how do you all like to relax around here?" I ask Billie, seeing three of the guys chatting loudly, laughing, and I assume this is an everyday occurrence.

"Food, drinks, and a little friendly competition," Eryx replies with a wink. "We have a pool table, darts, and plenty of space to unwind, but the twins keep us all busier than we've ever been."

"In truth, I forgot what it's like to sleep a full night." She leads me to a cozy couch area near the fireplace. "I'm so glad you're here." She nudges me, taking my hand in hers. "I miss us living together and all those late-night chats. You gotta tell me everything that's been happening with you."

"Hey, I do a pretty good job of keeping you up all night," Eryx interrupts and gives us a wink when we glance over.

Billie shakes her head at him, smiling, her flowing white hair dancing across her shoulders. She's wearing a bright blue crisscross dress with a deep V-neck and long sleeves, and looks stunning, like she always does. Then she blows him a kiss. "That you do."

Khaos joins us, too, in midnight-blue dress pants and a fitted jacket. He offers me a drink of something honey-colored that smells strong. I take it and settle into the couch near the fireplace while Eryx stands by the flames, studying us with a curious gaze. Chowder scrambles down from my lap and in front of the flickering fire, looking around the room with wide eyes.

"Why don't we have more fire at home?" Chowder asks, staring at the flame, then back at Kaden.

"Oh, he talks?" Eryx murmurs, tilting his head as he studies Chowder with genuine curiosity. "My gryffin talks to me, but he's never spoken out loud." He leans down to Chowder, stroking his head. "You're a clever otter, aren't you?"

Chowder stands on his hind legs, enjoying the flames and staring at Eryx, seemingly unsure what to make of him.

"Is he magical?" Khaos asks, leaning forward, intrigued.

After a quick sip of my drink, which is a strong whiskey and burns my throat, I set it on the coffee table near the couch and explain in a low voice.

"I found him being experimented on, so I saved him and gave him a home. I couldn't bear to leave him." Looking over, I adore the way he wears his blue vest. While most of the cuts and experiments on his back have healed, he seems more comfortable wearing the outfit. It hurts me to think of his past, which is why I try not to bring it up around him.

Billie presses against me, her hand on my leg. "You are so sweet to take him in, but not surprising. You've loved animals for as long as I've known you."

"Yep. Remember that time I brought home a baby lion?" I reply, smiling at her.

She bursts out laughing. "Yeah, and you wanted to

keep it while there was a mother lion terrorizing the neighborhood, searching for her cub."

I shrug, laughing. "I gave him back, but he was so adorable."

She laughs and hugs me. "I missed you so much, you know that."

"Me, too. All our long chats into the night, our snacking, and your obsession with cakes."

Khaos laughs, a warm sound that fills the room. "That hasn't changed," he states. "We have our personal chef bake her new treats every week. Billie deserves the world." He squeezes in on the couch alongside her, and I love how caring they are over her.

"So as a gryffin," Chowder starts, glancing up at Eryx, drawing all our attention. "Do you lay eggs or give birth? How does it work for gryffins?"

Eryx bursts out laughing, his head thrown back. The sound is contagious, and soon, we're all joining him, even Chowder, who seems pleased with himself.

"Why do you ask?" I say as Kaden and Tallis join us by the couch in front of the fireplace. Kaden sits on the edge of the couch, close to me, while Tallis stands behind Billie. Billie told me he's a demon, and he would definitely be scary to encounter alone, but then all of her mates are slightly intimidating. Yet when I look at Kaden, he fits in perfectly alongside them because he's just as terrifying and unpredictable.

"Who isn't curious?" Chowder replies, staring up at Eryx. "Gryffins are part bird and lion, so..."

Eryx wipes his tear-filled eyes, still laughing. "Thing is, I can't say I've experienced it personally, seeing as I'm a male. But my kind lay eggs in burrows, if that answers your question."

Chowder turns to Billie, then back to Eryx. "So, your two babies came in eggs?"

Billie bursts out laughing, shaking her head. "Definitely not," she says. "They were a natural birth, thank goodness. I might have freaked out if I was laying eggs."

As Tallis makes a joke about the eggs, Khaos approaches me, kneeling near me, and I feel Kaden leaning in closer to me, protective.

"Are you okay after your first transformation?" Khaos asks gently.

"It was a complete shock, to be honest," I admit. "But I woke up back in my human form. I'm not too sure yet how to change into my wolf, but I feel her just beneath my skin."

Khaos smiles, nodding in understanding. "Yes, I can sense her, too, and she's strong. It might take a bit of time to learn to fully control her, which is why you were running in the woods earlier. She was scared and wanted to hide somewhere familiar. For transforming, the best I can recommend is to close your eyes and reach out to her. Talk to her in your mind and just ask her to come out. It sounds like she's ready."

"Thank you. I'll have to try. I would hate for her to always take off toward a forest when I transform."

Kaden rubs my back in small circles.

"Just remember, while you share a body with her, you are in charge, and she needs to know this."

Khaos places a hand on mine, and instantly, I feel the vibration of my wolf inside me, recognizing another wolf shifter. I sense a rumble inside my chest, and I grin. Having a wolf side is so different from my mermaid side, which lies dormant until I transform. My primal side now is more vocal, making her presence known.

"Once, when I was injured," Khaos begins, "my wolf took over and led me back home without me realizing it. You're very fortunate to have yours as your protective backup. She will take care of you."

I smile at the thought. "It's already a bit strange to have a wolf and a mermaid side."

"It's beautiful," Kaden says softly. "Unique and spectacular."

"He's right," Khaos adds. "You have something not many shifters do—the ability to balance both power and grace. Your strength comes from embracing all that you are."

Billie turns toward us. Chowder hops onto my lap, and the warmth of the fire creates a cozy atmosphere. If I lived closer, I could see myself doing weekly dinners or even game nights, just like Billie and I used to do back in South Africa.

"When do we meet the gryffin?" Chowder pipes up.

Eryx's eyes light up with excitement when I glance his way.

"You want to see my gryffin? Of course!" he exclaims, clearly thrilled by the idea, his chest puffing out, chin high.

"No, Eryx, don't—" his brothers simultaneously shout.

A crackling energy surges through the room, and in seconds, Eryx bursts out of his clothes. I try to look away, but my eyes are glued to the transformation. Kaden instantly places his hand over my eyes just as Eryx's pants shred away, but I push his hand aside, unable to look away from the spectacle.

Now, in front of us stands a massive gryffin whose head almost rubs the ceiling. His body is that of a lion, golden and powerful, while his head is that of a majestic eagle, fierce and noble. His enormous black wings stretch wide, and when he beats them once, a flurry of wind rushes against us. His talons scratch the wooden floorboards, clenching and unclenching on the spot.

My mouth might have fallen open in awe. I'm speechless, and even Chowder is pressed up against my side as if he wasn't expecting him to be so huge.

Eryx steps away from the fireplace and bumps into a small table, knocking my drink over and sending it tumbling, the glass smashing.

"Oh, shit, I'm so sorry." I move to get up, but Billie has my hand, pulling me back.

"We'll clean it later. Better to just let Eryx do his thing first."

Back in my seat, we all turn around, following him strutting toward the windows.

"Wow," I breathe, unable to take my eyes off him.

Tallis rolls his eyes, a familiar exasperation in his voice. "He's going to break everything in here. Again."

Beside me, Billie watches with admiration but resignation. "He always does," she says. "His gryffin side has a mind of its own and isn't always controllable. But I adore him, and things can be replaced and fixed."

Chowder's eyes are huge, and he makes excited

chirping sounds. "So pretty! He can fly? Who doesn't want to fly?"

As if hearing him, Eryx unleashes a sharp birdlike screech with a growl, then stretches his wings out, reaching the walls. He eyes the large floor-to-ceiling window with a curtain drawn across it.

"Fuck, Eryx, don't do it," Khaos warns, getting to his feet, but it's too late. Eryx charges the window. The room erupts in chaos as he smashes through the glass, shattering it with a deafening crash. Glass sprays outward, and a cold breeze rushes into the room.

Eryx soars out into the night, his wings catching the air effortlessly. The moonlight glints off his feathers as he flies upward, powerful and free. He disappears into the sky, a dark silhouette against the stars, leaving us in stunned silence.

Adrenaline rushes through me, my heart racing as I watch him vanish into the night sky. It's a breathtaking sight.

Chowder claps his hands, bouncing with excitement in my lap. Kaden stands nearby, ready to act if needed, but Billie just smiles.

"It's okay. He'll be fine, and we have a whole team in the mansion who fix up all the breakages he causes." She laughs, a fondness in her eyes. "As much trouble as he causes, I adore him to bits."

Her words resonate with me, reminding me of the acceptance and love she has for Eryx, despite his wild nature.

Tallis stands with a deadpan expression, staring at

the now-broken window, letting in a cool breeze. Khaos turns back to us.

"Well, he'll be back in his own time. Let's move the party to the parlor."

They're all so casual about it, showing how much they respect Eryx just as he is.

"I like Eryx," Chowder chants, and I giggle at him, wondering if he sees a part of himself in Eryx—the wild, untamed side that refuses to be caged.

Kaden approaches Khaos, asking, "What can I do to help?"

He shakes his head, grinning. "Nothing at all, my friend. Just enjoy yourself."

That's when Kaden catches my eye once more, and I realize that he's my chaos, just like Eryx is to his mate. He's grown on me so much that I'm obsessed with him just as much as he is with me, and I don't think I'd have it any other way.

It's past two o'clock, and I'm snuggled up in bed when Kaden crawls in behind me because he won't take no for an answer. "You can share the other bed with Chowder," I say to him sarcastically, knowing he won't do that. I glance up at him in the blue darkness of the room, lit up only by the moonlight pouring into the bedroom and onto the large four-poster bed.

"You think I'm not sharing a bed with you?" he chuckles. "You haven't been listening to me."

He climbs under the covers, causing the whole mattress to jump around. As I try to pull away, mostly because I'm only wearing my underwear, his large hand loops around my middle and scoops me across the bed and up against him. My back and ass collide with his chest, and I let out an *oomph*.

"Kaden, geez."

"Would you have snuggled me otherwise?"

"Hell no."

"My point is proven," he says, his arm around my middle, his leg over mine, keeping me pinned in place. His chest is flat against my back, the blankets over us, and as much as his dominance drives me crazy, I can't help but admit there's something comforting about lying in his warmth, all cuddled in the blankets.

"Did you have fun tonight?" he asks, his breath in my ear, which heats me up. Nothing about Kaden keeps me calm; it's the opposite, especially when he's wearing nothing and isn't shy about pressing against my ass.

"It wasn't how I expected the day to go, but I loved seeing Billie again. And you know what?"

"What's that?" he whispers, his fingers tracing across my stomach, leaving me covered in heated goosebumps.

"Here I thought my life was chaotic with you and Chowder, but Billie has had her fair share of crazy, too, it seems. So maybe it's a sign, you know."

He chuckles, the sound so delicious it leaves me trembling. "So, you're saying you now approve of us?"

"Well, I approved of Chowder long ago, but I'm still getting used to you," I tease, knowing that we're still figuring things out, and this isn't some fairy-tale ending.

"I know she has lots more stories to tell me," I say about Billie. "And I think, being this close to Finland, I might come over to visit her more often."

"We'll make it a regular trip," Kaden replies. "And once the mansion is fixed up on the exterior, we can invite them over."

I smirk to myself at his assumptions that I'm doing everything with him. Then again, I have no clue how to unglue him from me, either. But do I want to?

Just as his lips press against my shoulder, a small bounce at the end of the bed makes us both glance over the blankets. Chowder is there, coming toward us on all fours.

"Why you sleep here without me? Family stays together," he says, his voice full of mock indignation.

I laugh while Kaden grunts.

"Come and join us." Pulling back the blankets in front of me, I make a small area for him to snuggle under the covers.

"Really?" Kaden grumbles, and I laugh at him.

"Maybe you can back up a bit," I suggest, wiggling my ass.

"You keep doing that, and you're going to be in trouble."

"Ain't happening. Now squeeze on over so Chowder can fit."

With a groan, he moves a smidgen of an inch, still glued to me, his arm and leg on me. Chowder is now sharing my pillow, curled up and facing away from me. I stroke him so he settles down. Before I got moved out of my cabin, Chowder would sleep in bed with me and keep me company most nights.

"He better not get used to this," Kaden says, pressing in close to me, his breath on my neck. "You smell so beautiful. You're so soft against me."

"Why you talk so much?" Chowder asks.

Kaden groans.

I burst out laughing.

Right now, I'm surrounded by the two men in my life, and despite everything, it makes me incredibly happy.

The next morning, I wake up alone in the bed, blankets bunched up around me like I'm the filling in a burrito. I'm sweaty, hot, and a little annoyed that no one woke me up. Stretching my arms over my head, I kick off the covers and get up, pulling on pants, a bra, and a shirt to appear semi-decent.

As soon as I open the door, I'm hit with the mouth-watering smell of cooked eggs and bacon, and my stomach growls. I figure Kaden and Chowder probably followed the smells, so I do the same.

I find myself in a large kitchen, half of it dedicated to an island covered with several cakes in glass stands, and nearby are counters with lots of gleaming appliances. The other half of the room features a round table for six, holding dishes filled with food. The spread is impressive—fluffy scrambled eggs, crispy bacon, buttery croissants, fresh fruit, and steaming coffee. The rich aromas fill the air, making my stomach rumble with hunger.

A brunette maid is bringing more coffee to the table, along with muffins. Billie is there in a robe, enjoying the food with Tallis in jeans and a wrinkled T-shirt, both of them sitting close, chatting and giggling. He kisses her brow, and they both look up when they see me.

"Come join us," Tallis suggests, gesturing to the table. "We have way too much food."

"Where is everyone else?" I ask, choosing to sit on a chair adjacent to Billie. I instantly pour myself a glass of juice and start serving food onto my plate because I have no shame. Billie knows me; I inhale food.

She grins at me, amused. "Khaos and Kaden left super early this morning to visit King Kaspian, as it's the only time he is free. Eryx and Chowder are outside, getting along like two peas in a pod."

He left without telling me. Something stirs in my gut, though I remind myself that I'm not his keeper and he can do what he wants.

As I take a sip of my juice, I notice movement outside the window.

There, I spot Chowder riding Eryx in his gryffin form, soaring through the air.

My fork falls from my hand, clattering against the table.

"Oh my God!"

Billie places a reassuring hand on mine. "He's safe. I promise. He asked Eryx to ride him this morning because he wanted to know what it felt like to fly."

"Oh," I say, feeling both worried and slightly guilty

for having Eryx entertain Chowder. "Sorry," I say to Billie, shaking my head. "Seriously, I can't control Chowder any more than I can Kaden. They just do the craziest things sometimes."

She laughs, serving herself from the big bowl of fresh, chopped fruit and yogurt. "I know how that feels more than anyone."

Munching on bacon, Tallis is watching the pair outside doing spins in the sky.

"The things I faced with Eryx when I arrived at this mansion I'll never forget." Billie bumps her shoulder into Tallis, smiling. "Not to mention this one!" she adds in his direction.

"I'm an angel compared to him," Tallis protests, his demon eyes glinting with a playful darkness.

"Right..." Billie says, rolling her eyes. She breaks into a story about how Eryx once grabbed her from the house, burst through a window, and swooped her up to a mountaintop.

I ease back in my seat, realizing that we're fitting in with Billie and her mates better than I could ever have imagined. At the end of the day, it's become obvious that they're *our* kind of crazy.

# TWENTY-THREE



We're at the gates of Billie's mansion, and a cool breeze blows through my hair, making it flutter around my face as I hug Billie tight. Chowder is already in a town car with the driver at the front, and Kaden is off saying goodbye to Billie's mates. He had been gone half the day, spending more time with the king than intended, then Khaos gave him a tour of Lapland. Now, we're rushing as our flight is scheduled to leave in less than two hours.

"I'm going to miss you so much," Billie murmurs, squeezing me tightly. "I loved seeing you. We really need to do this more often."

"We will," I promise her, returning the hug with equal fervor. "Especially now that I'm working out of Norway. Last night's catch-up was amazing."

We hug again, and as Kaden reaches my side, Billie hugs him, too. Then Kaden and I head into the car where Chowder waits.

"What took so long?" Chowder asks, waving out of the open window. Then he's suddenly calling out, "Bye, Eryx!"

"He's obsessed with him," Kaden mutters as he leans into his seat as the car takes off.

Kaden's reclined, legs spreading, taking up most of the back seat, glancing at me silently. I shift in my seat, still buzzing from the morning's rush.

"So, how did it go with the king?" I ask, breaking the silence. "You came back so late, and I need to know if it's all sorted."

"It couldn't have been easier," he admits, smirking. "The king is admirable and someone I highly respect. I would happily serve under his reign while living in the House of Gold and Garnet. I mean, I also have an agreement with the Siren Goddess permitting me to use the seas for now. Her insistence that I relocate to the House of Sea and Serpentine is something I'll deal with later."

I swallow hard at how blasé he is about such matters, but Kaden isn't someone to be pushed into doing something he doesn't want to.

"And what happened?" I ask as Chowder continues to stare out the back window at the mansion disappearing behind us, while I'm curious about how Kaden handled meeting a king.

"Well, with Khaos, who is evidently very close with King Kaspian, he arranged for me to meet with him as a favor to Khaos. All I had to give him was a few drops of my blood—the currency in this House." He's smirking, and I can't recall the last time he spoke so much in one breath. "Through Khaos, he was able to affirm that I spoke the truth along with confirming your identity, and that took all but ten minutes. The king's passing through Finland, so I didn't spend as long with him as I'd hoped, but he welcomed me back anytime. I'm the first kraken in his House, and he's proud of it. Seems everyone wants me in their Houses." He grins, chest sticking out. "And he'll ensure that I'll be left alone by all mercenaries. He put out orders to spread the word when I was there."

He's talking rather excitedly and proudly—cocky, too—but I guess it's not every day one gets to meet a king. Regardless, I'm smiling at the thought that he'll have those mercenaries off his back.

"Well, I'm glad that's sorted and no more attacks. Though you should have woken me up when you got up."

He grins, reaching over to squeeze my thigh gently. "Do you know how beautiful and innocent you looked, all curled up? It broke my heart to wake you."

With Chowder curled up near the rear window of the car, Kaden wraps an arm around my back, drawing me closer to him.

"I'm contemplating swimming back to Norway," he says with no amusement in his voice.

I laugh. "Are you crazy? How long is that going to take you? And we'll be there so fast on the plane."

The corners of his lips pinch, and he sighs. "I don't think I'm made for flying. I sweated so much on the way here."

"I promise it'll be all right, and you can hold my hand the whole time. What do you say?"

He's not teasing me or anything, and I can tell he's

dead serious and scared. I like this more vulnerable side of him.

I press in against his side, and we enjoy the ride, me holding his hand. "It's going to be all right," I murmur.

"You really are incredible," he whispers in my ear, then holds me tighter.

I find myself lost in the moment, wrapped up in the warmth and safety of his presence. But beneath the surface, a flicker of fear stirs. Everything is moving so fast —what if things go wrong, like they did with my parents? The thought nags at me, a shadow on the edge of my happiness, reminding me that nothing is ever truly certain.

As we drive toward the airport, a comfortable silence settles between us. I'm trying to plan what we need to do once we're back when suddenly, Kaden stiffens beside me, his eyes rolling back into his head.

"Kaden, are you okay?" Panic lurches in my chest. "What's going on?"

He slumps against the door, his body trembling. Fear slams into me, tears springing to my eyes as my stomach turns to ice. I've never felt so scared before, and just as I thought maybe things were finally perfect, he passes out for no reason. Has he been drugged?

"Wake up, please," I plead, my voice trembling. Chowder senses my panic and scrambles onto Kaden's lap, his tiny paws pressing against Kaden's chest.

"Kaden, Kaden... What's wrong?" Chowder calls, his voice high-pitched.

My mind races with possibilities, fear clawing at my insides. Has he been poisoned? Is it some kind of attack?

"Please, Kaden, wake up," I murmur, tears slipping down my cheeks. The fear grips me so tightly it's hard to breathe.

I knock frantically on the tinted glass divider between us and the driver, desperation clawing at me. Just as the driver lowers the glass, his concerned eyes meeting mine in the rearview mirror, Kaden starts to groan.

"Is everything all right?" the driver asks.

But I'm focusing on Kaden as he opens his eyes, staring at me, his breaths coming fast and shallow.

"It's okay, I think," I reply to the driver. "He's just... not feeling well."

The driver nods, watching us through the mirror. "I can pull over if he's going to be sick."

Kaden expels a gasping breath, as if he's been holding it. He looks confused for a few moments, as though he's unsure where he is.

"Kaden, are you all right? What just happened? Are you okay?" I ask urgently.

Chowder is still there, peering into his face. "Why did you pass out?" he asks.

Kaden rubs his face and breathes heavily. "I'm fine," he finally says.

"No, you're not. People don't just pass out like that," I say, tears stinging my eyes. I'm shaken to my core, imagining the worst.

He smiles, reaching for my hand. "This is why I know you want me as much as I do you. You're crying for me. Do you know how much that means to me?"

"Kaden," I say louder, trying to keep my voice steady.

"Tell me what just happened. If you're pulling some stunt, I swear to the gods that I'm going to throw you out of this moving car. You really scared Chowder and me."

"I-I have visions," he finally admits.

The admission catches me off guard. It's not what I expected him to say at all.

"Like seeing the future?" I ask, trying to wrap my head around it. I've never heard of anyone having visions, so I'm not sure what it really means.

"I have what's called genetic memory," he explains calmly. "It's a gift that runs in my family line, where random snippets of my ancestors' experiences are passed down to each new generation. I mostly get visions from my grandfather's life, like he wants me to know something."

He rubs his face again, his brow furrowing as I absorb what he's saying.

"So, it's like you get a glimpse into his past? Do you think it's related to you trying to discover who got him put into Tartarus?"

He shrugs. "It might be," he admits, a hint of uncertainty in his words.

"So, what did you see?" I ask, my heart still pounding from the scare.

Chowder curls up in his lap, and Kaden rests a hand on him, a gesture that makes my heart warm with tenderness.

"It's hard to make sense of it," Kaden admits. "I see him either with his business partner or his lover. And I feel like I'm missing a major clue. His business partner is the woman you spoke to at the wharf, so I really need to find her again and discover what's going on."

I blink at him, noticing the slight tremble in his hands, worried about what all of this means.

"I feel like she's the key," he continues. "Like she might know what happened to my grandfather. So, once we're back, I need to concentrate on finding her."

"I'll help you," I say, determined. "There have to be records of her somewhere."

Pressed up against him, I can't believe how quickly I reacted, how much he means to me.

We fall silent. I remain glued to him.

The road stretches out ahead of us, but I'm worried about him—about us.

For now, though, I squeeze his hand tighter, grounding myself in the moment, and hope that he's right... and that I'm nothing like my mother.

We step out of the airport into the late afternoon sun, which casts golden hues dancing on the horizon. Norway looks stunning in this light. The more time I spend here, the more it feels like home.

Kaden is back to his friendly, jovial self, dragging me close to his side, stealing kisses, bantering with Chowder. He sneers at any man daring to look at me as we walk toward the parking area where we're getting picked up by a driver.

He leans in to whisper in my ear, "I'm going to cut their eyeballs out for daring to stare at you."

"You need to calm down," I answer, secretly amused by his protective nature.

We move toward the sign indicating the pickup area, and I notice how quiet the underground parking area is. There aren't many cars or people around, which is strange so late in the day. Suddenly, I spot two men in black hoods heading straight for us with purpose, and my heart skips a beat.

Kaden's posture changes instantly, his muscles tensing as he sees them.

"You gotta be kidding me," he mutters, mostly to himself. "They better not be mercenaries."

The men charge at us with menacing intent, and Kaden steps forward. The first man swings a fist at Kaden's jaw, but Kaden ducks beneath it with fluid ease, responding with a quick jab to the man's ribs that makes him grunt in pain. Kaden charges after him, slamming those powerful punches into his face and chest, and once the guy falls, he doesn't get back up.

I'm recoiling, my body on high alert, scanning our surroundings... we're still alone.

The second man lunges with a knife. Kaden twists aside, grabbing the man's wrist and using his momentum against him. The man stumbles, and Kaden drives an elbow into his back, sending him sprawling onto the pavement.

"Stay back," Kaden snarls at me, glancing over his shoulder to ensure I'm out of the way. I clutch the straps of my backpack with Chowder sitting over my shoulder. Fear courses through me as I watch the fight unfold. I hate seeing him continuously being attacked, but then again, he is disposing of them quickly.

The first man recovers, dragging himself up, and charges at Kaden again with a wild swing.

"Fuck!" Kaden growls and catches the man's arm, twisting it sharply until I hear the sickening crack of bone. The man cries out, dropping to his knees.

The second man rolls to his feet, brandishing the knife with renewed determination. He slashes at Kaden, but Kaden sidesteps, grabbing the man's arm and slamming his knee into his midsection. The air rushes from his lungs in a wheeze as he collapses, clutching his stomach. Kaden doesn't let up, grabbing the man by the throat and lifting him off the ground.

"Who the fuck are you?" Kaden demands, throttling the man like a rag doll before tossing him into a stone pillar. Seeing he's still moaning, Kaden goes after him and lifts him to his feet by his fisted shirt.

"Didn't you get the message, asshole? King Kaspian's called all hits off me. I'm a damn citizen of the House of Gold and Garnet now. And you're getting your asses kicked for being stupid."

"We were hired, man," the man gasps, his words choked as he claws at Kaden's grip, gasping for breath, looking pale as a sheet.

Kaden's grip tightens, and the man's thrashing for

release. "Who sent you?" Kaden barks, his voice as hard as steel.

The man coughs, a strangled noise, and Kaden drops him, letting him collapse to the ground. "I don't know," the man croaks, clutching his throat.

Kaden looms over him, snatching him by his dark hair. "You're going to regret that," he promises just as the guy's eyes roll up into his head, and he passes out, just like his buddy.

"What the hell's going on?" I ask, unsure why anyone would be coming for us.

Kaden's gaze turns to me, concern flashing across his features. "Are you hurt?" he asks, his voice softer now.

I shake my head, though my heart is still racing, and my grip on the backpack straps is white-knuckled. "I'm okay," I reply.

From behind a parked car to my right, movement catches my attention. I swing around to a third hooded man darting toward me with alarming speed.

"Watch out!" Kaden is already bolting forward, but the man reaches me first. I twist around, shoving my fist into his face and kicking his knee. But the bastard already has his hand on my backpack, yanking it off my shoulder with such force that I stumble sideways.

Then he's gone like lightning.

"Chowder!" I scream, darting after him. The bag's clutched in his arms. Panic surges through me as I dash after him, Kaden hot on my heels.

Kaden sprints past me and reaches the man in a flash, tackling him to the ground. They roll across the stone floor, the bag tumbling free and skidding to a stop a few feet away. I scramble to it, my heart pounding in my chest as I rip it open.

"Chowder!" I call, relief flooding me as I find him inside, frightened but unharmed. "It's going to be fine," I murmur, trying to soothe him.

Chowder doesn't respond, just curls up tighter, and my heart breaks at his fear.

"No one's going to hurt you. I promise." My throat croaks.

Turning back, I find Kaden pinning the man to a stone pillar near a parked car, growling in his face. "What the fuck do you want? Are you after me? Why did you steal her bag?"

The man spits blood at Kaden. "Fuck, I don't want you, you idiot." He glances over at me, and a shiver runs down my spine at his stare.

Kaden's gaze flicks to me, then back to him. "Who sent you?"

"Fuck you," the man snarls, his response dripping with venom.

Kaden grips his wrist harder, then bends it backward instantly, the snap loud, and the man howls in agony. "Every time you don't answer my question, I'll break another bone. Now, who sent you?"

The man's cheeks blanch, and he mumbles, "Fuck... It's the otter she wants and for the girl to leave town."

Kaden cracks the man's fingers back, and the man screams. "You didn't answer my question. Who the fuck sent you?"

Shaking, I hold the bag with Chowder tighter. My mind races, starting to suspect the worst. They're here for Chowder. My mind flashes back to the asshole, Zane, who traffics and experiments on animals. And whom I didn't catch on my last mission... the one who got me relocated to Norway. Did he track me down?

"I asked a damn question," Kaden roars in the man's face.

"Lilia," he cries out, literally sobbing as Kaden holds him by the throat. "Lilia sent us to get the otter and to scare her out of town."

"What the fuck?" I mumble, my mind spinning with confusion. Who's Lilia, and why does she want me out of town? Is she working for Zane?

"Keep talking," Kaden demands. "What does she want with Sasha and the otter? Where can I find her?"

The man chokes for breath as Kaden releases his grip slightly.

"Someone hired her to retrieve the otter, and Lilia said to deliver you a message... that Sasha is being watched, and she wants her out of town, or she'll get rid of her. And you won't like how she does it."

I'm trembling, trying to piece together what this means, but I'm left just as perplexed.

"Where do I find her?" Kaden commands.

"Man, I don't know that. She found me at a bar and hired me. That's all I know, honest to God."

Kaden drags the guy farther from my sight, and I hear the dull thuds and groans as he interrogates him further, I assume. When he returns alone, he appears grim, shoulders bunched up, shadows dancing across his face.

"Did you get anything else from him?" I ask, my voice trembling.

He shakes his head, darkness clouding his features.

"I think I know who's after Chowder, but I have no idea who Lilia is. Maybe a local mercenary Zane hired?"

"I know who she is." Kaden's lips pinch tight. "She's my grandfather's business partner. The woman you met on the wharf and who's been in my visions."

# TWENTY-FOUR

## KADEN

I'm back at the mansion, pacing the basement like a fucking caged animal. Sasha's taking a shower, and Chowder's in the kitchen, eating his weight in food. She was all worked up after the attack, and I didn't want to discuss the situation until we got back, not when we were so exposed in the parking area. I needed to get us home, to know she and Chowder were safe, before I started dealing with this shit.

The basement is cool and dark, the air thick with the scent of salt and the distant roar of the fjord just outside. It calms me, the water and the stone. I stroll around the enormous room, past the table Sasha jokingly calls the sacrificial stand. It makes me grin every time, the way she teases me about it. But right now, my thoughts are a tangled mess of questions with no answers.

*Lilia.*

She's involved with Sasha somehow and has put out a threat on her to leave town. What the fuck for? What threat does Sasha pose to her? What am I damn missing?

I think back to the vision in the car, the one that was different from the previous ones. My grandfather was alone down here in this same basement, and then suddenly, he was heading down a set of dark steps into a hidden area. Inside was a room filled with books he'd written in, line after line of names that made no sense. He was mumbling about a pendant, furious, throwing things about, books strewn everywhere. Frantic and scared. I'd never seen him that way before.

I feel like I'm close to something, something that involves Lilia and somehow Sasha, too, which is the part that boggles my mind. Why her? What connection does she have to this whole mess? And is it connected to my grandfather ending up in Tartarus?

I'm in the back of the basement, the stone walls cool and solid under my hands. The entire place is polished stone—floor, walls, ceiling. Paintings grace some of the walls, ships at sea, mermaids in the water, krakens drowning sailors.

I go around the walls, patting them, pushing, trying to find the hidden door I saw in the vision. It has to be here, right? Frustration gnaws at me.

I don't remember Grandfather ever telling me about a secret room in the mansion. He told me about the place being grand, about the entrance to the fjord for an easy escape, but not about this room. There must be something he didn't want anyone to find.

I search every inch of the walls, looking for a trigger or a hidden latch, anything to reveal the room. But by the end, I tense, not finding anything.

I'm not giving up. I'll find this damn room. There are

still rooms upstairs I haven't touched, some with my grandfather's items, and maybe there's something up there that'll give me a clue.

Upstairs, back in the main part of the mansion, I enter the living room, only to catch a quick glimpse of aquamarine hair and a bare leg disappearing down the hallway from the bathroom. I grin, unable to help myself, and go after my beauty.

I find her in the bedroom, her back to me as she pulls a pair of jeans up over that beautiful curved ass. She grabs a lace bra, fastening it before she turns and startles at the sight of me.

"Fuck, warn someone before sneaking around like a damn stalker," she scolds, her eyes narrowing playfully.

"I didn't want to ruin the perfect moment," I reply, my gaze locked on the way those lace cups hold her breasts in place.

"Hey, eyes up here," she says, lifting an eyebrow.

"Oh, I know," I reply, grinning. I can't stop studying her bra, knowing it's slightly transparent, trying to make out her nipples.

She drags a shirt down over her head, covering herself, and I groan, unable to get enough of staring at her. She's perfect in every way.

She rolls her eyes, but I can tell she's amused by my persistence, a playful grin on her mouth.

I find myself captivated by the little things—like the way the water droplets cling to her skin.

"We've got shit to talk about. This Lilia business," she says. Her expression shifts, worry creasing her brow. I can see her mind turning, and I nod in agreement.

I flop down on the bed, patting the mattress for her to join me.

She laughs softly and sits close. The fish in the glass aquarium at the end of the bed swim closer as though they're fascinated by my every move, their eyes fixed on me with an unblinking stare.

"Seems you have a fan base," she jokes, nodding toward the aquarium.

"They'll go away soon enough," I reply, watching as they continue to hover as if they're captivated. Her hand is warm against mine, and I stroke it gently.

"Tell me more about Lilia?" she asks, her gaze lifting to mine. "Why would she want me out of the city? And how is that connected to you, to Chowder?"

"Lilia was my grandfather's partner for the business they ran," I explain, thinking back to what little I know. "From what I understand, it was something about imports and exports by sea, but he rarely spoke about it to me. I've seen in my visions that he and Lilia didn't always see eye to eye on things."

"I remember meeting her at the wharf," she says, her brow furrowing in thought. "Maybe it's a coincidence that I asked her questions about sirens attacking sailors, and I remember she got hostile with me. But she left it at that... Oh, and I had Chowder with me, and she saw him. No idea what that means except that she knew about Chowder after I met with her."

She gnaws on her lower lip, and I can see the gears churning behind her gaze.

"Lilia holds the answers to everything we need to know."

"Do you think she's in cahoots with that asshole Zane, who tortured Chowder? Otherwise, I can't understand why she'd want Chowder and me out of town." She blinks, looking at me, as confused as I feel. "Maybe she runs a mercenary company, and dickhead Zane put a threat against me… I mean, it would make sense after I burned down his warehouse."

I listen, trying to piece it all together, but the puzzle is mostly gaps right now.

"I suspect that somehow it's all connected, and maybe with my grandfather… Don't ask me how, but something feels really off," I say, then think of the lists of names in my vision with my grandfather. "Something happened with her and my grandfather, and he was involved in something, in trouble. But the only way to find out is to track her and this asshole Zane down."

"You think he's in town? I assumed he hired her all the way from South Africa, seeing as that was where I last saw him," she explains, her voice tight.

I study her, the way she appears when she thinks, how her brows furrow in concentration. It's cute, endearing, and I take in every word she says.

"Zane might be easier to track down than Lilia, and he might lead us straight to her. So lay it on me. I need to know everything about him."

She swivels to face me more, a leg bent between us. She rattles off his full name, details about the psychopath he is, and the animal-trafficking ring he was running, along with his description and a bunch more info I didn't need to know about his broken past. She's passionate and furious at him, but I also sense a flicker of fear from her shaking hands.

"He can't take Chowder back, ever. I'll kill him myself before I allow that to happen," she states.

I take her into my arms, sensing how tense her body is. "I promise I'll keep you both protected."

She pulls back, blinking more, her eyes glistening with unshed tears.

"I keep thinking about the whole siren incident and my mother. Could this be related to that? Is it someone who doesn't want me to find her?"

I ponder her words, a heavy silence settling between us. The thought worries me because why would someone try to hide a siren's actions?

"It's time we find out what that is," I say finally.

She nods, determination etching her features, and fire burns in her eyes.

I squeeze her hand. The room is silent except for the gentle bubbling of the aquarium filter. I watch her, the way her chest rises and falls with each breath, the way she worries her lip as she thinks. I want to protect her from everything, from the dangers lurking in the shadows of our world.

"What if it's more than we can handle?" she whispers, her eyes meeting mine with a vulnerability that tugs at something deep inside me.

"There's nothing I can't handle, my little mermaid. Trust me," I reply firmly.

She leans into me, her head resting against my shoulder, and I hold her close, absorbing the warmth of her body. Her hair smells like the ocean, and I close my eyes, breathing her in.

"I'm going to start searching for Zane tomorrow," I admit, the decision settling in my bones like a promise. "It's late now to do anything, and after everything today, I'm going to make you dinner and give you a massage."

She eyes me, smirking, a playful light in her gaze. "You are?"

"Of course," I reply with a grin.

"Well, I'm not one to say no to a massage, especially a foot one. And maybe a bit of time to relax might be nice." She leans against me, and I kiss her brow, taking in her scent once more.

"I'm worried," she admits, her voice barely above a whisper. "But I'm happy I'm not alone."

I cup her cheeks, staring down at her, adoring her so much that it hurts.

"Do you realize how mental I'll go on anyone who dares to touch you? You are my world, Sasha, my everything. Around me, you don't need to be scared, okay?"

She smiles, a small, soft grin that lights up her eyes. She snuggles closer, and I wrap my arms around her, holding her tight. It feels right having her here in my arms.

"Come on," I say, pulling back slightly and taking her hand. "Let's get something to eat."

We head to the kitchen, and as we step inside, we find Chowder sprawled out at the table, patting his fat belly with a satisfied grin. Four empty sardine cans lie discarded in front of him, evidence of his feast.

"Looks like someone's had a good meal." I chuckle, reaching out to rub Chowder's head.

"He's always hungry," Sasha says with a laugh, shaking her head in amusement. "You're going to turn into a sardine one day, Chowder."

He chirps in response, looking utterly content. His little paws rest on his belly, and I'm laughing at the sight.

"Why would I become a sardine?"

She's laughing louder. "It's only a saying. I'm joking."

I chuckle again as he studies her, clearly confused.

"All right, let's see what I can whip up," I say, moving to the counter where I left the mushrooms I'd bought just before we went to Finland. "How does mushroom and bacon carbonara sound?"

"Sounds delicious," Sasha replies, settling at the table, pulling out a deck of cards she found in the living room, and starts playing a game with Chowder, who watches her intently.

I start preparing the meal, the sound of boiling water and sizzling pans soon filling the kitchen. Sasha's laughter rings out as she plays with Chowder. The sound of laughter in my home is something I never thought I'd hear, something I didn't realize I needed until now. It fills the space, turning the cold stone and steel into something warmer, something more alive.

Watching her play with Chowder, seeing the way her eyes light up with joy, makes me realize more than ever how much I want a family with her. I want this laughter, this warmth, to be a permanent fixture in my life. I want to see her happy every day, to wake up beside her, to build a life with her.

The bacon sizzles in the pan, the rich aroma of garlic and butter filling the kitchen. I move around the space with ease, adding pasta to the hot water and stirring the creamy sauce.

As I cook, I think about the future, about what it would mean to have her by my side, to build something lasting together. It's more than a want; it's a need, a deep, primal urge to make her mine in every way possible.

I plate the food, carrying it over to the table where she and Chowder are still engrossed in their game. She looks up as I set the plates down, her eyes sparkling with delight.

"This looks amazing," she says, her gaze shifting from the food to me, warmth and gratitude in her eyes.

"And mine?" Chowder pipes up.

"Definitely," I say and bring his small plate of chopped-up bacon. "Because you haven't eaten enough already."

His eyes are only for his serving.

We dig in, and for a while, everything else fades away. It's just us, sharing a meal, sharing a moment, and it feels perfect.

"This is heaven," she murmurs, her voice dreamy.

"I aim to please," I reply, smiling down at her.

At this moment, everything feels right. We might be facing an oncoming storm, but here, with her in my home, I know we can weather it. We have to because losing her is not an option. I'll fight for this—for her, for Chowder, for us—with everything I have.

# TWENTY-FIVE

KADEN

Lying across her stomach on the bed, I'm lost in admiring the way Sasha's muscles relax under my touch. It helps that she's completely naked for me, and as much as I've been focusing on kneading the tension from her shoulders and along her spine, my cock is rock hard at touching her, at taking in the smoothness of her skin, at the way her waist narrows in, the curve of her ass, the softness of those cheeks, the toned legs that I've been willing to spread for me in my mind. But nothing yet...

"How are you feeling, my little mermaid?" I whisper, leaning in closer to her ear. I don't know how I got so lucky to have such a sweet, beautiful angel end up being all mine. Not that I had a choice from the moment I first met her.

She lets out a soft moan, the sound sending a thrill right down to my balls. "Why have you stopped?" She's pouting as she turns her head to give me a contented look. "You promised me a massage."

"I've been doing it for the past hour," I tease, watching the way she flutters her eyelashes at me, propping herself up on her elbows, where I catch a glimpse of her side boob.

"Oh, I didn't realize there was a time limit on it." She pokes her tongue out at me, giving me her mischievous pout.

She's going to be the end of me.

"You're temptation incarnate." And she knows it, the way she stares at me with those bright eyes.

I pull back and slide my hands down the back of her calves, then up again, tracing her legs, my fingers skimming under her ass before I slide over it, kneading her.

"You like that, don't you?" She almost purrs the words, pulling herself up on all fours, already swiveling away from me as my gaze drops to her ass.

But she's facing me now, and it's hard to look away from those delicious tits dangling there, calling for my mouth.

"How are you going to clean up the mess you're about to make in your pants?" She's staring at me with those dreamy eyes, driving me wild.

"You're going to do it for me because my cock is pulsing with need like a fucking drum." I draw back and sit on the bed, leaning against the mountain of pillows behind me. Then I'm reaching down, unzipping my pants, gripping my cock, tugging it out, presenting it to her. "How about you slide that pretty little mouth of yours over him?" I tug a few times, the tip glistening and ready.

Like a cat, she slinks closer to me on all fours, coming

up between my spread legs, and in moments, she's breathing over my dick. She rubs the tip of her index finger down the ribbed sides of my cock, the sensation sending a buzz of exhilaration through me.

"Oh, you want me to kiss here?" She lowers her lead, her puckered mouth brushing the tip. I tense, hissing, then she pulls back, licking her lips.

"Why don't you try again and put him all the way into your mouth? My balls are so fucking full."

Her eyes grin up at me, and she takes her time, pulling herself up to her knees, rewarding me with a full view of her sensual body. My dick hardens to the point of pain as I take in her bouncy, curvy tits, those tight pink nipples, and the thin strip of aquamarine between her legs, barely covering her pussy. It glistens. She's so ready for me. If I bent her over now, I'd slide easily into her cunt. And she'd cry for me to fuck her like a beast.

"I have something for you," I explain, already reaching over to the drawer of the bedside table.

"In my room?"

"Technically, it's now our room." Digging into the drawer, I pull out a bright pink dildo, not as thick as my monstrous cock.

"Oh," is all she says, her eyes captivated by the toy, following it as I bring it to her.

"Show me how you put it into your sweet pussy. I want you to wear it as you suck my cock, to grip it so it doesn't pop out. Otherwise..." I grin as she accepts the dildo. "You're not coming tonight."

She arches an eyebrow. "You've always been a control freak?"

"Is that a yes?"

She stares at me, placing the pink toy into her mouth, elaborately licking it, taking it deep in, and then pulling it out completely moist.

I'm breathless, studying every movement she makes.

Then she leans back on her ass, spreading those sexy legs for me, my gaze falling to her plump lips from her arousal. She's so ready for me that it must be aching... as much as it does me.

My hand's on my cock again, squeezing as I watch her spread herself, showing me that sweet little hole.

"Is this what you want?"

"Fuck yes!"

She slides the tip into her pussy and slowly works it deeper, in and out, a moan in her throat. Her hips work to take the vibrator, her breaths escalating.

"All the way, gorgeous. I want it in deep so you feel it as you come undone."

She's staring at me, challenging me, yet her eyes are hazy with desire, and as she works it deeper into her, the wet sounds she's making are captivating.

With it now fully embedded inside her, only the wide tip handle sticking out, she's gasping for air.

"Did you go for the biggest one? Damn!"

"The biggest one is here, waiting for you. Now, turn it on."

Heaving for breath, she flicks the switch on the end of the toy, and instantly, she's moaning, her chest sticking out, her body shuddering. She's spectacular. Sexy as fuck. All mine.

She gently rolls onto her side, squirming, and with

another push of it deeper into her with a small cry on her lips, she's back on her hands and knees. Damn, I've never seen anything so erotic in my life.

"You love to see me tortured, don't you?"

"You have no idea," I answer, reaching over with my hands, brushing her hair off her face, and taking it into a ponytail. I wrap the strands around a fist and hold her, guiding her lower. I fight the urge to push her down harder, controlling her completely.

"How does it feel to have your pussy filled as I'm about to fuck your mouth?"

She bares her teeth at me in a primal response. "You better not hold back on me once I'm done."

"My Sasha, I'm going to fuck you until you pass out, until you're so sore I'll have to rub lotion on your pussy. Now, wrap your sweet mouth around my cock."

There's no fight from her, just her complete submission. I'm damn loving her this way during sex. I want her to do as I demand, to satisfy every fantasy I've had, to make her weak, to make her mine.

She leans into my erection, and with a final smirk my way, she opens up and slides her mouth down over my huge offering.

I hiss, calling out, "Fuck!"

She goes deeper, her lips slipping over the ribbed bumps on my cock, her beautiful mouth stretched over them, her tongue lapping at my underside, and my fist around her hair tightening. I wait for her to go down the full length, and when my tip hits the back of her throat, she doesn't stop but takes me that bit further.

My hips are moving, grinding into her, and I notice hers are rocking, too, turned on by being plugged up.

"Fuck, I love seeing you filled up. You're so damn beautiful at my mercy."

She moans and starts moving up and down my shaft, and I can't help myself. With her hair wrapped around my fist as my guide, there's something exhilarating about controlling someone as powerful as Sasha. To drive her mouth over my cock as she sucks me relentlessly while knowing her pussy's dripping. To know she's going animalistic on me.

I keep rolling my hips toward her hungry mouth, tingles rushing through my balls because I know I'm not too far. How can I be with such beauty sucking on me?

"Your mouth is too good to be real, created by the gods for me." I've never fucked a more delicious one.

She's moving faster now, and my balls pull in tight, my nostrils drowning in her scent. When I feel the first jolt of a climax about to crash over me, I pull her back by her hair, and she releases my cock with a popping sound.

"My turn."

She licks her lips, her cheeks flush, her eyes hazy like clouds. "Please, I'm about to die from the ache at how turned on I am."

"You have no idea how ready I am." I climb off the bed, and she just watches me, still on all fours, her hips moving from the buzzing of the vibrator working her pussy.

I move to the end of the bed where her ass is high, her legs spread, and that tight hole buzzing. The dildo is half sticking out, looking ready to come out, and I slip it out of her. Slick stretches out from her, her opening dripping for me.

"My little mermaid, you're so ready for me, aren't you?"

She makes a crying sound as she sticks her ass higher and lowers her chest to the bed.

"You better not break your promise," she murmurs between her moans. "Fuck, I've never been this turned on in my life."

Reaching over, I grab her hips and drag her over to the edge of the bed to where her lush cunt craves me, quivering for me.

My cock is hard as I push him down, the tip instantly dipping into her hole.

I might think she's lost control, but I have none either because I'm salivating at the anticipation. She's soaking, bare, and engorged. An image I will forever imprint on my mind.

Pushing forward, I drive myself into her without mercy. I can't prevent what's coming. My balls are slapping into her pussy as I bury myself so fucking deep that she's already screaming for me.

Not wasting time, I pull out and start plunging into her like a wild animal, fast and powerful, the whole damn bed and her ass shaking with each thrust.

I go at it like a damn animal, thundering into her, unable to get enough, not caring who hears us fucking. I'm convinced I can keep going like this all night. She pushes back against me with each thrust, her greedy little cunt hungry for me. She's making those delicious horny sounds, her throat raspy, as I claim what's mine.

"I love how tight you are, how excited you are for me. I fucking love you, Sasha."

She's bouncing forward and back with each powerful thrust, saying something, but I can barely hear her when she's suddenly squeezing my cock, screaming.

"That's it, come for me, coat my cock in your juices, suck me in deeper." I don't dare stop. I hammer into her faster, harder, when my own orgasm takes me over. It's coming out whether I want it to or not.

I slam into her, my fingers digging into her hips, both of us bellowing our climax, and I'm bursting inside of her, roaring.

"Fuck, you're..." She's gasping for air. "You're breeding me, aren't you?"

I laugh, then growl, and keep on pumping my seed into her, my cum jutting out of me and filling her insides.

"You're mine, Sasha, and I told you I would start trying. Now, take it like my good little mermaid. I'm going to love you for eternity and take care of you and bring you to orgasm every damn day so you never forget how obsessed I am with you."

She's suddenly laughing, then crying out again, and instead of fighting to pull out, she's pushing back against me to take more of my cock.

My heart has never felt so full to have her give herself to me fully.

Finally, I pause, waiting for her to calm down, too. When her breaths steady, I draw out of her, some of my white magic sperm dripping out. I push it back inside of her where it belongs.

She turns and stares at me. "There's no stopping you,

is there?" Her chest is pumping fast up and down with each breath. Despite her words, she's smiling, and I take that as her approval.

"Not when it comes to claiming what's mine. You want to deny the inevitable, while I want to start our lives together." I lean my body over her, covering her, my mouth on her neck, then moving to her mouth. "Do you want to go again or have a rest?"

She chuckles, attempting to crawl out from under me, but I've got her in my arms. "I may need a rest first."

"Okay, shower first. I'll clean that beautiful pussy and show you that you are my world. Whether you want to fight me, it doesn't change that you are my light, Sasha. I will always love you."

As I carry her, she leans into me but is staring up at me, yet she's not saying anything. There's only a glint in her eyes.

"It's all right," I explain. "You don't need to say it back. I can wait."

CHAPTER

# TWENTY-SIX

SASHA

Hurtling down the road in the early morning light, the car engine roars as I grip the steering wheel. Kaden sits beside me, his expression stoic. Chowder's back home, curled up safely. My mind races with thoughts of what lies ahead. Kaden woke me with an urgency this morning, and now, here we are, on the hunt for Zane.

"Are you sure you found him?" I ask, glancing over my shoulder at Kaden, who's staring out the window. "I mean, how?"

He turns to me with a wink. "You doubt my ways?"

"No, it's just that after a long night of sex..." I'm tingling between my thighs at the memory of how many times he brought me to orgasm. "And did you even sleep? So how did you find where Zane was?"

He smirks. "My head wouldn't rest, so once you fell asleep, I contacted Khaos."

"Oh, you did?" I try to keep the surprise out of my voice, though Kaden always seems to amaze me.

"We're buddies," he jokes, flashing me a grin. "He's a great guy. Sure, now I told him I owe him big-time, but he delivered the goods."

I blink at him, then refocus on the road. "And?"

"He has contacts on the king's team and was able to track down who entered Norway in the past few weeks, specifically Zane. They found him fast. I have the address he put down of where he's staying."

"That's genius." My knees bounce with nervous energy, memories of the last encounter with Zane flooding back—the warehouse, the caged animals, the fury I felt. The fact that he can move into another country without being hunted down says my old bounty company has closed the case on him. Of course, they would... but I want revenge against that asshole.

Kaden's hand lands on my knee, steadying me. "He'll pay," Kaden assures me. "But first, he's going to tell us where we can find Lilia."

I nod, ready for this. I feel the blade tucked in my boot and another at my hip. We're heading to the industrial district of the city, not far from the wharf.

"Maybe he's moved his business to Norway," Kaden states.

"Or he's just finally found me and is coming back for what I stole from him—Chowder. Whom he's not getting. Under any circumstance." My gut twists at the thought.

"I promise you he won't."

We soon pull up to a smaller industrial building made of weathered wood, just one among several lined up along the road. The docks stretch out in the distance in front of the buildings.

I park at one end of the street, and we get out, the chill of the morning air biting at my skin. Kaden takes the lead, and a sense of déjà vu washes over me, reminding me of the first time I went after Zane with that idiot Scout. But this time, I have real support by my side.

We move quietly as we approach the property. The door is locked, but Kaden doesn't hesitate. He shoves his shoulder into it, breaking the lock with a splintering crack. We slip inside quickly, finding a small warehouse and office space, but it's empty. Devoid of life, as if no one's been staying here.

Dust clings to the surfaces, and the air is thick with the scent of the place being closed up for a long time. I scan the open area, taking in the metal shelves lined with nondescript boxes and a small, cluttered desk shoved against the far wall.

Kaden moves deeper through the place, only lit up by sunlight pouring in from the high windows, scanning every corner, every shadowed recess.

My attention fixes on the office door. Kaden's footsteps echo softly behind me. The office is empty, with no sign of life. I move cautiously, rifling through the drawers, but they're all empty except for a few scraps of paper and pens rolling around as I yank them open. I kneel down, running my hand underneath the desk, hoping for a hidden compartment or something out of place, but there's nothing.

Kaden's outside the room, keeping an eye out.

My stomach churns with disappointment. We were so sure we'd find something here, some clue to point us in the right direction. I straighten up, wiping my hands on my jeans, and head back into the main area.

"Nothing in here, just an empty storage area." I sigh, feeling the heaviness of failure settle over me. "This place hasn't been used in a while."

We cross the floor, checking behind the shelves and peering into the dusty corners. The air is still, silent except for the soft creak of the floorboards under my feet.

Kaden's expression mirrors how I feel on the inside—disappointed.

"Sorry to get your hopes up, but I think this is a fake address," he murmurs.

I sigh heavily.

"If Zane was here, he's long gone now," he adds.

"Let's go to the docks, then," I suggest, not ready to give in. "We can ask around for him."

With his nod, we move back outdoors, the sunlight bright. Just as we emerge, I spot someone familiar crossing the road toward us.

It's Zane. A massive man with a handlebar mustache, wearing blue overalls, filthy with what look like black grease stains, his eyes narrowing as he takes us in.

Our gazes clash, and he pauses mid-step. Recognition flickers in his eyes, and a split second later, after sizing up Kaden, he turns and bolts in the opposite direction, heading back toward the wharf.

"Fuck, that's him," I shout to Kaden, taking off after Zane with a burst of adrenaline. Kaden's there in seconds, thundering like a train behind me.

We chase Zane through the bustling dock area, weaving between crates and containers. My heart pounds in my chest, a savage determination driving me forward, Kaden's footfalls a steady beat beside me. The salty sea air fills my lungs as we sprint past workers loading and unloading cargo, their confused gazes following our frantic pursuit.

Zane is fast, his bulky frame surprisingly agile as he darts around the shipping containers like a rat fleeing the light. The docks are alive with activity, workers shouting instructions to each other, forklifts beeping as they move pallets, and the low hum of ships idling in the harbor. The sound is almost over-whelming, but my focus remains fixed on Zane's retreating figure.

We dodge past a group of men unloading a crate of fish, their shouts of surprise barely registering as we race by. One of them tries to grab my arm, probably thinking I'm a thief or worse, but I jerk free, the urgency of our mission driving me onward. I can hear Kaden behind me, cursing under his breath as he pushes past obstacles with brute force.

"Out of the way!" I yell, ducking under a crane arm that swings overhead. The operator shouts something in Norwegian, but I'm already past him, my eyes locked on Zane, who's slipping into the shadows between two stacked shipping containers.

For a moment, I lose sight of him in the maze of metal and rust. My heart skips a beat, panic rising in my chest. But then I spot a flicker of movement—a flash of his overalls disappearing around a corner.

"There!" I shout, pointing as Kaden skids to a halt beside me, his gaze following my gesture.

We take off again and burst into an open area, a loading bay where a ship is being prepared for departure. Workers pause to watch us, more curious than surprised. The smell of oil and salt hangs heavy in the air. Zane is just ahead, slipping through the crowd, his gaze darting around as he searches for an escape route.

Kaden and I split up, flanking him on both sides. I duck behind a stack of wooden pallets, my breath coming in ragged gasps as I watch Zane attempt to blend in with a group of sailors, but his broad shoulders and distinctive gait give him away. I lock eyes with Kaden, who nods in understanding.

We converge on him, moving swiftly through the throng of people. A sailor steps in my path, asking if I'm lost, but I brush past him with a hurried apology. There's no time for explanations, no time to lose our target. Zane's red, round face flickers with recognition as he spots us closing in, his lips curling into a sneer.

Just as he's about to slip away again, Kaden lunges, his hand grazing Zane's shoulder. The impact spins Zane around. He stumbles back, crashing into a stack of crates, sending them tumbling to the ground. Zane regains his balance and bolts to the edge of the dock.

Fuck!

I'm breathing heavily, my legs pushing after him, Kaden close by. We're gaining on him, the distance between us shrinking with every stride.

He rounds a corner, disappearing behind a towering pile of rusted shipping containers. For a heartbeat, I fear we've lost him again, but as we sprint forward, I catch a glimpse of him slipping into an alleyway that leads toward another section of the wharf.

"This way!" I shout, and we pivot, our feet pounding the pavement as we close the gap. Zane glances over his shoulder, his face twisted with frustration, and pushes himself to run faster.

*Fucker, you're not going anywhere!*

The alley opens onto a quieter part of the docks, a place where abandoned ships bob listlessly in the water. Zane's footsteps echo hollowly as he races toward a derelict vessel.

Kaden veers left around a container left near the road, motioning for me to take the opposite direction. I nod, turning right, and as I round the corner, I find myself face-to-face with Zane.

"Fucking bitch, you found me." He gasps the words breathlessly. "But big fucking deal... because I've got you now, and you have no idea what shit you're in." His voice is a low growl. He lunges at me, swinging a massive fist at my face.

Breathing fast, I duck to the side, driving my elbow sharply into his ribs. He grunts, spinning around, and I take the opportunity to kick the back of his knee, sending him sprawling onto his hands and knees.

Fury surges through me, hot and fierce. As he struggles to get up, I can see the trembling in his limbs, the telltale signs of a shifter on the verge of transformation.

I catch a glimpse of Kaden approaching, his eyes blazing with fury, and the wolf inside me stirs, a growl rumbling just beneath my consciousness. I can feel her power, a fierce command urging me to let her out. The sensation is overwhelming, a primal instinct that resonates through every fiber of my being. It's as if she's speaking to me in my mind, and I find myself whispering, *You can come out.*

I surrender to the call, allowing my wolf to emerge. The transformation is swift, a rush as my body begins to change. It's not painful, but I feel every shift, every stretch of muscle and bone as they rearrange themselves. My skin tingles, the sensation spreading through my limbs as white fur erupts.

There's a moment of disorientation as I drop to all fours, the world tilting to accommodate my new perspective. I'm grounded now, paws digging into the gritty surface, my senses sharp... sounds louder, sight crisper. I inhale the salt of the sea, the sweat of exertion, the metallic tang of Zane's fear.

It's only the second time I've transformed in as many days, but the wolf feels natural, as though she's always been a part of me, waiting for her moment. My ears flicker, catching the sound of Zane's ragged breath and the scuffle of his boots as he tries to scramble away. But he's too slow, and I'm on him in a heartbeat.

I lunge at Zane before he can completely rise to his feet, a growl rumbling deep in my chest. He throws an arm up in defense, but I bat it aside with ease, my claws raking across his sleeve. He cries out, the sound music to my ears as I snap my jaws, catching the fabric of his shirt and tearing it away.

I bowl him over, and he's rolling to his back, arms up to defend himself. A growl rumbles in my chest, and I snap at his arms again, my teeth tearing at his skin. He cries out, and I latch onto his throat, pressing down just enough to draw blood but not kill him. He's not transforming because in his vulnerable position, I could rip out his throat if he tries... and he knows it.

I let out a low warning growl, my eyes on Zane's, daring him to make a move. It's an ultimatum, a demand for submission, and he seems to understand.

"Fuck," he gurgles. "Fine, just let me go."

A shadow falls over us, and I inhale Kaden's scent—a mix of pine woods, seawater, and something uniquely him. He steps on Zane's forearm, and when I glance down, I see the glint of a blade in his grip.

"Don't even think about it," Kaden snarls down at him, his voice a low, dangerous snarl. "Now, I've got some questions for you. How you answer is up to you, but if you don't give us what we want, she'll rip you to bits. Understand?"

White spreads over Zane's face, the panic flaring in his gaze.

"I know you've been working with Lilia," Kaden presses.

Zane grunts, refusing to speak, and the next moment, I sink my teeth deeper into his flesh. The coppery taste of his blood floods my mouth, and it's odd not to be repulsed by it. Instead, it only feeds my anger, the wolf inside me relishing the taste of revenge.

"Told you what's going to happen," Kaden snaps. "You willing to die for her?"

I spot a few people watching us from a distance.

Kaden snarls at them to fuck off, and they quickly scatter, leaving us alone once more.

My gaze is fixed on Zane, my heart pounding, anger burning through my veins. All I can think about are the atrocities he's committed, the suffering he's caused. I want to make him hurt, to see him beg.

"Hell, call her the fuck off," he gurgles, desperation coloring his words.

"Then talk," Kaden growls.

"I-I can't..." Zane gasps, bleeding profusely.

I loosen my hold on his throat, pulling back just inches, my breath hot against his skin.

"There, now talk," Kaden barks. "You're wearing my patience down, asshole."

Zane coughs, struggling to get the words out. "I don't really know her... fuck, but she found me."

"What does that mean?" Kaden demands.

My ears perk up, straining to catch every word.

"Look, man, I just want that damn otter. I paid big for him and invested so much in the magic technology used on him. He's my property. Whatever beef you have with Lilia is none of my damn business. Tell me where my otter is, and I'll tell you where you can find her."

Anger surges through me, and I bite down on his shoulder, feeling the crunch of bone beneath my teeth. Blood bursts into my mouth, its metallic taste stirring a hunger I never imagined. Zane's howl pierces the air, his body trembling beneath me.

As I pull back, I see the extent of the damage I've done. His shoulder is a mangled mess, blood seeping through the torn fabric.

*Oops.* A dark satisfaction of hurting a monster like him after he hurt all those animals curls through me.

Kaden pats my head. "Good. Next time, rip it the fuck off."

"No!" Zane screams. "She's crazy…"

"You're in no place to negotiate," Kaden warns, his tone icy. "Now, are you ready to talk and tell me where I can find Lilia, or is Sasha going to rip your fucking balls off next?"

I rather enjoy being the bad guy in this situation.

Zane's face drains of color, fear etched into every line of his features. The stench of his fear fills my nostrils, bitter and acrid.

"I-I put out a call for someone to track down Sasha and the otter, and Lilia replied to my request. She sought me out, sent someone to come collect and bring me here to Norway."

*Hell!*

"Why?"

"Fuck if I know, but she hates Sasha, wants her out of town, is all she told me. She's been watching you both."

A shiver runs down my spine, wondering what this means for me.

"Is that meant to scare me?" Kaden growls. "Where the hell is she?"

"How the fuck should I know?" Zane pleads, desperation in his eyes. "I've only seen her two times. Both times, we met on a boat here in the harbor."

"What's she got against Sasha?"

I glance up at Kaden for a split second, seeing the same confusion on his face as I felt in my mind.

"Who the fuck knows? Because she's a bitch and sticks her nose where it don't belong," Zane mutters.

I snarl in his face, lips peeling back, and he recoils against the ground.

"Fine, fuck," he snaps. "It's something to do with some damn sirens. I don't know. I just overheard them saying something about sirens and getting Sasha out of town or taking her out before she finds out."

"Finds out what?" Kaden voices my exact thoughts, his gaze burning into Zane's.

"Didn't you just hear me?" Zane protests with a crackling tone. "I only heard snippets... who knows? Lilia is fucking psycho, and I wouldn't deal with her if I were you."

Kaden huffs, his hand resting on my back. "Okay, he's got nothing more for us. You can finish him off now."

"What? Hell no!" Zane screams, attempting to wriggle away, but Kaden's got his foot planted firmly on his chest. "Man, I just told you everything. I don't know anything else. I can't even tell you how to contact her since her minions find me when she wants to see me. She knows every fucking thing!"

I stare down at the man who deserves the worst, contemplating the justice I could deliver. However, the more he talks about Lilia, the more my skin shivers at what we don't know. But the thought of executing Zane to get rid of him twists something inside me, a darkness I can't embrace. I have a different plan for him.

I shift back to human form. Fur recedes, leaving me cold and exposed and naked, but Kaden's already ripping off his shirt, handing it to me.

"Put this on fast," he instructs. I pull it over my head, the fabric falling to my knees. My clothes lay nearby, shredded and useless.

"Thank fuck someone is sane," Zane bellows.

"I'm going to take him to my work... I want my old boss to see that I can complete a job and that he's a fucker for getting rid of me. And my ex-partner, Scout, can go suck it!" I declare, fire burning in my veins.

Kaden smirks, a proud glint in his eyes. "I love how vengeful you are. That's my girl."

"What? No, just..." Zane protests weakly.

"Shut the fuck up," Kaden interrupts, bending down to wrench him up by his hair. "Now, be a good horse. You're coming with us."

Zane pushes against Kaden's grip, but it's impossible. He stumbles, bleeding heavily, sweat on his brow.

We move quickly, and at the car, I retrieve ties from the trunk, binding his feet and wrists behind his back, then shove him into the rear seat. Kaden holds me close, his warmth seeping into my skin.

"You did amazing out there, such control of your wolf. You have no idea how much I admire how..." Kaden's words trail off as he kisses me quickly on the lips, and it's hard not to melt against him. "Your instincts, your power, you're incredible."

"That means a lot to me, but right now, I just want to be done with this asshole."

"You got it!"

In the trunk, I find a bag I always keep with backup clothes—pants, a shirt, a jacket, and boots. In my business, getting dirty and hurt is part of the job, so I'm always prepared. I quickly change, giving Kaden back his shirt so he's not walking around bare-chested. As much as I love it, there's a time and a place.

Dressed, I dive into the driver's seat while Kaden climbs into the back with the bastard.

"I don't trust him," Kaden sneers. "So, I'm going to keep an extra-close eye on him. And maybe if you're smart," he adds, addressing Zane, "you'll tell me anything else you know. It might sway us differently on what we're going to do with you next."

Not that it was going to sway me, but I figure he's negotiating, hoping there's more he can reveal.

"Look, the last I saw Lilia was a few days ago, and she looked ready to head out on the boat again with her crew. The boat's called the Siren's Vengeance. So, I doubt she's even in the city right now."

We drive toward my workplace, the information swirling in my mind. I try to piece together how I'm involved, why the sirens attacking boats feel connected to this. Including my mother... and why Lilia wants me out of the picture. Of course, I'm guessing, but right now, my mind is on alert because someone wants me to either disappear or die. The why part is what baffles me.

# TWENTY-SEVEN



I'm back home after dropping Kaden off in the city. He mentioned he had a few people to ask about Lilia, so he took off while I took Zane to my work. After handing him over to my boss, I felt an enormous weight fall off my shoulders. My boss was ecstatic, singing my praises, which I'd never had a boss do before. She even called up my old work in South Africa with me standing in her office, putting him on speaker. My new boss knows that this is the first mark I ever missed and hence, it got me transferred to Norway. I didn't say a word, but hearing my old boss stammer and sound honestly surprised made me smile so hard my cheeks hurt.

The authorities are involved now, and there's a comfort in knowing that something that has haunted me for so long is finally being resolved. Sure, Zane has others he works with, but catching him is a huge step toward stopping his animal-trafficking operation.

With a lingering smile, I stroll through the mansion, calling out, "Chowder?"

In seconds, he comes scrambling toward me, chirping excitedly. His little legs can barely keep up with his enthusiasm. I scoop him into my arms, hugging him tightly. "Today has been a great day," I murmur into his fur. "Sure, there are other issues, but that asshole who hurt you is now caught."

Chowder stares up at me, his gaze innocent, as if he's trying to comprehend the gravity of the situation. I kiss the top of his head, unable to resist his adorable confusion.

"I think we need a celebration," I announce, the thought of a carefree evening lifting my spirits even more.

"Food!" Chowder chirps instantly, his eyes lighting up at the prospect.

I laugh, shaking my head. "You're insatiable with food. But I was thinking we could go swimming down in the basement pool afterward."

His tail wriggles with excitement, his entire body vibrating with anticipation. Chowder loves the water almost as much as I do, and a swim sounds perfect after such a tense day.

I set him down, watching him scurry around my feet, and head to the kitchen to whip up something quick. My thoughts drift back to the confrontation with Zane and the information he spilled about Lilia. There's a nagging feeling in the back of my mind, a sense that things are far from over.

As I prepare a simple sandwich, I keep one ear tuned to the soft sounds of the house, listening for any sign of Kaden's return. The shadows in the corners seem darker today, the usual comfort of my home tinged with unease. There's something about the quiet that feels charged, like the air before a storm. I can't work out if it's me or that I know she's still a threat to me and is out there somewhere.

Chowder and I are at the table while he munches happily on smoked salmon. After we finish eating, we head to the basement, and I'm ready to dive in and unleash my mermaid side. It feels like an eternity since I've done so. The corridor is dimly lit, and the sound of our footsteps echoes softly against the stone walls.

"When do we go back to visit Eryx?" he asks.

"Not sure," I reply, smiling at his enthusiasm. "Why? Missing your new friend already?"

"Yes! I like him. And flying! Do you think we can do it again?"

I chuckle at his eagerness. "We'll see, buddy. I'm sure Eryx would love to take you on another flight. But first, we've got to figure out some other things."

The hallways seem darker than usual, the shadows looming larger as we descend the stairs. I try to shake off the feeling, focusing instead on the plans for our swim. But my instincts are screaming at me, a subtle warning I can't ignore.

As we reach the bottom of the stairs, a creaking noise behind us makes me stop in my tracks. The hairs on my nape prickle with unease. Chowder spins around, a hiss on his lips.

"What is it?" I whisper, my voice barely audible.

Before I can react, something hard slams into the back of my head. Pain explodes across my skull, and my vision blurs. The world spins and darkens, swallowing me whole as I fall to the ground, unconscious.

A dull ache throbs across my head as I slowly regain consciousness. I groan, blinking against the dim light of the room. The space around me seems to sway, but I can't tell if it's the room or just my pounding head. I struggle to sit up, rubbing the sore spot on my skull, trying to piece together what happened.

"Chowder?" I call out, my voice hoarse.

A small squeak answers me, and I look to see him curled up beside me. My heart aches at the sight. I reach over and scoop him up, holding him close to my chest.

"Where are we?" I murmur, glancing around the room, trying to ignore the pulsing pain in my head.

"Why he bring us to boat?" Chowder asks.

The room sways again, and the salty scent of the sea fills the air, confirming Chowder's words. We're on a boat. The walls are wooden, creaking softly as the ship moves on the water. It's a small room, empty except for a single door.

"Who brought us here?" I ask, though I'm not expecting Chowder to know.

"Big man," he squeaks. "Why did he throw us into this room?"

"I don't know," I reply, moving to the door and finding it locked. I place my ear against it, listening for any sounds outside, but all I hear is the muffled creak of the ship. I glance around for anything useful, then find a pin in my pocket. Thank God for my paranoia. I always keep tools on me just in case things go bad.

Chowder watches intently from my shoulder as I fiddle with the lock, his whiskers tickling my cheek. My hands work quickly, and soon, I hear the satisfying click of the lock giving way. I open the door cautiously, peering out into a narrow wooden passage lined with several other doors.

"Stay quiet," I whisper to Chowder, moving stealthily toward the small steps.

The ship's creaks grow louder as I ascend, my heart pounding in my chest. Fear claws at me, but I push it down, knowing I need to stay focused. Chowder clings tightly to me.

When I reach the deck, I emerge into the open air, staying low. The fishing boat we're on is large but in need of maintenance, its wooden hull groaning as it cuts through the waves. The salty breeze tugs at my hair, and I take in the vast expanse of the sea surrounding us. Norway's coastline is not too far behind us, meaning we just left shore.

I keep my eyes peeled for any signs of life on the deck, my heart hammering in my chest. The boat's rusting rails and peeling paint tell me it's been a while since it was last cared for. The deck is cluttered with ropes and equipment.

"We have to get off this boat. We're going to swim back," I whisper to Chowder.

The air is cold, the chill biting through my clothes as I edge closer to the railing. I spot a set of stairs leading up to the captain's area.

As I near the railing, I hear voices—a low murmur that sends a jolt of fear through me. I freeze, straining to make out the words, but they're too distant, too muffled by the sound of the sea. I can't risk being seen, not now.

I edge closer, my movements slow and deliberate. The voices grow louder, but they're coming from the other side of the boat, near the stern. I peer around the corner, careful to stay hidden, and catch a glimpse of figures—two men, their backs turned to me as they talk.

Suddenly, a tightness squeezes around my throat.

Panic surges through me, and I'm frantically reaching for my neck, but there's nothing there... yet the tightness squeezes as if invisible hands are choking me. I scratch at my neck, gasping for breath. Chowder hisses and growls while clinging to me.

"What's happening?" I manage to choke out, struggling against the invisible force. Fear pulses through my veins, and my mind races, desperate for a solution.

The world spins as I'm yanked away from the railing, my back slamming against the wooden deck. Pain explodes through me, and I gasp for breath, the grip around my neck unrelenting.

Chowder's terrified squeals pierce the air, but they're almost lost in the rush of blood in my ears. Terror tears into me, and I struggle against the hold, my fingers clawing desperately at the invisible force.

This time, it's different—stronger, more relentless. I feel myself being dragged across the deck, the wood scraping against my skin.

"Chowder!" I choke out, my voice barely a whisper. But he's still with me, his little body a warm presence against my skin.

I fight with everything I have, thrashing against the hold, refusing to give in to the darkness closing in around me. Chowder's terrified cries surround me.

# TWENTY-EIGHT



I'm lying on my back on the boat and glance up at someone standing there—Lilia, the woman I spoke with at the pier last week, the same person in the photo at the library. Her blonde curls bounce lightly around her shoulders. There is an ageless beauty about her, though the deep lines at the corners of her eyes and mouth reveal her older age.

The tightness around my neck loosens just enough that I'm not choking, and I reach for Chowder, frozen on the spot for a moment.

Lilia's gaze blazes with anger as she watches me struggle. Behind her, a few bulky men stand close, their expressions hard, their eyes fixed on me.

"Sasha." Lilia's voice cuts through the chaos like a blade, smooth and sharp. "I would have thought you were smart enough to heed my warning and not keep looking into things that aren't your business. I gave you a chance to leave the city, to go back to South Africa, stay where you belong."

The coldness in her words sends a shiver down my spine, and my breath comes in short, panicked gasps as I continue to struggle. I scream inside my head for my wolf to come out, to help me break free. I feel her growling, pushing for release, but something's holding her back. And that worries the hell out of me.

"Don't waste your time," she mutters casually. The invisible grip around my neck completely releases, and I breathe easy. My vision swims as I struggle to regain my footing. Chowder hangs on to my shoulders, perched there, pressed close to my head.

"What the fuck do you want, Lilia?" I rasp, my voice hoarse from the struggle.

She laughs, a sound that cuts through me like shards of ice. "Oh, so you know my name. Good, you've done some research. Or was it that buffoon Kaden feeding you lies? Though he's as useless as his grandfather, so let me give you a piece of advice, girl to girl. Dump his sorry ass because he's only going to betray you in the end and rip your heart out."

"What the fuck do you want? And how are you wielding such magic?" I shout, frustration and fear making my voice tremble. My wolf is still silent, trapped by whatever magic she's used on me.

Before I can demand more answers, Chowder leaps from my shoulder, his mouth opening to reveal rows of sharp teeth as he lunges at Lilia. The woman's laughter rings out again, and one of her men steps in front of her, intercepting Chowder's attack with efficiency.

Panic grips me as I see the man's hand reaching out to catch Chowder. I lunge forward, yelling for Chowder to stop, but he's already biting down on the man's fingers.

Ouch!

Blood sprays as two fingers hit the deck, and the man screams in agony, clutching his mangled hand.

He reels, his face twisted in pain and rage, and he aims a vicious kick at Chowder. I throw myself between them, taking the brunt of the blow to my thigh. Pain explodes up my leg, sharp and burning, but I push through it, grabbing Chowder and tossing him toward the ship's edge. I throw him overboard. He hits the water and bobs back up, staring at me with those huge, terrified eyes.

And just as fast, I'm scrambling up over the railing.

But the noose tightens around my neck again, dragging me back in a flash. I cry out, clawing at my neck for release.

I hit the deck with a bone-rattling thud, my vision swimming as tears burn my eyes from the pain stinging across my back. The shadow of Lilia looms over me again, her smile triumphant and bitterly cold.

"Forget the damn otter," she snarls. "You had your chance, and now it's too late."

I struggle to focus, the fear in my veins turning to ice as I stare up at her.

"Kaden will find you. He'll come for me."

"That idiot?" Her laughter echoes in the open air. "I dealt with his kraken grandfather, and I will deal with Kaden, too, have no fear. Where you're going, he won't be able to reach you."

Two of her men grab me under the arms, hauling me

to my feet. I fight against their hold, my fingers brushing the blade hidden at my waist. With a swift motion, I whip it out, slicing one of the men across the middle. He recoils, cursing and clasping his wound, but the other man retaliates with a punch that snaps my head back, sending stars dancing across my vision.

The world tilts, and I drop to the deck, the pain radiating through my skull like a lightning strike. I blink up at Lilia, trying to focus, trying to comprehend the chaos around me. Her presence feels like a storm sweeping over me with endless force.

I'm choking for more air, the tightness around my neck never giving up.

"Well, just like your mother, you're a fighter," Lilia murmurs. "Which is good. The more you fight, the better you'll be."

The mention of my mother sends a jolt of electricity through me. "My mother?" The words leave my lips in a gasp, my chest tightening as memories flood back—the day I watched her drown my father, her transformation into a siren, the day I was left alone.

"You asked me earlier what I was," Lilia continues, her tone smug. "I'm part harpy, part fae, so powerful magic runs through my veins. I can control energy, but I can also force someone into a transformation. Do you know what happens when a mermaid finally takes on being a siren?"

Anger surges inside me, hot and consuming, mixing with despair that feels like it's ripping me apart from the inside.

"You turned my mother into a siren?" I cry out in a raspy voice. "Who gave you the right? She killed my father!"

I push myself to my knees, ignoring the throbbing ache and the pain in my neck. That's when I catch a glimpse of movement to my left. Chowder, hanging on to the side of the ship, dripping wet but still here. My heart aches with fear for him. *Why did you return, little man?* But my focus swings back to Lilia, the woman who turned my life into a nightmare.

"Yes, well, unfortunate consequences, but I needed her," Lilia says carelessly with a shrug. "And now you'll get to see her again. Isn't that exciting?"

Fear knots in my stomach, icy and cruel, and as I try to back away, the invisible cord around my throat pulls me back. Chowder hisses, ready to pounce again, but I shake my head at him, a silent plea for him to stay safe.

"Chowder, go, leave now!" I gasp, my voice firm despite the panic coursing through me.

But Chowder doesn't move, his eyes locked on me, determined to stay by my side.

"Why?" I demand. "Why the fuck did you do that to my mom, to me?"

Lilia's lips twist into a cold smile. "I have a business to run," she admits in a matter-of-fact way. "I've never been more profitable since I took over the reins all those centuries ago."

My mind reels with the knowledge of siren attacks, the stories of boats lost at sea, of sailors drowned or driven mad.

"Money," I blurt out, the pieces falling into place. "That's all this is for you?"

"Riches, gold, magical artifacts," Lilia replies, her eyes glinting with greed. "You have no idea what it can buy in this world. How those things mean you live like a queen! And no one can ever hurt you again. Besides, everyone has a price. Everyone can be bought, you know that?"

"Fuck you!" I spit, rage burning in my veins. "Not everyone!"

Lilia steps forward, her hand reaching out to my throat once more. I shove it away, but she's like steel and unmovable. Her touch is cold, a chill that seeps into my skin and makes me shudder.

"Now let's do this because your sad face is ruining my day. I have things to do."

One of her men is there, forcing my mouth open as Lilia leans in, whispering words in a language I can't understand. Her breath is cold against my skin, and I watch, horrified, as black smoke pours from her mouth into mine.

I thrash, a scream in my throat, and I see commotion at my side, which I know is Chowder and the other men stopping him.

The black smoke, the breath... it's suffocating, a bitter taste that coats my throat and fills my lungs. I shove against the hold, terror making my heart race, but the darkness wraps around me, squeezing tight.

"What did you do to me?" I gasp, stumbling back as they release me. I stagger, my body heavy and barely responsive, fear thrumming through my veins as

Chowder rips free from a guard and scrambles back up on the railing.

"Sasha!" He keeps calling my name. "Run!"

I try to take a step and find myself glued to the spot. Lilia's laughter grows louder, a sound that promises nothing but more pain. The world tilts, threatening to swallow me whole.

I pound at my chest with my palm, trying to dispel the acrid taste of smoke that seems to cling to my insides. My vision blurs, and I fight to remain standing, to keep my focus.

The boat rocks beneath me, but there's nothing comforting about the sway. It feels like the world is tilting on its axis, dragging me down into an abyss. I glare at Lilia, standing just a few feet away, her foot tapping on the deck as if this is merely a mild inconvenience to her. Her sharp gaze cuts through me like knives. Every muscle in my body is tense, my breath shallow and rapid as panic coils around my heart.

"Sasha," Chowder calls.

"Go home, Chowder," I whisper, my voice barely audible over the sound of the waves slapping against the hull. "Do it for me, please…"

Lilia's voice is a whip crack, slicing through the air. "Get that fucking pesky otter… just kill it already."

"No!" My voice cracks. "Chowder, leave the boat, now!"

"Sasha," he pleads, his small voice trembling with terror. "Danger here. You must leave with me!"

His words pierce my heart, and I'm torn between the desperation to protect him and the inability to move.

Tears burn in my eyes as I struggle against the invisible bonds holding me, my limbs heavy and unresponsive. I can't let them take Chowder. I won't let them hurt him.

A guard steps forward, and a cold wave of dread washes over me.

"Chowder, leave me now! Go get Kaden!"

Chowder's eyes are filled with fear, his body quivering so hard I'm afraid he might collapse, but he needs to run. My heart aches with the weight of our parting, and I'm choking on the fear that this might be the last time I ever see him.

The guard lunges, and Chowder looks at me one last time, his eyes glistening. "We always stick together... we family." His voice breaks.

"Go, now!" I scream, tears streaming down my face as he dives into the sea just as the guard's hand swipes through the air where he was. Chowder vanishes beneath the waves, leaving behind a splash and my shattered heart.

"You idiot... can't even catch a damn otter," Lilia snarls at the guard. "I should make you dive in after it for that. Knowing your luck, you'd get eaten by a damn shark." She shakes her head, turning back to me with a mock pout on her lips. "Oh, how sad... boo-hoo."

Her words ignite a fire within me, a burning rage that surges forth with a force I didn't know I possessed. My skin tingles, and I feel my body start to change, an overwhelming sensation of something powerful pushing through me. My fingers extend, claws ripping through my skin, and darker, murky scales ripple across my flesh. I scream out from the pain of the forced change.

I'm convulsing, my body twisting under the force of the transformation. I recognize it, the change I'd feared all my life. It's not just a shift; it's a violent rip, tearing away the parts of me that are familiar, replacing them with something monstrous. A numbness spreads through me, swallowing my emotions and leaving behind only hatred and an unbearable hunger.

"Good girl," Lilia coos, her eyes gleaming with triumph.

"No!" I shout, my voice shattering as I cling to the last threads of myself.

Lilia's laughter rings out. "You will work for me now, Sasha, do my bidding, and no one will ever be able to take you from me."

Fear roots itself deep within me into a suffocating vine of thorns wrapping around my soul. Everyone knows that once you turn into a siren, there's no turning back. That dread coils tighter around my heart, and my mind drifts to thoughts of my mother, the day she drowned my father, the day she abandoned me.

All my life, I feared becoming like her. I thought it was in my blood, a curse I couldn't escape, but now I see the truth—Lilia was responsible. It wasn't my destiny; it was her doing. But this doesn't lessen the terror gripping me now.

And when Kaden finds me, as I know he will, I'll do what sirens do best. I'll drown him with my kiss, stealing his life.

The darkness sweeps over me like a tide, suffocating the light from my mermaid side, replacing it with the icy chill of the siren. It creeps into every corner of my being, an unstoppable coldness that's driven by magic, a change I can't control or reverse.

In my last moment of clarity, as the final tendrils of who I was slip away, the truth settles over me like a shroud.

I am lost, and there is no coming back.

# TWENTY-NINE

## KADEN

The late afternoon chill clings to my skin as I step up to the front door of my mansion, my heart pounding in my chest. Left ajar, the front door swings slightly in the breeze, and a knot of dread tightens in my gut. Sasha's car is parked out front, but the silence inside the house is deafening.

"Sasha?" I call out, my voice echoing through the stillness. "Chowder?"

Only silence responds, and the dread unfurls in my chest. I rush through the place, searching every damn corner, even the basement.

Nothing.

"Motherfucker!" The word tears from my throat as the realization crashes over me—I'm alone. I should never have left her side. I was chasing a lead, and it turned out to be a goddamn waste of time. Now she's gone, and it's my fault.

A roar of frustration escapes me, reverberating off the

walls as I charge through the house again, hoping I missed something. Anything. My heart is a sledge-hammer against my rib cage. She's my world, and without her, everything feels wrong. The fact that Chowder is gone, too, only deepens my dread. Zane's been dealt with, so this only leads me back to Lilia.

I bolt back outside, diving into Sasha's car. It's after midday, but the world feels like it's collapsing around me. I yank the seat back, barely avoiding getting stran-gled by the seat belt, and drive like a man possessed. I never learned to drive properly, but I've watched it enough times. I careen down the road, jerking and swerving the car as I shift gears too quickly.

"Get the fuck out of my way!" I shout at the cars I speed through intersections without stopping. The city blurs around me, but all I can think about is Sasha.

I skid into the parking area behind her workplace, tires screeching as I park across three spots. I pry myself out of the car, barely noticing the skid marks from my tires. I'm too angry, too terrified, to care.

Inside, I demand to see her boss, who just happens to be walking past the reception area.

"Can I help you?" she asks, her eyes widening as she stares at me, bewildered.

"I'm looking for Sasha," I say, trying to keep my voice steady. "I'm her... fiancé. Did she come in here today?"

"Oh, she never mentioned she was engaged. But yes, she was here earlier when she brought in a felon. Then she headed home."

I grind my teeth, nodding tightly. "Okay, thanks."

"Is everything all right?" she calls out after me.

"I really hope so," I mutter over my shoulder, rushing back to the car.

I drive to the wharf, my mind racing. I have no idea where to start, how to find her. My insides burn, my heart squeezing so tight I feel like I might pass out. But anger fuels me, driving me faster. The world outside is a hazy streak as I weave through traffic. Every second feels like an eternity.

At the wharf, I park and leap out, charging down the pier where Sasha told me she last saw Lilia. The wooden dock creaks under my weight, my footfalls heavy and urgent. My heart trembles with fear that something awful has happened to her. If it hasn't, and she's just out shopping or something, I'm going to lock her up for good for scaring me like this.

I stop a couple of wharf workers, demanding answers. "Have you seen the Siren's Vengeance boat?" I bark.

The men exchange glances, pointing to an empty spot along the pier. "Yeah, it was here earlier today... guess it must've headed out again."

Pushing past them, I sprint to the far edge of the pier. I scan the sea, but there's nothing. Just the flat expanse of blue, burning under the sun. It's too glorious, too bright. It mocks me, and I stand there, feeling myself fall apart.

Loving someone this much was supposed to be a gift, not a weapon slicing through my soul. I've let her into my heart, let myself love her, and now it's shredding me to pieces. The rage inside me is a hurricane, threatening to tear everything apart.

I'll destroy this city, the ocean, the entire fucking world if I have to. I won't stop until I track down my little mermaid.

Grinding my jaw, fists balled tight, I turn away. I'll go to the wharf office, find out if there are records of the boat's journey and when it's returning. Something deep inside confirms that Lilia is behind this, and it makes my blood boil.

I march away, the feeling of helplessness gnawing at me. The sea is vast, and I'm directionless, aimless. I hate it. I hate feeling so fucking useless. But I won't let it stop me.

"Kaden."

Then I hear it—my name called out, faint but unmistakable.

I pause, ears straining, heart pounding. There it is again, the familiar voice. I spin around, scanning the wharf, my eyes finally landing on the water. There, swimming frantically toward me, is Chowder. His eyes are wide with terror, and my heart leaps into my throat.

Chowder climbs a set of metal stairs, and I rush over, stepping down to reach him. I scoop him out of the water, his little body trembling, collapsing in my arms.

"Chowder," I say desperately. "Where's Sasha?"

He's shaking. "Evil woman take Sasha on boat," he squeaks, his words trembling with emotion. "They hurt her, they change her... you have to find her... help her."

The words slam into me like a train, my blood

turning to ice in my veins. I struggle to breathe, my heart a lead weight in my chest.

"Who?" I manage to ask. "Lilia?"

Chowder nods, his little body quaking in my arms.

"Why she hurt Sasha, why?" he whimpers, his eyes darting back to the sea. "I try to protect her, I try... family protect."

His words are a knife to my heart, each one twisting deeper, and I fight to keep my composure. The sight of him so broken, so afraid, shatters something inside me, and I struggle to hold back the tears that threaten to spill over.

"Which direction did they go?" My question is raw with desperation.

Chowder points toward the horizon, his tiny paw trembling. "That way."

I glance out past the mountains and into the North Sea. A chill settles over me, colder than the wind whipping off the water, and I know I have to move. I have to find her before it's too late.

"Why she turn into siren?" Chowder says suddenly, the words a death knell in my ears.

"What did you say?" I ask, dread churning its way up my spine.

"Siren. Woman make Sasha siren."

The world spins around me, a dizzying blur of fear and disbelief. If this is true... if she's become a siren... then I've already lost her. I fall to my knees, the weight of the realization crushing me. I can't breathe, can't think, can't even begin to process the magnitude of what's happening.

"Kaden," Chowder whispers, his voice a soft plea in my ear. "Why don't you go find her? She told me to call you."

The words cut through the haze of despair, and I lift my tear-filled eyes to his. I never cry, but right now, half of me is ready to burn the world to the ground, while the other half is about to shatter like glass.

"I'll find her. I promise," I murmur. I have to find her. I don't fucking give up. Not now, not ever. Maybe it's not too late.

Frantic, I run back to the car with Chowder in my arms. I put him inside, leaving the window cracked for air. But Chowder clings to me, shaking.

"I have to find her," I say urgently. "You stay here, okay? Don't leave the car, and don't let anyone inside. Lock the doors."

Chowder nods, and it breaks my heart to leave him, but I have no choice. Without a backward glance, I turn and sprint back to the water like a madman.

Past the workers, I dash to the end of the pier, the world a blur around me. I strip off my clothes, tossing my boots aside, and without hesitation, I dive headfirst into the ocean's cold embrace.

The water hits me like a shock, but I welcome the chill. It sharpens my senses and fuels the fire inside me. I barely feel it, the pure fury consuming me like a living thing. I unleash my kraken, the transformation pouring out of me like an avalanche. I expand and grow, the ocean roiling around me as I dive deeper into its depths.

The waves ripple outward, but I don't care. Not when I have to track her down. I move through the water with fluid grace, my massive form cutting through the sea like a knife.

Fish and sharks dart out of my path, the darkness of the ocean swallowing me as I race through its depths. I have no time for anything else. I lift my head above the water, scanning the horizon for any sign of the boat.

Up ahead, I spot a large fishing vessel, hope flaring in my chest. I dive under, the water churning around me as I surge forward. The boat rocks violently from the waves I create, but I don't give a damn.

I rise to the surface, peering over the edge at the sign across its side—Kingfisher. Frustration gnaws at me, the hope I felt slipping away like sand through my fingers. I watch the fishermen run around in panic. It's not them.

I dip back under, pushing through the water with a fury that makes the ocean churn. Each powerful stroke propels me forward, but the water feels as if it's tightening around me, suffocating.

I surface, scanning the horizon for any sign of her. My heart thrums inside me with urgency.

I've been searching for hours, the sun's golden light slowly dimming as it dips toward the horizon. The longer I search, the more my frustration builds, and a storm gathers strength inside me. I'm a creature of the sea, yet here I am, lost and powerless. I surface once more, the water rippling out around me as I let out a guttural bellow of rage and despair.

The noise is thunderous. I'm a monster, a beast, but I can't find my true love. I can't contain the emotions tearing through me.

In the distance, I stare at the outline of the shore, the

lights of the city twinkling against the darkening sky. My heart is a lead weight in my chest as I begin the long journey back, my strokes heavy, each movement a reminder of my failure. I promised I'd protect her, and I've failed. The thought hammers at me.

As I near the wharf, something inside me snaps. A raw fury explodes from deep within, and I rise from the depths, the full magnitude of my kraken form towering over the land. The sea heaves beneath me, waves crashing against the pier with the force of my storm.

The people on the shore scream and run away. I doubt they've ever seen a kraken before, never witnessed the monstrous power that lies beneath the surface. I'm enormous, a dark silhouette against the horizon, and their panic only feeds the fire raging inside me.

I unleash a furious screech, the sound reverberating through the air, a primal roar that shakes the very foundations of the city. My tentacles thrash against the water, striking with the force of a hurricane, and I watch as the waves surge forward, crashing into the piers with a deafening roar.

Boats are torn from their moorings, the wooden structures shattering under the onslaught of my rage. The sky darkens, clouds gathering as if in response to the chaos below, the world echoing my tumultuous grief.

I'm losing control, the anger consuming me, and I embrace it, letting it wash over me in a tidal wave of emotion. I don't care about the destruction, about the people fleeing in terror. All I can think about is Sasha, about the gaping void where she should be. She's my world, my everything, and now she's gone.

I dive back under, the water rushing over me as I twist and turn, the fury propelling me forward. I lash out, my tentacles striking the remnants of the boats, tearing them apart, but it brings no relief, no comfort.

I rise again, breaching the surface, and for a moment, I pause, staring out at the destruction I've wrought. The world seems to hold its breath, but the emptiness remains, an aching chasm that no amount of destruction can fill.

Slowly, the anger ebbs, leaving in its wake a hollow void. I let the water carry me back to shore, the weight of my failure pressing down on me, a suffocating presence that refuses to relent. I am a kraken, a creature of myth and legend, yet I am powerless.

As I wash up on the water's bank, already in my human form, the world around me is a blur of confusion. The wharf is a disaster—people running everywhere, the air filled with the sound of screams and the crash of waves. I've done this, but it doesn't matter. Nothing matters without her.

I drag myself up. My body feels heavy, my limbs trembling with the effort, but I push forward. No one notices me, their fear too consuming to pay attention to the man who rises from the waves. They've seen a monster, a beast from the depths, and it terrifies them. It might be funny if I wasn't dying inside, if my world wasn't falling apart around me.

I reach the car, my breath coming in ragged gasps as I collapse against the door. The weight of my grief is suffocating, the knowledge that I've lost her a constant, unrelenting ache. I cling to the metal, my vision blurring as tears fill my eyes.

Then, just as I go to open the door, darkness edges in, creeping at the corners of my vision. The world tilts, spinning, and I'm ripped away from the present, the weight of the ocean pressing down, dragging me under into a vision.

CHAPTER

# THIRTY

KADEN

I'm standing in the living room of the mansion, watching my grandfather with his red-haired mermaid lover, Nixi. The room is filled with a warm glow, casting a golden hue over everything.

Nixi is laughing, tears of happiness glistening in her eyes, as she smiles at my grandfather and rubs her small belly. I can see it in the way my grandfather tenderly caresses her, the way his eyes light up with a brightness I've never seen before, that he must have just discovered she's pregnant.

"I can't believe how lucky I am," my grandfather coos. He lifts Nixi into his arms, spinning her around with a joy that's infectious, her giggles filling the room like a melody.

"So you're not upset?" she asks, her voice a sweet, lilting sound that seems to dance in the air.

"Why would I be? Having a family is everything I've wanted. You are my stars in the sky, Nixi, my reason for being. That's why I'm going to change things and start my own business, something with less travel, so I can be at home with you more."

*I wonder why he never spoke of her to me, why this part of his life was hidden away like a precious secret.*

*The vision blurs, a whirl of colors and emotions that leaves me reeling, and suddenly, I'm standing on a quiet shore with my grandfather and Lilia. Her face is a mask of fury, her eyes bright with unshed tears as she glares at my grandfather.*

*"You fucking asshole," she spits, her words a venomous hiss that cuts through the silence.*

*My grandfather stands there, looking truly bewildered, a frown creasing his brow.*

*"Lilia, I thought you would be happy for me, for Nixi and me."*

*"You really are clueless, aren't you?" Her response is sharp, coated with bitterness. "I actually thought we were building something together, and this whole time, you've been with someone else? And now she's pregnant, and you want to leave the business we built from the ground up?" Her hands are fists at her sides, trembling with rage.*

*My grandfather reaches out, his face a mask of confusion.*

*"Lilia, we were never an item. You know this. I told you this in the past. We've always been close business partners, good friends. Why are you making a bigger deal of this than it is? I never led you on."*

*The hurt in her eyes is raw. Her jaw clenches, and I see her struggling to contain the tears that threaten to spill over.*

*"You're a fucking liar, or you're simply too stupid to notice how I felt about you all these years."*

*Oh, fuck!*

*"Lilia, I'm sorry things turned out like this." My grandfather sighs, a heavy, weary sound that seems to carry the weight of the world. "I never intended—"*

"I don't care," she snaps, pulling away from him with a jerk of her shoulders. She turns on her heel, her steps hard and deliberate as she walks away, leaving him standing alone on the shore, the waves crashing quietly at his feet.

The scene shifts again, a dizzying whirl of confusion that leaves me breathless, and I find myself on the deck of a boat.

Nixi's there, too, groaning in pain, clawed hands cradling her belly, her skin a patchwork of scales and flesh. Blood pools at her feet, and more runs down the middle of her legs, staining the deck.

I turn cold at the sight, at the implication that she lost her child.

My grandfather is a storm of fury, his face flushed with anger as he turns on Lilia, who stands nearby with a smirk on her lips.

"What the fuck have you done, Lilia?" he bellows, rushing to Nixi's side as she collapses into his arms, her cries a piercing wail of despair.

"The baby," she sobs. "It's gone... I can feel that I lost my child." Her body convulses once more, and her face is changing slightly, too—elongated features, thinner cheeks, sharper cheekbones, darker eyes... and pointed teeth.

A siren. For fuck's sake, she's changing into a siren.

Nixi cries frantically, and my grandfather cradles her, terror blanching his face, but fire burns behind those eyes as he glares over at Lilia.

I want to reach into the vision, to rip her apart for what she's done, to make her pay for the devastation she's wrought. But all I can do is watch, helpless, as my grandfather endures his own nightmare.

He sets Nixi down and lunges for Lilia, his hand closing

*around her throat in a grip that promises death, but she remains calm, her lips curled in a cruel smile.*

*"You fucking bitch," he thunders so loud that the air around seems to shake. "Undo what you did to Nixi! Now! Change her back to a mermaid, or I'll destroy you!"*

*"What are you going to do?" she gurgles. Her laughter is a chilling sound. She shoves against his grasp, loosening the chokehold. "Destroy me more than you already have? You know as well as I do that once a mermaid turns into a siren, she can't go back. And, well, a small side effect is that she lost your baby. What a damn shame. Every decision has a consequence!"*

*The callousness in her words is like a dagger to my heart. My grandfather throws her against the wall of the boat with savagery, his anger a living thing.*

*Nixi cries out, and my grandfather rushes frantically to her side, taking her into his arms just as her expression shifts from one of pain to something more sinister, more terrifying. Her eyes glint with an unnatural light, a twisted grin spreading across her face as she reaches for my grandfather.*

*"Kiss me," she whispers, her voice laced with the siren's call, seductive and deadly. "Take me into the water with you. Please, I need this..."*

*"No!" I scream, though I know he can't hear me. My grandfather's hands tremble, tears streaming down his face as he turns back to Lilia, but she's gone. And he's left with the woman he loves, now lost to him forever. A tragedy is unfolding before my eyes, and I'm powerless to stop it.*

. . .

The vision shatters, the world around me dissolving into a haze of light and sound. I'm thrown back into the present, the real world crashing down around me with a force that leaves me breathless.

I'm kneeling on the pavement beside Sasha's car, the cold, hard reality of the world pressing down on me like a suffocating weight. Chowder's frantic cries pierce the air, a desperate plea that slices through the fog of my mind, bringing me back to the here and now.

"Kaden!" His voice is a lifeline.

I blink, my gaze focusing on the small otter staring at me from inside the car, his paws pressed against the window, his eyes wide with fear and worry.

My mind is a whirl of emotions, a maelstrom of rage as I process the horror of what I've just seen. Lilia's betrayal, the cruelty of her actions, the way she stole everything from my grandfather, just as she's trying to do with Sasha.

I replay so many visions in my mind, trying to piece together the puzzle. Nixi turned into a siren and lost her baby, and now, Sasha's fate is intertwined with the same evil. Is it because of me? Is that why Lilia has turned her attention to Sasha?

The realization hits me like a punch to the gut, the cold, hard truth sinking in with a finality that leaves me reeling.

Then I recall the one vision where my grandfather was searching through a secret room, sifting through papers, looking for something. *A pendant*, he called it.

Was it the key to reversing the curse? Could it be the answer I need?

My hands are shaking as I fumble with the car keys and get into the driver's seat. Chowder is frantic, his small body trembling with fear as he looks up at me.

"You find Sasha?"

I take a deep breath. "We need to find a hidden room, Chowder. Maybe, just maybe, we can find a solution. Maybe we can save her." I reach over and scratch his head. Chowder rushes over to my lap, clinging to me, and I sense the poor thing shaking.

I throw the car into gear, the tires screeching as we peel out of the parking lot.

"Go faster if it saves Sasha," he urges. "Why you so slow?"

I grit my teeth, pushing the pedal to the floor, the city blurring past us in a haze of colors. My thoughts are a chaotic jumble of desperation. I can't lose her, not like this. Not to Lilia.

We crash into the driveway, the car skidding to a stop as I leap out, Chowder close on my heels. Together, we sprint into the house, the door slamming shut behind us as we race to the basement.

"It has to be here somewhere," I mutter, my voice a low rumble of urgency as I search the walls, my hands tracing every surface, every nook and cranny. I'm frantic, needing to find the damn room.

The basement is dimly lit, shadows stretching across the floor as I work, my heart pounding with every passing second. I can sense the clock ticking, and after an hour of nothing, my insides are ice, and I collapse against the sacrificial table.

Then I feel it... a faint breeze against my back, a whisper of air coming from somewhere behind me. I twist around, my fingers brushing against the stone floor and where the stand meets, and there it is—a hidden seam, a concealed entrance.

My heart leaps in my chest as I push against it, the floor easily shifting with a low creak, revealing a set of dark stairs leading down into the depths. Chowder is at my side, peering into the shadows.

"What is that?" he says.

"Are you fucking kidding me?" I breathe as I stare into the darkness. This is it. The secret room.

We descend, the light above fading as we plunge deeper into the bowels of the mansion. Dust hangs in the air, the scent of old paper and forgotten secrets filling my lungs as we reach the bottom. I find a string hanging from the ceiling near the entrance, and I pull on it, recognizing it instantly. The light in the room flicks on. Nearly every room in the mansion had these until I had them updated.

The room is a mess, papers and books scattered across the floor.

"Why so messy?" Chowder asks, staring at the chaos around us.

"My grandfather was trying to find something down here," I reply. I run my fingers over the books and papers scattered across a table.

I start rifling through the stacks of papers, flipping through books filled with scribbled notes, searching for anything that might give me a clue about Sasha or what my grandfather was involved in. Every name, every date, every location feels like a thread, and I'm hoping they will lead to an understanding of how to reverse what's been done.

I find a ledger filled with names and dates, meticulously recorded alongside locations. There's another book with names of ships and their charted paths.

Wait a minute...

I'm thinking back to the news articles Sasha was investigating, of boats being targeted by sirens, of sailors killed and everything precious stolen. I flip the book pages madly, and there are so many entries. There are other books, too, older, fading... There must be years' worth of records.

My heart sinks as I realize the enormity of what I'm holding.

This wasn't just a business; it was a carefully orchestrated operation targeting ships, and what's the bet the names are mermaids who changed into sirens. Which tells me they must've been controlled somehow. Forced to board ships and kill sailors, stealing anything of value.

It's one thing to have sirens randomly attacking a boat, but these books with records tell me there was nothing accidental about those attacks.

And my grandfather must have been involved.

"Son of a bitch!" I breathe, my voice barely above a whisper as I stare at the names. I slump down heavily on a creaking chair. My grandfather's involvement, Lilia's betrayal—it's all connected. The vision of my grandfather wanting to leave this business makes sense now. He wanted out to start a family, to stop the death and destruction he and Lilia caused.

It guts me to think he's not innocent in this ordeal.

As I sift through the papers, Chowder's falling asleep on an open book in front of him. But my attention is caught by something colorful on those pages.

"Hey, can I look at that?" I ask, my curiosity piqued. I slide it out from under him as he shifts onto his side, curling up.

There's a hand-drawn image of a round pendant, beautiful with colored stones. The longer I study it, the more familiar it seems. I blink at it, narrowing my gaze as it comes back to me.

My grandfather had given me something similar, a trinket he'd said was precious and unique, something to keep safe. I brought it back from Tartarus with me, never thinking much of it until now.

The realization hits me like a thunderbolt.

"Chowder, this might be it!" I exclaim, gathering the book and Chowder as I race back upstairs, my heart pounding with a newfound sense of hope.

I dash into the living room, pulling open the glass cabinet where I had placed the charm for safekeeping. My hands shake as I retrieve it—a deep violet and golden pendant, its spiral pattern wrought in white gold, the stones shimmering like captured stars.

Flipping through the book again, I find a section in handwritten notes.

*Sirens can be reversed to mermaids, but only within twenty-four hours of being turned and only by one who is true of heart.*

What the fuck does that mean? I skim the rest of the page, my heart racing as I find another scribbled note.

*The pendant, when covered in blood, can reveal any siren you seek. Whisper her name into the pendant...*

My breath catches in my throat as the significance of this discovery sinks in.

"Chowder, I think we might be able to find Sasha. Once I do, I'll need to bring her back to heal her... somehow. But first, let's find her."

Chowder nods, his eyes filled with a mix of hope and determination. "We find her, we save her."

I grab a small knife from a nearby drawer, my hand trembling slightly as I make a shallow cut across my palm. The blood wells up, dark and crimson, and I press the pendant against it, feeling the cold metal warm under my touch.

"Sasha," I whisper, my voice a soft plea carried on the air and picture her in my mind to make it clear who my intended is.

The pendant glows faintly, its stones pulsing with a life of their own as the magic within it stirs. For a moment, nothing happens, and fear scratches at my throat, then the glow intensifies, casting shifting patterns across the room.

The pendant's magic reaches out, weaving through the air, and in my mind's eye, I see her. Sasha curled up on the deck of a ship in her siren form... her tail flapping, her face emotionless, her eyes wild. I don't see my Sasha in there, only someone controlled and cursed. My heart clenches at the sight of her.

"She's out there, Chowder, on a ship. I'm going to

find her with this pendant," I murmur. I have to reach her and figure out a way to bring her back before it's too late.

Chowder jumps onto my shoulder, his small form a comforting weight. "We go now?" he asks.

"Sorry, buddy, you're staying home for this one," I reply, my resolve hardening into something unbreakable. I set him back down on the couch. "I have to focus on her, no distractions. You stay here, and I'll bring her home."

He stares at me with those huge eyes that tear me apart.

"Stop staring at me like that. Trust me, you're safer here. I got this." I quickly scratch his head, and with the pendant clutched tightly in my hand, I stride toward the door.

"You bring her back," Chowder pleads.

Heading outside, I lock the door behind me. I waste no time and am at the wharf, which is a complete mess because of me. I should feel guilty, but I'm drowning in the ache for Sasha and have no space in my emotions for anything else. After I save my little mermaid, I swear to pay for all the damages.

The afternoon sky is already dimming. The pendant glows softly in my hand with a faint line of golden magic pointing out to the ocean.

I strip down and prepare to dive into the icy water, and I feel the familiar pull of the kraken, the power coursing through me as I shift, my body expanding, limbs lengthening, until I am one with the depths. The ocean sings to me, and I know that here, in this element, I am at my strongest.

With the pendant wrapped in one of my tentacles, I follow its path, moving fast through the sea, knowing Sasha needs me. And her time is running out.

As I swim, the water darkens, the depths deeper, and I sense the pull of the pendant growing stronger, its magic a constant pulse in my grasp.

Hours pass in a blur of motion and water, the relentless push forward the only thing that matters. I surface occasionally, checking my bearings, the cool night air a welcome reprieve from the pressure below.

Finally, I spot a ship on the horizon, bobbing on the water. The Siren's Vengeance is written on its side beneath the moon's gaze. I grin, gliding forward. I approach cautiously, the water concealing me from view as I circle the ship from beneath the surface.

I drift silently, but I fear that in my kraken form, I'll be easily spotted. If I'm going to save Sasha, I need the element of surprise. I won't take down the boat until I know she's off it and safe. I let the shift take me, limbs retracting, tentacles pulling back as I become human again. The water feels different against my skin now—cooler, more personal.

Gliding in the water, I peer up occasionally, just enough to break the surface and assess what I'm dealing with. It's an older vessel, its hull weathered and worn. It won't take much to destroy it, but not before I get my girl.

The pendant in my hand pulses with a gentle glow, guiding me toward her, the anticipation like a fire in my chest. Every second that ticks by is torture, every heart-beat echoing in the space between us.

I spot someone leaning over the railing, eyes scanning the water, and I slip back beneath the surface, allowing the ocean to close over me. I swim under the boat, deciding to climb on from the side. It's less risky to be spotted that way. In my head, I play out the plan—find Sasha, steal her off the boat, then deal with Lilia and her crew. It seems straightforward enough.

Just then, the movement of the water changes. A ripple of bubbles ahead signals someone entering the water with me. Even in my human form, my sight is strong enough to see the dark waters, and right now, I'm tensing, muscles coiling, ready for whatever's coming.

I'm no longer alone.

A solitary figure moves through the water with a captivating grace. Her flowing, glittery tail trails behind her like liquid gold. Her dark aquamarine hair dances around her face, framing eyes that see through me, piercing and profound. Those perfect, perky breasts bounce in the water, clawed fingers extend from delicate hands, and her lips peel back to reveal a predator's smile.

My heart lurches painfully as I recognize her—Sasha, my Sasha, transformed into a siren.

Seeing her like this, knowing the horror she must feel trapped in a form she dreaded, it's killing me. A piece of my heart shatters with every second that ticks by, with every moment she stares at me with cruelty in her gaze. The very gaze that once softened with love now turns hard.

"Sasha," I plead with her.

Her eyes focus on mine, and for a moment, her expression shifts. Then, slowly, beautifully, she swims toward me, her teeth hidden behind a smile that has my heart racing. The temptation she offers is impossible to ignore.

She begins to hum in the water, the song twirling in my mind, wrapping itself around my heart, my very soul. It's a siren's call, seductive and beautiful. My resolve wavers, my purpose blurred by her melody. For a moment, I forget why I'm here. All I see is Sasha, gorgeous and deadly, swimming circles around me.

"Come to me," she purrs, a melody that dances along my skin.

I remind myself to resist the pull of her song, but the desire to give in is overwhelming. It's like being burned alive from the inside, a torture I can hardly bear. My skin itches with the need to reach for her, my heart splintering in two. I want her in my arms, desperately, an ache I can't escape.

For a fleeting second, I remind myself that this isn't truly Sasha—she's a siren under control, sent to end me. But as I watch her lips, the thought crosses my mind—would dying by her kiss be such a terrible way to go?

I shake my head, trying to clear the fog.

"Sasha, stop this. It's me. I know you're in there somewhere." Desperation paints my voice.

She doesn't flinch, doesn't bat an eye at my words. She begins to sing again, the tune making me forget myself. It's as if each note is a thread, pulling me toward her, away from reason.

The world narrows to a single point—her. Sasha, the center of my universe, the siren of my destruction.

Rushing to her, closing the distance, I reach for her waist.

"Let me take you from here." My plan to rescue her, to destroy this damned boat and whatever control Lilia has, slips from my mind as I gaze into Sasha's eyes.

Her teeth bare at me for a split second, claws digging into my chest, scratching the skin. Then, as quickly as the hostility appeared, it vanishes. She morphs back into the goddess she is, pressing herself against me, those breasts so delicious, so soft, making me lose my mind as she sings softly in my ear.

She doesn't recognize me under Lilia's curse; that's clear. My heart cracks open, the pain unbearable. Her attention holds me captive, her eyes offering the promise of my destruction, yet all I can see is the love we shared.

She lifts herself, bringing our faces close. My pulse races, memories of our time together flashing through my mind—our laughter, our banter, the love that once burned brightly. I can't imagine a life without her, without those moments.

My throat thickens because I'm so close to her, yet I feel we're worlds apart.

The thought of pulling away slips from me, replaced by an overpowering obsession to be with her.

I lean in, whispering, "I've never been able to resist you."

Her lips suddenly meet mine, and electricity jolts through my body, a current so intense it sends us both into convulsions. In the chaos, the pendant in my hand glows fiercely. Sasha thrashes against me like she's trying to pull away. Her kiss should have ended me, should have stolen my life, but it doesn't.

Holding the back of her head, I refuse to let her break the kiss. I shove the pendant against her chest, figuring it needs to touch both of us, praying it works as a burst of magic surges between us like electrical currents.

Her body shudders violently, and in a heartbeat, she collapses, going limp in my arms.

Dread crashes over me like a wave, cold and relentless. I break the kiss, panic rising as I call out, "Sasha!"

# THIRTY-ONE

KADEN

A rush of panic grips me as I hold Sasha in my arms, her body limp and unresponsive. The transformation is complete—her scales shimmer in the water, the claws have vanished, and she's back to her mermaid form.

Yet she's not responsive!

What if it's too late? What if I've lost her forever?

"Sasha, don't do this to me. You better not fucking leave me!"

Dread consumes me, and in my desperation, I barely register the signs of a vision coming. I've never hated the damn thing more than I do now.

"Fuck no, not fucking now!" I shout into the void as the world spins around me, dissolving into darkness.

· · ·

I'm standing at the front of the mansion. Authorities in crisp, dark navy uniforms surround my grandfather, their expressions stern, weapons drawn, charged with magic.

My chest tightens with dread at the scene in front of me.

Nearby, Nixi clings to my grandfather, tears streaming down her face. "Don't take him! He hasn't done anything wrong."

The lead officer steps toward my grandfather, meeting his gaze. "You are under arrest for running an illegal racket, for forcing mermaids into sirens, and for orchestrating horrendous killings and crimes through them."

Stunned, my grandfather stares at them, eyes wide with disbelief. Shock etches into his features. "You've got the wrong person!" he bellows. "I have no such ability! It's Lilia Acker—she's the one with the power to do this!"

Nixi is beside herself, sobbing uncontrollably. She clutches his arm, trying to shield him with her presence. My grandfather's rage burns like wildfire, his face reddening.

A guard jabs my grandfather with a weapon that zaps him with magic, his body convulsing violently as he drops to his knees. Nixi screams, a heart-wrenching sound, as they drag him away, two more guards snapping a metal brace around his neck.

My heart pounds in my chest, anger boiling inside me. I watch in horror, wanting to intervene, yet I'm powerless to do anything but witness.

"Release me!" he roars, struggling against the guards. "It's Lilia! She's framing me!"

"There will be no hearing for your crimes," the officer in

*charge states with no remorse. "You are going straight to Tartarus Prison," the officer commands.*

*My stomach drops, and the rage within me intensifies. My grandfather tried to redeem himself, and it cost him everything. He was far from perfect, but he didn't deserve this. I want to scream, to tear down the very sky in fury at how everything crumbled around him, how the world he tried to escape from swallowed him whole. And that payment ended up being something my parents and I  paid for as well by being born in Tartarus.*

*As they shove him away, I catch movement in the shadows by the trees. There, watching it all unfold with a twisted smile, is Lilia. That fucking bitch! Of course, she backstabbed him, orchestrating his downfall and sending him to Tartarus.*

*Thinking back, it all makes sense. Her jealousy destroyed so many lives!*

*In front of me, my grandfather fights with every ounce of strength he has left. The guards use their weapons relentlessly, driving him back to the ground. Nixi stands there, screaming for them to stop hurting him.*

The vision darkens, fading away like smoke in the wind, and I'm plunged back into the ocean. Disoriented, I float in the cold, dark water. I glance around, whipping around on the spot, to find no sign of Sasha or my pendant.

Despair engulfs me, a suffocating weight dragging me down into the depths. The ocean presses in from all sides. The vision lingers in my mind, a haunting reminder of everything I've lost, everything I might still lose.

But I can't lose Sasha. I refuse to let this be the end.

Blinking away the water and the tears that mix with the salt, I force myself to focus.

Fire ignites within me. I kick hard, surging upward, breaking through the surface, and instantly, I hear Sasha's voice from the boat. From my distance, I can't make out her words, but she's on the ship... Why the hell did she return?

I haul myself up the side of the boat, the metal cold beneath my fingers, keeping low as I peer over the railing. Night cloaks part of the deck, but there are lights strung across the back of the boat, casting a sickly yellow glow over the scene.

There she is. Lilia, hands on her hips, with that sneering, arrogant look on her face. Rage boils inside me at the sight of her, my muscles coiling tight with the desire to leap over the side and rip her to pieces. But I know she deserves worse, much worse.

Farther back, near the stern, I notice Sasha. My heart lurches at the sight of her in her human form, surrounded by several other women. One of them makes me do a double take—a woman who looks just like Sasha but older.

Realization hits me like a punch to the gut—her mother. The woman Sasha feared she'd become like. I inhale a steadying breath, my mind racing as I take in the scene.

Lilia's voice cuts through the night, sharp and commanding.

"Tomorrow, we'll cross paths with the Queen's Fortune ship." Her words are dripping with malicious glee. "It'll require all five of you to take it over. Sasha, you'll lead, with your mother guiding you."

My heart clenches at the way none of the sirens react. They sit, faces blank, like puppets waiting for strings to be pulled. There's only one guard sitting among them, his attention on Lilia. The others must be inside, but I don't care about them. My focus is on Sasha, sitting stiffly next to her mother, hands in her lap.

The charm, my precious pendant, is nowhere to be seen. I can't tear my eyes away from her. Back in the water, I could have sworn I saw her mermaid form. But here, in human form, I can't tell if she's back to herself or still under the siren's curse. It gnaws at me, the fear that I failed her, that I didn't do enough.

I wait a bit longer, biding my time, watching as Lilia turns her back, speaking to someone inside before heading in. This is my chance. I swim around the boat quietly to the side where the guard is seated among the women.

I climb up onto the boat and over the railing behind him, snatching him into a headlock and squeezing tight. He thrashes, his fists beating against my arms, but I hold firm, hissing curses under my breath. None of the women pay attention, not even Sasha. It's like they don't see me or don't care.

*My little mermaid. I'm going to save you, and we're going to try again. I'll die trying to bring you back to me.*

The man goes limp in my arms, and I drag him overboard, letting him slip silently into the water. I take a deep breath, glancing around to make sure no one else saw.

Now's my chance. I dart past the empty chair, leaping toward Lilia. She has to die. Until then, Sasha will always be in danger. I rush at Lilia just as she turns, her eyes widening in surprise. But a guard comes charging out from the side, gun drawn.

A bullet tears through the air, hitting me square in the arm. Pain explodes, sharp and excruciating. I grit my teeth against the agony, growling through clenched teeth.

"You fucker," I snarl, but I don't stop. I don't care about the pain, about the blood dripping down my arm. All I care about is ending Lilia.

I slam into her, knocking her off her feet. She goes down hard, crying out as I land on her, but I don't let up. The bullet's sharpness is killing me, but I took it so she wouldn't escape.

I'm on top of her, fists to her face, mostly to keep her down. I get up in seconds, wrenching her up by the hair and shoving her in front of me as a shield from the two gunmen who are now facing me. I smile at them. Fuck, my arm stings so bad, but I push past that.

"Step out of my way, or you'll regret it." I hold Lilia, and she's stumbling, groaning, holding the side of her face that's bleeding from my hits. "And don't try anything, or I'll snap your neck," I threaten her.

One of the men approaches me, and I hear the groan of steps behind me.

But I warned them.

My tentacles burst out from my back, striking out

simultaneously with brutal precision. The man behind me is slammed in the face, sent crashing into a window, shattering the glass as he tumbles overboard with a splash. The ones in front of me barely have time to react.

I whip a tentacle into the face of the first man with the gun, sending him sprawling backward. His weapon clatters to the deck as he hits his head on the side of the boat, unconscious before he even hits the ground.

The third is suspended in midair, dangling upside down by his ankle in my grasp, his screams cutting through the chaos. I give him a good shake, watching as his gun slips from his fingers, tumbling uselessly into the ocean.

With one powerful toss, I hurl him out into the open water. He arcs through the air, disappearing from sight, his screams fading into the distance.

"Now, where were we?"

Lilia laughs. "You think you can save your precious Sasha?" She spits the words. "She's mine now, Kaden. And if you kill me, she will still be lost to you. That gives me so much satisfaction because, after all these years, I still hate your grandfather, and that includes you. But if you're smart, you'll keep me alive because maybe I can help you with getting her back."

"Shut the fuck up!"

The rest of the sirens rise as if commanded, moving toward me like specters in the dim light. I shove them away with my limbs, holding them at bay, careful not to hurt them. They are the innocents in this, victims of Lilia's cruelty. But they keep fighting, slashing at my tentacles with their claws, biting into me like damn beasts. Sasha ducks beneath one of my tentacles, darting across the deck so fast it startles me.

"Sasha!" I call out, panic seizing my chest.

Lilia's chuckle cuts through the air, a chilling sound that raises the hair on my arms.

"Kill him, Sasha." Her voice is poisonous. "End this now!"

Heart in my throat, my tentacles coil in preparation, but I hesitate. Instinct screams at me to defend myself, to strike before I'm struck, but the thought of hurting Sasha is a knife twisting in my gut. I can't bring myself to harm her.

Then I see it—a glint of something in her hand. The pendant. In that split second, Lilia stiffens, her confidence faltering. She must have seen it, too.

"Sasha, stop!" Lilia bellows. "I command you!"

Sasha grins, a defiant light in her eyes, and I want to kiss her so much my heart aches. Under the boat, our kiss, our pendant—it worked. Somehow, it brought her back. Here she is, my girl, faking still being under Lilia's control until the moment came to strike.

Her stoic expression breaks into a grin, and in a heartbeat, she rushes at Lilia with a determined ferocity. Her movements are a blur. In one fluid motion, she slashes the pendant across Lilia's throat, a trail of crimson following in its wake.

A gurgled scream tears from Lilia's lips as she stumbles into me. Her hands fly to her throat, trying to stem the flow of blood, but it's too late.

I shove her aside, and she falls over.

Sasha stands over her, panting. "You won't control me anymore," she says. "Not now. Not ever."

Lilia's body shudders on the deck, blood pooling around her. Her eyes fix on Sasha, a final flicker of defiance burning out as life drains from her.

A part of me is disappointed I couldn't deliver the final blow myself. But seeing her writhing there, dying slowly, her life draining away, there's a certain satisfaction in knowing she's finally suffering, finally going to face the darkness she wrought upon so many.

"Die, bitch!" I growl.

Sasha grins.

The pendant Sasha used to kill her lies nearby, covered in blood, its sharp ends glistening with the crimson that had torn her throat apart.

A surge of magic rises out from Lilia's mouth, dark and thick like smoke. As she chokes and bleeds out, the energy pours from her faster, threading and spiraling out in five directions. It funnels into the four sirens on the deck, each thread seeking its target, curling around them, seeping into their being, and another strand spears off the boat into the night. Most likely to other sirens she's cursed.

The sirens on the boat stumble, blinking as though waking from a long nightmare. They appear to be shaking off the curse that had them under Lilia's control, but while they look lost, they are still dark sirens, still trapped souls. Three of the sirens glance around frantically and jump overboard, vanishing beneath the waves.

Sasha's mom remains, staring at her with a sense of recognition and something deeper. My understanding is that sirens still remember some elements from their lives, even if they may slowly forget emotions over time. She looks at Sasha as if she remembers, as though she misses her.

"Mom," Sasha says, stumbling toward her.

Her mom blinks at her, and I step closer behind Sasha's back, just in case. Sirens are unpredictable, and while her mother may not remember much, the natural darkness of their form still lingers.

"I forgive you, Mom," Sasha finally says, her voice breaking. She sniffles and wipes at her cheeks. I hold on to her shoulders, letting her know I'm behind her, supporting her.

Her mom stares at her, her expression filled with something akin to sorrow. "I will always think of you." Then she dives into the water, vanishing into the depths.

Sasha rushes to the railing, staring down into the pitch-black ocean. I'm at her side, embracing her with my good arm. She turns and cries into my chest, her body racked with sobs, and my insides are breaking for her.

Around us is death, chaos in the making for centuries, so much hatred and jealousy, and it's finally come to an end. I left Tartarus to do two things—find my fated mate and discover who put my grandfather there. I have those now, coming at a huge cost, but with Sasha by my side, it's something I won't ever regret.

"You did incredible today," I whisper to her, and she glances up at me, tears in her eyes. It kills me to see her this way.

"I'm so happy," she says.

"Oh, you are?" I question, reaching up to wipe some tears away from under her eyes.

"I got to see my mom again, knowing that she's out there, but she's no longer trapped. I know she didn't kill my father of her own doing..."

I nod, understanding the bittersweet relief she's feeling. It's a small comfort, but a comfort nonetheless.

"I don't think I'll forget today for a long time," she continues. "But most importantly, you saved me, Kaden." She grins, reaching up to kiss me. "I have no idea how you worked out how to bring me back from being a siren, but is there a chance we can use it on my mother, on other sirens?"

I shake my head, the weight of the truth heavy on my shoulders. "The magic only works on those turned within twenty-four hours and only by those true of heart." I smirk, trying to lighten the mood. "That's me." I pat my chest.

She's laughing and crying.

I lift her into my arms. "I've got you now, Sasha, and you want to know something?"

"Yeah, what's that?" she asks, giving me her cheeky grin.

"Today, I gave myself to you, willing to let you kill me, because I'd rather be gone than be in a world without you."

She frowns, her eyes narrowing in playful scolding. "I don't like you saying that because if I go, who's going to look after Chowder?"

I chuckle, the sound rough but genuine.

"Seriously, though," I say, looking deep into her eyes.

"Today made me realize how much you are my world and that I am never letting you out of my sight."

"Well, you know what I learned today?" she says, leaning in to kiss my cheek, then the corner of my mouth.

"Go on."

"That you, Kaden, are my pain in the ass, my stubborn kraken, and I have fallen completely and utterly in love with you."

My heart might have just exploded. I capture her lips, kissing her, pushing past the aching pain in my arm. She's what matters, and she said she loves me, too! It's a promise of a future together, one where we'll fight for our happiness, where I'll fuck her every damn day. And one where she might stop fighting me.

**Three Months Later**

The morning sun streams through the open balcony doors, casting a golden glow over my reflection, and I realize with a flutter of nerves and disbelief that today, I'm marrying the man I once thought was only a dream.

Since moving to Norway, life has been turbulent, messy, and chaotic. I grew up my whole life believing things that weren't true and facing tragedy because of a stranger's greed. It's been months since we eliminated Lilia, yet my mind still goes back to the discovery that she caused so much tragedy for no reason other than greed, for revenge. She chose my mom, like other random mermaids, to exploit and turn into a siren, in turn destroying so many families.

I tense, trying to remind myself that my mother is free of her clutches, though I still lost her to being a wild siren now. And my father is never coming back. As I think that, my wolf stirs inside me as though reminding me that part of him will always be with me.

I'm moving to Norway permanently now, making this my home, and somehow, after everything, I seem to be catching a break and finally getting that perfect-ever-after life.

I lift my gaze to the full-length mirror in front of me. I'm alone in the hotel room, the French doors open to a glorious sunny day, the high balcony overlooking the ocean. The breeze rushes inside as I stare at myself, about to cry.

I'm wearing a stunning dress the color of azure to match my sea. It's covered in crystals, with a long train—electric blue at the top, fading into white as it goes down to my feet. There are patterns of starfish and shells sewn into it with glittery thread. Thin straps crisscross my back, while the front has a low, sweeping neckline and tiny pearly buttons going down my bust that cinch in the dress across down to my waist. From there, the dress opens up, fluttering, revealing my pearlescent white swimsuit underneath, shimmering iridescent colors when the sunlight hits it. My legs are completely on show, so wearing no shoes fits the beach theme perfectly.

My diamond necklace and matching earrings glint in the sunlight, and more of them are dotted through my flowing hair, which has been set in waves and perfectly frames my face. I still can't believe I look this amazing. But if I'm going to get married to my true mate, I want to blow him away, to have him never forget this day.

Smiling, I wipe a tear, not wanting to ruin my makeup. I have tiny diamantés along my eyelids and curling upward from my eyes, and my lips are a rosy pink and glistening.

The door suddenly opens, and I turn to find Billie there. Her eyes are beaming at seeing me, and she shuts the door, rushing over.

"Oh my God, Sasha! You look so beautiful. You're giving me goosebumps right now with how stunning you are. Kaden is going to go insane when he sees you. And that dress, wow!"

"It's not too much skin? I rubbed glitter all over my legs for extra shine." I'm laughing nervously now, and she's at my side, hugging me.

"I love you so much," she says.

"I love you more, and I am so excited to be sharing this moment with you. And look at you." I break away, taking in the strapless white lace dress following her stunning curves, the fabric see-through to her bikini underneath. With Billie having gorgeous, almost-white silvery hair, she looks like an angel.

"Are you ready?" she asks, smiling. Her presence calms me.

"I'm so nervous but excited, and I'm trying really hard not to cry."

Billie's suddenly fanning her face. "Don't say that," she says, "I'm already tearing up at seeing how beautiful you are and that you're getting married. But we have to go; everyone's waiting."

"I guess it's happening now."

"Yep, and you make a striking bride."

I take her hand, and we head out of the room. I lean into her, saying, "Thank you for agreeing to walk me down the aisle."

"Of course, you are my family, girl. I am so grateful to be doing this."

Her words fill me with warmth, and I squeeze her hand, feeling the soft tremor of nerves mixing with excitement. The reality of what's about to happen swells inside me, almost overwhelming. Together, we start our journey down the corridor.

We descend the grand staircase of the hotel, my bare feet against the cold marble. As we pass through the lobby, everyone stops to look at us, their smiles warm and encouraging.

Billie squeezes my arm gently, whispering, "They can't take their eyes off you. You're radiant."

I giggle nervously, my cheeks flushing. "I hope I don't trip," I confess, and Billie laughs softly.

"You'll be fine. Just keep breathing," she advises.

We head out the back entrance of the huge hotel, my heart fluttering like a bird in my chest. The large glass doors open directly onto the beach, revealing a breathtaking view of the ocean stretching to the horizon. The sound of waves gently crashing against the shore is captivating, and I take a deep breath of the salty sea air.

As we step onto the sand, a soft breeze tugs at the hem of my dress, and I feel the grains beneath my feet.

The path to the altar is lined with delicate flowers. Together with Billie, I walk forward, each step taking me closer to a future I never dared to dream would be mine.

Standing at the edge of the beach, I gaze out at the shimmering crystal-blue water ahead of me. The calm sea stretches into the horizon as I take in the sight before me. A handful of cherished guests—Billie's mates, her adorable twins, colleagues from work, and the friends Kaden and I have made—are gathered on the shore. Dressed in hues of white and blue, they look beautiful, all smiling warmly at me.

The guests are parted, leaving a clear path that leads into the shallow water. The sea is unusually still, almost like a mirror, which isn't surprising when you have a kraken who can influence the ocean. At the end of a circular design of white flowers floating perfectly on the water, anchored in place, stands Kaden, the love of my life.

As we approach, Chowder pops up, floating along-side Eryx. When he sees me, he rushes over, holding a small black box in his hands.

"You're beautiful," he tells me with a wide grin. "And Eryx and I are flying later."

I laugh softly at his excitement and watch as he paddles down the path ahead of me, making his way to Kaden. Waiting with him is Khaos, who agreed to marry us. As part god, he is qualified to be the celebrant, and he stands there in a white suit, barefoot in the ankle-deep water.

I turn my attention to my soon-to-be husband, and

my stomach bursts with butterflies from the anticipation. I want to run to him, to feel his arms around me.

Kaden's wearing fitted blue pants to match the color of my dress, and he's shirtless. A necklace made of shells hangs around his neck, accentuating the tattoos that cover his muscular chest, collarbones, and arms. His long hair flutters in the light breeze, and even though I asked him to have his back to me until I arrived, he clearly had no intention of doing that. He's smiling so widely, his eyes gleaming with joy.

Soft music begins, a beautiful melody played by a woman in a flowing white dress seated with a golden harp. The sound drifts through the air, setting the perfect tone. Billie and I walk down the sandy aisle, my legs shaking with excitement and nerves.

The crowd oohs and aahs over Chowder, who waddles closer in a little white vest with a flower pinned to the front. He looks utterly adorable. As he reaches Kaden, Khaos takes the ring box from Chowder, who swims around in the shallow water.

Billie squeezes my hand, whispering, "Ready, gorgeous?"

"I've been ready for so long," I admit, feeling the truth of my words deep in my heart. "I just didn't know it."

I smile at everyone around me. As I step into the water, its cool touch caresses my feet, and my smile stretches as I move toward Kaden. His grin is enormous, those white teeth gleaming, and his eyes glint with barely contained emotion. It's as though he's holding back tears, and it touches me deeply.

The moment I reach his side, he scoops me up, his mouth finding mine instantly. I giggle against his lips, whispering, "This is supposed to come after we marry."

"I can't help it. I was about to die watching you come down here like a goddess. I'm not an emotional man, I'd like to think, but right now, I'm about to bawl my eyes out that I found you."

I kiss him back, lost in the joy of the moment, while Khaos clears his throat, and the crowd chuckles softly.

Sliding back to my feet, I stand beside this huge man who towers over me, who loves me so much that I'm ecstatic. Kaden holds my hand tightly, as if unable to bear even the smallest distance between us. Just then, Chowder pops up, floating between us, a cherished member of our family.

Khaos begins the ceremony.

"We gather here today to witness the union of Kaden and Sasha, two souls intertwined by fate and love. May their journey together be filled with joy, strength, and endless adventure."

Tears well up in my eyes, happiness overwhelming me. This is the kind of joy I never thought I'd experience.

Kaden squeezes my hand gently, his thumb brushing over my knuckles in a soothing gesture. As Khaos speaks, the words flow over me like a blessing. I glance up at Kaden, my heart full of love and gratitude. His eyes meet mine, filled with an emotion that takes my breath away. We've been through so much to reach this point, which makes me love him that much more.

Khaos smiles at us both, then nods to Chowder, who offers the rings with a proud little chirp. We each take one from the box, then slip them onto each other's fingers, the circle of gold covered in diamonds a symbol of the endless love we share.

"With these vows and the exchange of rings, I now pronounce you married," Khaos declares, his voice carrying over the sound of the gentle waves. "You may kiss your bride... again."

The crowd laughs while Kaden draws me to him, capturing my lips in a passionate kiss that weakens my knees. The world fades away, leaving only the two of us and the ocean's embrace. Cheers and applause rise from our guests, but all I can feel is the warmth of Kaden's arms and the certainty that this is where I belong.

This is the best day of my entire life.

Hours later, I'm sitting on one of the stone seats that have been set up in the shallow end of the calm sea at a long, transparent table stretching out in front of me, long enough to accommodate everyone. The cool water laps gently around us. Bundles of white and blue flowers run down the center of the table, and food and drinks are flowing, brought out by the hotel staff. Laughter and music fill the air, and I can't remember the last time I've been this happy.

Kaden's hand rests possessively on my thigh. He hasn't stopped touching me since I arrived, and I'm drowning in his love. I can't get enough of it. I feel his eyes on me even as I laugh with Billie, who sits across from me, cradling one of her adorable twins, Dante. His tiny wings flap like he's ready to take off, making those cute baby noises that suddenly have me wanting to hold him.

Then I notice Kaden's gaze shift away from the table, and I follow it to see, standing in the water, the Siren Goddess herself, Asbesta. My mouth drops open at her ethereal beauty and her body-hugging dress of jewels shimmering in the sunlight. Most of the guests notice her presence, too, and a respectful silence falls over the gathering.

"Give me a moment, beautiful," Kaden explains, standing and moving through the knee-high water to meet her. They speak quietly, their conversation private, yet they aren't arguing. It reminds me of the first time I saw them talking in Kaden's underwater cave in the fjord.

Chowder leans closer, drawing my attention to his little, serious face.

"You will have a baby like Dante one day. With wings?" he asks in his adorable, inquisitive manner.

I laugh, and Billie chuckles from across the table.

"Not with wings, Chowder," I say, patting his head.

Chowder tilts his head. "You marry, you have baby? Is that how?"

"Not exactly, but close enough." I grin at his innocence.

A short while later, Kaden returns as the Siren Goddess walks into the sea, vanishing beneath the waves. He sits beside me.

"Everything all right?"

Leaning in, he whispers, "Even better than I thought. I explained that I have found my fated mate and don't plan to leave Norway. That I'm a citizen of the House of Gold and Garnet now. I asked if she'd be open to dual citizenship since I have no intention of not using the ocean."

"And?" I ask, eager to hear more.

"She agreed with the proviso that I visit her House regularly and set up a home there, even if it's just a holiday retreat."

"Oh, I love the sound of that."

"That's what I thought." Hugging me, he kisses me softly, lingering there.

The guests start cheering, and I laugh, breaking our kiss to see them all looking our way.

"You're all going to make me blush the entire day at this rate," I say, and Kaden chuckles.

"Please keep cheering. I need to kiss my new wife a lot."

"Kissing is good. Keeps you happy," Chowder chimes in with perfect timing.

The crowd erupts in laughter. The celebration goes on for hours, and as the sun begins to set, tiki torches are set up along the beach. I never want this day to end.

Standing, I take Kaden's hand. "Come with me. Let's go for a stroll."

Chowder instantly joins us, climbing up on Kaden's shoulder, his tail curling around the back of Kaden's neck. The three of us walk along the water's edge, the gentle waves lapping at our feet.

"I've been thinking about where to take you for our honeymoon," Kaden states.

"Anywhere with you is perfect," I reply, leaning into his side.

As we walk a little farther from the party, I gather my courage and just come straight out with my thoughts.

"I think I might be pregnant."

He freezes, turning to look at me, his eyes wide. "Are you being serious, or is this one of your jokes? Because if it is, it's not funny."

"I'm being real. It's been three months since I last bled, and well... I think I might be. I have to get tested, of course, but I've been thinking about it, and..."

His arms envelop me, and he kisses me fiercely, stopping my rambling. Chowder, perched on Kaden's shoulder, looks between us.

"Do you think there's too much kissing today?"

We laugh, and Kaden ruffles the top of his head.

"This is serious, you know," I say, playfully swatting at him.

"I know. I have wanted a family for as long as I can remember, and I want a small bundle of kids."

"Bundle?" I echo, raising an eyebrow.

He kisses me again. "We'll start with one, but I want the kind of happiness I never had growing up. And I want the same for you and Chowder."

His words touch me deeply. I stare at him, my heart full of bursting love.

"I've never been this happy," I say softly. "You've given me a life I never imagined, Kaden."

"I feel the same way. We've both needed each other more than we realized."

We continue our stroll along the beach, the water cool against our feet.

"I love you, Kaden," I whisper, glancing at him. "I love you, too, Chowder."

"I love you more, Sasha," he replies, his voice filled with emotion.

"And I love you both the mosterest," Chowder coos, sending us both into laughter.

And in that moment, surrounded by the beauty of friends and the warmth of love, I know that I've finally found my forever family.

# MERMAID SEA SALT BROWNIES

### Ingredients:

8 oz. [228g] (2 sticks) salted butter

2 cups granulated sugar

1 cup unsweetened cocoa powder

4 oz. [124g] 70% dark chocolate bar (chopped) or chips

1/4 cup brewed coffee or espresso

1 tsp vanilla bean paste

3 large cold eggs

3/4 cup all-purpose flour

1 tsp cornstarch

Flakey sea salt for sprinkling

*Optional chocolate chips for extra chocolate goodness*

### Instructions:

- Move rack to bottom third of the oven, then preheat to 325°F (162°c). Line 8x8 pan with nonstick spray and/or parchment paper.
- Place butter in a large heatproof bowl set over a pot of simmering water (a makeshift double boiler). When it begins to melt, add in sugar, cocoa powder, coffee, and chocolate bar. Stir occasionally until the butter and chocolate have completely melted and mixture is well combined and glossy. May still appear grainy; that's okay!
- Remove the bowl and let cool slightly. Add in vanilla and stir. Then add in one egg at a time, mixing well with a whisk to incorporate well.
- Sprinkle in flour and cornstarch and mix until well combined. The batter will be thick. At this point you can sprinkle in extra chocolate chips and mix in. Then pour into your prepared baking dish and sprinkle flakey sea salt over the top.
- Bake for 30–40 minutes, until the toothpick inserted comes out mostly clean. Let cool slightly, then remove from the dish. Serve warm or cold!

*Enjoy*

# CHOWDER'S CHOWDER

### Ingredients:

4 cans minced clams w/juice

1 tbsp butter (salted)

5–6 slices of bacon, chopped

2 cups diced onions

1 cup carrots (diced)

1 cup celery (diced)

1 can, drained corn

½  cup flour

½  tsp black pepper

½ tsp ground thyme

1 tsp Old Bay Seasoning

1 tsp smoked paprika

1 tbsp minced garlic

1 ½ cups chicken bone broth (or stock)

3–4 peeled and chopped potatoes

1 bay leaf

2 cups heavy cream

## Instructions:

- Strain clams from juice. Save the juice.
- Start prepping all ingredients first.
- In 6-qt. pot, add butter and fry bacon over medium heat until the edges are crisp.
- Add in onion and sauté until soft.
- Reduce heat and add carrots, celery, corn, and flour, stirring constantly.
- Add in dry seasonings, garlic, clam juice, chicken broth, potatoes, and bay leaf. Stir to incorporate, then cover and bring to a boil.
- Reduce heat to simmer and cook until potatoes are tender. Approximately 15–20 min.
- Remove bay leaf and add cream. Simmer for about 10–20 min.
- Add in clams and cook 3–4 min.
- Remove from heat and serve.

***Enjoy***

# MARK ME

## DISCOVER BILLIE'S STORY...

**I'm marked...but I won't be tamed.**

Loss has scarred my life. I've trained relentlessly, endured unimaginable pain for one goal—to face the beast who watched me, who came for me. But took my family instead.

There's nothing I won't do for vengeance.

Until three sinful and unhinged monsters find me, emerging from the shadows with sharp teeth, and with claws that could pull apart my life as easily as they do the buttons on my dress.

They think they can break me... Absurd.

Yet I'm caught in their twisted war in a world in ruins and

fraying at the edges. They won't leave me alone, insisting I belong to them. That they'll make me irrevocably theirs.

Resisting the fantasies they promise grows harder with every passing day, and it scares me how easily I've started thinking of them as my own monsters.

But I remind myself I obey no one. Especially when I'm starting to suspect that they had a hand to play in my family's death.

They aren't the first monsters I've faced. They'll most certainly be the last...

**Mark Me is a STANDALONE book.**

9 781923 093225